THE SPIRIT OF REJECTION

A SPIRITUAL WARFARE NOVEL

ERIC M HILL

SunHill
PUBLISHERS

Published by SunHill Publishers

Atlanta, Georgia 30312

The Spirit of Rejection: A Spiritual Warfare Novel

(The Demon Strongholds Series)

Copyright 2016 by Eric M. Hill

ISBN: 978-0-9673189-9-8

Unless otherwise noted, Scripture is from the *King James Version,* public domain; or **NKJV**: Scripture taken from the New King James Version®. Copyright © 1982 by Thomas Nelson, Inc. Used by permission. All rights reserved.

Cover Design by Cora Graphics

OTHER BOOKS BY THE AUTHOR

Spiritual Warfare Fiction

The Fire Series

Book 1: Bones of Fire

Book 2: Trial by Fire

Book 3: Saints on Fire

The Demon Strongholds Series

The Spirit Of Fear

The Spirit Of Rejection

The Spirit Of Ugly

General Christian Fiction

Out of Darkness Series

The Runaway: Beginnings (Part One)

The Runaway: Endings (Part Two)

Three Sisters Detective Agency Series

Finding Angel

Christian Non-Fiction

Deliverance from Demons and Diseases

What Preachers Never Tell You About Tithes & Offerings

10 Mistakes We Make When Casting Out Demons

You Can Get Answers to Your Prayers

General Dystopian Fiction

The Great Crime Spike

1

The demon gazed hungrily at the pregnant woman's belly.

The mood in the room among the angels was as dark as the expression on the demon's face. He wasn't the least bit concerned about them and their empty glares, or of their swords and daggers. One of the three angels even had a spiked ball of metal hanging from a chain gripped by his large hand.

And just what are you going to do with that? he thought. The demon cast the three angels a look that could've been spit. Actual spit would've been better. But why waste good spit? They had the weapons, but he had the power. Everyone here knew this. Well, make that everyone, but the new angel. He'd learn soon enough who had the power.

And that's what this warfare was all about.

Power.

And people.

Hurting people. Hurting as many of them as possible before that great day of God's judgment. And despite the three armed impotents staring at him with murder in their eyes, he was going to do some hurting today. His yellow eyes met the gaze of the angel whom he assumed by his scars to be the leader of this little trio. He turned up his lip and traced the long scar on the angel's cheek with critical eyes. He could tell that Scarface was proud of his slash.

Ridiculous. Just ridiculous, he thought. *The way you angels wear your wounds like badges of honor.* The thought that followed made his lip turn up more than the holy fools deserved. *But then why shouldn't you display your wounds suffered for the sons and daughters of Adam like trophies? The Son of God Himself walks around with a hole in His side and those wretched holes in His hands. It's all so perverted. Making a big ado over suffering.* He ended his thought with a dismissive, *Whatever.*

The demon's eyes left the angel's hideous scar and joined the angel's stare with a disregard that caused the newest of the angels to make a move forward before being held back by Scarface. The demon said nothing, but his amused expression was blowing a bugle. The new angel didn't like this. The demon smiled as Scarface held the angel back a second time.

Enough of these angels, the demon thought. He had given them too much attention already. It was time for business. And since angels loved suffering so much, once the parents gave him approval to afflict their child, they could watch him begin the child's suffering.

His yellow eyes again bore into the woman's abdomen. Specifically, it was her uterus that commanded the demon's attention. He had been stalking the child and staring at Heather's uterus for weeks now. Ironically, he never would have known the child existed had he not been pulled to the house by the dark energy of negative words. Words spoken by the child's parents about the baby one day as he roamed the neighborhood in search of prey.

The demon's breaths increased until he was nearly panting. The conversation between Heather and Vincent was progressing wonderfully. Words. Words. Oh, the power of words! *Come on,* he coached the couple. *Keep talking. Give me the baby.*

"I just *can't* be pregnant," said Heather. "I can't. This just isn't the right time."

"But you're telling me you *are* pregnant," said Vincent, his narrowed eyes carried suspicion.

Heather looked up at him, whipping her straight black, shoulder length hair. "What? Don't give me that look. I didn't get myself pregnant."

"We talked about this, Heather." He spoke the next words with slow emphasis, as though each word was its own sentence. "I am in medical school."

Heather wasn't the fiery type, but the prospect of an untimely and unwanted pregnancy, and her husband blaming her for it, lit a fire under her. She returned her husband's offensive cadence. "And don't I know it."

Vincent heard the unspoken accusation. "What? So we're back to blaming me for you not passing the bar? That's getting real old, Heather. And anyway, what does that have to do with you getting pregnant?"

Heather's blue eyes flared. *Me getting pregnant!* she heard herself scream in her mind. She crossed her arms and slammed them onto her chest. "*Me* getting pregnant? I got *myself* pregnant?"

"You want some water?" Vincent asked.

"What?"

"Do you want some water? I'm going to get me a cup of water. All of this arguing has made me thirsty."

She hesitated. "Yes, I do want some water."

Vincent got a couple of cups and went to the refrigerator door.

Yellow eyes stared beneath Heather's folded arms as her husband pushed each cup against the black lever. He watched the baby's agitation like a wolf watching a wounded deer. It hadn't happened yet. So he couldn't move too soon upon his prey. He had to wait for the right words. The words that would kick wide open the door to this child's life.

"Look at him—how the beast peers at the baby, Justis. Like she's a piece of meat," said Gabron, his concern moving him closer to the baby's threat. "We can't let this demon hurt the baby." The angel's eyes widened in alarm as he looked at the baby. "Did you see that? What this animal is doing to the baby?"

The baby's body was tiny. Only the size of a pea. Nonetheless, the Creator had placed an eternal spirit within this tiny person. It wasn't the pea-sized body that caused the angel's alarm. It was the cringing of the eternal spirit within the child that gripped Gabron's heart.

"She knows she's in danger," he said, surprised at this revelation.

Justis was as concerned and angry as Gabron, but his voice was controlled with understanding and experience that Gabron didn't have. "Yes, she knows."

"But how? How can an unborn child know such things?"

Krasa, the other of the three angels, looked at Justis. Justis nodded once. Krasa stepped closer to Gabron. "In the blessed book, it was written by Luke that when Mary visited Elizabeth, the baby in her womb leapt for joy."

Gabron's eyes showed his amazement. "John the Baptist."

"Yes, John the Baptist," said Krasa.

Gabron thought on this a moment. "If a baby in the womb can feel one emotion, he can feel another. If he can feel joy—" He looked at Krasa.

Krasa finished the thought. "If he can feel joy, he can feel sadness... and fear."

Gabron turned his head slightly left, then right, all the while vigilantly aware of the demon. He let the revelation run its course. If children in the womb could feel emotions, it was only because they were somehow stimulated by events outside of the womb. If this was true, and it was, he thought of the effects of the pregnant mother's environment upon the child. Hadn't it been the presence of the baby Jesus in Mary that had caused the baby John in Elizabeth to be filled with joy?

Filled.

Oddly, something about that word filled him with dread. He looked at Heather's trembling baby. He looked at the demon. *Filled? Filled?* What was it about being filled that was so unnerving? The only thing that came to mind was John the Baptist being filled with the

Holy Spirit even while he was in the womb. Well, that didn't make sense. There was nothing about a baby being filled with the Holy—

That was it!

He didn't understand it, but he didn't have to understand it for it to be true. How many other things had he accepted as true simply because they were true and not because he understood why they were true?

"Justis, if John the Baptist could be filled with the *Holy* Spirit in the womb," his words were urgent, as though any moment the demon would make his move, "then this child can be filled with an *evil* spirit."

That was the moment Heather and Vincent said the words the evil spirit had been waiting to hear for a week.

"I can't deal with this right now," said Heather. "Vincent, I don't want this baby."

Vincent heard the words like fingernails scraping over the chalkboard of his heart. They were harsh, but Heather was right. Yet, he could tell from her expression that she heard the same scraping. "It sounds horrible, honey, but we have to be honest with ourselves. We can't have this baby."

The demon snatched two daggers from his waist and took a step toward the baby.

Gabron was on him before his first step touched the floor. The slashings were too fast to qualify even as blurs. An overhand downward blade across the neck. A backward double-handed scissor motion that began its slicing on both sides of the demon's body.

The avenging angel stood before the evil spirit with widened arms, a short sword in both hands, waiting for the dismembered body to fall onto the floor in four pieces.

The demon looked at Gabron with a puzzled smile.

Gabron looked at him in shock and total confusion.

"What? No one told you?" said the demon. He looked at Justis. "You angels don't talk to one another?"

Justis stepped forward and rested his hand on one of Gabron's forearms. He gently pushed it down. Krasa pushed down the other arm.

Gabron's eyes bore into the demon as he asked, "Justis, why is this demon still standing?"

"So you angels don't talk to one another," said the demon. "I really hate to be the demon who says something good about angels, but I can't help myself." He looked at each of them. "It's amazing that you angels get so much done without talking to one another."

"Ignore him," said Justis.

The demon stepped forward. He was less than a human yard away from three armed angels, and yet confidence oozed from his evil pores. "Listen to your leader, angel. Since I am beyond your reach, it only makes sense that you should ignore me." He smirked. "That'll give all of you more time to not talk to one another."

"What does this demon mean beyond our reach? How is he able to do this?" Gabron needed answers before the evil spirit made another move for the baby. A move that he knew was only a moment away.

Krasa put his hand on the new angel's shoulder. "He's a spirit of rejection."

"And what does that mean? That we let him have the baby?"

"It means he's protected," said Krasa.

"Protected by whom?"

"Not who," said Krasa. "What. He's protected by rejection itself."

Gabron couldn't accept the hopelessness that was trying to drape him. This was only a child. She hadn't even been born yet. "How?"

Krasa wasn't dispassionate, but these were just the facts. "Sometimes a rejection spirit causes rejection and then attaches to or enters his victim on the strength of that rejection. But in this case, he didn't cause the problem. The problem caused him—as it is with many demonic problems. He has a right to be there. The rejection is his protection."

Gabron's eyebrows furrowed. He shook his head. "No. No. It can't be."

The demon sighed and bunched his lips together. How often did a demon get an opportunity like this to stick it in an angel's face? He jutted his head out. "Yes. Yes. It can be. In fact, it is. You can't touch me."

"He's in another dimension," said Justis. "Rules of engagement. We can only touch him if he violates the conditions of his protection."

"What are the conditions? Tell me," Gabron pled, hoping there was still some way to stop this demon before he attacked the baby.

The demon stuck a long finger into his meaty nose and scooped out a gooey, darkened wad. He looked at the angels as he placed his thumb atop his finger apparently in preparation of flicking the wad on them.

Justis looked into the demon's eyes with a dare. "We can engage him if he attacks, hinders, or otherwise seeks to materially impede the work of angels." The angel's next words carried his hope. "Or if he does anything directly or indirectly that results in an angel being touched by his actions—no matter how slight."

The rejection spirit flicked his finger carefully away from the angels and lifted both palms toward them as he stepped backward. "I wouldn't want to complicate our relationship."

Gabron was incensed. "We have to wait for him to do something that we know he isn't going to do? There must be something else." He begged Justis with his eyes.

"There is," said Justis.

The demon didn't like the sound of this. His pores of confidence instantly dried as he waited for the angel's next words.

"What is it?" asked Gabron.

"Truth," said Justis. "The truth of God's love and of being accepted by Him destroys rejection."

The angel's answer was met with an involuntary growl from the demon. He took a slow step backward. "Excuse me, angels, but Heather and Vincent have used their authority to declare the child unwanted. I have a baby to take care of."

The demon turned and walked away.

Gabron leaped forward and swung his swords desperately through the demon. It was like slicing through a rainbow. Nothing changed except the distance between the baby and the demon got smaller with each of the demon's steps.

"I'll get you!" Gabron screamed. "I'll find a way! You won't be able to hide forever! I'll find you!"

The spirit of rejection answered the angel's threats without looking back. "You don't have to find me, angel. I'm not hiding. I'll be right here with the baby controlling her thoughts, desires, and actions. My control will grow in her until she sees everything through my eyes. Then she will never be what God wants her to be. And do you know why, angel? Because she will never know what God wants her to know."

The demon's last words were too much. Gabron's right and left hand slung knives one after the other that passed through the spirit's skull. The demon turned right before he entered Heather's belly. "Now you have to go find those knives. If you want me, you know where to find me. But there will eventually be many of us in the wretched child. So you'll have to call me by name. My name is Unwanted."

The angels watched the spirit of rejection press against Heather's belly and disappear. Gabron dropped to his knees and lowered his head in dejection. He had failed the baby. Justis and Krasa stood beside him on either side and both lowered to one knee. They placed a hand on each of his shoulders.

"This warfare is hard and cruel, Gabron. There are rules of spiritual warfare that cannot be circumvented." Justis waited a few moments. "You understand, my brother?"

Gabron looked at the ground through watered eyes. "Rules that allow evil spirits to attack defenseless children?"

"It is a difficult thing to accept, but yes," said Justis. "The same rules that physically endanger children work in the spiritual realm, too. A mother drinks alcohol or takes heroin while she's pregnant, this hurts the baby. It's not fair, but it's real. And no matter how difficult it is for us to accept this truth, we have no power to make it untrue by denying its existence."

No one said anything for a couple of minutes.

"What's going to happen now?" asked Gabron. "This vile demon has the baby."

Justis and Krasa shared looks.

Gabron heard the troubling silence and raised his head. "I've overlooked the obvious, haven't I? Heather and Vincent are going to kill the baby."

2

---

*T*erminating the pregnancy should've worked. It didn't. Neither did *ending* or *stopping* the pregnancy. Getting rid of the *problem* never stood a chance. A new word auditioned.

Process.

Heather lay across her bed, unaware of the afternoon's sunlight that shone with force through the small rectangular windows above the closed vertical blinds. She had an empty gaze as she stared at the ceiling. The gaze was empty, but her heart was filled with emotion. Her mind filled with doubts and questions she was too afraid to ask, but too honest to ignore. A sole tear left her eye and tickled her neck before it settled.

Humph...process, she thought.

Terminating the pregnancy hadn't worked for the same reason ending and stopping it hadn't worked. It wasn't that one word was any better than the other. Sure, *terminating* was the most popular word, but it was no less accurate or precise as *ending* or *stopping.*

Heather had always been good in English. Something she was told would be helpful to her in law school. Her eyes blinked and twin tears exited each eye and rolled down opposite cheeks. Terminating, ending, and stopping were all verbs. Verbs acting on an object. The object was *pregnancy.*

Transitive verbs, she thought. But these verbs wanted more than to act on the object. They wanted to get rid of the object. The problem was the object was a person.

A baby.

Her baby.

This thought led her to that other word. The one that was most offensive to her sensibilities.

Problem.

Getting rid of the *problem.*

Heather wasn't an "It's either black or white," person. Her world-view had neighborhoods of gray. In fact, on some issues of morality, she deliberately chose to live in those neighborhoods. This was more out of convenience than blindness. But in a sense, she had come home to her gray neighborhood and found all of her furniture outside on the lawn. The pregnancy had evicted her from her home, and the document tacked to the front door forbade her reentry not only into her home, but into any gray neighborhood. It was now black or white. No gray.

Heather offered no resistance to the moral demands of the pregnancy. She was naturally averse to intellectual dishonesty. That is why she found it unacceptable to refer to the pregnancy as a problem. As untimely as the pregnancy was, the pregnancy wasn't *the* problem, and it wasn't *a* problem. The problem, she admitted to a mind that would have it no other way, was her and Vincent. They weren't ready for a child.

Furthermore, the pregnancy wasn't a problem, it was a baby. And the existence and demands of this baby couldn't be covered with the sheer curtains of denial, even if that denial was reinforced with camouflaged patches of terms of misdirection.

Heather's bluish-gray eyes didn't blink for a long time. Then they did, and she kept them closed. She thought on that last word. For some reason, *process* was the most morally offensive and intellectually dishonest of them all. At least the others alluded to a pregnancy, and thus a baby—even if it was in the most indirect terms. Yet process was abstract. It referred to nothing in particular. But Heather wasn't built that way. Her mind was incapable of such mental gymnastics.

It had been three months since she'd found out she was pregnant. Three months of pure emotional hell. Three months of arguments. Three months of going back and forth on what to do about the baby. Twice she had made appointments to have the baby aborted. And once she had even gone to have the abortion and backed out minutes after the doctor entered the room.

Oh, what was she going to do about this baby!

Heather didn't see the small ball of brilliant light appear in her bedroom and hover at the foot of her bed. Nor did she see the light grow larger and more brilliant until an angel of truth stepped out if it and went to the left of the bed and look down at her. He had a message from the Holy Spirit.

"Look at the picture," he said.

Heather knew it was a mistake to get a sonogram of the baby before she did it. But she had foolishly followed the urge, without her husband's knowledge, and now she found herself sneaking and looking at the picture all throughout the day. She didn't know why she continued to do this. Each time she looked at it, she ended up crying until her guts almost emptied onto the floor.

No, she told herself, *I'm not going there.* But she felt herself already going there. Tears rushed out of her eyes like convicts breaking out of prison.

"You must face your decision, Heather," said the angel. "You have always made decisions with your eyes wide open. You can't close them now—not with your child's life at stake."

Heather took a deep breath. She raised and looked around and through the angel. She was right. She had to be honest with herself. That was why she had gotten the sonogram. She wasn't going to hide behind lies. She had always owned up to her decisions. But she knew that wasn't the only reason she had gone to the closet and was now unzipping the inside pocket of a purse. The truth was that as painful as it was, she was going to look at this picture again because there was a baby inside of her. And no matter what she did to this baby, it would never change the fact that she was this child's mother—*now*.

She sat on the bed with closed eyes, holding the small picture with both hands, as though it may tear itself away from her grasp and fly away. She braced herself and opened her eyes. She looked at the picture.

"There's a little girl inside of you. She's two and a half inches long. Her feet are almost half an inch long. You can't feel it, but she moves around a lot. If you could see her fingers and toes, you'd see soft finger nails and toe nails." The angel was heavy with the importance of his mission, but this didn't stop a grim smile from appearing as he said, "Her face looks like a baby's face now. She even sucks her thumb some. This is what you plan to kill, Heather. You will have to live with this all of your life. You will never be able to hide from this everlasting crime."

Heather's thoughts broke her heart. The weight of what she knew she had to do doubled her over and pulled her to the floor. She fell to her side with great sobs and wailing that gave her no relief.

Vincent's head felt like it weighed a hundred pounds. His face rested in his hands over an open four-inch thick medical book, with his elbows propped on the table. He had been fighting a losing battle against sleep all night. He had even resorted to physically holding his burning eyes open with his thumbs and index fingers. His cemented eye lids testified that he had lost yet another battle.

Wake up, son of Adam. Your wife is in distress.

Vincent journeyed deeper into sleep.

Wake up, son of Adam. Your wife is in distress.

Vincent didn't move.

"Vincent, wake up!"

Vincent's head popped up. "What? Huh?" Momentarily startled, he looked around from the kitchen table into the living room. He could've sworn he heard a man yelling for him to wake up. He looked down at the book and shook his head. This crap was trying to drive him crazy.

"What time is it?" he said. He pressed the side button on his phone and cursed. "We gotta get to the clinic."

He stood up and remained still, taking a deep breath with his eyes closed. He was heavy with exhaustion and heavy with what he and Heather were about to do. He was six years removed from Regina's suicide, but it seemed like yesterday. He had told himself ten thousand times that his girlfriend didn't kill herself because of the abortion he had talked her into getting. But something deep in his soul wouldn't stop pointing an accusing finger at him.

Vincent opened his eyes. Then just what was he supposed to do? Drop out of medical school? Heather was in no condition to care for a baby. She had nearly had a nervous breakdown when she failed the bar exam the second time.

Vincent's face hardened. He sat back down. Honestly, he didn't know if they were going to make it through this. Here they were living in one of his dad's rental properties, which wouldn't have been bad if he didn't hate the drunk, irresponsible SOB. He had a wife whom he loved with all his heart, but a wife who was as fragile as an eggshell. If she kept the baby, knowing her, she'd probably fail the bar again. And she'd probably be back in the hospital—or worse.

And what would happen to the baby? Would Heather be capable of loving their child? Under these circumstances, would he be capable of loving their child? He wished he could reject this thought as outrageous and hated himself that he couldn't. Anger rose in Vincent's heart. He knew all too well what it was like growing up in a house where you weren't wanted.

I'm as bad as Heather is weak, he admitted to himself. *Of all people, I should know better.*

"Be strong," said the angel. "For once, be a man. Lead your wife in the right way. She will follow you if you are strong."

Vincent narrowed his eyes at the sound. He listened closer. Heather. She was wailing. He ran up the stairs. "Heather," he called out before bursting into the room.

She was in a fetal position on the floor and clutching something to her chest.

Vincent dropped to a knee. "What's wrong? What's wrong?" He glanced around her for any signs of blood. Nothing. He scanned her from head to toe. Nothing. In the loudness of her cries, he heard a whisper in his heart. *The baby.*

He wouldn't try to get her to stop crying. She needed to cry. So he instead placed a light hand on the side of her rocking head. He stroked her wet face. He stroked and stroked until the last wail became a tired whimper.

Be a man, Vincent.

"What's this?" He spoke of the paper she held against her chest.

"Just a paper," she said.

He nodded after a pause. "Okay."

Lead your wife, Vincent. She needs you to be a man.

"What are we going to do?" Heather's voice was weak. "What are we going to do about this baby?"

Vincent's soul trembled. He knew he was at a moral crossroads with a broken compass. He took the coward's way out. "What do you want, Heather?"

She was still on her side. "I don't know. I want to be more than I am. I want to fill this hole in my heart."

Vincent took a mental step backward as he thought on her words. He knew she wanted to be a lawyer, but this was more than that. This was the peeling away of a new layer of vulnerability. And what he saw scared him. She wanted something he feared she would never get if they had the baby.

"Honey, I'm going to call the clinic and tell them we're running late. We're going to terminate the pregnancy. You're going to study for the bar, pass it, and in a few years, after you've gotten established in your career, we're going to have a beautiful baby."

"Really?" asked Heather.

"Really?"

"Then everything's going to work out okay," she said, with a weak hope that she wanted desperately to be true.

"Yes, everything's going to be okay," said Vincent.

"Yes, everything's going to be okay," said Unwanted.

A chill gripped the baby's spirit. She pulled her thumb from her mouth and kicked and thrashed, looking for an escape from a danger she felt closing in on her.

3

The angel walked into the kitchen.

Nancy's eyes became so heavy she could hardly continue chopping celery. She fought the sudden tiredness and continued chopping. Finally, she said, "This is ridiculous. If I'm this tired, I'm going to take a nap." She went to the living room. "Bill," she said to her husband, "I'm going to take a nap. Don't worry. Lunch isn't in jeopardy."

Pastor Bill, as everyone called him, sat in his favorite chair and wore a baseball cap that said something about retirement and fishing. He flipped the page of his *Field & Stream* magazine without looking up. "Woman, it's eleven o'clock. You just got up."

"Bill, close your mouth. You're attracting flies."

"Now that's a nice deer," he mumbled, looking at his magazine. "If I'd married a younger woman, she'd have my food ready when she's supposed to, and she wouldn't give me any lip about it."

Nancy looked in his direction. *Oh, yeah?*

Pastor Bill's face was buried in his hunting magazine. A wet dish rag hit him in the head and landed on his magazine. "Woman, you can't treat the pastor like that. If these were Old Testament days, I could have you beaten."

Nancy lay down and closed her eyes. "Yeah, but they're not Old Testament days. And if you're ever feeling lonely, put your hands on me and I'll introduce you to my two friends, Smith and his brother, Wesson."

He looked at his wife of thirty-five years and smiled. "I think you'd do it, too." He went back to his magazine. "They don't make 'em like they used to."

Nancy didn't hear him. She was sound asleep immediately after *Wesson* left her mouth.

The angel blew a long breath on her face, then slowly disappeared.

Vincent stopped at the red light. He stared straight ahead, his instincts on the traffic, and his mind alternating between his old girlfriend's suicide and him taking his own wife to get an abortion. He jumped slightly when Heather's phone rang.

Heather looked at the number and decided no, but mistakenly pushed answer. She grunted at herself and shook her head in angry disbelief at her unfaithful finger. "Hi, Mom."

Pause.

"What am I doing? Oh, I'm just out running errands."

Pause.

Heather looked at Vincent. "You had a dream?"

Vincent tensed.

"About us," said Heather.

Vincent pounded the steering wheel with a hand and looked for the nearest place he could pull over. He sped through a yellow light and turned into a gas station. He turned off the ignition and fidgeted in a simmer while Heather spoke to her mom.

"What? Mom? Are you serious? No, I'm not pregnant."

"That's it!" Vincent got out, slammed the door, and ruffled both hands through his curly brown hair before walking away. He took about twenty steps before he turned around and walked back toward the car. About ten feet from the car, he slapped twice at the air before turning back around and walking away. He rubbed the hair on his face and stopped, mumbling something about the CIA. He looked at Heather. She was talking with her hands. When she did this with her mother, it meant Mom had her cornered. He hurried back to the car and got in.

"Mom, of course, I remember. How can I forget?"

"What? What?" Vincent whispered.

Heather silently mouthed the answer.

Vincent rolled his eyes. "Oh, my God."

"No, Mom, he doesn't ask me to do that any more. Yes, I'm sure. Of course, I'm sure. How would I not be sure?"

Vincent wanted to get out of the car again. Heather saw his agitation and put her hand on his leg. He looked at her with bugged eyes and waited.

"He knows its perversion. Yes, Mom, he knows God destroyed them with fire."

Vincent wanted to scream.

Finally, mercifully, Heather pushed the button, ending the call.

Vincent was out of the gate like a race horse. "She did it again, didn't she? She knows. She knows what we do in our bedroom. She knows if we smoke a little weed. She knows we're pregnant, doesn't she?"

"Yes, she knows."

"But how? How, Heather? How does she do it?"

"You know, Vincent. She has these...dreams. She's always had them. She's a Christian."

Vincent bounced an index finger at Heather. "Uh uh. Uh uh. I know some Christians, too. None of them are in our business like this. What about Aaron? He's a Christian. Is he in our business?"

Heather looked at him in disbelief. "Really? Aaron? Our marijuana supplier. Oh, Vincent."

"She knows about the abortion, doesn't she?" he asked, knowing the answer.

Heather took a deep breath. "Yes, she knows."

Vincent covered his face with his hands and rubbed up and down.

He came out of it and looked up as far as he could before letting out his own deep breath. "Did you tell her?"

"Did I tell her? Are you nuts? Tell my mom that we're aborting her grandchild? No, I didn't tell her."

"Good," he said in relief.

"Look at me, Vincent."

He did.

"And we are never telling her. We can never tell Mom and Dad that we aborted their grandchild. Do you understand me, Vincent? Never. After today we never talk about this again. It never happened."

Vincent heard his wife's words, but remembered his girlfriend's funeral. He'd never speak of this abortion again, but he knew from experience that some things refused to be silenced. "It never happened," he said.

As soon as Vincent got back on the road, Heather said, "Mom says the baby is a girl, and her name is Becca. She says the baby knows what we're up to and is terrified."

Vincent's face twisted. "What? You said you didn't tell her."

"I didn't."

"She's named it," said Vincent. "She's named the unborn baby she's not supposed to know about."

"She says she's praying against the abortion," said Heather.

"Oh, just great! She's given the baby a name, and she's praying against the abortion."

"Vincent."

He didn't answer.

"Vincent," Heather said louder.

"Yeah."

"She can pray, but this is our decision to make. She can't stop us."

Vincent kept his thoughts to himself.

———————————

Chelsea Women's Medical Clinic.

Vincent and Heather didn't see the thick darkness that

surrounded the clinic. They didn't see the hordes of bloodthirsty demons that swarmed in and out of the place in a frenzy that resembled flying, black piranhas. They didn't hear the spiritual screams and natural cries of babies being chopped with scissors and crushed with forceps and sucked out of their mother's bodies with vacuum cleaners created for this specific purpose. They didn't see the eternal spirits of lives cut short ascending from the bloody crime scenes to return to their Creator. Nor did they hear the wails of God Himself as the sound of His grief joined the sounds of hundreds of millions of murdered children as they cried out for justice.

Vincent and Heather were in no position spiritually to hear the urgent request of the victims spoken under the heavenly altar before the Judge of all the earth. "How long, O Lord, holy and true, until You avenge our blood on those who dwell on the earth?"

Nor were they aware of the powerful angel who was proclaiming God's promise throughout the heavens until His appearing. "It is a righteous thing with God to repay with tribulation those who trouble you...when the Lord Jesus is revealed from heaven with His mighty angels, in flaming fire taking vengeance on those who do not know God, and on those who do not obey the gospel of our Lord Jesus Christ. These shall be punished with everlasting destruction from the presence of the Lord and from the glory of His power."

Vincent and Heather exited the car and walked with determination through the darkness toward the clinic's doors with only enough perception to see what they wanted to see.

The baby felt them coming.

"I'm sorry, Mrs. Jennings, that your husband couldn't come in with you. It's clinic policy. Our experience has proven that it's a much more healthful environment to not allow anyone else in the room but medical staff during the procedure. We want to do everything within our power to make sure you receive optimal health care. Okay?"

She heard the words and said nothing, staring straight ahead at a spot on the wall.

"Are you okay?" asked the nurse. She didn't get an answer. "It's okay. The worst is already over," she smiled. "Three hours is a long time. But the actual procedure will be over in less than ten minutes. Then you'll sit in recovery with your husband for an hour, and you can go on with your life."

"Will you hold my hand?"

"Of course," said the nurse, grasping it just as the doctor entered.

The baby couldn't see the attractive face of the young, female doctor as she sat facing her mother's spread legs. Nor did she understand the words she spoke. But she felt their energy, and mysteriously she knew the person from whom the words came had instruments she would use to destroy her body.

There's still time to say no, said the angel.

But she didn't say no.

The baby spiritually saw the instrument and tried to get away. But there was nowhere to hide.

The nurse had seen the glazed post-procedure look in hundreds of women's faces—maybe even thousands. So she wasn't surprised. But women were resilient. They were strong. The woman would recover and give herself a pat on the back for taking control of her life. She looked at the patient and smiled at her as the husband held her under her arm and guided her away.

"You two have a nice day," she said.

A doctor walked by them on his way to perform another procedure. "You take care of her," he said with a professional smile. "Get out and enjoy the sun, Mrs. Jennings. It's a beautiful day out there."

There was no return smile from her. No return of a customary remark about the day. The nurse had been mistaken. The hour of recovery contained sixty minutes, but no recovery. She and her husband passed through the exit door with a numbness of soul that made them feel like zombies.

A couple walked toward them from the parking lot.

She looked at the approaching woman and when she was close enough, she grabbed her arm. "Don't do it," she said. "Don't let them kill your baby. Please, I beg you. It's not...it's not—"

Vincent looked at the woman who was squeezing Heather's arm. He looked at Heather, then at the man, signaling that he would appreciate it if he took his wife away. It was hard enough doing this without having a crying mother—or an almost mother—come out of an abortion clinic begging his wife not to get the abortion.

"Come on, honey." The man pulled his wife's fingers loose from Heather's arm. "I'm sorry," he said. "It's—" He didn't finish.

They walked away and Vincent and Heather continued into the darkness and entered the clinic.

This was Vincent's second time at the clinic. Funny...really, not so funny, it felt worse this time. He wondered why. Then he stopped wondering—Nancy. How could it not feel worse than the first time? The first time he didn't have to worry about Mom and her dreams.

How does she do it? How does she dream about stuff that's going on in our lives? This isn't that horoscope, Nostradamus, one-size-fits-all crap. This woman is like a cruise missile.

"You think your mother's dreams are—"he searched for the right word—"real?"

Heather heard an unspoken question submerged below the surface of Vincent's query. She put the magazine down. She wasn't reading it anyway. "You mean do I think God told her we're getting an abortion?"

The clinic's pager lit up into bright colors and vibrated on the table.

Heather picked up the vibrator and stood.

Vincent stood.

"Yes," she answered.

He kissed her on the cheek, watched the receptionist disappear with his wife, and sat down. He bent over, with his elbows on his knees and his head in his hands.

If this is God... He shook his head. *Great. Just freakin' great.*

"And how have you been since I last saw you?" Dr. Lí wore a radiant smile. "Done anything exciting? Been anywhere?"

Heather appreciated the doctor's energy and smile, but she wondered now, as she did the last time she was here and had cut the abortion short, how the woman could be so joyful working in a place like this? She was about to kill someone's baby for a fee, and she was asking her had she done anything exciting or been anywhere exciting lately? Had the world gone completely mad?

"No," said Heather.

"Well, honestly, neither have I," the doctor spoke through her large smile, "but we've got a cruise planned."

"Where to this time?" asked the nurse. The same nurse that was there when Heather had called the last abortion off at the last minute.

"Mediterranean," she beamed. "Can't wait to see Greece. Lots of Bible history."

Heather felt like she was pricked with a pin. Her husband sitting in the abortion clinic's lobby asking about God. The doctor who was to perform the abortion talking about Bible history. What was next, the nurse singing *Just As I Am?* "I'd like to get this done as soon as possible," she said.

"Of course." Dr. Lí's smile lessened only slightly. "No changing our mind this time, huh?"

A determined look came to Heather's face. "Could you give me something? Something to put me to sleep?"

The doctor pushed back on her stool. "Yes...we could, but it would be unnecessary, and it would make the process longer. If we begin now, we can empty your uterus of fetal matter in three to five minutes." Dr. Li's full smile was back.

For a moment, Heather thought of pressing the matter. If she was asleep, she couldn't change her mind. Not that she was going to—she wasn't—but it would be impossible for her to change her mind if she was sleeping.

"Okay, no drugs." She looked into the doctor's eyes. "But Dr. Li, I need this baby dead today."

The smile left the doctor's face. She'd never heard a pregnant woman speak so candidly about an abortion. She rolled the chair closer and reached for her instrument.

'Empty your uterus of fetal matter' pounded on the door of her conscience like a firefighter trying desperately to awaken drunken residents from a burning home. Heather looked at the working light above and wondered why the room seemed to have gone dark.

Nancy put down the phone. "Bill, I've got everybody praying, but I don't feel good about this. I know that daughter of ours is pregnant, and I know she's planning to have an abortion. That's what I saw."

Bill turned his head, with a little twist of the face. "You sure about this, hon. Abortion? That's a lot even for Heather. You think she'd do something like this?" He shook his head. "I just can't see her doing something like this. That's not how we raised her. She knows better."

Nancy's eyes were filled with water and trouble. "I know we didn't, Bill. But I know what I saw." She recalled the dream and shuddered. "I saw her sitting on a table and letting some woman chop her baby to pieces. Bill, the baby, our granddaughter, our *granddaughter*, was fighting for her life."

Bill didn't want to believe their daughter was capable of this. But the tormented look on his face said that time had proven that his wife's dreams were something to not take lightly. "Nancy, we gotta pray. I don't know what would make her do a thing like this, but we gotta pray right now!"

Nancy started by reminding God of a Scripture.

Unwanted found himself in an odd position. Like the last time Heather had come here, he was rooting for the baby. For what good was a dead baby to him? He couldn't live in the soup of a dismembered baby who was sucked from Heather's body. He needed this baby to be born. Only then could he enjoy years of expressing himself by tormenting her with rejection. But what could he do to stop the instrument of death in the medical assassin's hand? He looked on in futile anger as the tool prepared to close on the baby's body part it located.

"Wait," he said, hopefully. "What is that I hear? Scriptures? Someone quoting—no, praying Scriptures for the baby?" The demon trotted sideways a few steps in the direction of the words. He listened intently, his eyes lighting up in dark hope.

"Arise, O Lord, do not let man prevail!"

"Yes! Yes!" the demon encouraged whoever was praying this Scripture to the enemy. "Don't stop. Don't let this murderer have my baby!" The demon listened, his fidgeting body begging for more. There was more.

"Have mercy on me, O Lord, for I am weak…O Lord my God, in You I put my trust. Save me from all those who persecute me. And deliver me, or they will tear me like a lion, rending me in pieces, while there is none to deliver."

Unwanted took on a momentary calm, wondering at the baby. He wasn't sure, but it seemed like the prayers were now coming from the baby. *Praying babies?* He didn't know of anything in the cursed book that talked of such things one way or the other. But why not a praying baby? The vermin was alive, after all. *Fascinating*, he thought.

The demon shook himself. "What am I doing? I don't have time for a Bible study. This wench is trying to kill my baby." He looked around in every direction. "Do any of you worthless angels hear this defenseless baby crying out to God for help? Can we get a little help here?" he yelled.

———

Dr. Lí inserted a pair of embryotomy scissors into Heather. The scissors had long handles and short ends, perfect for reaching babies and clipping off heads, arms, and legs. The ends found the baby's left arm.

You are my hiding place! You preserve me from trouble! You surround me with songs of deliverance!

"That's it! Don't stop, you cursed baby! Pray! Pray!" yelled the rejection spirit. "Maybe you can get somebody off his holy, sanctified butt to do something about this woman!"

Heather and Dr. Lí jumped at the sound that blared through the building. The nurse gasped and clutched her chest. Dr. Lí looked at the nurse and rolled her chair backward. The ever-present smile was gone. In its place was a look of pure anger. She lifted her hand. "What is that?"

"I don't know," said the nurse. She looked up at the new speaker. "Music."

"Yes! Yes! It is obvious that it is music, Carol. What I want to know is why does the clinic now sound like a rock concert? Will you—?" She cursed again. "I'll do it myself."

Heather was leaning back on both elbows, her feet still in the stirrups, and her expression one of total disbelief.

"I've never seen her like this," said the nurse. Then it dawned on her why Dr. Lí was acting like this. "Oh, I'm sorry. I don't know what this is. The intercom system is new. It's not even supposed to be ready until tomorrow. The guy said the speakers won't be wired until then. At least that's what they told us." She shook her head. "I'm really sorry for this."

Heather said nothing. She laid back down and stared at the ceiling. *Mom, I know this is you.*

———

Vincent looked around from his seat, wondering what madness was going on in this place. Why was the 1979 AC/DC song *Highway to Hell* blaring throughout the abortion clinic like this was an auditorium? He watched with perfect understanding when a heavyset woman with too much make-up and too little attention given to purchasing her wigs took a girl by the arm and jerked her out of her seat. He assumed by their similar features that the girl was her daughter.

"Lord Jesus, forgive me," said the woman. "Come on, girl. Get your fast behind up. We are getting out of this place. God will just have to make a way." The woman walked across Vincent's line of vision, staring at him like there was a monkey sitting on his head.

What. Is. Wrong. With. You? he thought of the woman as he looked into her wide eyes. The last thing he heard her say was, "Come on, girl. This place is full of the devil."

Vincent looked at the receptionist sitting behind the glass and Heather's doctor blasting her out, presumably about the unplanned concert. The poor woman was nearly in tears as they spoke—really, as the doctor screamed at her. There wasn't very much back and forth conversation going on. Finally, the music stopped. He watched the doctor march down the hall on the other side of the thick glass which separated the waiting area from the hall of patient rooms. She put her smile on and disappeared into a room.

The doctor opened her mouth to apologize to Heather.

"Dr. Lí, I don't mean to be rude, but I don't want to hear it. What I need is an abortion. I need it now. I *need* you to take this baby from me. Will you do this for me?"

Dr. Lí looked at the tears in Heather's eyes and broke out of her momentary frozen position. "Yes," she said with steely resolve.

The doctor picked up the scissors and sat in front of her patient.

Vincent wasn't a Christian, and he wasn't trying to pretend to be one. He was just trying to live his life the best he knew how. Pay bills. Keep wife from nervous breakdown. Finish medical school. Don't piss God off.

That last one wasn't added to the list until he heard *Highway to Hell* pop out of nowhere a couple of minutes ago. Mom and her dream had stuck a nail in his butt that he may have been able to at least try to ignore. But *Highway to Hell* blaring out of nowhere right when he had prayed—he guessed that's what his mumbling was—where was this abortion going to take them?

He looked at the glass door to the left and the receptionist to the right. He knew she wouldn't open that door for him. Plus, why did he want to go back there? To talk her out of it? To talk her through it? He didn't know. All he knew was that he had to get back there—and now!

The receptionist was still shaken. It was apparent she was embarrassed at being screamed at by her boss in front of everyone in the waiting room. She kept her head lowered as she did her work. She turned to the side to get something when she heard a bunch of commotion on her desk.

A man had jumped through the large opening and landed on her desk, sending things flying everywhere. The receptionist screamed and jumped up. She ran screaming out of the office through the waiting area and into the parking lot. Others in the waiting area followed her lead, sprinting for the door to the parking lot the moment they saw the man jump through the opening.

Vincent ran for the door that stood between him and his wife and baby.

Dr. Lí was light-years beyond frustrated. The scissors wouldn't close. What else could go wrong? She put the scissors down with a slight slam and picked up the forceps. She looked inside and found one of the baby's arms. She closed it on the arm and prepared to tear it off.

The door burst open.

"Stop!" Vincent ordered, looking at the doctor's hand.

The startled doctor turned, but her hand didn't move from its lethal location. Something evil appeared on her face. Vincent couldn't explain it, but he saw it.

"What are you doing?" said Heather.

"Doctor, if your hand moves one inch...if it twitches...if you sneeze, I will kill you right here, right now. Do you understand me?"

Do it! Do it! He has no right to be here! No right to stop this abortion! The murderous spirit shouted so loudly and frantically that its sounds almost became audible to the doctor.

The doctor looked at Vincent's eyes. Common sense prevailed. "What do you want me to do?"

Without taking his eyes off the doctor's hand, he said, "You slowly open your hand."

"I don't want any trouble, Mr. Simmons."

Vincent noticed her hand didn't open. "I didn't say there would be trouble. I said I would kill you. Slowly open your hand and let my baby go."

"Okay," she whimpered. "I'm not moving, Mr. Simmons. My hand is trembling because I'm scared. I'm opening my hand now."

He watched her hand open. "Get that thing away from my baby."

The doctor slowly pulled the forceps away from the baby and out of Heather. She let the instrument drop to the floor.

The nurse's back was pressed hard against the wall.

Heather couldn't believe what she was seeing. Vincent threatening to kill someone? A woman? Her mind hadn't yet concluded that there wasn't going to be an abortion. Her legs were still in the stirrups. "Vincent?" was all she could say.

Vincent took her legs out of the stirrups and swiveled her to the side of the table.

"Vincent?" Heather studied his face as though he were an imposter. "What are you doing?"

"I don't know." He hugged her and kissed her on the forehead, then kissed her hair several times. "I don't know."

"You threatened to kill Dr. Lí."

Vincent looked at the doctor and nurse, his expression showed that whatever crazy state of mind he had been in was now gone. He searched for what to say. "I'm sorry. I didn't know what else to do. I couldn't let you kill my baby."

The nurse didn't move or say anything. She wasn't convinced the danger was over. Dr. Lí sat on her stool, gazing at the patient table with a blank stare, her whole body trembling hard. "Get out of my clinic," she found the strength to say.

"I'm really sorry," he said.

"If you are here when the police get here, I will press charges. If you are not here when they arrive and you ever return—"

"Dr. Lí," said Heather.

Still looking blankly at the table, the doctor continued, "If either of you ever come back to my clinic, I will have you arrested."

"Dr. Lí, I'm so sorry," said Heather.

"The police should be here soon," said Dr. Lí.

———

"I thought you angels would never show up," said Unwanted. "I liked what you did with those scissors. You have such liberties."

Kraśa ignored the demon. Hopefully, he'd have the opportunity one day to show this demon that they were never far away from the baby. And, hopefully, he'd be able to exact the vengeance of the Lord upon this demon for the permanent damage this failed murder had inflicted upon the baby.

Unwanted watched the angels ascend. "I hope it's okay for me to thank you for saving my house," he yelled after them.

4

Vincent deliberately didn't look at Heather. He sipped a cup of coffee that he knew from experience must've tasted good. Same French roast. Same number and level of scoops. Same amount of water. Same cream and sweetener. But the foul mood interfered with the coffee's taste. He'd have to rely on his memory to enjoy it. He took another angry sip. *What was the guy's name who wrote that crap about Sunday mornings being easy?* he thought. *He ought to have his—*

The guy's name popped into mind. Lionel Ritchie. His thought softened. He liked Lionel. Lionel was cool. No need in taking it out on him. But that didn't change the fact that he needed to change his song. There was nothing easy about dealing with a bitter, complaining woman in her eleventh month of pregnancy.

Eleven months!

It wasn't common, but it wasn't exactly a medical miracle either to go this far past the due date. But of all the women in the world to be the exception, why Heather? Why someone who absolutely hated being pregnant?

Vincent held the cup steady near his lips, continuing to beam his angry gaze at a lamp directly ahead of him. Without turning his head, he squinted a Clint Eastwood look and stole a long gaze at his angry wife lying on her back on the sofa. He watched her try a few times to find a comfortable position. By the scowl on her face and the way she let out a curse word in rapid machine-gun style, she wasn't successful.

You hate your own baby, don't you? he thought. He knew the answer to this. *And you hate me for stopping the abortion, don't you?* He knew the answer to this, too. He had a response. Vincent didn't say it. He didn't have to. The revulsion that took the place of his blood and circulated through his body in hot liquid fire said it for him. *I hate you, too.*

"We could always use her for fish bait," said Vincent.

"What?" Heather wasn't as comfortable as she would have liked, but she knew she was probably as comfortable as she was going to get. So she didn't want to reposition herself. But anger beat practicality. She lifted herself up to an uncomfortable sitting position. She looked at Vincent. "What is that supposed to mean?"

Vincent took another sip of coffee. It was no longer hot. He didn't like warm coffee. But his anger increased the coffee's temperature. His heart hardened and he sipped again. The coffee was good. "It mean's having a baby girl doesn't have to be a total loss."

Heather's eyes glared. "Fish bait?"

Vincent put the glass cup down hard on the wood table. He joined her glare with one of his own. "Yeah. Fish bait. You've been out fishing with your father a hundred times. I'm sure you know what fish bait is."

She scooted up a little on the deep sofa. "Why would you say something like that?"

"Oh, I don't know," Vincent bordered on yelling. "Beeeecause you act like this child is the worst thing that has ever happened to you. Because every day and night for the past seven months I've heard you talk about our baby like she's a disease destroying your life. Or maybe it's because, ohhh, I don't know, you're the only pregnant lady I've ever known to hate her own baby."

The baby felt the hate and balled up as best she could, trying to make herself as small a target as possible.

That was it, enough to push Heather into full waddle. She placed her hand on her belly and waited for the moving to stop. She hoisted that mountain of a belly up and walked as fast as she could to Vincent —which was quite slow. Vincent waited in silence as she made her way around the coffee table in slow, wide steps, with a hand on one side nursing an ache.

"You know what I hate, Vincent?"

"Well, actually, yes. I think I do."

"No, actually you don't. What I hate, Vincent, is being trapped in this condition. And do you know why I'm trapped in this condition?"

Vincent didn't let her finish. "I'm sorry. Am I missing something? You're not on the *Titantic*, Heather. We had sex. Like billions of women before you, you got pregnant. You don't have a *condition*. You're having a *baby*. *We* are having a baby. It's not the end of the world."

"It is the end of the world!" she screamed.

The sudden scream pushed him back in his chair. He watched her waddle away as fast as her anger would take her. He let out a long, slow, guilt-heavy breath. This non-abortion had turned their marriage into one intermittent, but persistent argument, sliced, diced, tossed, and served in a hundred different ways and times. He was sick of this diet. He buried his face in his hands. When he looked up, Heather was standing before him with her iPad.

"The end of the world," she said, handing it to him.

He took it. A site was opened. *The Supreme Court of Georgia Office of Bar Admissions.* Vincent felt everything drain from his body before he looked closer. He knew from her behavior what he was going to see. The names were in alphabetical order. He scrolled down, then up, then down again. There was one name conspicuously missing.

Heather had failed the bar exam for the third time.

Vincent looked at his wife's face and emitted a low gasp that came from deep within his throat. He stood up in slow motion and put his arms around her. He fought back his own tears as he tried to calm hers. He held the back of her head as he pressed it into his chest. She couldn't see his face, so he let his pain show in a grimace. "I'm sorry, honey."

"I can't pass this test, Vincent," she cried. "I can't pass it. Three times."

"You're going to pass it, honey. You have to hold on to your hope. You're going to do it." He was ashamed that he felt so little conviction that his words were true.

"How can you say that?" she said. "I looked up the stats."

"It doesn't make a difference what the stats say. It's what we say that matters."

"Georgia State has an eighty-two percent pass rate for first-timers. Eighty-two percent, and I was in the eighteen percent that failed! Thirty-six percent of people who retook the test a second time passed. I didn't. And it's even less for people like me who have to take it three times. And now a fourth, Vincent?" She pulled away and looked at him with drooped shoulders.

He had never seen such brokenness in her. Such finality in her submission to failure.

"He said I was stupid," she said under her voice as she turned away. "I guess I am."

Vincent stiffened. "Who said you're stupid?"

"Nobody," she mumbled. "It's not important." An apologetic smile that was only supported weakly by one cheek surfaced on her face. "I'm sorry, Vincent. I really am. I'm empty inside. I don't have anything for this child. I can't love it. I'm going to lie down."

Vincent didn't want to let this go. He couldn't let it go. *Who called her stupid? Where does this emptiness come from?* But under the circumstances, it would probably be more humane to let her lie down than to force her to talk about this now. Hopefully, she could fall asleep. *God, let my poor wife go to sleep*, he prayed, without realizing that he was praying.

He helped her up the stairs and onto the bed. He consoled her, or at least tried to, for several more minutes, and ended his efforts with a light kiss on the lips before going downstairs to call Heather's mother. Maybe she could help him understand what was going on with his wife.

Heather was in a deep sleep before Vincent reached the bottom stair.

———

The baby didn't understand with her mind the many comments and conversations about her that were said in her presence. *"I don't want this baby." "This is not a good time for this baby." "We have to get rid of this baby." "The baby's ruining my life." "Maybe I'll have a miscarriage." "This baby's making me feel miserable. I can't study like this." "She's going to make me fail the bar again." "Why did you stop the abortion?" "I don't love this baby." "We can always use her for fish bait."* And the most recent words from her mother: *"I don't have anything for this child. I can't love it."*

These words were unintelligible and meaningless to the baby's mind. But the communication wasn't mental. It was spiritual.

And it was painful.

Becca couldn't see the spirit with her natural eyes, but she knew he was there. She could feel his form, hear his words, smell his death—and feel his blows. Savage and sadistic.

First, the words. *Your mother hates you. They both tried to kill you. Nobody wants you.*

Then the knife.

Unwanted looked out of his dimension and at the angels who were watching what he knew they interpreted as a horror show. Well, it was. And it would only get worse. He lifted the knife over his head and looked into the angel Gabron's eyes for a few contemptuous moments. Without turning from the enraged angel, he brought the knife's tip down hard on Becca's spirit. Over and over and over, enjoying each stab of the knife more than the one before it.

Becca's pain was sharp, traumatic, agonizing. But it was so much more. The pain took her beyond the boundary of miserable suffering into the place of intolerable rejection. For as monstrous as these afflictions were, they were done at the hands of a demonic creature who was incapable of doing anything other than what it was doing.

But the knives in the creature's hands had been supplied by her own mother and father.

Becca writhed in pain. Her screams seemed to only enrage the demon more. She lifted her spiritual eyes to the heavens. To the God who had said of the prophet Jeremiah when, like Becca, he was yet in the womb, "Before I formed you in the womb I knew you; before you were born I sanctified you; I ordained you a prophet to the nations."

Her communication to God wasn't in English. It wasn't in any earthly language. She didn't know any earthly language. But this didn't mean she couldn't communicate. For communication with the Creator would not be dimmed, and pre-birth prayers forgotten, until *after* physical birth.

Help, O God, my Savior. Arise, and do not let man prevail. Do not let my parents take my life. For life and death are in Your hands, O God, my Creator. Have mercy on me, O Lord, for I am weak; a child in great danger from those who seek my life. Rise up, great God, and see my calamity. See the plottings of the one who hates me. Relieve me from this demon who wrecks my soul. Remove his cruel words and the blade will cease. Speak life to me and I shall live forever more. Tell me of Your love and my heart shall sing. Yes, Your love and kindness toward me will set me on high, and I will laugh in the face of great evil. Then I will shine as the sun in the darkest of night. Then I will be full in the greatest of famine. For my strength comes from the Lord. It comes from my Creator who rescues me from the evil one. My trust is in You. I declare that I will live and not die. Though my father and mother forsake me—

The demon stood over the suffering child. He was worn out from his savagery. He held the knife loosely at his side, taking deep breaths. He'd have to rest before lifting the knife again. But his tongue was not as tired as his arms.

"No one wants you, Becca! You're all alone!" he yelled.

Becca felt the crushing, suffocating weight of the demon's words.

She looked into the darkness of her pain and said, "Lord, I don't feel You. I don't know where you are. I don't know what will happen to me, but I trust in Your love. I will hide no longer from those who seek my life. Praise to the Lord Most High."

The exhausted demon peered at the rebellious child with renewed energy and lifted his knife.

Vincent was just about to punch in Nancy's number when his phone rang. It was Nancy. "Hey, Mom, I was just about to call you."

He and Heather had survived—barely—Bill's and Mom's blistering interrogations about their secret, not-so-secret abortion plans. They had lied as if their lives depended upon it, and the suspicious questions had ended months ago. But every time Vincent spoke to them, especially Mom, he felt like it was the day before Thanksgiving and he was a fat, wobbly turkey trying to convince the farmer that he was a pigeon and not a turkey. He'd be careful not to reveal too much, but he needed Mom to give him some backstory about Heather.

"You were?"

"Yeah, um," he looked up the stairs, "hold on." He went into a bathroom, put down the toilet cover and sat down. He turned on the fan. "Mom, I wanted to ask you something."

"Okay."

"Um, has Heather talked to you about her test scores?"

There was a pause. Then, "Lord, yes." Mom's voice was heavy with regret.

Vincent sighed. "Yeah, well, that's not good. We had a talk today and…" his voice faded before picking up again, "she said something about herself that I'm trying to understand."

"What she say?"

"She called herself stupid. She said, 'He said that I was stupid. I guess I am.' And she's mentioned more than once that she's empty. It's like she's hollow inside."

"That's what she said?"

"Yeah," he said. "I know she just failed the exam again. So I can see how she'd have a crisis of confidence, but," his voice trailed, "it sounded deeper than this. It sounds like there's something else going on."

"Where's Heather?"

"She's upstairs sleep."

"Sleep? Good. The poor girl's exhausted. We need to talk in person."

Vincent twisted his mouth. This was not the answer he wanted. He needed something before Heather awakened. "I was hoping—"

"Come outside," said Mom.

Vincent's head popped up. "Outside? You're here?"

"Yeah. The Lord gave me a dream."

A dream! "Oh, God," he said, like a man discovering he had just stepped in a big pile of dog poop, the words leaving his mouth without bothering to say goodbye.

"Come on out, Vincent. We need to talk. You can't miss us. We're the only big black truck in your driveway. Hop in the backseat."

Vincent put the phone in his pocket so slowly that his movement almost didn't qualify as movement. It *was* Thanksgiving. The farmers *had* discovered that he wasn't a pigeon after all. The turkey had been outed by another one of Mom's dreams.

Vincent looked over his shoulder and up at their bedroom window before getting in the backseat of the Ford-150. Closing the door had the sensation of hearing a prison cell door close—his cell. But instead of sitting on a metal bench attached to a drab, concrete wall, he was sitting on soft black leather.

"Hey, Vincent," said Bill.

Vincent didn't detect anything amiss in Bill's voice. He sounded like his usual jovial self. "Hey, Bill. I thought you were going to get a smaller truck." He knew Bill had never said anything about getting a smaller truck.

Pastor Bill's eyes rolled. "Now why would a man buy a small truck if he can buy a large truck? Nancy, I told you I had my doubts about this one. And now we're stuck with him."

That's what Vincent was hoping to hear—some wisecrack. So whatever their reason for popping up like this, it couldn't be as dire as he had feared. "What brings you by? I thought you guys weren't coming by until tomorrow."

"Is there a problem?" said Pastor Bill. "Do we need to give you time to get the marijuana smell out of the house?"

Vincent dropped his head.

Nancy punched Bill on the shoulder. "Bill!"

"Yeah, bad joke. I guess it's just my carnal man trying to hurt him for saying I'd get a small truck."

Vincent looked at Nancy who had turned in her seat to look back at him. She looked at his raised eyebrow and silly expression. "Oh, never mind him. Let's talk about Heather. You said she said someone called her stupid."

"Yeah," said Vincent. His eyes went wide momentarily as he thought, *Oh, what if it's Bill?*

Not much got by Nancy. "Lord, no. Not this one. The one before him."

Vincent's eyebrows tried to meet across the bridge of his nose. "The one before him?" He went from Nancy's face to Bill's, pondered a couple of moments, and returned to Nancy.

Pastor Bill broke the silence. "Believe it or not, I'm not Nancy's first true love. There was a scoundrel before me who drank like a fish and beat the crap out of her and little Heather."

Vincent had to work to remember an extremely brief and veiled reference Heather made early in their marriage that only now made sense. *Bill was her stepfather.*

"Bill, you don't have to be vulgar to get your point across," said Nancy.

"There are worse words than crap in the Bible, Nancy. Hell is in the Bible. Damn is in the Bible. Bas—"

"Are you going to go through all of them?" Nancy snapped.

"You cut me off at the second to last one." His expression was plain, except for a tell-tale sign of a slight upturn in the corner of his lip that revealed he was a skilled comedian taking advantage of the moment."

"Well, let that be the last one," Nancy ordered.

"Yes, ma'am," he said.

"Pastor Bill's right," said Nancy. "He used to beat the crap out of both us."

"Nancy!" said Pastor Bill. "I thought we weren't using that word."

"Well, it's already in the atmosphere. You put it out there."

Pastor Bill looked at Vincent with a twinkle in his eye.

"For some reason, he hated Heather. Can you believe that? Someone hating his own child?" She was looking into Vincent's eyes when she said this.

Turkey.

"He'd beat the poor child for the littlest of reasons—sometimes no reason at all. Come in the room and smack all sense out of her. Then he'd say all kinds of mean things to her. He used to love to tell her that she was stupid, and that the only thing stupid girls were good for were having babies."

Vincent flinched.

Nancy noticed.

"That explains why she's having such a hard time shaking this feeling—that she's stupid." That's all Vincent dared say. There was no way he'd say this monster, whoever he was, was also the reason his wife saw having a baby as an admission that she was stupid. Or as she had called herself another time: *nothing.*

It was time for Pastor Bill. "Didn't hunt. Didn't fish. Didn't go to church. Drove around in a little girly truck. Signs were there that he was no good."

Nancy ignored him.

"What happened to him?" Vincent backed up as soon as he finished the sentence. "I'm sorry. That's none of my business."

Pastor Bill smiled. "Tell him what happened to your true love." He looked to Vincent like he couldn't wait for Nancy to tell him.

"Smith & Wesson," she answered.

Pastor Bill watched in glee as Vincent's mouth widened.

"You killed him?" asked Vincent.

"No, I was already a Christian."

Vincent waited impatiently for the rest.

"He came home drunk and started his foot in Nancy's butt routine. He knocked me out. When I woke up, I went downstairs with the gun I had secretly purchased. He didn't know it, but I was at the range when he was at work. I heard a loud slap and him calling Heather stupid again. I heard what he had done to her, but I guess I was still in shock or something because even though I was dizzy and found it hard to stand, I made it to the living room.

"Little Heather was sprawled out on the floor. Blood's coming from her nose, and this worthless drunk's standing over her with a beer in his hand still calling her stupid. I raised the gun and told him to turn around. 'I'm going to kill you, Biggie,' I said. Everybody called him Biggie—from high school. He turned around and when he saw the gun, he quickly turned his back to me. He said, 'You won't shoot me in the back.' Then he started walking backward toward me."

"What did you do then, First Lady?"

"Why do I tolerate you?" she said. She didn't like the title First Lady. It was silly. But it didn't bother her nearly as much as she pretended. Pastor Bill knew this.

"Because I'm your new true love. That's why. Finish the story," he said.

"The good Lord gave Biggie his first butt hole. I gave him his second," she said.

"You shot him?" said Vincent. "In the butt?"

"Would've been the chest had he turned around. Good Lord gave him more sense than I thought he had. Anyway, I'm glad I didn't kill him. Seems the new butt hole was just what he needed. He came to the Lord a couple of months later."

"In Windsor Church of God," said Pastor Bill.

"Windsor? Your church?" said Vincent, certain that Bill had to be talking about another Windsor Church of God.

"Yep. Rascal got saved in my church. Good, strong salvation, too," Pastor Bill said.

Vincent's eyebrows did their touching business again. "Biggie got *saved*? In *your* church?"

"Yep."

"Then where is he? What happened to Biggie?"

"Got hit by a church bus of all things. Died on the spot," said Nancy.

This was like a soap opera. Vincent rubbed his forehead and blew out a breath that could be heard. "You shot Biggie in the butt. Biggie gets saved in your church. Biggie gets run over by a church bus. You marry Mom."

Pastor Bill saw a long runway. He came in for a landing. "I know how it looks," he smiled, "but I assure you I wasn't driving the bus, if that's what you were thinking."

Vincent sat back in the seat and pushed his back into it. "Whew, that's…" he shook his head, "wow."

Pastor Bill had one last thing to say before coming to a complete stop. "This is not one of those *Lifetime* movies. Nosiree, I married Nancy purely to get my hands on the insurance money, but I didn't kill anybody."

"Bill," said Nancy, in mock exasperation that may have had some real exasperation mixed in with it.

Vincent chuckled.

"Got a nice fishing boat and camper out of it," said Bill. He looked at Nancy and had trouble keeping a straight face.

They'd been married a long time. Nancy knew what was going on under that stoic look. She switched gears and looked at Vincent.

He saw the change in her eyes. *Uh oh. The dream.*

"Did we fill in enough blanks for you about Heather?" she asked.

He wanted to prolong the conversation. To steer away from any talk about her dream. He couldn't think of any way to do this. "Yes."

"Good," said Nancy. "I told you I had a dream." She looked at her watch.

"Yeah," said Vincent.

"God showed me that the baby's coming tonight."

"Tonight?" Vincent was intimidated by Mom's dreams. He'd rather they just go away. But one thing he knew was that he would never ignore them.

"Yes, tonight. I also saw in my dream that the baby was scared to be born. That's why Heather's nearly in the *Guinness Book of World Records.*"

"The longest pregnancy is three hundred and seventy-five days," said Vincent.

Nancy looked at him as though he was missing the point.

"I mean of a baby born alive and healthy," he said, trying to deflect attention off of he and Heather.

"Heather is fifty-eight days past her due date because the baby is scared of something. What have you and Heather been saying around this baby?"

Was Vincent really as drenched in sweat as he suddenly felt? Ten thousand little prickles erupted over his body. He dared not look at Mom. He looked at Bill and was sorry he did. What had happened to nice, always ready with a joke Bill? Bill looked at him like he was Superman focusing his x-ray vision to look through a steel door. Vincent dropped his eyes. *No, don't drop your eyes. You'll look guilty.*

"We can talk about this later," said Mom. "We need to get Heather to the hospital. Becca will be here at 5:22 p.m."

"Five-twenty-two?" Vincent's voice was weak.

"Five-twenty-two," she answered, her eyes looking through him. "I looked all over the Bible for fifty-two-two and five-twenty-two. For some reason I keep being drawn back to Psalm 52:2. It says, 'Your tongue devises destruction, like a sharp razor, working deceitfully.'" She closed her Bible. "I don't expect to get a straight answer from you or Heather. I'll just tell you this, Vincent. Your wife and my daughter is still haunted by my ex-husband's cruel words. I've tried everything I know to help her, but it's like something evil is clinging to her, sucking the life out of her, making her think she is less than she is. She can't believe God's love because this rejection thing inside of her won't let her see the truth. Biggie screwed up my little girl with his evil words. I hope you and Heather have not been speaking death over my grandbaby. If you have, it's going to show."

Vincent wilted under each word. Mercifully, she finally stopped. There was a long, awkward, scary, guilt-heavy three-hour pause during the several seconds Bill and Mom stared at him.

"I hope to God you haven't ruined my grandbaby," Mom said.

"Come on." Bill opened his door. "We gotta get Heather and our grandbaby to the hospital."

Vincent opened the door and followed them with quiet lips, but not a quiet mind. All he could see was Mom shooting Biggie in the butt.

5

Vincent saw what Heather was planning. Uh uh. Not happening. No go. Not today. She got him yesterday, but not today.

These weren't thoughts jumping out of the water of his mind, twirling in the air like dolphins for all the world to see—for him to see —before splashing back into the depths. They were more like crabs or lobsters on the dark ocean floor, aware of predators and running from exposed places to find safety in tight crevices. Besides, no good father would entertain such thoughts. So although he instinctively followed their orders, he wouldn't let himself acknowledge their presence.

Vincent hopped up the stairs two at a time, hurried into the bedroom, grabbed his Mac and stuffed it into his bag, and hopped back down the stairs. Even in her condition, Heather took long showers—he heard the water still running—so he was ahead of the game. This time he'd be able to make his break without an argument. He wrote a note, put it on the table, and hurried to the front door. He shook his head and pushed out a breath.

The plan wasn't perfect. He couldn't just leave a four- and a five-year-old by themselves, even if their mother was upstairs. He put the bag down by the door and ran back into the living room. The water was still running. Both girls sat on the floor looking at Saturday morning cartoons. Well, actually, that was when he was little. Cartoons were now any time a kid wanted to watch cartoons. This time they were watching a couple of carrots and tomatoes fighting for their lives.

Becca looked up at her daddy. "The man wants to put them in a salad."

Vincent looked at Becca. She had her mother's black hair and slightly angular face and bluish gray eyes, but that's where it ended. Everything else was him. The full eyebrows and lips. The nose, ears, and chin. Well, honestly, the eyebrows were obvious to him. He didn't know about the lips, nose, chin, and all that other stuff that women seemed to recognize at a glance whether it was the mother's or father's trait. But they knew better than him, and since every female above the age of twelve within a ten-foot-perimeter of Becca saw him in her, it must be true that she looked like him.

Becca stared at Daddy, waiting for a response other than his silent gaze.

"But he's not a bad man. He's hungry. It's lunch time."

This was Danielle. Heather had put yellow ribbons in her hair. It was long, too, like Becca's. But her hair was brown and curly. Vincent smiled. Brown and curly like his hair. A mental alarm went off and interrupted his smile. He picked her up and squeezed her to his chest. He kissed her forehead, nose, cheeks, eyes, and started over in quick fashion. The water had stopped. He only had a few more seconds before he had to make a run for it.

"I love you, baby," he said to Danielle, putting her down and planting one more kiss on her forehead.

Becca watched the whole thing from her sitting position. She waited eagerly, hungrily for Daddy to hug and kiss and tell her he loved her. He did it all the time to Danielle. She couldn't make his eyes look at her. So she said, "Daddy," and stretched out her arms to him.

He looked at her. Her outstretched arms asking for something he couldn't give. "I'm sorry," he whispered to himself. "I can't."

Vincent hopped to the door and waited for Heather to make her way halfway down the stairs before he closed the door deliberately hard behind him. A moment later he and his Mac were out of the driveway and onto the street.

Heather watched his car drive away and walked immediately to the kitchen table. This is where Vincent left his notes. She read it and balled it up, holding it in her clenched fist, and holding her scream in her clenched lips.

"Fine!" she spat. "I'll take Becca with me."

Becca's eyes were pointed toward the talking bright orange carrot and bright red tomato that filled the wide television screen. The carrot ran; the tomato rolled. Both sliding around a corner as the fork gained on them.

"Run faster," said Danielle.

Becca's eyes did a slow blink and looked without focus onto her pink dress. The dress was pretty. She knew it was pretty because she had worn it before, and Grandma and Grandpa had said it was pretty. They said she was pretty, too. But she didn't feel pretty. She couldn't. He wouldn't let her.

You're an ugly little girl. That's why no one loves you.

"Grandma and Grandpa love me," Becca answered aloud. She usually answered the voices aloud when her mother and father weren't around. She used to do it around them, but they told her to stop talking to herself. Mommy said only a crazy little girl would talk to herself. She didn't know what crazy was, but it was bad because when she told Mommy what the voices were saying, she screamed at her.

No, they don't love you, Becca. If they loved you, they would come over more to see you. They would ask you to go to their house more often. Unwanted watched Becca and focused on perceiving what her five-year-old mind was thinking. But more importantly, what she was feeling.

Daddy didn't hug you. He didn't kiss you, said the demon, knowing the thoughts were loud in her mind. *He hugged and kissed your sister. Why didn't he hug and kiss you?* The demon let the tip of that spiked question press painfully against her tender heart before bringing the hammer down and driving the spike deep inside. *There must be something wrong with you!*

Becca didn't know what it was. She put her little hand on her chest. She got up and walked toward Mommy, who was adding two more ribbons to her sister's hair. Heather saw her coming and started feeling sick. A frown formed. "What Becca?"

"My heart hurts."

"Your *heart* hurts? Becca, your heart is on the other side of your chest."

"It hurts."

Heather took a deep breath. "You know what I think, Becca? I think you see me busy with your sister and you're just trying to get attention. Now go sit down. We're going to the park. You want to go to the park with me and your sister, don't you?"

"Yes."

"Then go sit down."

You're nothing, Becca. You're not like your sister. You're ugly. Nobody likes you.

Becca sat down in front of the television.

Unwanted stood before the child with a dagger in each of his crusty hands. The stabs and slashes followed each of his proclamations.

Daddy hates you! SLASH.

Mommy hates you! SLASH.

You're ugly! SLASH.

They love Danielle more than you! SLASH.

Nobody likes you! SLASH.

You're alone! SLASH.

They wish you were dead! STAB.

Becca's whole left arm started aching. She rubbed it up and down, but the pain didn't stop. It never stopped when she rubbed it. It only stopped when it wanted to stop. She rubbed anyway. She went back to Mommy.

"My arm hurts again."

Heather sighed with helplessness. She could tell by how the arm was hanging by her side that it was limp again. "Can you move it?"

"No, Mommy. Can we go to the doctor?"

"We went to the doctor. Remember? She can't do anything. She doesn't know why your arm does this."

Heather looked at her child. She knew she should feel more sympathy for her, and she wished she did. Deep down she wished she could. But this was like wishing she could drink all of the Atlantic Ocean. She could try, but it would kill her. This is how she felt whenever she tried to love Becca. She could only last a little while before her self-survival instinct kicked in to keep her from drowning. Plus, there was something about Becca that literally made her sick sometimes.

"But it hurts, Mommy. Can they do another test?"

"Becca," Heather sighed and picked her up, "Becca, they've done every test they know to do."

Becca's arm didn't just ache; it felt like something was trying to pull it off. She felt something clamp around her upper arm and squeeze. She would've cried. She would've moaned. But Mommy had picked her up. She was in Mommy's arms, on her hip, looking into her face.

Heather's and Becca's eyes met and Heather started drowning. It was too much. She put her down. "I'm sorry, Becca, I can't."

Becca's arm ached, but though she was no longer in her mother's arms, she could still feel the warmth of her mother's touch. For the moment, the past warmth was greater than the present pain. A little smile formed on Becca's face. "It's okay, Mommy. I know you can't fix it.

"You're right, Becca. I can't."

6

Rachel poured the vodka into the shot glass and emptied it into the highball glass. She poured in the cranberry juice and pineapple juice and left a little room for the lime garnish. She grabbed a little straw and stuck it in the glass and with a smirk pushed it to the evergreen flirt on the other side of her station.

Harold was a regular. Nice guy. About a hundred and fifty pounds overweight. He got away with the flirting because he wasn't vulgar, and everyone knew, including Harold, that he couldn't back up anything he threatened or wished for. The girls also liked him because he was funny and was a fabulous tipper.

"Your twin, Crystal, would've filled the shot glass to the top," he said. "I saw you short me."

Rachel cocked her big, black hair to the side and sneered at him. "What is this? True confessions? Don't blame me. Blame your father."

He slid the drink closer. "Oh, now that was low. Even for you. We need to start calling you Crystal. Sound just like her. You ought to get that tongue of yours registered. It's a deadly weapon." He saw what she was thinking. "Don't say it." She exhaled and let her shoulders drop. "Good. I'm gonna make a lady out of you yet, *Crystal*—even if it kills me." He looked at her big hair. "It's amazing you don't tip over with that thing on your head. How'd you keep your balance?" He looked at her chest. "Never mind. A lifetime of practice."

Harold smacked thirty dollars on the counter before razor tongue could cut him. He smiled. "You were saying?"

Rachel scooped the money up and sang, "Thank you, Harold."

Harold gave her a huge, fake one-second smile. "Thank you, Crystal." He fluttered his hand backwards. "Now go harass someone else, will ya?"

There must've been something about the way Rachel "harassed" her customers tonight. She knew the tips were landing heavy, but she didn't know how heavy until it was time to go. "*Holy* crap," she said, and put the money back in her pocket.

"Hey, hold up and I'll walk you to your car," said Johnny, the other bartender. "I just need to hit the restroom first."

Give it up, Johnny. How much more strongly do I have to say I'm not interested? She walked quickly toward the door. "I'm a big girl, Johnny. See you tomorrow," she said, with a wave over her back.

Tomorrow was really later today. It was three o'clock in the morning.

Rachel walked quickly out of the tavern and turned the corner.

"That's her," the man lying across the back seat of the car said to the guy lying across the front seat and to the other on the phone who was hiding in the dark recess of one of the little shops. "That's the girl I saw in the bar. I saw her up close. I heard somebody call her Crystal. She got the black hair. The black make-up. Everything, man. That's her."

The *empty* car was parked on Rachel's side of the street.

She was half a block away from the tavern and directly across from the car when she remembered that in her haste to get away from Johnny, she'd left her purse. She turned around. A man in a hoody stood before her. He had a gun in his hand.

"Crystal, I'm going to count to three. If you're not in that back seat when I get to three, I'm going to shoot you in the face."

Her mouth opened in terror. Her lips smacking against one another with cartoon speed. "I'm not Crystal."

The man put the gun's barrel under her nose and pressed it above her top lip. "One, two—"

The man was at two before Rachel could even believe this was happening. She looked into the man's cold eyes and knew he had killed before. "Wait!" She hurried to the car door, opened it, and jumped in. The car door closed behind her and her terror went to whatever was worse than terror.

A man was waiting in the back seat.

A man was waiting in the front seat.

She was being kidnapped by three men.

"Put yo' head down," the man in the back ordered Rachel.

She lowered her head.

"All the way down. Across my lap. Put yo' hands behind yo' back."

She obeyed.

He grabbed her wrists and put a plastic tie around them and tightened. He then tied a scarf around her eyes. He slammed her head onto his lap. "Now keep yo' mouth close."

The driver sneered and glanced over his shoulder. "Told you I'd get you. You got a debt to pay, and you gone pay it."

"I'm not Crystal. My name is Rachel."

The man in the back seat slapped her hard. "What part of keep yo' mouth close don't you understand?"

Rachel was too filled with terror to regard her stinging face. The man had told her to be quiet, but she had to let them know she wasn't Crystal or they'd kill her. "Look in my purse."

The back seat man balled his fist this time. "Oh, so you stupid *and* hard of hearing." He raised his fist.

"Wait," said the driver. "Check her purse."

"What?" said the back seat man. "B— ain't got no purse."

Rachel's heart sank when she recalled leaving her purse in the tavern. "I'm not Crystal," she pleaded. "Please believe me."

"Now just the heck you ain't Crystal," said back seat man. "I was in there. I heard them call you Crystal. You answered when Humpty Dumpty called you Crystal."

Rachel didn't know whether her hysterical crying would make it worse or better, but she had no control over it. They were going to kill her because of something Crystal had done. She had to find a way to convince them she wasn't Crystal.

Her name tag!

"Look at my name tag."

"Shut the—"

"Please...just look at my name tag."

Back seat man jerked her up by the neck. All three men looked at the tag, even the driver.

Rachel's crying went down a couple of levels. "See? I'm not Crystal. My name is Rachel."

The one who had stuck the gun in her face looked at the driver. "Do you believe this hoe?"

"What?" Rachel's voice trembled. "Why would I wear a name tag that says *Rachel* if my name is Crystal?"

Back seat man slapped her harder than he did the first time. "B— what we want to know is if yo' name is Rachel, why you wearing a name tag that says *Crystal?* Or maybe you just think we too dumb to know the difference between *Ra—chel* and *Crys—tal.*" He looked at the guy who had gotten into the car. "You white as *Leave It To Beaver.* You'd think this b— would have at least thought you could read." He bent down to Rachel's ear. "You don't respect nobody. Runnin' over niggas, and just doing whatever you wanna do."

Rachel's disorientation added to her terror. Why were they saying these things? Her tag— *Oh, my God! My tag!* "No, no, no! It's a mistake. It's just a joke. Me and Crystal, we're like fake twins. I dress up like her and—"

One of the men finished for her. "Die your hair black and wear it in the same style. Wear your make-up like her. Wear her name tag. And answer to her name when someone calls you."

"Yeah, it's just a joke," Rachel begged.

"Yeah, well, what you did to my brother wasn't no joke," said the driver. "And we ain't no joke."

The car and Rachel disappeared into the darkness.

7

Becca's eyes released none of the emotion that filled her mind. The years had proven that tears were worthless. Instead, her chest rose up and down in rage. She looked at the four unopened envelopes and picked up the latest one. She looked at the return address. It should've made her smile. It didn't. She dropped it on the stack and lay across her bed on her back.

A tear defied Becca's commands. Its rebellion was immediately met by an angry swipe of her hand. *Tears don't do anything but show you're weak.*

Knock. Knock. Knock.

Becca knew who it was. There was only one person who knocked on her door. Only one person who came to her room. "Come in, Danielle," she said, without moving.

Danielle came in, shut the door, pulled out Becca's new high-back office chair and sat down. She rested both arms on the rests and swiveled around, looking critically at the room. "You really ought to do something with this room. People are saying you're bringing down the property values." She pushed her back against the chair. "Gosh, this thing is like a throne. Queen Becca." She smirked at her big sister.

"Makes you feel important sitting on a throne while you do homework?"

Becca hadn't lifted her head off the pillow yet. But she knew what smart-butt expression awaited her. Anger was still on the line, but Danielle's drop-in had put the call on hold. She turned to her side, plopped her elbow, and rested her head in her hand. Yep. There it was. Head cocked. A smirk, punctuated by deep dimples. And a raised eyebrow.

"You're not cute, you know," said Becca.

"Yeah, I know. I'm beautiful."

"You're only sixteen. You don't even qualify for beautiful until you're seventeen—like me," said Becca, making a joke she wished she felt.

"In case you haven't noticed, I'm an exception to that rule." Danielle shook her hair with exaggeration and twirled some in her fingers as she gave her a side pose.

Becca studied her and rolled her eyes before dropping her head back on the pillow and looking at the ceiling. "Okaaay, I confess. You're beautiful."

"Well now, you are both intelligent and honest," said Danielle.

"Okay. Okay. Enough already," pled Becca.

"Oh, there's more to come…" Her sing-song voice trailed with an unspoken offer.

"Unless?"

"Unless you come down and eat with us?" said Danielle.

Anger was back on the line and with a bullhorn.

"Did Mom or Dad ask you to come get me?" asked Becca, knowing they had not.

Danielle thought of a few mental gymnastics flips with the truth and knew she couldn't stick the landing if she lied. Becca was the type to get down there and ask their parents if they had sent her up to get her. "No," she answered, then rushed to get the next word in. "Becca, you eat up here by yourself all the time. You never eat with the family. Never."

Becca sat up and planted her feet on the floor. She hoped her eyes didn't reflect the fire in her chest. She wasn't angry at Danielle, and didn't want her to think she was. "The reason I don't eat with *the family* is because you're the only part of *the family* who cares whether I live or drop dead."

Danielle looked horror-stricken. "Why would you say something like that?"

"Danielle," said Becca, her sudden impatience with her sister's naïveté heard in the way she thrust out her name, "come out of the clouds. You're a nice person. I get that. But does that mean you have to see everything as you wished it were? Could you for once just see this as it is?"

Danielle's changing expressions showed that she was struggling with what to do with the bear that had just come out of nowhere. "Becca," she said, and then her response was exhausted.

Becca got on one knee before her and clasped both hands over one of hers, resting them on Danielle's thigh. "Danielle, I don't blame you, and I'm not mad at you. Mom and Dad love you. They should. You're a wonderful, smart, beautiful girl. I'm glad they love you. I'm glad you don't have to live with a hole in your heart. But I am suffocating to death. I need you to stop pretending that I am part of this family. I'm not. I just live here. You have parents. I don't. You are loved and wanted. I'm not."

Danielle's soft heart was crushed. Her large eyes filled with water. "Please don't say that, Becca. Please."

Becca allowed an expression that resembled a smile. "You're a junior. Where are you going to college?"

"What?"

"Where?"

"UGA if they'll have me," said Danielle.

"And if they won't have you?"

"Dad and I think I should go to Georgia State and then apply later as a trans—" Danielle stopped and looked at her sister with an open mouth.

Becca saw the ugly realization on her sister's innocent face. "Hand me those envelopes on the desk."

Danielle didn't turn from her sister. "I'm sorry," she said through tears.

"Don't be. This isn't your fault." She crawled a few steps and got the envelopes herself and crawled back to Danielle. "These are letters from universities I've applied to. Here's UGA. Here's Tech. Here's Stanford."

"Stanford?" Even in such an emotional moment as this, hearing Stanford in the mix was exhilarating. "You didn't open it."

"And we even have one from Duke."

"You didn't open that one either. Why haven't you opened them?"

"Others are on the way, too." Becca took in a deep breath and exhaled. She got up and sat on the edge of the bed. Danielle rolled the chair closer. "I don't know why I didn't open them. I guess I just wanted to see how long they'd sit here without one of your parents saying something about them."

"Did you tell them about the letters?" Danielle asked.

Always hopeful, thought Becca. "Did you put these letters on my desk?"

"No," said Danielle.

"Then either the postman put them there, or one of your parents put them there."

Danielle's squinched face showed that she was still struggling to find another explanation other than Mom or Dad placing her letters from university admissions offices on her desk and saying nothing to her.

"The shortest distance from point A to point B is a straight line, Danielle. They don't care."

"I don't understand," she said, shaking her head in denial. "You're so smart. You spend virtually every free minute studying or practicing. You're brilliant in everything you do. You probably have full academic *and* sport scholarships in one or more of these envelopes. Why…?" Danielle couldn't get her head around this.

"Kiddo, I'm not asking you to understand my suffocation. I'm only asking you to admit that Mom and Dad have their hands around my throat."

Danielle's glow was gone. Her shoulders slumped. She looked like she was the one with all of the problems.

"You want me to go downstairs?" Becca asked.

Danielle wasn't so sure now.

"Okay, I'm going," said Becca. "But I'm going with these envelopes. Let's open them up and make sure there's no surprises. There's Stanford, Tech, UGA, and Duke. Which one is the farthest from here?"

"Stanford."

"That's the one they'll both agree I should attend. No questions asked about scholarships, academics, athletics, nothing. They want me as far away from this family as possible."

Danielle looked at her big sister with sad eyes. "I don't think we should do this."

"We have to. I have to. I need you to see what I feel."

They opened and read the letters—no surprises—and went downstairs.

———

Vincent was first to see her. He looked up and did a double-take. He tried to cover his surprise by stuffing food in his mouth. But he couldn't resist the urge to look at Heather who had seen Danielle, but hadn't yet seen Becca.

"Satisfied?" Heather said to Danielle in a *That's why I'm Mom, and you're not* playful dig.

"Sure am," she said, answering in the same tone.

"Satisfied about what, Mom?" asked Becca, surprising her mother, who was looking to the left at Danielle when her question came from the right, just behind Mom's chair.

It was an instant replay of Vincent's response. Heather was obviously surprised, and then just as obvious, tried to hide her surprise. She started by closing her gaped mouth. Then it must have dawned on her that staring into a plate of spaghetti was odd. She put some in her mouth and chewed long past the time to swallow, like she was driving a car with the needle on E and trying desperately to get one more block out of an empty tank.

Guess that was a hard question, thought Becca.

Becca was a survivor. And like all survivors, she noticed things that needed to be noticed. She noticed Dad's surprise at seeing her. She also noticed that he was eating quicker than usual. He was going to do his disappearing act. The one he did whenever she was around. And Mom, she wasn't like Dad. She didn't physically leave when she was around. She emotionally and mentally left. *Must be some spaghetti. To look at it like that,* thought Becca.

Danielle sat down and put food on her plate, while Becca went to the cabinet and got a plate and glass, then to a drawer to get a knife and fork. She preferred to cut her spaghetti before eating. Danielle waited for Becca to fix her plate before speaking. "Guess what? Becca's got responses from some of the universities she's applied to."

Danielle pointed the fork into the plate and twirled the spaghetti. She smiled and put the food into her mouth. The few seconds of silence from their parents made Danielle widen her smile—to keep from crying. She didn't break the silence. She knew if she did, her tears would betray the smile. The smile that was keeping her from screaming to her parents, *How can you just sit there? Did you hear what I said? Your firstborn daughter has responses from university admissions offices. Don't you care?*

Becca had her own calculations going on. She was invisible to Mom, but only intolerable to Dad. At least with Dad, she existed. He'd be the one to say something. He dabbed his mouth with a napkin and put a hint of a smile on his face. Becca saw it and felt her heart go warm. She hated this about herself. So needy. So thirsty for attention and acceptance. But she couldn't help it. Trying to not respond to his smile, if that's what it was, for whatever reason it was, nervousness, habit, clumsiness, whatever, was like a flower in parched ground trying not to respond to a rainfall. It was impossible.

"Oh yeah?" Vincent said, looking at Becca.

Becca's elbow was on the table, with a piece of garlic bread in that hand. She looked at him and stopped chewing. She was certain that his smile had widened. No, she wasn't certain, but it looked like it did. Maybe. "Yeah."

"What schools?" he asked.

Becca looked at Danielle for a short moment that shared a long story. She smiled like an innocent person about to be burned at the stake in the name of justice. Danielle didn't share the smile. There was not one thing funny about this moment. Becca and Danielle looked into one another's eyes as Becca answered the fateful question.

"UGA, Tech, Duke, and Stanford. I'm waiting on some others, but that's what I have so far."

Danielle saw Mom look at Dad.

Becca saw Dad look at Mom.

"So what do you both think?" said Becca.

The silent mom with the invisible daughter spoke up as she and Vincent looked into one another's eyes. "I think Stanford is an excellent choice."

Vincent shook his head. "That's exactly what I was thinking."

"Thank you," said Becca. She pushed her chair back and went upstairs.

Danielle looked at Dad for several seconds. She said nothing because her brain hadn't caught up with her heart. There was no way to articulate a tornado. She turned to Mom. If anything, the tornado gained strength. The best thing to do, the only thing to do that would guarantee she didn't say something she'd later regret, was to get out of this room as quickly as possible. She pushed her chair back.

"You're not going to finish your food?" asked Heather.

Danielle was too stressed to try the placeholder smile. So she offered no smile at all. "Becca thought both of you would recommend Stanford. I think I need to help her sort things out."

Becca lay across her bed with the admissions letters on her chest and belly. Her heart and arm ached. She was like an airplane with no instruments in a cloud. She was moving fast. Toward what she didn't know. A mountain would be good. She didn't care. At least then it would be over. She heard the mumblings of Danielle saying something about this couldn't be true. Some naïve and unrealistic something or other about how Mom and Dad had to love her.

"Trust me. They love you. They're your parents. They have to love you."

She heard Danielle's hopeful voice as though a wall separated them. Loud on one side, barely audible on the other. Her sister's hope filtered out and pinned somewhere against a cynical stud. She felt a light kiss on her forehead and a drop of water on her closed eye. She heard the door open.

'You'll see, Becca. They do love you."

Danielle left the room and closed the door, leaving Becca alone.

Becca was not alone.

Unwanted was there, too. But he was not alone. Seventeen years, plus the pregnancy, was a long time to strengthen his position from a *hold* to a *stronghold.* It was a thing of dark beauty, which meant it was ugly and oppressive.

The rejection spirit was smug in his fortified castle. Its walls ever thickening. Its defenses ever growing. Unwanted considered his position. He smiled. *They can't touch me*, he said, as he looked from the relative—he'd say absolute—safety of his dimension of rejection.

An angel said something to another about his arrogance. Unwanted heard it and try as he may, he couldn't keep himself from answering. Not that he put a lot of effort into not saying something.

"It's a matter of perspective," he said. "Some would call it arrogance," he bobbed his head with a smug look, "some would call it confidence." He looked at them as though he expected an answer. His lips turned up. "Oh, that's right. Daddy said you couldn't talk to strangers."

"I'd like to open his belly," said Gabron to Justis.

"I like you, Gabron," said Unwanted. "You're the only one I can get a word out of. Your short bus brothers aren't friendly at all."

The angels talked among themselves as though Unwanted didn't exist.

"Oh, now that hurts," he said. "You know how painful rejection is. I can't believe—" He shook his head and one hand. "Never mind. We're getting off track. Back to my *arrogance* as you call it. I have reason to be arrogant. We are many. Let me introduce you to my friends."

Still no response from the angels.

"I know you're listening, angels" said the demon. "Come out, my friends," he said to the other demons afflicting Becca. "Introduce yourselves to my angel entourage."

First out was Alone. He looked at the angels and pulled back his long neck and studied them from head to toe. "They look like the three stooges."

Unwanted laughed. "They do, don't they. The one over there is Moe." He pointed to Gabron.

"The one pointing his sword at us?"

"Yeah," said Unwanted. "He's the mean one. He doesn't like me."

"And the other ones are *nice* and *do* like you?"

"Not as much as I would like," Unwanted answered with a sneer.

"True love is hard to come by," said Alone.

"I feel so rejected," said Unwanted.

The demons looked at one another wondering who was going to laugh first. Their laughter burst forth simultaneously.

"Oh, Alone, you're too much," said Unwanted, his dying laughter finally allowing his shoulders to stop bouncing. "Tell them what you do."

"Whew," Alone shook his head, 'I feel so rejected,'" he repeated. "That was good, Unwanted." He looked at the angel he thought looked like Moe. "I'm Alone. I'm a rejection spirit, too. I help Becca feel alone and out of place in the world. Even when she's in a room full of people, I help her feel alone."

The spirit opened his mouth for further commentary. Unwanted patted him on the back. "Okay, that's good, my friend," he said.

"That's it?" asked Alone.

"That's it. There are so many of us, and I want the angels to meet everyone. They're quite irresponsible. They pop in and out all the time without telling me anything."

"Of course," said Alone.

Next up was Hopelessness. He spat out his introduction. "I am exactly what my name says I am!" He leered at the angels.

Alone leaned into Unwanted's ear. "What's wrong with him?"

"You heard him," he whispered. "Hopelessness—it eats at you if you let it."

"What are you whispering about?" said another demon whose head was sticking out of the darkness.

"We're not talking about you," said Unwanted. "Stop hiding and come on out. Tell the angels who you are."

This spirit looked at his demon colleagues with as much suspicion as he looked at the angels. Unwanted started to hurry the spirit, but he was so skittish and easily offended that he may run back into the darkness. So he masked his impatience, barely, and waited for him to talk. Finally, satisfied that he was safe, the spirit spoke.

"I'm Run Away. Sometimes I'm Hide." The spirit's eyes bounced around looking for threats.

Unwanted saw the difficulty he was having and finished for him. "He's a fear spirit. I've got tons of them helping me. This one anticipates offenses and makes Becca hide or run away. There's a lot of them like him in her." A smile inched onto Unwanted's face. "Unfortunately, Run Away is often wrong about his suspicions. So Becca sometimes runs away from things that aren't really there."

Alone looked at Unwanted in mock surprise. "Nooo. Really? This must make it quite difficult for anyone to get close to her."

Pain was up next, but Unwanted's fun was over. The angels were gone. "See, what did I tell you, Alone? Did they tell me they were leaving?"

"Look at her?" said Alone. "Crying like a little baby. Holding that crippled arm of hers. I don't see what the enemy sees in these creatures. He promises this dirt that she can sit with Him on His throne, but kicks us out for wanting the same thing. We were angels!" He felt his hatred of God erupt over his being. He had only one way to hurt God, and that was to hurt the ones He loved. "Unwanted, I have work to do."

Alone heard nothing from his friend. He turned around and froze. From the corner of his eyes, he saw that the others were frozen, too, watching the imminent threat.

Three mercy angels stood motionless, staring at them from the other dimension. Big? Yes, they were big. Armed? Yes, they were armed. Ferocious? Yes, more lethal than truth angels, at least in the short term. For truth angels did their devastating work only in support of the truth. But these murderous creatures were proof of God's double standard of righteousness. They did whatever they wanted to do.

"Unwanted," whispered Alone.

"What?" he snapped in a whisper.

"Are these—?"

"Yes, they're mercy angels. Shut up!"

Run Away stood as motionless as the others. He knew the danger. He knew how unpredictable mercy angels were. But…his…nature… to…run…away…and…hide…was…pushing…him…to… Run Away took off before any of the mercy angels could react. He zigged and zagged, dipped and twirled, looped and counter-looped until he disappeared as a black dot in the horizon.

That was the plan.

The plan didn't go as expected.

Run Away made his move. A mercy angel was on him the micro-moment the demon's body tried to turn his thought into an action. The demon wasn't aware that he had moved. But he was painfully aware that he was pinned under a mercy angel being ripped apart by large, clawed hands. He was not aware that the large-mouth angel had bitten his head off.

This quick, violent commotion was not enough to make the other demons move an inch.

"Come out!" one of the other mercy angels commanded.

Immediately, hundreds of demons stood before the three mercy angels. The thought never crossed their minds to bum rush the angels. A face-to-face attack on God's mercy? No thanks.

"The Lord God Almighty has declared a brief moment of mercy for this daughter of Adam. Leave!"

The demons were gone before the mercy angel's mouth closed.

<hr>

Unwanted and Alone followed the same life-saving path, and now both were doubled over and leaning heavily with their hands on their knees as they let the weight of the car keep them from falling to the ground. Both of their burning lungs struggled for air.

Alone fell over onto his side on the asphalt. "It's not," he gasped a breath, "fair. How those," he gasped again, "mercy angels can do that. Come into our space like that."

Unwanted pushed himself off his knees and stood against the car. He knew the angels hadn't pursued them. Logic wasn't enough to overrule his fear, however. He scanned in every direction before answering with enough anger to kill—if he could.

"When has this ever been fair? The enemy makes these rules. Rules that no one can keep up with. Changes them whenever it serves His purposes. And makes Himself a catch-all exemption."

"Mercy!" spat Alone.

"Yeah, His beloved mercy," said Unwanted, with a low growl through clenched teeth. "We're the only ones who really have to follow rules. He has mercy on whoever he wants."

"You just quoted a Scripture. Romans, I think," said Alone.

"What?" Unwanted growled.

"Pretty sure of it," said Alone. "Paul and Moses. 'What shall we say then? Is there unrighteousness with God? Certainly not. For he says to Moses, I will have mercy on whomever I will have mercy, and I will have compassion on whomever I will have compassion.'

Unwanted twisted his face into a new level of ugly. "Never knew you were such a student of the Bible."

Alone got to his feet and leaned against the car. "Hey, don't look at me like I'm a son of an angel. If the enemy's going to use that cursed book against us, we need to know what's in there."

"So then what's the point, Alone? If He can use this mercy crap whenever He wants to invade our space?" He thought of Becca. "Loving these maggots and being kind and compassionate to whomever He wants!" His question turned into a statement. "I'm sick of it! Sick of it! If He can stick His hand in the garbage can and pull out anyone He wants—?" He jumped thoughts. "What does that leave us, Alone?"

Alone patted his friend on the shoulder. "Deception and lies. That's what it leaves us. God has mercy on whomever He so willy-nilly chooses. But sooner or later, He demands submission to truth. His truth. This girl, Becca, sooner or later she has to go the way of all the earth and choose for or against the truth. We just need to keep her so messed up that she's never in a frame of mind to seek the truth."

Unwanted knew this was true. He felt a little better. "Thank you, my friend. I just needed to hear someone say it again."

Alone smiled. "Deception and lies. A demon's best friend."

"Deception and lies," said Unwanted. His relative tranquility lasted all of two seconds. "But I *hate* mercy." A thought popped into his head. "What pretext do you think the enemy used to show mercy to this trash? You're the Bible scholar. What do you think He's using?"

Alone thought for several seconds, rubbing his chin. "He's God. He doesn't need a pretext. But if He did use one…"

"What? What?" Unwanted urged.

"His favorite is prayer?"

Both demons looked at one another with an unspoken acknowledgement. The mercy wasn't random. It was Bill and Nancy again.

Alone's dark eyes darkened more and narrowed. "Deception and lies."

Unwanted's dark eyes darkened more and narrowed. "Deception and lies."

8

Seven dinners later Danielle sat at the table, chewing in silence, as Mom and Dad made small talk. It had been more than a week since Danielle talked Becca into the lion's den. But Danielle was having a hard time dealing with her sister's blood and strewn body parts on the floor and both her parents dealing with the horrific scene by ignoring it. Danielle, however, was too sensitive a soul to get over witnessing a tragedy and not being affected by it. She wasn't built that way.

"How was school today, sweetheart?" asked Heather.

Dad looked up, his eyes joining Mom's question.

Danielle hadn't been built that way, but obviously her parents had. Her mind raced here and there, wondering about her parents. How Dad never missed their school Father-Daughter banquets. She didn't notice it then, but now she could let herself see and not deny the truth. He wasn't there for Becca. He was there for her. It showed in the pictures. It showed in his mannerisms. It showed in how his face lit up when someone said something about her.

He'd squeeze and hug her to himself as only a proud father could. But he never did that with Becca. How could he? He was never alone with her. And when he was, the time was always, *always*, cut short by something. Pressing work. An up-till-now forgotten appointment. A sighting of Godzilla. Anything to get away from Becca.

Danielle remembered how Becca would bravely stand to the side alone as Dad hugged her and gushed to others about how proud he was of her. She remembered how she'd glance at Becca and see her standing in a room full of people, yet alone. She remembered her big sister's watery eyes, and how she'd try to hide how hurt and humiliated she was. But she couldn't hide it, not from her anyway. How many times had she seen her sister casually rub her arm and hastily retreat to a spot alone or a restroom stall? And how many times had she tracked her down and found her crying and grimacing in agony as she tried to stroke the pain from her suddenly limp arm? And what a coincidence that this only occurred when Mom and Dad rejected her?

Dad, you missed Becca's Father-Daughter high school banquet. Funny how you never missed another one when I started going there, she thought. Her mind was asking no permission and seeking no assistance in digging up these memories.

And, Mom, I'm only sixteen, but I've never seen anyone go from hot to cold or from on to off as quickly as you. You can be so animated...talking and carrying on, until your other daughter walks into the room. Immediately you're cold and off.

Danielle's jaws closed and opened on the mush in her mouth that was once a bite off a yeast roll. The food had long ago ceased being a solid and begged to be swallowed. She kept her slow chew going, like a cement truck slowly twirling its load. There was a purpose to the twirl. Danielle was thinking.

"Well, how about them Braves?" said Vincent.

"Earth...to Danielle," said Heather.

Danielle blinked and she was back. She'd only been gone a few seconds, but she felt that she had grown ten years. She was no longer afraid. She was no longer a coward.

Danielle swallowed. "School," she said.

"Yes," Vincent said, half word, half laugh. "A place where people sit in a classroom and try not to sleep while a teacher talks."

Danielle looked at her parents. It was time for everyone to grow up.

"Honey? School?" said Heather, her head cocked, with raised eyebrows and a half smile.

"I can never get my chicken to taste like this," Danielle said truthfully.

Vincent and Heather waited to hear what was going on in the school world of sixteen-year-olds. Something may have changed since they were that age.

"You're gonna be sorry you asked," said Danielle. It was obvious she was teasing.

"Try us," said Vincent gamely.

"We're having a concert."

"That's it?" said Vincent.

Danielle looked surprised. "Soooo does that mean you're coming?"

Vincent made an *Are you serious?* look. He looked at Heather. "Of course, we're going. You're our daughter."

"But you don't know when it is. What if you've got something else planned already? You, too, Mom."

"Don't be ridiculous, Danielle. Have we ever missed any of your events?" asked Heather.

Danielle's body immediately declared independence. There were too many emotions attacking at once. Too many body parts allying with the rebels. Eyes. Voice. Heart. Pores. She had to get away from the table while she still had a façade of control. She popped up. "Restroom," she creaked out.

Once inside the restroom, Danielle turned on the fan and cried into her hands. "I'm so sorry I wasn't there for you. How have you survived this long by yourself? You've been through so much already. I hope this concert doesn't break your heart."

Danielle managed to labor through the meal without a meltdown. She knocked on Becca's door.

"Come in, little sister."

Danielle entered and sat on the carpeted floor with her feet crossed. She leaned back on her hands. "In an absolute sense," she said, smiling, "I'm the big sister and you're the little sister."

"I'm seventeen. You're sixteen. I'm five-foot-nine. You're five-foot-eight. How do you figure I'm the little sister?" A low-down thought volunteered for duty. "Unless you're talking about weight." Becca held the smirk in check.

Danielle twisted her face about five hideous ways, ignoring the insult. "You are *not* five-foot-nine."

"Ask coach," Becca said, her hand pressed against the little kid's forehead as she swung wildly at the air.

"You are five-foot-eight…and one-half inch, Becca. You know it. And I'm five-foot-eight and five-eighths."

Becca was lying on her back. She closed her eyes and put a hand over her face. "Ask coach," she said, with exaggerated sleepiness in her voice and faking a yawn.

"Ask coach? Coaches lie all the time about their players." There was a pause in the banter. "And what do you mean 'Unless you're talking about weight'? I know you're not saying I weigh more than you."

Loud, fake snores came from under Becca's hand.

Oh, so now you're sleep, thought Danielle. She got on her knees and reached a hand under Becca's hand and pinched her nose shut. Becca compensated by breathing from her mouth. Danielle compensated by using her other hand to pinch the fake five-foot-niner's lips shut. No problem. Becca compensated continuing to breathe out of the corners her mouth.

Something went wrong with the plan. Becca found that the two slits she had available for air on both sides of her mouth had no problem pushing air out, but a whole lot of problems sucking air in. She jumped up, gasping for air.

"Are you trying to kill me?" Becca asked, with eyes widened by the joy of having at least one person in the house who didn't want to throw up or run away when they saw her. "Okay, if it makes you happy, I'm five-eight and a half."

Danielle had started laughing when Becca jumped up sucking for air. But then Becca had said, "Are you trying to kill me?" Amazing how quickly midnight could replace noon. Her heart turned heavy for her sister. *I hope not, Becca.*

"I need to talk to you about something," said Danielle.

"What?" she asked, sensing the change in her sister.

"My concert."

Concert day, or rather, evening, arrived like the first mortgage note of a new homeowner who had just discovered there was no way he could afford the house. Danielle had never been so scared. What had she been thinking to talk her sister into this?

"This is so exciting," Heather said to no one in particular. "I can't wait to hear you, Danielle."

Becca didn't think it. She felt it. *Here I am. In the car with Dad, Mom, Danielle. My family. But only Danielle is my family. I don't know who Mom and Dad are. I don't belong here. Why am I in this car?* Becca subconsciously pushed her back into the car seat. She wanted to disappear. Oh, if only she were as small as she felt. Then she could hide. She could get out of this.

Vincent drove into the school parking lot and followed the directions of the guy motioning him with the orange thing. He turned into the parking space. "Yep, me too. You have a lovely voice."

Danielle looked at Becca and squeezed her thigh. "Thanks, Dad." She looked into Becca's hurt eyes and mouthed, *I love you.*

I love you more, Becca replied with silent lips.

The car stopped.

"Let's go." Dad was in a cheery mood.

"Dad," said Danielle, "I'm going to the restroom. I'm taking Becca with me. There's reserved seating in the front for the families of people who are performing."

"And they're going to know we're family?" He had his doubts.

"That's why you and Mom have lanyards hanging around your necks," she said. It felt good for a teenager to scold her parent.

He looked down. "Oh, yeah."

"Oh, yeah," said Danielle.

Danielle and Becca took off in a hurried walk.

"I thought that by now Danielle would've grown out of being ashamed of us," he said, only half joking.

"She's not ashamed of us," Heather smiled.

"I know. Let's go get our seats before the people with no lanyards take them all. Our girl is the star of the show. I want to be so close I can see her tonsils when she sings."

"What is it with doctors and tonsils?" said Heather.

There was no actual discussion between Vincent and Heather as to who was going to sit next to Becca. They both knew it was going to be a mixture of luck and maneuvering. The end seats were all taken. The front rows were all taken.

Vincent grimaced. *Get here early and I still have to sit on the second row.* He looked at the stage. *Aw, it's close enough, I guess.*

The immediate problem was there were enough available seats for two possibilities. He knew Heather. If he let her go in first, she would go all the way down and sit next to the man. He'd then either sit next to his wife and have Becca sit next to him—Heather's plan, he knew— or he could leave a seat between them and Becca would sit in the middle.

It was a no-win scenario. Becca sits between them. Or Becca sits next to him on his left. The first scenario would be awkward and undesirable. The second scenario would be awkward, undesirable, and promised an argument later with Heather. He chose the second scenario. Argument or no argument, they were sharing the misery.

They sat leaving a seat in the middle.

Heather looked at the chair's seat, huffed, shook her head, and rolled her eyes. She was cold and off. She couldn't wait until the lights went out. At least then, she wouldn't have to see her.

Fortunately for them both, Becca was still gone when the lights went out. The thought went through both parents heads that maybe she had pulled another disappearing act. Or maybe she was sitting with friends. Both parents felt lightened at the possibility. One also felt guilty. Only one.

Vincent and Heather were expecting a concert. It wasn't a concert. It was a musical. But, actually, that was even better. Danielle was an outstanding actress. They waited impatiently for her appearance on stage. How could the star not be on set for ten full minutes?

Finally, there was a change in the music's tempo. It rose to a slow crescendo and ended with a sophomore striking a bass drum.

Heather looked at Vincent in the dark and stretched her arm across the empty seat. She and he clasped hands. He smiled and scooted into Becca's empty seat. Then he squeezed Heather's hand until she had to use the other hand to pull free of him. This was hard to do because at the same time she had to keep herself from passing out onto the floor.

There were now around twenty young people on stage in elaborate costumes, equally divided between boys and girls. The cast was quite good. It was obvious that parts were not passed out to whomever showed up first. These young people could sing, dance, and act. But there was one girl in particular who was sucking the air out of two people in the second row of the section reserved for the family of performers.

The cast formed a straight pathway of adoring fans of the girl. On one side, boy, girl, boy, girl, and on down the line. On the other side just the opposite. Girl, boy, girl, boy, and so on. The boys wore all black and carried large white feathers. The girls wore all white and carried large black feathers. Together they formed a whispery canopy for the girl who danced so gracefully from one end of the canopy to the next that she seemed to defy gravity with movements unimpeded by the normal limitations of bone and muscle.

The girl wore a headdress of white and red and black feathers that matched the makeup on her face. Her long bracelets spanned from her elbows to her wrists. They didn't move because both were hugged tight enough to assure they wouldn't.

The girl stopped a spin and the short dress's long, slender pieces finally caught up, joining her kneeling, head bowed to her chest, waiting for... The music qued. In one fluid movement, the girl was on her feet, head still bowed. But now a beautiful song came out of her mouth.

The girl sang like a professional.

The girl was as tall and beautiful as a runway model.

Then the girl picked up a guitar that was lying behind a prop.

She played.

The girl played with such skill.

"Vincent," said Heather.

"Heather," said Vincent.

The girl was Becca.

———

Three mercy angels stood on stage, one on each side of Becca, and one behind her. Bill and Nancy were out of town, but they had promised to pray for Danielle's concert.

———

Becca wasn't on this stage because Danielle had talked her into it. There was no way she could have been *talked* into something this dangerous by anyone. She had listened to Danielle, sure. But she was on this stage for two reasons. One shamed her. The other scared her.

First, she was brilliant at everything because she had nothing. Her drug of choice had been busyness and accomplishments. Hopefully, she would be so busy and get so tired that there'd be no time and energy left to feel sorry for herself. But this was only partly true.

The other part, the part that she was ashamed of, was she was jumping through these hoops trying to make her parents love her. If they couldn't love her, could they at least notice her? Maybe that would be enough to stop the stabbing in her soul.

Then there was the part that scared her. She didn't know what would happen if this evening turned more horrible than it was. But she knew in her heart that she was at a tipping point. If they crushed her tonight, her life would go in another direction. What that direction was, she didn't know. She only knew that she was at a place of such torment, loneliness, and rejection that she couldn't live like this much longer. So Danielle's foolish idea to trick Mom and Dad into coming to her musical was perfect for bringing the monster out into the open, and for bringing the inevitable to its long overdue conclusion.

Still, Becca was a child looking for love. It wasn't going to happen. She knew it wasn't. She *knew* it wasn't. They were cruel monsters incapable of love. But as she held the guitar and sang, she found Mom and Dad and looked directly at them.

Vincent looked at his daughter and was horrified. She was beautiful, talented, and looking at them with such hunger in her eyes. All she wanted was for them to love her. His mind wandered. He was holding her in his arms and crying. She was crying, too. He was telling her how sorry he was for treating her so badly.

I do love you, Becca. More than you can imagine. I've always loved you. But I die every time I see you. Every time I see you, I see me trying to kill you. I see me pushing your mother to have an abortion. Yes, Becca. An abortion. Twice. The last time we tried to have you killed, it almost worked. He saw himself offering the one good thing in this miserable confession. *But at the last moment, I jumped through a window and over the receptionist desk and ran to the patient room where your mother was on the table. The doctor had something in her hand. She was in there where you were, trying to kill you, Becca. But I told her if she moved one inch, I'd kill her. I told her that, Becca. I told her if she hurt you, I would kill her.*

· · ·

Becca didn't hear that confession. In fact, she didn't hear anything after he stood up, stared at her like he wanted to say something, and left. The room went mute. But her eyes still worked. Mom sat for a half minute after Dad left, staring at the floor in front of her. Then she, too, got up and left. That's when Becca went into a standing coma. Somehow her brain kept her right hand stringing the guitar. Then the old pain grabbed her shoulder.

"Ask God to help you, Becca," said the mercy angel. "All you have to do is ask."

Becca's mind was half on, half off. She was going up and down at the same time. She was in and out. She was here and nowhere. Dizzy. Falling. Dying.

God.

Grandma.

God loves you, Becca. He sets the solitary in families.

She felt the thoughts of God and Grandma push against her chest from the inside.

No, she thought in her stupor. *He doesn't love me. No one loves me.*

Becca stopped stringing the guitar and robotically tried to rub away the tearing pain from her limp left arm.

The lights came on when Danielle screamed and ran to her sister's side.

9

Becca was dead.

She had always felt almost dead. Always felt like she was in a crude, shallow grave, and fully aware that the dirt that daily landed on her rising chest and barely fluttering eyelids came from the shovels of heartless parents eager to erase her presence, and perhaps memory, from the world. But when her parents publicly walked away from her tonight, their last lethal dose of earth landed over her face, covering her nose and mouth. She searched for air and inhaled only dirt.

Danielle held the warm corpse close to her body in the backseat as though she were protecting it from vultures circling overhead. Every now and again her eyes cut to the front seats. The vultures weren't overhead. One of them was driving.

But death was in the front seat, too.

Words were too precise, too limiting to capture the maelstrom of emotions that had fallen upon Vincent and Heather like an avalanche. A surprise avalanche, as most avalanches are. But this was an avalanche orchestrated by Danielle. The daughter they had loved with their whole hearts, holding back nothing. How could she do this? *Why* would she do this?

Angry? Were they angry at Danielle? Oh, yeah. Plenty. But she was only sixteen. Passionate, idealistic, sometimes to the point of being unrealistic. Often impulsive, and always fond of her sister. And that, no doubt, is what led her astray. She was a good girl and had never done anything like this before. How had Becca convinced their daughter to do this?

Yet, as disturbing as Danielle's behavior was, the worst part of the evening was that Becca's sting operation had goaded them into crossing the line. She had forced them into the open. It was like those shows where the undercover cop gets the spouse to offer money to have him kill the other spouse. No amount of creative spin could outtalk the video. *Becca had tricked them into showing themselves in public!* And Danielle holding her sister when the lights came on and screaming out after them, "Why are you doing this to her? She's your daughter! What kind of parents are you?" may as well have been a Super Bowl ad.

Once in the house, Vincent and Heather immediately headed for the stairs.

"Wait," said Becca, her voice absent of any fight. Rejection having taken it all. She rubbed her left arm as Danielle hugged her around her waist. "I'll make it short."

Vincent slowed down, but didn't stop. Heather was behind him. She didn't break a stride. She may have even sped up.

"She asked you to wait!" yelled Danielle.

Vincent turned around and looked at Danielle in disbelief. "Excuse me, young lady. Talking to your mother like that?"

Her fiery eyes met his. "Young lady? Mother? Now you're parents again?"

Neither parent was prepared for this Danielle. How could they be? They'd never seen her before. Becca heard the muffled sound of her sister's yelling. She would have been as astonished as her parents were she not still in a stupor and fighting disorientation. Why had she not fallen out? The floor seemed to be grabbing at her.

Heather was arrested by the anger in her little girl's voice. She was afraid, too. She had poured her very life into that child. They both had. Her heart constricted at the thought of losing her and didn't let go until she took her hand off the top of the large wooden stair rail and joined her husband.

Becca didn't notice the different looks in each of her parent's eyes. One, she didn't look them in the face. She looked at the floor as she spoke. And, two, she didn't really *see* anything at all. Everything was like a bad reflection in murky water. Every image was distorted and untrustworthy.

But the images were crystal clear to Danielle, especially her parents' eyes. Dad's eyes were sad and guilty and tired. Mom's were angry and defiant and detached. "Becca, they're listening."

The third time she heard the voice in the tunnel, Danielle's voice, she heard it clearly. She held her arm and looked at the floor as she spoke. "Thank you, Danielle, for making your parents listen to me."

Danielle gasped, moved her lips to say, "No. No, Becca, don't say that! You're my sister. We're sisters. This has been a terrible night, but we're still a family. Mom and Dad love you," but her sister had been insulted enough. Besides, she wasn't living with her head buried in the sand any longer. She closed her mouth and let Becca continue without a protest.

"I didn't ask to be born into your family," said Becca. Her head raised. She looked at each parent's eyes. A grimaced smile stood solo. A perfect representation of her life. "But here I am. Both of you hate me." Becca shook her head with a slow and painful realization. "You have always hated me. I don't know why. I try to be everything you want, but..."

Danielle stood at a forward stoop, holding her heart, pulled down by the weight of her sister's sadness. Her mouth was open with trembling lips. She was unaware that there wasn't a dry place on her cheeks.

Becca's cheeks, surprisingly, were desert dry. Her soul was so parched by the long, unnatural drought of love that dust clogged her tear ducts. "Sometimes I have dreams that I'm a baby in your womb, and I'm talking to God, and He's talking back. I'm telling Him that I'm in danger…that I'm all alone…that He has to help me, or they'll get me."

Becca smiled. This time there was actually a hint of something to smile about in her smile. "And He's talking to me. Telling me that He's with me. Then I wake up and I'm here. It's like being on death row and dreaming that you're free and waking up to see that it was your mind playing a cruel joke on you. Vincent, you're in agony whenever you're around me. Heather, you don't have that problem because for you I don't exist. Except I know I sicken you."

Vincent winced when she called him by his name instead of Dad.

"If there is a God out there somewhere, I thank Him for what happened tonight. I needed this to happen. I needed to accept the fact that it's not me. That I'm not bad. And that I'm not crazy. I needed to finally accept the fact that you are monsters. As far as I'm concerned, you're now as dead to me as I've always been to you."

Still giving her arm deep rubs, she walked slowly toward the hallway with her head down. Her mother was directly in her path. "Please move, Heather."

She wasn't deliberately ignoring Becca by not moving. It's just that she was stunned by the power of her daughter's words, and mostly by her recounting having dreams about being in danger while she was in her womb. *What if God gave her dreams with more details? What if He told her about the abortion? Is she like Mom?*

"Heather?" Becca said.

"Oh," said Heather, standing aside so Becca could pass.

Vincent's eyes went large when Becca mentioned dreams and hadn't returned to their normal size yet.

Danielle watched her sister walk past her mom, and had to try twice to speak before she could free herself enough from her emotions to do so. "Becca," she said, as though she was out of breath.

Becca stopped, stood motionless for a few seconds, then turned partly around.

"Wait," said Danielle. "I have something to say."

Heather's throat narrowed. It was impossible to swallow. She waited with fear. Her fear was well founded.

Danielle looked with calculating eyes from one parent to the other. They waited before her like an accused criminal does when asked to rise to hear the jury's verdict. A verdict delivered after the jury had heard overwhelming evidence of guilt.

"Becca had nothing to do with this. She didn't want to do it. It was all my idea." Danielle saw her mom's expression. She didn't believe her. "It's true, Mom. She didn't want to do it. You know why? Because she knew you and Dad would humiliate her in front of everyone. I told her that was ridiculous. I told her that she was mistaken. That she was seeing things that weren't there." Danielle took two steps toward her parents. "But I was wrong. Boy, was I wrong. I still can't believe you did this. It's the most cruel and mean thing—"

Danielle looked at Becca. She could tell by her body language and the new life in her face that the slow process of recovery had begun, and that her words were helping. She saw gratitude in her big sister's eyes.

"Becca, I'm sorry," she said. Danielle lowered her head and reminded herself that she wasn't living in denial or fear any longer. She looked up. "All these years…" Tears welled in her eyes. Her face tightened with the weight of what she was about to say. She let out a loud breath. "I knew it was wrong. I saw how they treated you." Now she was crying. "And I saw how they treated me, and I never said it, not out loud. But I didn't want them to treat me like that. I thought that if I spoke up too much, they'd turn on me." She shrugged in guilt. "So I pretended everything was okay. It was wrong, Becca. It was so wrong. You're like the perfect big sister. You've always been there for me, even—even—" Her hands went to her face as her cries burst forth.

Vincent and Heather said nothing, guilt and fear clamping them shut. Besides, what could the criminal do after the guilty verdict? Make a run for it?

Becca went to her little sister and hugged her with her good arm. They stood cheek to cheek as Danielle emptied her Dead Sea of guilt and shame onto her big sister's shoulder. Becca couldn't cry. She could only hurt. When Danielle finally stopped crying enough to speak without having to work to catch her breath, she pulled away from Becca.

Becca kissed her on the forehead and said softly, "You see. Admit it. I'm a full half-inch taller than you. So either I'm five nine, or you're not five eight and a half."

Danielle smiled through new tears. "If you say so."

"Danielle, what you did tonight, I," she shook her head, "I don't know how to thank you, except to say that Vincent and Heather have crushed my soul, and honestly I don't know if I'll ever find it. I don't know if I ever had it. But if I do find it, it'll be because of what you've done for me tonight. I love you…and I'll never forget you."

Becca gave Danielle a last smile and turned away. As she walked past her parents, she stopped and whispered to them, "Vincent, you'll never have to run from me again. And Heather, you'll never have to ignore me again. I'm leaving." Her eyes narrowed. "If you hurt my sister, I swear to you both, I'll find someone to kill you." She thought her ability to cry was gone, but now she felt her eyes threatening to betray her. How could she say something so evil—even to people like them? She could never do something like that. Then the thought of Vincent and Heather turning on her little sister made her face tighten with menace.

Vincent's and Heather's eyes popped open.

Becca smiled coldly. "You're not the only person who can hate. The old Becca is dead. You killed her. Don't—hurt—my—sister."

Danielle didn't hear what her sister said, but she saw shock on her parents' faces, and wondered what she had said. Whatever it was, she knew none of them would ever tell her. She said to them both before walking past them, "No one treats their own flesh and blood like this unless they are pure evil, or…" she waited, "unless they're hiding something. Whatever your reasons, it's too much for me. There's no way I can live here in this house with you. I'm going to live with Grandma."

Vincent and Heather both opened their mouths to protest, but the protest died as soon as Danielle snapped, "I hope we don't have to get

DFACS involved. And I haven't yet decided whether I should tell Grandma."

Becca would suffer one more day behind enemy lines. But it would be different. Saturday would be the first day of her new life—alone.

Or so she thought.

10

Becca was on the fiftieth floor. The building was hopelessly on fire. It was burn or jump. She had told her parents with more resolve than she knew she had on the night of the musical that she wasn't going to let them burn her any longer. She was going to jump, and she meant it. But knowing she had to jump and making the jump were two different things. Jumping was not without consequences.

She let her mind continue to ponder the metaphor. Was it possible to jump from such a dizzying height and land safely on an inflated rescue pad below? Problem was, from her height she couldn't tell whether there was a rescue pad below. Maybe she had merely exchanged one form of death for another.

Death.

Becca took the reins of her imagination. No rescue pad waiting. Twirling body slams horrifically into pavement. Life gone. Pain gone.

She stopped, lifted her head with closed eyes, and just let the crisp, early morning's March air refresh her. Funny how little, often taken for granted things like crisp morning air could brush aside thoughts of death. Even if only for a little while.

She made her way up the few concrete steps to the coffee shop and entered. She placed an order for a coffee, fixed it up, and let the backpack drop from her back. She sat at a table in the back next to a wall and the hallway to the restrooms. The only plan she had was to escape the fire. To leave that torture chamber called home. *"Okay, I've jumped. Now what?"*

Two spiritual forces were hard at work to answer that question for her.

The darkness had not seen this coming, but it was definitely a win for them. Becca was running from the pain. She was running from the stabbing accusations that something was wrong with her. That as horrible as her parents were, there must be something wrong with her to have caused their behavior.

Becca sipped the coffee as she passed the time people watching. Then she heard—she really heard!—a sick, stupid, no-talent poem in her mind.

Run, Becca, run.
   Run as you may, you can't get away.
   Run, Becca, run.
   Run as you may, we are here to stay.
   Run, Becca, run.
   Run as you may, you can't hide.
   Run, Becca, run.
   Run as you may, we are inside.

"Oh, no," she thought, *"now the voices?"* A guy glanced at her. Then so did a girl. The guy got a micro-glance. The girl a second more. Becca stared blankly, wondering what those people would say if they knew she wasn't alone at her table. That she had a sick, tormenting poet in her head. And a bad one at that.

Unwanted was obviously displeased with the lack of focus. He lowered his head, but raised his eyes at Run Away. It was that same lack of focus that got the other Run Away spirit eaten by the mercy angel. These Run Away spirits had such low attention spans. He cleared his voice.

Run Away finished the poem and laughed at one of his own jokes. He heard Unwanted's gurgling, but didn't know it was directed at him.

"You really crack yourself up, don't you?" said Unwanted.

Run Away turned from Becca. "What? Huh? You were talking to me? I didn't know. I was just having a little fun with Becca."

"Fun, huh? The reason I called this meeting is because truth angels have taken a sudden liking to our girl. They've been spotted in the area. In fact, they are out there right now, strategizing how they're going to take her from us."

There was an eruption of murmurs at the news of truth angels in the area. There were only two classes of angels who were of concern to Alone and the demons that comprised his stronghold.

The first were those hideous cannibals God deceptively called mercy angels. They came and left without regard to proper protocol or God's so-called rules. They behaved as though mercy trumped everything. They made a mess of the rules.

The second were angels of truth. From a strategic view, these posed more of a long-term and comprehensive threat than mercy angels. For as lethal and as arbitrary as God's mercy was, it had time limits, conditions, and lines in the sand. People received it all the time, escaping the judgment of God for their actions, but failing to stop the behavior that warranted the judgment in the first place. So at best, they just postponed the inevitable. The wretched book was filled with such examples.

Truth, on the other hand, was the great uncompromising constant that brought divine light to those who walked in darkness. Unlike mercy, which only delayed judgment when there was no change of behavior, truth actually got rid of the offending root. It brought offending behaviors and false beliefs into the light. When the offending behavior and false belief were forsaken through repentance and faith in Christ, the power of sin and deception was broken.

Oh, to be sure, that class of demons known as seduction spirits had been quite successful recently with their false grace doctrines! Many so-called Christians, mostly false converts, had gloriously bought into the lie that God's unconditional love meant unconditional forgiveness. Thus, stripping God's truth of its convicting power.

The dupes never considered that if God's forgiveness was unconditional, then the dark kingdom would not be doomed, Adam and Eve would still be in the Garden of Eden. The flood would never have destroyed the world. The whole Jesus fiasco would have been unnecessary. And the Lord would not have declared so many times in that wretched book of His that He is coming back to earth with His angels in flaming fire to take vengeance on the ungodly.

Unwanted considered all of this in an instant. *Better to have one of my demons eaten by a mercy angel than to have to deal with these truth angels,* he grimly thought. *Left to themselves, they'd dismantle the whole stronghold.*

He continued with his meeting. "They want Becca. We want Becca. Who's going to get Becca?" No volunteers. Incredible. A room full of demons and no one wanted to talk. This had to be a first. "I see that truth has put sandbags in your mouths. Well, I guess that's not a bad thing. At least you're taking it seriously."

"We've been with her for a long time. There are many of us. Do you really think we're in danger?" asked Self-Hatred.

Unwanted considered the source of the question. He knew this demon wasn't asking from a position of ignorance. He looked at the demon's exceptionally long claws. The thick points curled at the tips. He knew that once this demon got his claws into a person, the person would probably never be set free. It was the *probably* they had to talk about.

"Self-Hatred, you are a great demon." Unwanted saw the demon's agreement with his assessment. "Many of us are great demons. We are powerful. But the issue here is not *our* power. It is the power of *truth*." Alone looked at the demons of his stronghold with peering eyes. He jabbed his finger to make his point. "We must not make the fatal mistake of believing our own lies. It is no dishonor to recognize our limitations or what gives us our power—or what can destroy that power."

"Go on," said Self-Hatred.

"This is a stronghold because we have a strong hold on the worthless wench. It will stay strong only if we continue to work together and take the threat of truth seriously. This means we must double our efforts."

"Double them?" some demon murmured too loudly.

"Yes! Double them!" Unwanted yelled, the diplomatic gloves off. "Did you not hear me say there are truth angels in the area? Double them! Yes! I will spell it out for you. Whatever lie you are telling her, tell her more. This is a rejection stronghold. Our success is based solely on her believing what we want her to believe, and this means what?"

No one answered. Then Self-Hatred prepared to answer. Alone motioned with the hand. "No, Self-Hatred, you know this already. You are a great," he now looked accusingly at the murmuring demon, "and *intelligent* demon. I want to hear from a demon who is not as intelligent."

The demon who had unwisely murmured his doubts a bit too loudly tried to look away, but his guilty eyes made contact with Unwanted. "Yes, that would be you!" said Unwanted.

The demon seemed totally unprepared for the question.

"My darkness," an irritated demon offered. "I'll answer it for you. We can only get her to believe what we want her to believe if we keep her from believing what God wants her to believe."

Unwanted looked at the demon and twisted his face and shook his head as though the evil spirit gave off a pungent smell. "Who *are* you?"

"Cutting," he answered. "Cutting."

"Cutting?" said Alone with surprise. "Well now, we haven't seen much of you, now have we?"

"Cutting?" barked Self-Hatred. He marched to the spirit and slapped him to the floor. His claws left a trail of dark ooze as they ripped through the shocked demon's face. "You are an expression of me. Where are the cuts? Where's my expression in her body? Don't you ever disgrace me like this again. Now you better get to work."

The demon hadn't yet returned to his feet. "Yes, my lord."

Self-Hatred yelled into the crowd. "Any eating disorder spirits here? Bulimia? Anorexia Nervosa? Overeating?" he said, as he searched the crowd with a stretched neck. "Recklessness? Suicide?"

Hopelessness spoke up like he was protecting his turf. "Suicide is mine."

Unwanted liked the way things were progressing. The major demons under his control—since he had been first to enter; although sometimes this rule was violated—stepped up to the moment and made their demons give account.

Unwanted wasn't overconfident. He knew the threat. But he did smile. Those truth angels had another thing coming if they thought Becca was going anywhere other than to hell. That is, once they were through with her.

Now to make sure she met the right people.

Justis, Krasa, and Gabron looked up at the three brilliant beams of light that shot from the heavens toward them. The lights weren't like shooting stars, large masses followed by a glowing but diminishing tail. Instead, they were three single, unbroken lights that began in the horizon of heaven and stayed constant as they got closer. The lights weren't large, but they were brighter than the earth's sun.

The angels' mouths were agape at the sight. Being an angel didn't mean you weren't awed by God. On the contrary, it meant you were in a state of near constant awe. They looked directly into the immeasurable brilliance. No blinking. No squinting. No shielding of the eyes with their hands.

When the three lights touched down before them, three bubbles of light formed at the base of each beam. The beams retracted back into the heavens, leaving three brilliant bubbles. The bubbles disappeared and three angels stood before Justis, Krasa, and Gabron.

Three angels of truth.

Heaven was a place of infinite diversity and wide ranges of distributions of power and honor. Yet, unlike Earth, there was no competition in heaven. No envy. No condescending attitudes. No backroom politicking for power. No undermining of another's position. No willingness to step on another to satisfy a selfish desire.

Angels of truth were among the highest orders of angels. Every angel was literally a perfect expression of God and a representative of heaven. However, a perfect representation or expression of God did not mean it was complete.

The only perfect and *complete* representation and expression of God was done by the Lord Jesus Christ. And even then, the expressive mission of Christ had not been to show all of God, but to show all that humanity presently needed to know of God prior to seeing Him face to face. For how could an infinite God be fully revealed in three years?

Nonetheless, angels of truth were more than angels assigned to represent or express God. Nor were they merely on assignment to do something for God. A something that could be one thing today and something else tomorrow. No. Angels of truth were infinitely more.

Although created beings, they were created solely to express not an attribute of God, but the very essence of God. This was more than mercy. More than wrath. For there could be no mercy, and there could be no wrath, but there could never be no truth. It was the ever present core of God and foundation of His kingdom and rule.

Justis, Krasa, and Gabron knew this. It was why their mouths were agape as they looked at the angels. They were no more majestic in appearance than most angels. In fact, the three angels who had been fighting for Becca had seen many others with more commanding appearances. But there was something about these angels that differed from all others. It was difficult to make sense of it, even to Justis, Krasa, and Gabron. *The angels were solid, but transparent.*

And there was something else. Justis said, "You are…God," he stammered.

There was no need among the angels to correct the statement because it needed no correction. They all understood what he was and was *not* saying.

"Yes," the angel answered. "We are. I am Inteegrus. This is Mark."

"And I am Alphus."

"We were told truth was coming," said Justis, still in awe, but now smiling. "Now there is hope for Becca." Justis saw Gabron asking him with his eyes. "My brother here has many questions. And I must admit, so do I. The demons have such control over her."

"I understand," said Inteegrus, his tone encouraging their questions. "Where can we talk?"

Justis led them to a safe spot. "Did Nancy and Bill send you?"

"Yes."

Justis nodded approvingly. "The stronghold is rejection. There's so many of them. Praise be to God for their prayers."

Gabron couldn't wait any longer. "How will you free her?"

"Truth," said Inteegrus.

"You can attack them? You can enter their dimension? There are only three of you. Are more coming?" Gabron had many questions. They couldn't be answered fast enough. He wondered whether there was some way he'd finally get his hands on Unwanted.

"Actually, Gabron, the truth is everywhere. The heavens declare God's glory, and the skies declare the work of His hands. God's moral law is written in the hearts of the sons and daughters of Adam. There is no one who does not have," he paused, "or *had* a witness of God's truth in their heart. So we *can* and *do* go everywhere. But you were asking about something more specific."

"Yes," said Gabron.

"Becca's troubles," said the angel. "We can *go* anywhere. We can *attack* anywhere. But we can only free those who embrace us. My brothers and I can enter Unwanted's dimension any time we desire. We can destroy them on the spot this very moment, or we can chase them away."

"You can?" Gabron's smile was wide, his eyes full of joy, his movements full of energy. He thought of Unwanted. "Can we enter his dimension with you?"

Inteegrus knew what Gabron was thinking. He rocked his head slowly one time. "Yes," he said, the word dragging out of his mouth, "if we entered, you could go with us."

Gabron caught the "if." He looked at Justis. His friend seemed to know something he didn't. He looked at Inteegrus. "If?"

"God is merciful," said the angel. "He can send mercy angels to destroy these demons any time He desires. But they'd only come back with reinforcements. The last state would be worse than the first. The only way to get rid of them for good is through truth. The person must submit to truth to stay free. This strips them of their legal right to be there. Fighting demons without removing their right to be there is like trying to get rid of a mighty oak tree by plucking its leaves. We're going after the roots."

"You're going to attack rejection," said Justis.

"Yes."

"How is this done?" said Gabron.

"It will be extremely difficult. She will have to repent of her sins, and trust Christ for salvation. And she will have to believe what the Lord says about her." The angel knew that his proposed solution was not the solution Gabron was hoping for. He saw the angel's troubled look and knew a question was coming.

"But there is no greater victory in our warfare than salvation," said Gabron. And though he said this, and though his heart was nearly as heavy now as it had been before he had heard that truth angels were coming for Becca, he knew there was no other way. He had simply asked questions that his love for Becca demanded.

"No, there is no greater feat than this," said the truth angel. Then he added something that Gabron, Krasa, and Justis knew, but would rather have not heard. "And there is no guarantee of success."

"You have to succeed," said Gabron, pleading for something he knew even a truth angel couldn't guarantee.

"We must be going now," said Inteegrus. He pulled out his swords. The other truth angels did likewise. "We have to make sure Becca meets the right people."

11

The demons had all heard Unwanted's orders: "We must double our efforts." They did not double their efforts. They tripled and quadrupled them—with an energy and resolve that showed they believed the truth angels were serious about putting them on the streets. It was also with an understanding that there were specific things they must achieve to prevent this.

First, salvation. This was always the first objective. Keep the sons and daughters of Adam from salvation. And how was this to be done with her? She had a background in the things of God, with those grandparents of hers. So they'd have to keep her distracted enough to not allow any of the cursed seeds of truth to be watered by her contemplations. *Keep her from thinking about the things of God!*

Fortunately, Becca had so many felt problems that it should be no problem to keep her mind focused on her problems instead of the answer to her problems. She'd have to see through her problems to see the Christ on the other side. Fat chance of that happening! Even the cursed book agreed. What did it say? Yeah, that was it: "But if our gospel is hid, it is hidden to those who are lost, whose minds the god of this world has blinded." Yep, and that's the way it was going to stay!

Second, God's love. Darkness forbid that she should somehow find her way to the Christ! But if she did—a demon had to admit the possibility—she had to be kept in the dark about His unjust love for her. This at first glance seemed an impossibility. How could a rescued sinner be kept in the dark about the love of God?

Dark smiles. Demonic grins. Hellish smirks and snickers.

It was most definitely an obvious truth that could not be denied that the darkness had failed miserably in keeping *everyone* from God's love. However, it was also an undeniable truth that they had kept *almost* everyone from knowing His love. That was a great victory indeed.

But perhaps the greatest victory was that of those who had fought through the darkness and had come to know His love, their understanding of His love was so miniscule that it never allowed them to progress to a level that radically changed their identity. They were truly saved, but that was all. Like the thief on the cross when Jesus was crucified. Saved, but still pinned to a cross that prevented them from becoming all that God wanted them to become.

Third, identity. Becca must never be allowed to understand the depths of God's love for her. She must never be allowed to know that she is fearfully and wonderfully made. She must never be allowed to know that she is insanely loved by the enemy and made acceptable to Him through the blood of Jesus Christ. She must never be allowed to know that through Christ she is a literal daughter of Almighty God.

This third point of Christian identity was a hotly contested area. That diabolical traitor and enemy of darkness, the apostle Paul, had mentioned in his infamous letter to the Ephesians how the enemy's eternal purpose from the beginning—proof again that He has always been a liar!—was to change their identities from slaves of darkness to sons and daughters of light through their ever growing knowledge of God's love for them:

For this reason I bow my knees to the Father of our Lord Jesus Christ, from whom the whole family in heaven and earth is named, that He would grant you, according to the riches of His glory, to be strengthened with might in the inner man that Christ may dwell in your hearts through faith; that you being rooted and grounded in love, may be able to comprehend with all the saints what is the width and length and depth and height—to know the love of Christ which passes knowledge; that you may be filled with all the fullness of God.

That last part was hideous, and it was exactly what these demons did not want to happen. It was bad enough that traitors by the multitude regularly escaped their clutches, but to have those same ex-slaves growing in God's love to such a degree that they were controlled only by God—well that was not going to happen with Becca!

Unwanted and Alone held daggers in both hands. The two demons worked well together.

———

Becca put her elbow on the table and leaned her head into her left hand and put the other hand over her chest. She felt an ache in her heart.

"You're all alone. You're always alone," said Alone.

Becca felt her sense of aloneness growing.

"You're all alone. You're always alone."

"There must be something wrong with you," said Self-Rejection. "Why else would your parents treat you like that? They don't treat Danielle like that."

"They don't want you," said Unwanted. "Nobody wants you. No one will ever want you."

"The only chance you have of someone wanting you is if you hide. You have to hide who you are and become who and what they want. No one wants the real you. You have to hide." This was Run Away, one of the surviving hiding spirits.

Becca rubbed her forehead as she continued with her hand over her heart. She began to wonder for the millionth time why her parents treated her so badly. Was there something wrong with her?

No, she told herself, *this has been going on all my life, even when I was little. What could a four-, five- or six-year-old do to be treated like this?* Then she thought of Danielle. They didn't treat her sister the way they treated her. Why?

"Danielle's really pretty," said Self-Rejection. He added nothing to it. He knew he didn't have to.

Becca knew it was stupid, but she let her mind wander into comparing looks with Danielle. They both were tall for girls. They kidded one another about who was taller or prettier or thinner, but there was no genuine competition between them. But now something inside of Becca was trying to make her see that Danielle was secretly envious of her. It was the reason she didn't believe she was five-nine.

What was it that Danielle had said recently? "You are five-foot-eight…and one-half inch, Becca. You know it. And I'm five-foot-eight and five-eighths." Why would Danielle say that? She knew Becca was taller than her.

"And she called you a liar," Self-Rejection finally added. "She said you and coach were lying about your height. Why is she so concerned about who's taller? It's bad enough they choose her over you, but then she has the hips to call you a liar?"

Becca knew this was ridiculous. She wanted to shut these stupid thoughts down, and she would've, but…

Alone swirled around Becca in a literal mass of dark thoughts, bad feelings, and aloneness. His swirling didn't make her feel *lonely*. He made her feel *alone*. She was the only person on a small, barren island in the middle of a vast ocean of rejection. This overwhelming aloneness made it nearly impossible to quiet these ridiculous thoughts.

When the thought rose in Becca's mind like a tide's wave against the shore that she and Danielle bantered about looks, but never about intelligence or talent or physical strength, she didn't hide from its splashings. It was true that she was more intelligent and talented and strong than Danielle. Danielle was smart, but her PSAT scores, though high, were much lower than her own. Plus, nearly all of her classes were honors or advanced placement courses. *She had enough credits already that she didn't have to go to school for one more day and she'd still graduate—with honors!*

And when it came to sports and music and—

A demon interrupted this line of thinking with another accusation. "Where was your sister when your parents were treating you like garbage? She said it herself that she knew they were doing this to you." Now the demon hurled the words at Becca. "She knew and she did nothing!"

Becca thought of time after time that she felt like an orphan as Danielle received all the love, all the praise, all the attention. Everything! Anger rose from beneath. It descended from above. She was being baptized inside and out with anger. No, not anger—rage. Pure rage.

Why are you thinking evil of your sister?

Becca didn't hear the thought. She was lost in one of her thousands of painful memories. She saw herself as a child looking at cartoons. She and Danielle. Dad picked up Danielle and loved on her. She held out her arms to be held by Daddy. He looked at her and said, "I can't." Then Mom came and did the same thing.

Why are you thinking evil of your sister? asked the angel of truth.

Becca thought back event after event where Mom referred to Danielle as "My daughter," but spoke of her as "Becca." Sometimes she even referred to her as "Vincent's daughter." Mom didn't know that she heard her speak of her that way, but she did. And she'd never forget it. And she'd also never forget that sometimes right after Mom or Dad would do something to hurt her, Danielle would ask them if she was loved. Why would she ask them if they loved her? Danielle wasn't the person being rejected; she was. What kind of person would rub it in her face like that?

"And she says she loves you," a lying spirit added. "She doesn't love you."

Why are you thinking evil of your sister?

Becca took her hand from her heart and buried her face in her hands. She fought to come out of this tornado of lies, accusations, and self-pity.

"Something is wrong with you," said Self-Rejection. "Deep down inside of you, there's something wrong with you. That's why your parents don't want you."

The thoughts and voices were relentless. Trying to dismiss them made her feel like a butterfly caught in a spider web—helpless. Trying to ignore them was like trying to ignore the approaching spider—impossible. Becca tried instinctively rather than expectantly to leave the voices in the coffee shop. She picked up her bag and put it on her back and went outdoors.

She walked into what was just about to become a bad scene.

An attractive young woman was sitting alone at one of the coffee shop's small tables alongside the large window. She was maybe twenty or twenty-one, but her eyes carried wisdom beyond her age. Like Becca, she had long black hair, but her hair was big. Her hair, eyeliner, and long narrow face gave her that Amy Winehouse look, but she wasn't as skinny. Actually, although she did physically resemble the deceased singer, it was her combined first-impression persona that made Becca think of her. Something about her said, "Piss off. I'm doing my thing." It was the sense that hers was a life going a hundred miles an hour with no brakes that made it eerily Winehouse. Just steering until the inevitable crash.

A lit cigarette was in one of her long-fingered, ring adorned, tattooed hands. Tattoos. Her black dress was short, as were its sleeves, which revealed that she had tattoos everywhere. That's what started the problem. One tattoo in particular.

The woman's foot was propped on the edge of a chair in front of her like a guy would do. Or like a woman not wearing a short dress would do. A black guy walked by. He was about the woman's age. He wore baggy clothes and a baseball style cap turned a little to the side. He liked a tattoo that was high on the inside of the woman's thigh. Becca heard him say something to her about licking the ink off of her. That's when Becca froze.

The Amy Winehouse look-alike's mouth was like a cursing machine gun. She let out a venomous burst that seemed to have been practiced. There was no way a person could curse so eloquently *and poetically* on the fly like that. She was a magician with words.

The guy's smug laughter died in the throat of a face that was struggling to decide what to do. He had kept his slow stroll as the woman's surprise volley hit him. But now he stopped and turned. That's when the woman's poetry went to the *Pulitzer* level. The fury in his eyes showed that he didn't appreciate what she was saying about limp noodles, little soybean sausages, and him having girl parts. The silence behind his trembling lips showed the frustration of wanting to respond with the same eloquence as his attacker, but being unable to do so.

The guy settled for, "Hoe, if I wanted yo' dirty skank butt, I'd take it."

Becca was only a few yards away from the action. She was terrified. The guy wasn't huge, but he was much bigger than the woman. She knew she was about to see a beating—right there on the street! Then the woman did and said something that shocked her even more. And from the way the guy responded, he was shocked, too.

The woman clapped her hands. "Parolee's got me mixed up with his mama. That must mean your father's white." She spread her legs wide. She wasn't wearing anything underneath! "Here it is, Mr. Noodle. Bring your worthless, ankle bracelet wearing, no good teeth, third-grade education, ghetto self over here to your white mama and take it."

Becca stared at the woman in absolute disbelief. Her mouth went wide. She looked at the guy, absolutely *not* looking back at the woman —she did not want to look at *that* again—then dropped her head.

The brazen move by the verbal magician freeze-dried the guy's tongue. But his eyes were working fine, and for several seconds they didn't leave the rabbit that had popped out of the magician's hat. But this wasn't for the obvious reasons. There was nothing sexual that kept his eyes there. What kept his eyes there was rage. When the white girl tapped herself and said, "Come to Mama," the rage exploded.

Becca gasped. Her hands went up like she was being robbed. She stumbled backwards a couple of steps, screams gathering in her throat, waiting to emit the moment the guy closed the short distance to get to his tormentor.

The attack lasted all of one second.

In a flash, the woman whipped out a knife that looked like it came from a Rambo movie and landed on her feet in one swift movement. "I'm going to cut it off right here in front of the coffee shop." She sounded like a gladiator taunting an opponent.

Becca looked at the guy. He—did—not—move. His expression of rage now one of fear. Becca looked at the woman. This guy had reason to be scared…because the woman had no fear at all. She actually seemed to be enjoying it, wanting it to end in blood. Instead of backing up as most women would to get away from their attacker, she crouched and moved toward him. An Amy Winehouse lookalike wearing a short black dress and Converse sneakers crouched and looking at a man who had accosted her like she was going to carve a turkey.

"Still want to take it, little girl?" she taunted.

The guy glanced at Becca. Their eyes met. This unnerved her. He looked back at the woman.

"We're gonna have some drama or what?" the woman said. "I got things to do, ghetto Romeo."

The guy backed away slowly, saying everything with his eyes, but nothing with his mouth.

That was not the case with the magician. She stood there with that monster of a knife hanging by her tattooed thigh and used that poet's tongue of hers until the guy was half a block away. When she finished, she turned and several people from the coffee shop came outside and gave her a standing ovation. She looked at them with a wooden expression and said to Becca, "Canaries saw the whole thing go down. Then when it's over, they come out here and give me a standing O. Gotta take care of yourself, girlfriend. Nobody's going to do it for you."

The trouble was over, but Becca's feet didn't move. She watched the girl go to the table and pick up her cigarette. In that short moment, thoughts of light swirled in the dark tornado of her troubled mind like the reflections from a disco ball in a dark room.

She didn't know this girl, but it was as though she did. On the outside, they were as opposite as night and day. She was vulgar and violent and…fearless. Odd. Physically she was smaller than Becca. But her heart. Her heart was ten feet tall. If that guy would've done her that way, she would've kept her mouth shut and hoped he would keep walking. But this girl didn't shut her mouth. She didn't sit in a ball of weak fear and let the bully have his way.

"Hey," the girl interrupted her thoughts.

Becca snapped out of her private discussion with herself.

"What's with the bag? You look like Cheryl," she said.

Becca's eyes said, "Huh?" and so did her shaking head.

"Wild," the girl said. "The movie. Reese Witherspoon walking halfway around the world, doing drugs and screwing everything that moved."

"No," Becca said innocently, blushing.

The girl took a long drag off her cigarette. "Naw, you don't look like the drugs type." She gave her a quick look-over and chuckled. "Now the screwing part," she bobbed her head, "I don't know," she nearly sang the words. "If the priests are freaky, I just assume the nuns are too."

Becca hadn't been a nun in a long time. Nothing that could've gotten her pregnant. But that left a lot of other unnunly things on the menu.

"What's your name?" the girl asked.

"Becca."

"Well, Becca, I'm Crystal. Like crystal meth. But you don't ever want to go down that road. Make you ugly as a frog's butt after a few years." She smiled and her face gave off a light that caught Becca by surprise. "And we don't do ugly. Life is hard enough for a pretty girl. Can't imagine being ugly. Where you going? You need a lift?"

Becca felt herself being urged by some force to go. "No, I'm good."

"No, girlfriend, you're not good. You got thirty pounds on your back. No one with a car would walk around carrying that thing." She pointed down the street. "And Mr. Noodle Man looked at you like you don't want to bump into him again."

Becca hadn't thought of that. The guy did give her a bad look.

"I'd hate for him to come back looking for me and find you walking down the street with that sofa on your back. It's not like you're going to outrun somebody carrying that thing." The girl started walking. "Come on, I'll give you a lift."

Choices.

Angry black man. Angry *and* crazy white woman. She got in the car.

12

Little Five Points in Atlanta was physically close enough for it to be a periodic hangout of Becca's. But it was culturally too far away to ever be a serious consideration. Except for an incredible burger at a restaurant named *The Vortex*. That had occurred only twice.

This restaurant was as good enough a representation as any as to why the area wasn't on Becca's map. The front door of the place was made up like a giant skull. Want a burger? A drink at the bar? No problem. Enter the skull. Not that the restaurant's theme was had been a problem the two times Becca had eaten there. It hadn't.

And the problem wasn't that Little Five Points was *bad*. It wasn't. It wasn't a red light district. It wasn't a drug district. It wasn't a high crime district. It was simply a small east Atlanta community of bars, indie restaurants, shops, and theaters whose residents and visitors were of the alternative culture type.

This meant the usual physical attractions that scared suburbanites. Unconventional clothes. Green, orange, and purple hair. Lots of tattoos. Rings in noses and lips. A permanent contingent of homeless people sitting on benches or lying on the ground at the central location called *The Point*. And from time to time, a group of ever wandering young men and women wearing backpacks and tattered clothes that carried lethally pungent smells. Their hair long, matted, and filthy.

The problem was that although Becca wasn't a Christian, her grandparents' influence upon her, especially her grandmother's, had kept her from acting with abandon on her urges. Sometimes she felt as though there was a chain attached to her that kept her just out of reach of going too far. But she had found that the chain of conscience that held her in check was made of rubber and not steel. If she really wanted to do something, and she pressed against her conscience hard enough, the chain stretched and lengthened. That was the reason why she had done everything on the sexual menu minus anything that could get her pregnant. What the girls at her school called *nice girl sex*.

Little Five Points represented no boundaries. It represented a collective community of people who lived their lives without the low energy restraints that influenced Becca's thoughts and actions. Crystal's car was just reaching the edge of the community, and already Becca felt something tugging at her grandmother's chains.

They drove south on Moreland Avenue and passed a row of large townhomes on the left. A few seconds later and there was Starbucks on Becca's right. A gentle smile formed at its familiarity. *Hello, my friend*, she said silently to Starbuck's. Becca looked out Crystal's side of the window at Sacred Heart Tattoo and wondered if she had gotten any of her tattoos there.

Crystal pointed at a building on Becca's side. "That black building there's a restaurant. Burned down and took forever to reopen. Put me and my girlfriend out of work."

"Oh, that's too bad," said Becca.

Crystal shrugged. "No big deal. If you can mix a decent drink, you don't stay out of work long. We got another job just like that. At the same place. Not the place that burned down. Another place. She was an awesome bartender. Got crazy tips. Our resemblance was crazy. She looked just like me. She said I looked like her. But I'm older, so she looked like me. We used to dress alike and take each other's name.

The customers got off on that. A lot of the customers at bars are regulars." Crystal paused and said softly, "I miss her."

"She's not in the area any more?" Becca asked.

"Nobody knows where she is. Left work one night and never came back. Left her purse... Rachel's dead." Her voice was hard with bad reality.

"I'm sorry," Becca said softly.

They turned right at the corner and Becca tried to be inconspicuous about staring at the homeless-looking guy who was flailing his arms and having a horrible argument—with himself. "You eat there before?" Becca said, pointing to a tiny Thai restaurant, hoping that asking a question would mask how awkward she felt, and if she was honest, how afraid she was.

"They got good sushi. We'll check 'em out." The girl tapped her on the leg twice when she said it.

Becca spotted another tattoo shop before they turned a corner and wondered again whether those folks knew Crystal.

Crystal parked on the street. "We're here, girlfriend."

Becca's smile was only partially there. A mixture of *Okay, let me get my bag*, and *Have I gone absolutely insane?* She didn't know this girl. And the little she did know was scary.

Crystal saw how slowly Becca moved to get her bag out the back seat. "Hey," she said.

Becca looked at her with that nervous smile.

"You don't know me, Becca."

Becca looked across the hood at her.

"I don't know you," Crystal continued. "But you know pain, and I know pain." The girl didn't say anything for a while. "But I wear short dresses and no panties, and I carry a big knife." She smirked. "If I were in your shoes, I wouldn't do it. It's not the knife. It's the no panties thing. I couldn't get past that."

Becca laughed holding her belly. After a pause, she shook her head and asked, "Why don't you wear panties?"

"Don't want to."

"Well, we know that," said Becca. "Why don't you want to?"

Crystal looked at Becca, the question peeling scab from one of many old, but still painful wounds. Her mind told her to shut down. She didn't talk about it. And when possible, she didn't think about it. But something traitorous happened in her emotions. Before she knew it, she heard words coming out of her mouth that peeled back a thin layer of her shell. "My way of telling the world what I think of it. Somebody don't like it, screw 'em. Not trying to please anybody or make somebody accept me or—" She stopped.

Becca wondered whether her unspoken sentence was, "I'm not trying to make someone *love* me." She looked at her with a smile that masked her nervousness. Oddly, her mind went blank. It had literally stranded her without one single thought.

"Becca, you can stay as long as you need to. No strings attached. Somebody was there for me. Us girls, we gotta help one another. When you wanna go, go." She pointed floppily and dropped her hand. "It's a house; not a prison."

Something told Becca this was a bad idea. Then flashes of the scene with her confronting that guy at the coffee shop went across her mind. This girl was definitely not someone she would have chosen for a friend under other circumstances. Under *any* circumstances. But with all her tattoos and cursing and violent temper…

Becca thought of the aching in her heart and the pain in her arm she felt whenever her parents rejected her in a big way. She didn't want them to have that kind of power over her any longer. She didn't want to spend the rest of her life dying inside as she tried to make her parents love her. She wanted to be strong—like Crystal.

"I don't have a lot of money," said Becca.

Crystal shrugged with her shoulders and lips. "Money. No money. Who gives a—?" She went colorful with her language again.

Becca marveled at Crystal's creativity. *What this girl can do with curse words,"* thought Becca, as she grabbed her bag.

The house had about ten cement steps that led from the sidewalk to the large wooden porch that was covered with an equally large deck above. The porch and deck had white fencing and circular white columns that contrasted starkly against dirty red bricks. The full tree in the front yard provided privacy from the street. Privacy that Crystal used often when she wanted to cool out on the deck and smoke a nice, fat joint.

Becca stepped inside the dimly lit house.

"You can drop the body anywhere," Crystal said.

Becca was happy to comply. She let the bag slide to the floor from the one shoulder she had it on.

Crystal turned up the light dimmer. "Just in case you're not part vampire. That's a little better," she croaked. She carried her small bag to the kitchen. "And don't lie and say what a nice place I have. I know it's crap. You don't have to lie." She put a few things in the refrigerator and left the other stuff on the counter. She returned to the living room.

Becca was looking around like the place was a museum. "It's a really nice place you have," she said, turning from a small, ornate statue."

Crystal bounced her finger in Becca's direction before plopping onto a sofa. "I told you, you didn't have to lie. I swear, that's why I carry a knife."

"I didn't lie. It's nice. Why don't you like it?"

Crystal widened her arms across the top of the back of the sofa and used her hands to shrug. She looked toward the mantle over the fireplace. She pointed lazily at the statue Becca had been looking at earlier. "Him for one."

Becca looked again at the statue. "What is it? Why don't you like it?"

"Look at it," said Crystal.

She did.

"What do you see?" asked Crystal.

"A statue of a man with four arms. Sitting full lotus. Lots of hair. Got three eyes. Likes jewelry."

"I don't get it," Crystal said in a higher tone. "Everyone I ask that question says the same thing. I thought it was Vishnu."

"Who's Vishnu?"

"Vishnu's a woman. A Hindu god. *The Preserver*."

Becca looked again at the statue and frowned her face. "How'd you get a woman out of that face?"

Crystal shrugged. "I don't know. Vishnu's got four arms; the statue's got four arms. I just thought she was overweight and ugly. Do you know who *he* is?" She looked at Becca with a pause. "Shiva."

"Okay," said Becca. The name meant nothing to her.

"Shiva's *The Destroyer*."

"Okay." This meant as much as Vishnu to Becca—nothing.

"Becca," Crystal said as though it was obvious, "Shiva's a male. A man with two hands is bad enough. I have a man with four hands sitting on my mantle."

Becca's eyebrows went up. "And he got into your house under false pretenses." She nodded with an understanding grin. "You can't trust every man with four hands."

Crystal looked at Becca and said with an intensity that didn't fit the light mood. "You can't trust any man. If he's got a penis, you can't trust him."

Becca was surprised by the instant transformation of the moment. This girl had a lot of stuff going on just beneath the surface. A lot of anger. Her mind connected Crystal to a pit bull. Pit bull owners swore their dogs were wonderful and loyal pets. That was probably true. But those wonderful, loyal pets were regularly in the news for inexplicably attacking, mauling, and killing people. There was something in those animals that was on a trip wire. A trip wire that was better not tripped. Problem was, *what was the wire?*

The thought of the pit bull made Becca ask, "Were you really going to cut that guy?"

Crystal gave a half smile. "Remember I said if he's got a penis, you can't trust him?"

"Yeah."

"I was going to make him trustworthy."

"Oh, now I feel better," said Becca. "For a minute, I thought I might have gone home not only with a stranger, but a killer."

"Ahh, I'm not crazy. Just mean. Sometimes things happen that make you that way. I learned a long time ago that the world wipes its butt with nice people." She smiled. "I give you my word as a killer, if you don't have a penis, you don't have anything to worry about." Crystal popped up. "Come on. Let me show you around this dump."

"Guess I'm safe then," said Becca. "And you know, you can always get rid of ol' four-hands if he ticks you off so much."

Crystal stopped. "Naw. Not that easy. He's a gift. Gerald. You'll meet him." She went to the mantle and pointed a finger into the statue's face. "But that don't mean I won't cut you. Come on," she said. "The grand tour begins."

Becca lagged. "Don't worry, Shiva. She's not going to cut you." She smiled and turned to follow Crystal and clutched her chest, stopping for a moment.

Unwanted and Alone were at it again with their daggers.

Becca felt like something inside was butchering her. Not her flesh; her soul. Whatever it was that was the deepest part of her. It was being slashed and ripped and punctured a thousand ways. She pasted a grimaced smile on her face and followed Crystal. Following a stranger because she had no one else. Following a stranger because she was alone and unwanted in the world.

Becca could tell from the street that the house wasn't small, but it was even larger inside. Crystal took her from room to room, trashing the house the whole time. But she and Crystal must've been looking at different homes. There was nothing wrong with this house. It was clean, spacious, and although the furniture wasn't great, it wasn't bad. Probably the only thing Becca would've changed was the floor plan was a little too cut up for her. She liked more open spaces. Plus, it needed a couple of more bathrooms.

It was upstairs that she discovered there was something else about the house she didn't like.

"This is Gerald's hangout," said Crystal.

Hangout? It has a bed in it. It's a bedroom, thought Becca. "Gerald? It's a bedroom."

Crystal bobbed her finger and smiled at Becca. "When I saw you at the coffee shop, Becca, I said, now that girl there, she's a smart one." She laughed. "Bed. Room. You're right. It's a bedroom."

"Gerald lives here?"

"See. There you go again—showing off."

"What about what you said downstairs?" asked Becca. Going home with a woman she didn't know, and apparently crazily letting herself consider staying there for a while was one thing. But now there was a *man* in the house, too? Becca felt like she had taken a drug that makes people think and do crazy things, and the drug's effects were wearing off fast.

"What? You mean what I said about the penis?"

"Yeah, what you said about the penis. I'm assuming he has one."

Crystal bobbed her finger. She looked like she was searching for the right word. "Not really."

Becca's mouth opened with the speed of a drawbridge. Her tongue felt starched heavy. Finally, "Not *really?*"

"I talk too much. He'd kill me if he knew I told you that. Remember my big knife, girlfriend."

"How can I forget?"

"Gerald's one of the few good guys out there," said Crystal. She made a face like she was experiencing something good. "Cooks like a chef. Does all the cooking."

"Is he gay?" Becca hoped the answer was yes.

Crystal chuckled. "No, he's a whore."

"I thought you said—"

"He doesn't let that stop him." Crystal saw the questions. "Don't worry. He's harmless. Scrawny little guy—tender. Has three sisters. You'll like him. Trust me." She added. "Plus, he's in and out. More out than in."

"Okay," said Becca, unsure of what else to say.

"We're cool?" said Crystal.

"Yeah," lied Becca. She was getting out of this girl's house. And fast.

13

Danielle sat in the living room with her arms folded tightly across her chest. Her lips were tight. Her eyes were tight. She stared across the long sofa and out the large window that looked out the cul-de-sac. The sun was bright, but her mood was dark and angry. Grandma was blackmailing her. She was blackmailing them all.

Vincent sat on one of the love seats. He had nearly rubbed the skin off his forehead, and his hand and fingers were still nervously at work. He pinched the bridge of his nose and listened to Heather's side of the conversation. *Why didn't Nancy mind her own business?* he thought.

Heather was talking as much with her hand as her mouth. She cupped the phone and said to Danielle, "Are you sure you didn't tell her anything?"

"Yes," said Danielle.

"Nothing?" Heather pressed.

"Nothing, Mom. You know God tells her stuff." Danielle didn't know if this was true, but Grandma did know a lot of stuff, and Dad believed she had some kind of weird connection with heaven.

Vincent grunted.

Heather looked at him with irritation and shook her head and turned around and walked toward the kitchen.

"Danielle, you said if we let you stay a few days with your grandmother that you wouldn't say anything," said Vincent, with his hand still on his forehead.

"I didn't say anything, Dad. And I didn't say a few days. I didn't say any amount of days."

"Well, it can't be more than a few days."

"Are you and Mom going to start treating Becca the way you're supposed to within a few days? Like your daughter? The way you treat me?"

Vincent stopped rubbing and sat up. "Danielle, it's not that simple." He let out a long breath. "There are things…"

"Dad, Becca's your daughter. She's Mom's daughter. She's my sister."

This dad was getting tired of being bulldozed by his sixteen-year-old daughter. "It's not that simple!" he snapped.

Danielle popped up like she had a spring under her.

"What are you doing? You sit back down," he ordered.

Danielle's eyes flared. "It's not that simple."

"Okay, wait!" he tried to lower his voice after he'd already yelled. He pushed his palm in the air, calling for a truce.

Danielle stood rigid, waiting.

"Take as long as you need. Just please don't bring your grandmother into this. Let us work it out ourselves."

Danielle was hoping he'd have more to offer than this. She shook her head. "You're not going to do the right thing, are you?"

Heather walked into the room and held the phone out. "She wants to talk to you."

"To who?" Vincent jumped like a spooked cat.

"Don't worry, Vincent. Not you, Danielle." Heather's voice was laced with disgust.

Vincent heard it, but his greatest concern was not his wife's attitude. It was keeping Nancy out of their business. He looked at Danielle imploringly. "Danielle."

Danielle huffed and took the phone.

Both parents stared at her as though they wanted to fashion each word in her mouth like Play-Doh before she spoke. Why didn't she listen to them any more? Oh, what had happened to the old, sweet Danielle who obeyed? They listened to the conversation like soldiers listening to the whistling sound of enemy bombs dropping from the night sky, hoping none would find them. Their eyes were wide. Their movements were stilled. *Come on, Danielle.*

It appeared that the conversation was about over.

"She got out early this morning with one of her friends before anyone was up," said Danielle.

Vincent and Heather looked at one another. A dark secret in their eyes.

"Yes, I know strife is of the devil." Danielle listened in defeat, a lazy smile forcing its way to the surface by a pushy, but wonderful grandmother. Danielle looked at her father as she said this to help calm his nerves. "If that's what it takes to visit with you for a few days." Then her eyes bugged out. "Grandma, you want us to do what?"

"No, don't worry about it. This doesn't change anything," said Crystal. "We're friends."

"Really? You were so nice to offer me a place to stay."

Crystal looked thoughtfully. "Yeah, that was nice of me, wasn't it? Then you eat my Thai food and pull some crap like this."

Becca had gotten more used to Crystal's sense of humor.

"I told you," said Crystal, "if I were you, I never would've gotten past the no panties thing. Hey, I never would've come here."

"What?" Becca asked, surprise in her voice. "You never would've come?"

"Of course not."

Becca jutted her neck and laughed. "What?"

"You kidding me? People are crazy."

"I don't believe you," said Becca."

"I don't believe you," said Crystal. "Crazy white girl with a huge knife and wearing no panties about to cut a guy's nuts off right there on the street. You jump in the car with her. Go home with her," she stressed. "I don't know how you've lasted this long."

An angel of truth placed his hand on the back of Becca's neck. He got close to her ear and whispered, *I was found by those who did not seek Me; I was made manifest to those who did not ask for Me.*

The thoughts were as strong as the negative thoughts she often had, but these weren't pushy. She momentarily looked into the well of her soul. She could see its dry bottom. Another strong thought surfaced. *All day long I have stretched out my hands to a disobedient and contrary people.*

Crystal snapped her fingers. "Okay, mystery solved. You're not all there."

"Oh," Becca chuckled. "Sorry. Drifting."

"Hey," said Crystal.

Becca looked at her tattooed friend.

"Whatever you're going through, it ain't nobody's business but yours. You don't owe me or anybody else an explanation. But if you ever want to talk, you know where to find me."

"Oh," Becca was caught flatfooted by Crystal's kindness again. It didn't match her appearance and coffee shop drama. Becca shook her head gratefully. "Okay. Thanks. And if you ever need—"

Crystal's palm went up. "One-way street, sweetheart."

"Oh, so it's like that?" said Becca, smiling. "I can talk to you about me, but you can't talk to—"

Crystal cut her off again, not rudely, but still—off. "I don't talk about me."

Becca looked for a smile or a chuckle or something to show that Crystal was kidding. The look in her eyes—a look Becca couldn't decipher—had *serious* written all over them. "Okay, Crystal, but still, just so you know, you can always talk to me, too."

Crystal didn't acknowledge one way or the other that she heard her. "We better get you home."

Home.

Becca grabbed one of the shoulder straps of her bag. Home? What was that? She and Crystal both agreed that she was crazy to accept Crystal's offer to stay with her. But now Becca wondered whether it was more crazy to go back to her house—really, her parents' house. She knew that her soul was too fragile to survive their abuse. It was ironic. She was leaving a strange house full of kindness to return to a familiar house full of cruelty. *Crystal, you're right. I am crazy,* she thought.

Crystal was silent the whole drive.

Becca wasn't sure, but she got the faint impression that Crystal was hurt. She shook this off. This was the girl with the big knife and sailor's mouth.

They were now only one block away from making the turn down the cul-de-sac.

"Crystal, stop the car, please."

Crystal pulled over.

Becca's eyes were closed. Her head was bowed. It seemed to Crystal that her soul was bowed. She looked at Becca's hands. They were trembling—badly. Becca's breaths were short and rapid. She started hyperventilating.

Becca's eyes were still closed, but her mouth opened wide. Tears streamed down her face. Her heart ached. Her arm throbbed. Something was trying to pull her arm off at the shoulder. She didn't want them to have this kind of power over her. Becca didn't want to be weak. And she didn't want Crystal to think she was weak.

Crystal took her hands and squeezed. *What have these people done to you?* she thought. She quickly wiped the surprise tears away from her own eyes. "It's going to be okay. We'll sit here as long as you need to. Or we can leave." Crystal wondered whether her father was doing something to her friend. The more she thought of it, the angrier she became. The angrier she became, the more she thought of her knife.

After several minutes, Becca wiped her eyes. "I'm sorry."

"You don't have to be sorry for feeling pain."

"It's just—my parents and I—it hasn't been easy. They should've aborted me."

"No! I created you for My glory. I preserved you for My glory," said the truth angel.

Becca heard the thought, but felt the pain. She listened to the pain.

"I'm glad they didn't," said Crystal.

"I wish I could say me, too. I can't. I wish I could." She took a deep breath and let it out. "Okay."

"We're okay?" said Crystal.

Becca nodded.

Crystal drove down Becca's street. Three houses away. Two houses away. Becca looked at their large window that faced the street. One house away.

"Stop," she said. She shook her head and looked again. The ache in her heart got worse. She gritted her teeth, trying to ignore her arm.

———

"I don't know why Grandma's making us do this," Danielle said.

"If this is what it takes," Heather whispered.

"Anything to keep her out of our business," Vincent mumbled to himself.

Vincent, Heather, and Danielle did a group hug that had about as much life in it as three life-like mannequins being pushed together.

Grandma looked at her iPad and frowned. "That has got to be the most pathetic group hug of a family that I've ever seen. Now I want to see some love or me and Pastor Bill—"

"Okay," said Vincent. "Come on," he said, his voice urgent. He looked at Danielle. "We're going to work this out, Danielle…please."

She looked at him with a tight look.

"Please," he whispered again.

Crystal's car was parked in front of the house, but not in the driveway. They had an unobstructed view of all of the hugging and kissing going on among the Simmons's.

"Well, well, now. Would you look at that?" said a lying spirit to Becca. "What happened to that beautiful speech your loving sister made to your parents? She was furious with them...wasn't she? Maybe I'm mistaken."

Becca looked in disbelief at Danielle and their parents. It wasn't the kind of disbelief that denied what it saw. It was the kind of disbelief that saw the train coming and admitted in resignation, *I'm about to be hit by a train and there's nothing I can do about it.*

Becca dealt with the train by going numb. The last picture she consciously saw was Vincent and Heather kissing Danielle on opposite cheeks, and Danielle loving it.

Crystal started driving just when Danielle glanced out the window. Danielle froze, staring at the girl on the passenger side as the car circled away from the house. She bolted for the door without uttering a word. "Becca! Becca! Come back!"

Whoever was driving stuck her arm out of the window and gave her a middle finger.

"Take me home, Crystal," came the gutted plea.

They both knew she meant her new home in Little Five Points.

The demons of Becca's stronghold of rejection were gathered in the great room, awaiting the arrival of Unwanted and his number one demon, Alone. The meeting had been called with urgency, but not panic.

A couple of minutes later Unwanted and Alone entered the room. But they were not alone. The stronghold demons wondered at the trail of other demons that followed them carrying an assortment of odd things. Tables, musical instruments, banners, food, and party hats. *Party hats? And blowers? They were having a party?* Several spirits carried a large disco ball to the high ceiling and held it steady while another fastened it.

Unwanted stepped forward. His demons gave him their attention, but they were still clearly distracted by the activity going on around them. "It's okay," said Unwanted. "This is a day of celebration. My plan is working." His voice was triumphant.

Alone cleared his throat.

Unwanted gurgled a laugh. "*Our* plan is working," he corrected. He looked at his audience and put his hand to the side of his mouth and whispered, "He always feels like he's being left out." His shoulders bounced with a low laughter that didn't escape his chest.

Some of the more powerful demons laughed. Those considerably lesser in stature wisely passed on the temptation to laugh. Alone was easily offended and had a long memory.

"Why don't we let my friend give you the details?" Unwanted took a step backward and motioned to Alone.

Alone stepped forward and looked at Unwanted and said, "*Our* plan to further isolate Becca is working to perfection. Today we have done what every great stronghold of rejection does. We have distorted communication. We showed Becca something that didn't exist. Now she has turned from the very person who loves her. The only person who loves her." Alone pumped his fist as he spoke. "This is what we do! We destroy relationships and isolate. Becca is alone!"

Alone nodded to Unwanted that he was finished.

"What about that miserable grandmother of hers?" a demon from the crowd asked.

Unwanted saw a lying spirit waving his hand that he wanted to answer. A rejection spirit was doing the same. Unwanted waved them both off. "What about that miserable grandmother of hers? Becca has suffered all her life at the hands of her parents. How many times has she confided in her grandmother? Zero. How often has she listened to Granny's gibberish about Jesus and eternal life? Zero. Why is she with our girl instead of her grandmother? I'll tell you why." He peered into the audience. "No. No, I won't tell you why. I'll let Self-Condemnation tell you. Come up, my friend."

Self-Condemnation pushed rudely through the crowd. He had a twisted, permanent scowl, like a face after a bad stroke whose muscles had visited an area and now couldn't go home. Flesh frozen in place. He looked darkly at the crowd.

"I'll speak for my whole team of shame and condemnation spirits. Becca isn't with that ugly old woman because she is ashamed of herself. She doesn't feel right when she's in her presence. And do you know why she doesn't feel right when she's around that woman? It's because she knows that her grandmother is right," he waited for effect, "*and that she is wrong.*

"She doesn't understand why she feels this way. But she feels that every moment spent around that woman is another moment she may be exposed as the wretched person she feels she is." He pointed at each spirit as he called out their names. "Shame, Fear of Being Discovered, Self-Hatred, Self-Rejection, all of us, all of you," he roared, "we are the reason Becca is not with that hideous woman!"

The stronghold broke out into cheers and hisses and growls.

Self-Condemnation's twisted face couldn't show that he was pleased with himself, but he was. He took a slow walk back to the applauding crowd and stood at the front. He faced Unwanted and Alone.

"What's going to stop Granny from praying for her once she hears that she's run away?" a demon in the back asked.

"Don't ruin the party!" several demons shot back, as though they had practiced this response among themselves.

"Who said that? Who said that?" said Unwanted. "Get him out! Out! Out! Get him out of here! We are not going to let thoughts of prayer ruin our party!"

The demon was grabbed by several who saw him as a threat to their party and savagely beaten to a motionless pulp. Two demons grabbed him by the ankles and dragged him to the edge of the door. One motioned the other. They went to his top and placed hands under his shoulders, stood him up, and tossed him face first outdoors.

Unwanted and Alone watched the beating with satisfaction. But the damage was done. *That idiot had messed up their party by reminding them of the power of prayer.*

Gabron looked at Justis and Krasa, then at the truth angel. When he had first heard that truth angels were coming, he was expecting an army. The army turned out to be three angels. Three angels for a stronghold. Now he and his friends were looking at one truth angel. They certainly were frugal.

"Where are the other truth angels?" asked Gabron.

"Out working. Probing. Finding weak spots. Putting things in place."

"Two angels? Against such a mighty fortress of lies?" Gabron's words were more rhetorical than disbelief. He did believe. He had to believe. But the angels had said success wasn't guaranteed. *So why only one angel here and two angels out there somewhere? Why is Satan's power always so evident and ours so hidden?* "My brother, my I ask you a question about the operation?"

The angel of truth looked fondly at the warrior. He placed a hand on his shoulder and lifted the other to heaven. He looked up. "Lord, open his eyes that he may see."

Gabron's eyes stretched as wide as possible. He looked in every direction, with his hands outstretched as though what he saw afar off was within an arm's reach. "Justin! Krasa!" he laughed in gleeful joy and relief as he looked at the mighty armies of the Lord. "They're everywhere! Everywhere! Armies! Oh—I—I'm—my brother," he said to the truth angel, "I did not doubt—I knew—Satan's power. His power is always so there. In our faces. In the faces of the sons and daughters of Adam."

The angel of truth wore an expression that conveyed understanding. "It is all a matter of perspective," he said. "Satan must appear all powerful because he is weak. The Lord can appear weak because He is all-powerful. At the appointed time, everyone will see what is now hidden."

Gabron looked up to the heavens and lifted his hands. He dropped to his knees and cried and prayed and sang a song of worship. His friends joined him.

The angel of truth waited for the three angels to arise. "Truth is never alone," he said to the weeping angels. "The Lord watches over His word to perform it."

Then he and the armies were gone.

Or were they?

14

Crystal stood in the doorway of what was now Becca's bedroom. "It's crap, but it's yours as long as you need it."

Becca let her emotionally drained body plop heavily onto the bed. She felt like a bug fighting desperately against the flushed waters of a toilet. Fighting to live another day of life as a worthless bug. A pest. Still, when she heard Crystal call the room crap, ten percent of her face smiled.

According to Crystal, every room in the house was bad. This one was too small. Closet too small. Window too small. Bed was too hard. Dresser and two end tables too dark and too old. Paint color too bland. Too this, too that. But like the rest of the house, there was nothing wrong with this room.

"It's perfect," Becca said. It was a room attached to a house that didn't have her sister down the hall and didn't have her parents' name on the mortgage. That made it perfect.

"You probably need some time alone," said Crystal.

Becca nodded. She watched agreeably as the door closed. She took a deep breath and exhaled and anticipated the nice feel of the mattress against her tired body.

The door popped open.

"Uh, you want a joint or something? A beer? A drink? I'm not as good at mixing as Gerald, but... Whatever you nuns do," Crystal offered.

"A hunky priest with no collar," Becca teased, her voice carrying no energy. "No, thanks. I'm just going to crash a little bit."

Funny you should say that, thought Crystal. "Okay. Uhh, Becca?"

"Yeah?"

She thought for a few seconds. "Nothing. Close those eyes. Get some rest."

Becca's body embraced the mattress. She closed her eyes. She went to sleep. But she did not rest. There were monsters to fight.

The faces were horrible. They weren't human. They were monsters. Demons. They stood side by side, looking at her. They were hungry. Hungry for her. They wanted to eat her, but not as an animal eats another for food. They wanted to eat her because they hated her. They both held long black knives in each hand. Blood dripped from all four blades. Her blood. It was her blood that was dripping. The hungry eyes of the demons wanted more.

Becca looked at the monsters from inside something like a bubble. The bubble was filled with liquid. It was all around her, but she wasn't drowning—not from the liquid anyway. But then Becca heard angry and cruel words. She couldn't understand them, but she could feel them. They were like spears being thrust into her. That's when the dry drowning began.

There was a sensation of something akin to what it felt like for the ten percent of people who drowned without water in their lungs. Dying instead from suffocation when the brain detects the imminent threat of drowning and protects the body by closing the air passage. Something in her soul detected the darts, and to protect her from the threat, it shut down a part of her soul.

. . .

The scene abruptly changed to Becca huddling at the back of a wet cave and looking with terror at a huge hand carrying scissors. Becca knew this hand meant to use the scissors to rip her to pieces. The scissors opened its mouth at her shoulder.

She pushed as far back into the cave as possible and screamed.

Becca's door burst open. Crystal paused for a split-second just inside the room. Her friend was screaming and tossing and pushing into the headboard as though she were being attacked by wild dogs. She made it to her bed in three leaping steps. "Becca!" said Crystal, shaking her. Then shaking her more vigorously. "Wake up! Wake up!"

The scissors find Becca's shoulder.

"Becca!" said Crystal.

Blaring music. The scissors leave.

Becca was asleep and fighting as though she was awake. Crystal shook her roughly, putting niceness aside. This wasn't the time for it. "Becca! Becca! Wake up! It's a dream!"

Music stops. Odd shaped scissors return. "Oh, my Lord—"

Crystal shook Becca with all she had.

Becca's eyes popped open. "You are my hiding place! You preserve me from trouble! You surround me with songs of deliverance!"

"Becca, it's me—Crystal. You had a bad dream." Crystal looked into Becca's eyes and saw terror. She sat on the edge of the bed and cupped the back of her head with one hand and slid her other hand under her back. She hugged her close to her body. "It's okay. It's okay. It's okay."

Crystal said this a few more times and suddenly her own heart heard it. Tears formed and spilled from her eyes. She spoke to Becca and herself. "They can't hurt you any more. You're in a safe place. You're with friends."

Becca held on to her friend's embrace and cried desperately. She was so happy to be rescued from that nightmare. *They were trying to kill her. The demons. The scissors.* "Crystal," she said.

"Yeah, I'm here," she said, still holding her, and rocking.

Becca pulled back and sat up and propped two pillows behind her. She pulled her knees up and wrapped her arms around her legs. "These things…like demons, they were stabbing me. I was in some kind of thick bubble in a wet cave." She shook her head. "Giant scissors were trying to get me. They were about to chop off my arm. Music blasted out of nowhere and the scissors left."

Crystal looked at her friend and felt her own heart hurting for her.

"And this is weird." She sniffled. "I mean really weird. The music—it's a really old song. It was *Highway to Hell.*"

Crystal jutted her neck. "AC/DC? Girlfriend, you're going way back now. We weren't even born when that song came out. How'd you even know it?"

"I know. A guy in one of my classes used it for an assignment on censorship in media. Our class watched them perform on You Tube together."

Crystal smiled crookedly. "At school watching AC/DC sing *Highway to Hell*—for credit. No wonder you kids are so worthless."

Why did she call you worthless? said a rejection spirit. *She didn't have to use that word. She could've said something else. You better watch her.*

"Crystal," said Becca.

Crystal saw that Becca was back to the trouble of the dream. "Yeah?"

"When the music stopped, the giant scissors came back. They weren't really scissors, not like the first ones. These had funny ends. They were going to tear me to pieces with them."

"Who? The demons?"

Becca shrugged. "Yeah, I guess. But really it was somebody else. Somebody I couldn't see. Somebody being used by the demons." She didn't tell Crystal that although she didn't see or hear them in the dream, she felt her parents were somewhere in the dream's darkness. *That wasn't hard to believe.*

"Hey, you know you came out of that nightmare saying some wild stuff, girlfriend."

Becca looked at her with a question.

"Yeah, you were jammin' like you were Shakespeare's old lady, or praying or something. 'You are my hiding place! You preserve me from trouble! You surround me with songs of deliverance!'"

Becca's eyes widened. She hardly knew why. All she knew was that hearing Crystal repeat those words were like hearing someone read the words of her own diary. An entry made at a desperate time. "You surround me with songs of deliverance?" said Becca.

"That's what you said," Crystal laughed. She stood and mimed playing a guitar, complete with twisted face, exaggerated movements, and biting her bottom lip. "Maybe God answered your prayers and sent the *Highway to Hell* boys to chase the scissors away."

Becca smiled and giggled a little at Crystal's antics. It felt good to put some comic relief distance between her and the nightmare. But behind the smile and giggle, Becca wondered hard on Crystal's words.

The girls talked for hours, well into the evening. Becca doing most of the talking, and Crystal listening sympathetically, but sharing nearly nothing about herself. And the little she did share was done so cryptically that she sounded like a skilled spy passing secrets under the noses of those trying to sniff her out. One thing was clear, though. She was filled with rage.

The angel of truth looked intently into Becca's mind and heart, discerning her thoughts and intentions. Of course, the girls didn't know he was there. Neither did the stronghold demons. Nor the warrior angels. But this was routine. The work of truth was often imperceptible beneath the soil of God's plans until the moment of His choosing. *Nothing, then something.*

Becca finally rested her head on the pillow and closed her eyes for the evening. Alcohol on her breath. Confusion in her mind. Turmoil in her soul. And demons fighting among themselves for control of the new ground they were gaining in her.

The work of rejection was accelerating.

The angel of truth put his hand on the forehead of this daughter of Adam. "Rest for now," he said. "You will need your strength for tomorrow's light."

15

Crystal scooped up the omelet with a smile and put it on Becca's plate, where toast and grits were already waiting. She sat down and looked across at Becca. She was looking at her omelet like it had a pistol in its hand, saying, "Stick 'em up!"

"I'm starving," said Crystal, smiling and diving into her food. She looked at Becca. "What? You didn't get that body by eating lettuce, girlfriend. You carry dumbbells in that sack of yours?"

"It's just that I've never seen a six-egg omelet," said Becca.

Crystal had a mouthful of food. She raised two fingers.

"No way that's two eggs," said Becca.

Crystal swallowed. "Yes, there is a way." Her expression had a hint of humor. "These eggs come from free range chickens. These are happy eggs. And the chicken sausage I used in the omelet is happy, too."

Something dark rose inside of Becca. It started in her belly and spread to her chest, filling her. Then it moved to her head. *What difference does it make that the chicken died with a smile on its face? He's still on your plate about to be eaten. Like you, Becca. No matter how much you smile, you're going to be eaten.*

"You alright?" said Crystal.

"Huh? Oh, yeah." Becca shook her head and smiled. She lowered her head and said a quick prayer over her meal.

Crystal's phone rang. She hopped up and got it off the counter, answered, and sat down. She looked at Becca. "Little Five Points Convent. How may I direct your call?"

Becca put a piece of the dinosaur egg omelet into her mouth. She looked at Crystal's troubled expression and stopped chewing.

Crystal pushed away from the table. "I'll be right there. No, it's no problem. What? Girlfriend, it's going to be a problem if you keep asking me if it's a problem. We're friends."

"What's wrong?" Becca asked.

"Look, I gotta go. A friend of mine needs me. I gotta take her somewhere. Where's my purse?" Crystal said to herself.

"You're not going to eat your breakfast first?" Becca asked.

Crystal spun and looked at Becca with intense eyes. "Breakfast? Food? My *friend* needs me? She needs me now, Becca, not in thirty minutes. Not in an hour. She needs me now." She bounced her finger at Becca as she spoke. "Friends don't let their friends down. Ever!" she thrust the word like it was a spear into the side of an enemy. "Ever!" she said again. "You have to be there for your friends...or you're no friend at all."

Becca's eyes showed her surprise. She had obviously pushed a hot button. She didn't know what to say. So she just stared at Crystal.

Crystal's trembling finger was pointed at Becca. Her lips quivered. Her emotions trying to force water from her eyes. "She's my friend."

Becca knew Crystal had had a messed up life, too. She had dropped a couple of hints. Besides, nobody got the kind of rage she had by having a good life. But what was it that made her so fanatical about friendship and being there for her friends? "Okay," she said softly. "I'm going with you."

"No. She's my friend, not yours. You don't have to go."

"Yeah, but you're *my* friend." Becca shrugged. "So let's go."

Crystal froze, momentarily stilled, then tried to play it off. "Okay," she said, but the hardness she called for never showed in her voice. "I'm glad you're going. I don't like abortion clinics."

Crystal came off of Ivan Allen Jr Boulevard and crossed Northside Drive and went west on Joseph E. Boone Boulevard. The city had given Simpson Avenue the new name of Joseph E. Boone Boulevard for the same reason it had changed Stewart Avenue into Metropolitan Avenue. It was easier to rename a major street known for its violence and prostitution than it was to stop the violence and prostitution in those neighborhoods.

Becca saw and felt the change the moment the car crossed Northside. They literally went from affluence to poverty simply by crossing the street, and it only got worse the further west they went. The left and right sides of the street competed from block to block for the unattractive award. But the truth was it was a running tie for the ugly award, not the unattractive award.

Becca looked at the small shopping plaza on the right. A coin laundry. A supermarket. A cleaners. All resembling prisons behind iron bars and iron grates. She looked at the groups of black guys who hung out in front of stores and tried to ignore the awkwardness she felt. Or was it fear? Every black guy who wore baggy clothes and hung out on the streets wasn't necessarily a criminal, she told herself.

Becca noted the liquor stores and the drunks who hung out there like dying men hanging out at the graveyard. And, of course, there was a *Family Dollar* store.

"Go ahead and say it," said Crystal, interrupting her thoughts.

"Say what?"

"Say what?" Crystal said, like Becca knew what she was talking about. "Where are you taking this suburban white girl?"

"No. No. I wasn't thinking that at all," said Becca.

"Okay." Crystal sounded unconvinced.

About thirty seconds later, Becca said with laughter, "Okay! Where are you taking me, Crystal?"

"Uh huh. Thought so." Crystal gave her a sheepish grin. "Have you noticed we're the only white girls in this neighborhood?"

"Try the only white *people* in the neighborhood," said Becca.

Crystal smiled at Becca with the smile that had surprised her once before for its vibrancy. A smile that was deep and without reservation. One that enjoyed the present moment as though there had been no painful moments before it.

"Don't worry, girlfriend. Gas in car. Knife in purse."

"Knife?" Becca stretched her head back and looked at the top of the car, shaking her head with a slight laugh. "We're two white girls in the middle of the ghetto, but we're safe. Crystal's got her knife."

Crystal smirked as she looked straight ahead. "That's not all Crystal's got."

Becca's head came down fast. She looked at Crystal.

"Touch Crystal's right ankle," she said.

"What?"

"Go ahead. My right ankle."

Becca reached down without taking her eyes off Crystal's smiling face. She felt a bulge. "What's this?"

Crystal shook her head. "What's this? What a nun. Pull my pant leg up."

Becca's eyes popped. "Crystal! It's a gun!" she said, jerking her hand back as though touching it would cause it to shoot. Becca looked straight out the windshield. She pressed her hands hard into her lap.

"Don't freak out on me," said Crystal with a smile. "It's a gun, not a snake."

Still looking straight out the windshield, Becca said half joking with a wide mouth, "What—on earth—happened to you that you carry a knife *and* a gun?"

What on earth happened to you? The thought dug into Crystal's soul.

There were several seconds of silence. When Becca turned to Crystal, she saw stone where there had been flesh. Her friend's eyes were pointed toward the road in front of her, but she knew she was looking at something behind her. Something horrible in her past. Becca thought of trying to get Crystal to open up, but instead turned and began looking out her own side window.

"It didn't happen on earth," Crystal said icily. "It happened in hell."

She was opening up! Becca turned. "What do you mean?"

"This world is awful, but some things only happen in hell, Becca."

"Crystal—"

"I can't talk about it, Becca."

Becca's mouth remained open a few seconds before she said, "Okay," and turned back to her side window.

Crystal texted a message while she was driving. They crossed Chappell Road and turned into the second driveway on the right. Becca thought the apartments were public housing projects, but they weren't. They were around eight small, two-story brick buildings that gave good impressions of being public housing projects.

The building on the right was burned out on the second floor. It looked as though it had been in that condition for a long time. Crystal pointed to a black girl with long hair standing near the bottom porch of the building on the left. The girl was furiously tapping her head.

"There she is. That's Ta-Nisha. The one beating her brains out."

"Why is she doing that?" Becca asked.

"You really need to widen your circle of friends," said Crystal. "She's scratching her head."

Becca looked at the girl as she got closer to the car. "Oh."

Crystal stopped the car, jumped out, and hugged Ta-Nisha. She looked her up and down, as though appraising her.

Ta-Nisha wore a short, blue, skin-tight dress. Her bare thighs were big, but not firm. They had the texture of melting JELL-O. This was something she must've been proud of because she put her hands on her hips and snapped her body into a few seductive poses. Each snap sent pockets of cellulite crashing into one another like bumper cars at an amusement park that refused to stop when the ride was over.

Crystal shook her head. She looked at Becca and pointed across her body at Ta-Nisha. "Will you look at this? This is what I put up with."

Ta-Nisha said to Crystal, "Don't be hatin' cuz you flat."

"Ain't nothing on me been flat since I was seven years old," said Crystal.

Ta-Nisha looked at her with the blank face of a comedian about to give the punchline. "Then what happened? You better call Po-Po. Because somebody done stole yo' behind."

Crystal smiled, paused, bounced her finger in Ta-Nisha's face, and laughed. "See, see, I'm not even going to put up with this today. Becca, look in my purse and get me my knife."

Ta-Nisha looked in the car. "Becca, sweetie, don't waste yo' time. By the time you get it to her, all that's gone be left of her is one of those fake eye lashes."

"Don't make me hurt you, Ta-Nisha. Get in the car," said Crystal.

Tears appeared in Ta-Nisha's eyes out of nowhere. They rolled down her smooth brown cheeks. She smiled through a grimace and grasped both of Crystal's hands. "I knew you would come," she said.

Becca heard the girl's words and watched her hug Crystal as though she would never let go. How did Crystal know this girl? What had she done for her to make her...well, like her so much? It must've been something big.

Then Becca recalled how Crystal responded when she had asked her if she was going to finish her breakfast before coming here. It would have added ten or fifteen minutes at the most. But Crystal saw this as abandoning a friend.

Becca thought of how complexed Crystal was. On one hand, she was hard and guarded. But at the same time, she could be incredibly softhearted, especially toward those she considered friends. And even though she had a high wall around her heart, she'd invite a stranger into her home and instantly treat her like family.

Ta-Nisha got into the car and didn't waste a moment. "Okay, my name is Ta-Nisha. What kind of mess you in?"

Becca didn't turn around. Her eyes did funny things as she considered how to answer the forwardness of Crystal's friend. "Uh…"

Crystal jumped in with a schoolteacher's voice. "What my rude GHET-to friend means is, Hello. My name is Ta-Nisha Bottoms. It's nice to meet you. What is your name?"

Ta-Nisha put a silly look on her face and spoke with exaggerated Southern fakeness. "Hello. I know your name is Becca because I heard my skank friend call you Becca. My name is Ta-Nisha Bottoms. It's nice to meet you." She looked at Crystal and twisted up her nose before continuing the fake Southern accent. "If I was GHET-to rude, like somebody said I was, there would be blood in this raggedy car."

"That's what I have to deal with, Becca. I drop everything to drive across town to give somebody with no car a ride. Then that somebody with no car calls my car raggedy. Somebody with *no* car," Crystal repeated.

Becca was silent. They were kidding with one another, *weren't they?*

Ta-Nisha looked at Crystal with an open mouth, but she said nothing. Then after a few seconds she made a sound like she was coughing. "No you didn't," she said.

Crystal didn't look back. She just raised her right hand up over her shoulder with her palm up. "Lay it on me," she said.

"That was cold," Ta-Nisha said as she playfully smacked her hand. "I can't believe you said that. You know I'm sensitive."

"Uh huh," said Crystal. "We're going to that same clinic?"

"Yeah," she answered. Ta-Nisha went back to Becca, but in her regular voice. "What I was getting at before I was so rudely interrupted is that Crystal's got a habit of helping girls in trouble. You with her, I figure you must be in some kind of trouble."

This piece of information was like a flash of light. Becca turned in her seat to face Ta-Nisha before she knew what she was doing. "Is that how you two met?"

"Yep. My boyfriend put me in the hospital."

Becca's face went through at least three expressions of shock before she settled on the last one. "Your *boyfriend* put you in the hospital?"

"My ex-boyfriend."

"Her ex-pimp put her in the hospital," said Crystal.

Ta-Nisha chopped her open palm as she spoke. "Crystal, this—is—my—story."

"I'm going to keep you honest, girlfriend," said Crystal. "You know I am. Anyway, I'm part of that story. Just because you're the one that got the butt whipping, doesn't mean you own the story."

"Anyway, like I was saying," said Ta-Nisha, "my ex-*pimp*—you happy, Crystal?—was beatin' the crap out of me. Right there in the middle of the street. That nigga hit me so hard I literally saw stars. That ain't just on cartoons. I was on my knees trying to get back to my feet so I could run. He went to his car and got a tire iron. That's when I met Crystal. And that's when he met Crystal."

Becca felt like someone had pulled the plug right in the middle of an awesome movie. "What do you mean, that's when you met Crystal?"

"I mean she ran over my pimp."

Becca looked at Ta-Nisha in silence, like she was looking at an old rickety walking bridge over a dangerous river and deciding whether or not to cross.

"My friend's a nun, Ta-Nisha. You've got to make it plain," said Crystal.

"I bet you a nun," Ta-Nisha said with a suspicious little laugh. "Boss Man was about to kill me. That's when Crystal introduced herself. Ran his crusty, ugly behind over."

"Oh, so now he's ugly," said Crystal.

"And crusty," said Ta-Nisha.

"You ran over a man?" Becca said, looking at Crystal.

"Yeah." Her answer was simple, natural.

"Just like that? You didn't feel bad or anything," asked Becca.

"Nope," said Tanisha. She didn't feel bad. But he did. All she felt was a bump," she laughed.

"It's two o'clock in the morning," said Crystal. "You drive down a dark street and there's nobody there but two people. A man and a woman. The man is beating the woman like she's a man. Hitting and kicking and stomping her. He goes to his car and gets a tire iron. What do you do, Becca?"

Becca didn't answer.

"What do you do?" Crystal asked sharply. Becca didn't answer. "I couldn't do then what you're doing now, Becca. Ta-Nisha would be dead. So, yeah. I punched it to the floor and ran him over."

Becca waited a few moments. "Did he die?"

"Unfortunately, no," she said.

Ta-Nisha laughed and talked at the same time. "He may as well have died. He landed in a tree. Still had his hat on. He looked like a scarecrow, didn't he, girl?"

"If he didn't die, did he come after you when he got better?" Becca asked Crystal and Ta-Nisha.

"Nope." Ta-Nisha started making sounds and doing motions like she was driving a car with a stick shift. "Errrk. Mmmmm. Boss Man in a little chair with a battery and little wheels." She started laughing harder. "Never mind me. Whew." She wiped her eye. "It's just that nigga went from a Lexus to a—" She started doing the wheelchair thing again.

Crystal said, "He can't come after me, but he's got a thug brother who'd like to get his hands on me." She thought of a close call she'd had with him in a chance encounter. Fortunately, she had friends with her that would have loved nothing more than to give him his own scooter. "Can't let that bother me. You gotta do the right thing."

Becca had never been this close to this kind of reality. Pimping. Prostitution. A man trying to beat a woman to death in the middle of the street. And her new friend deliberately running him over. She looked at Crystal from the corner of her eye. She wasn't remorseful in the least way. And Ta-Nisha was in the backseat pretending to drive a scooter chair, and making jokes about her ex-pimp hanging in a tree with his hat on looking like a scarecrow. The whole thing was horrifying.

Crystal saw Becca's expression. "Let me ask you something, Becca," said Crystal. "The guy in the wheelchair, how many more girls you think he's put on the street since I ran him over?"

"None."

"How many more girls has he beaten like dogs?"

"None."

"Then it's a good story."

"Amen to that, sister," said Ta-Nisha.

Crystal and Ta-Nisha continued to talk to one another. Becca didn't say very much. She was trying to acclimate her breathing to this new world of pimping and vigilante justice. But when they were within a block of the abortion clinic, she felt suddenly nauseous. And by the time they rolled into the parking lot, her airway passages narrowed.

Crystal looked back at Ta-Nisha. Ta-Nisha looked at her like she knew what was coming, and like Crystal was crazy for asking. "Gotta ask, girlfriend. You sure about this?"

Ta-Nisha opened her door and got out.

Crystal looked at Becca. "Guess that answers that. You don't have to come in. I don't like these places myself."

Becca looked at Crystal, wondering what kind of expression Crystal saw on her face. Did it match the dizzying swirling that was spinning her like an astronaut in training? Did she look like she was about to throw up? Was she about to throw up?

"No, I'm going to wait here."

"Okay. She's been here before. So I don't know if she's got to do all that paperwork again. I'll let you know if it looks like it's going to be long." Crystal smiled a little. "I'm glad we're friends. I think fate knew I needed a nun in my life."

Becca wanted to say, "I keep telling you, I'm no nun," but she was afraid that if she opened her mouth, she may throw up.

Crystal closed the door and ran to catch up with Ta-Nisha.

Fifteen minutes later, an angel of truth touched Becca's shoulder and squeezed. "Be strong," he said.

Becca felt the sick feeling being pushed out of her like a tide pushing something out to sea. She put her hand on her belly and pressed. She opened and closed her mouth a couple of times. She hummed out loud. Whatever the sickness was, it was gone. Great! Becca quickly opened the door. She hurried toward the glass doors. *She was so tired of being weak.*

Becca looked up and read the abortion clinic's sign: Chelsea Women's Medical Clinic. A paralyzing fear exploded in her bones. She felt herself not losing consciousness, but losing parts of her being to a swirling force that was trying to suck her into a million directions. It was like a tornado of lostness. It was trying to separate her from herself.

She felt a blackness descending over her. It was everywhere, coming from every direction. She'd lost track of time, but she knew that shortly she would pass out. There. In the parking lot. She grabbed her suddenly throbbing left arm and prepared to fall.

Two angels of truth were there to make sure that didn't happen. They walked beside her, one on each side. The one on the left placed his right hand under the pit of her arm to hold her up as he used his free hand to rub and massage her aching arm. He couldn't make the pain go away entirely, but he could lessen it so she could get closer to the truth. Both angels guided her to the doors as their invisible armies worked to honor the prayers of Nancy and Bill.

Nearly forty sets of demon eyes watched this puzzling assault. That it was an assault was plain enough. *Any* action by an angel of truth was an attack, no matter how indirect it was. What was puzzling was that the truth angels had chosen to show themselves to the stronghold, and that not only were they not fighting to keep Becca from the abortion clinic, they were actually helping her into the clinic.

Unwanted knew why he and his demons wanted her to go the clinic. More torment, pure and simple. But why would angels of truth want this vermin to go to the clinic? What could they possibly gain by taking her to the scene of the slaughterhouse she had escaped?

"What are you up to?" Unwanted murmured.

16

Becca's limbs were moving, carrying her forward, opening the door, but not by her own power. Her invisible supporters led her to an empty seat in the far left corner of the waiting room. They sat her down. After three minutes, they removed their hands from her. She fell face first onto the hard linoleum floor, an angel's hand softening her landing.

"The truth, Becca. The truth can make you free," said the angel.

The quiet waiting room erupted into a frenzy of low-keyed commotion over the girl who had fallen out onto the floor, shaking and gasping for air. None of the several people in the room, all women, were Crystal or Ta-Nisha. And since they hadn't come in together, it was assumed the girl was alone.

One of the women joined the other three women kneeling around Becca. "Let me see her," she said, squeezing one woman out of the way.

"Are you a doctor?" asked the woman who had lost her spot.

"No. I work at Wal-Mart," the woman said, then started half tapping, half slapping Becca. "Get up." Smack. Smack. Smack. "Get up." Smack. Smack. Smack. Smack. "Get up."

Wal-Mart? You have got to be kidding me. The woman who lost her spot said indignantly, "I don't think slapping her is the appropriate thing to do." She turned to the receptionist desk. The receptionist was turned away and distracted by a phone call. "Hey! This girl over here needs help. She needs a doctor!"

A woman next to the slapping Wal-Mart woman said sharply, "Stop slapping her." This got her a funny look, but the lady did as she was told. The woman who had taken charge spoke softly to Becca.

Becca was on her back. Her eyes were open, but she saw nothing except monsters with knives. They slashed and cut and punctured every inch of her. She couldn't scream. She couldn't moan. She couldn't writhe. But she felt it all. Her torture was stuck in a body paralyzed by fear.

"What's your name, honey? Are you here with anyone? Who can we call? You have a phone?" The woman opened Becca's purse. She found her ID. She found her phone and hoped it didn't have a screen lock. It did. *But then it didn't.* She scrolled through the contacts. *Sister.* "I'm calling your sister, honey. We're going to let your family know where you are."

The lady punched the number. Danielle answered.

"Becca! Where are you? Why did you leave? Didn't you see—?"

"Hello? This is Amy. I'm calling from Chelsea Medical Clinic for Women. Becca is here and she's fallen out on the floor in the waiting area. We're waiting for the doctor to come out. Is she allergic to anything? Is she diabetic? Good. Good. No, I think she's alone. I think it would be a good idea for you to tell your parents. The way she looks, she could end up in the hospital. Okay, sweetie. The doctor's coming now."

Dr. Li walked briskly to the small crowd and kneeled beside Becca. She looked into her eyes first before conducting a quick examination of her. The moment Becca looked into Dr. Li's eyes, all of the pressurized torment that was snagged in her chest and pushing upward against the trap of her throat exploded into the loudest and most wrenched scream anyone in the room had ever heard. The stunned doctor bounced backwards. So did the few women still around Becca.

Becca's limbs came to life. The adrenaline of fear replaced the paralysis of fear. "Get it away from me!" she screamed. She crawled backwards on the floor, staring wide-eyed at the doctor as though the white-coated lady was a monster.

That's what Becca saw.

A monster.

A woman, but a monster. A hybrid of humanity and hell drenched in blood from head to toe.

Crystal ran out into the waiting area. Ta-Nisha was a few seconds behind her. Crystal ran to her friend and literally slid on her knees getting to her. She clutched her around her shoulders and head and hugged her tightly.

Someone said something about Becca being on drugs.

"She's not on drugs!" Crystal yelled at the onlookers.

Ta-Nisha hurried over thinking, *Crystal, do you know anybody who's not crazy?* "We need to get her outta here. We can come back. Huh, these people ain't goin' nowhere."

Becca was trying to scoot backwards as Crystal held her still. Dr. Li took a step forward. Becca balled up. Crystal ordered, "Stay back!" with her palm up. She looked down at her friend. "It's going to be alright. We're leaving."

Becca looked out from the safety of Crystal's cocoon. Her eyes were fixed on the doctor who she now saw as a woman. "I know her," she said. "I don't know how, Crystal, but I know that woman."

Crystal glared at the doctor with protective eyes, then narrowing, probing eyes. A crazy thought went through her mind. "What's your name?" Crystal asked.

"Dr. Li," the doctor answered.

"No. Your first name?" Crystal ordered.

Dr. Li hesitated, then answered.

"I know her," Becca said again, with fear in her voice. "I think I've been here before."

Dr. Li saw the warning in Crystal's eyes and decided not to speak directly to the girl she held. But she did say for the benefit of her patients, "I don't have any idea what she's talking about. I've never seen this young lady before."

"Oh God, my arm hurts so bad. Oh, God. Oh, God. Please get me out of here, Crystal. Something's trying to take my arm off. *Please. Please,*" she begged.

Ta-Nisha stood there with scrunched eyebrows and an open mouth, tapping her itching head. *Something's trying to take your arm off?*

"Ta-Nisha," said Crystal, looking up.

"Oh," she snapped out of it. "Let me help you with her."

Crystal and Ta-Nisha lifted Becca and walked her out of the clinic.

Becca walked toward the car feeling like her arm was going through a meat grinder. Yet each step away from the clinic brought a tiny, but discernible measure of relief to her limp, throbbing arm.

There's something about this place...there's something about that woman... she thought.

───────

The troubling but wonderful call had come at the beginning of her lunch period. Danielle put the phone in her purse and covered her face. She looked up with tears into the inquiring face of a girlfriend.

"What's up? You okay? Is it about your sister?"

"Yeah. I have to go," she said, popping up from the table and leaving her three friends. She went outside and found a place to sit. "God, what's going on?"

She was almost sure Becca was the other person in that car she had seen outside their home on Saturday, but when she had run outside, the car was already driving away. Then she called her on the phone and Becca didn't answer. She hadn't answered any of her calls. It was now Monday and she hadn't spoken to her since Friday. No one had spoken to her or seen her since she'd left Saturday. She found this out on Sunday evening when she had called from Grandma's. That's when Dad first called the police.

So many things rushed through Danielle's mind as she looked at her phone wondering who to call. Why did Mom and Dad wait a full day before they called the police? How long would they have gone without calling? If Grandma hadn't gotten involved, would they have ever called? Deep down inside she knew the answer was no. Her big sister was out there alone somewhere because of their parents.

Danielle felt something strange happening to her insides. It wasn't anger. Although she was furious. She knew it was something far more powerful and permanent than passing fury. The feeling that was spreading throughout her body and filling her was also hardening. It was like emotional wet cement nearing the drying point of no return. A picture of her sister standing on stage humiliated and abandoned by her parents came to her mind. Danielle's face mirrored her heart as the last bit of moisture evaporated from the cement.

I hate both of you, she thought bitterly.

She looked at the phone with a somber expression. She wasn't going to call those monsters. Why should she? They didn't care a thing about her sister. Her face twisted with a new realization. They didn't care a thing about either of them. She could just as easily have been in Becca's shoes and Becca in hers. It was only fate that she had won the coin toss. And what had she won, truly? The love of monsters.

And now Danielle considered something else. Even this love, this monster love of her parents, wasn't real love. It was something warped and polluted. Her mind didn't see the metaphor, but she felt like a puppy sitting on Hitler's lap, feeling his murderous hands patting her on the head and affectionately digging his fingers into her fur. It was enough to make her want to throw up.

She called her grandmother and told her what the lady on the phone had told her. When she finished talking to her, Grandma and Grandpa were already in the truck going to see after her sister. A warm feeling interrupted the hatred she felt. *At least Becca has Grandma and Grandpa,* she thought.

Danielle took a deep breath. Now what was Chelsea Women's Medical Clinic? She looked it up on her phone and gasped so hard and awkwardly that she coughed. "What?" she yelled. Her eyes stared at the small screen. "Family planning?" She paused in disbelief. "It's an abortion clinic. What is Becca doing at an abortion clinic?" Then another dose of reality that made her want to reach into the phone and pull her words out. "I told Grandma!"

Bill stopped at the light and turned to Nancy with a look of disbelief. "Nancy, are you sure that's what Danielle said? Chelsea Women's Medical Clinic?"

Nancy looked at him with an expression of anger and pain. "I know what I heard, Bill. She said Chelsea Women's Medical Clinic."

The light turned green and Bill drove on. He shook his head. "That's not our Becca. She doesn't serve the Lord, so I'm not so foolish as to say she's not having sex. She's seventeen. But even if she is, I don't think she'd be so foolish as to have unprotected sex."

Nancy wiped her wet eye with the palm of her hand, but said nothing.

"I mean, she's a smart girl, Nancy. There's something else to this story. I just can't see her having an abortion."

"She's not saved." Nancy thought on her words and started crying, her chest bouncing with the guilty emotion that she had failed her granddaughter. Maybe if she had prayed more or visited more or was more adamant about her going to church with them.

Bill patted her on the leg. "I just don't think it's what it looks like. I can't believe that about Becca."

Nancy squeezed his hand and tried to smile through her tears. "You're right, Bill. I shouldn't jump to conclusions. Love doesn't act like this. I'm sorry. I'm gonna believe the best until proven otherwise."

Bill gave her hand two squeezes. "Nobody loves that girl like you do."

The whole time Bill was driving, they both were silently hoping there was a mix-up with the name. But forty-five minutes later, they sat in the parking lot of Chelsea Women's Medical Clinic. They looked at one another in silence. Finally, they both silently conceded they couldn't look at one another forever. Nancy reached for the door.

"Wait," said Bill. "We don't know what we're going to find when we go into this place."

Nancy noticed there was no ambulance. She didn't know if that meant anything. Danielle had said Becca had fallen out and had some kind of a fit. She could've gotten better and left on her own. Or she could be in the hospital. "I hope she's okay."

"We can do more than hope," said Bill. He took her hand. "Let's pray."

They finished praying and went inside."

"Oh, God," groaned Vincent, the bullet tearing through his chest and collapsing a lung. But it wasn't a literal bullet that collapsed his lung. Nor was his lung really collapsed. It simply felt like it collapsed when he looked out the window and saw Bill's truck pulling into the driveway.

He didn't have asthma, but now he was struggling with a sudden wheeze to suck air into his now obstructed air passage. *What is wrong with you?* he scolded himself. He was a grown man. It was foolishness for him to be affected this way by the sight of Bill's truck. He held his chest with his mouth open as his eyes dumbly scanned the floor. The thought of a heart attack raced into and out of his mind, and carrying with it the idea of an easy getaway.

Hand still on his chest, Vincent looked at the tinted windshield. He could see the darkened images of Bill and Nancy. The backdoor opened. "Oh, God," he groaned again. It was Danielle. He'd forgotten what time it was. There could be only one reason they were here.

Becca.

Vincent could clearly see their faces now. Hard. Angry. *Vengeful?* As though prompted, Bill, Nancy, and Danielle's heads turned sharply and focused their eyes on him. They looked like they were on their way to the gunfight at the *OK Corral*. His first instinct was to duck, but what was left of his backbone held him steady.

This didn't mean he wasn't trembling. In a few seconds, that door was going to open and he and Heather were going to be skinned alive —by the truth. That's what terrified Vincent. It was all but certain that Danielle had told Nancy and Bill everything. And not just the musical or his delayed response when Becca ran away. Danielle had threatened to tell them *everything.*

Could he simply deny it? He knew the thought was both foolish and desperate.

Thinking time over.

The three angry people glaring at him in the window were now glaring at him face to face in the living room. A room name that now seemed ridiculously misnamed. It felt like the *dying* room to Vincent.

Bill was at least sixty, Vincent guessed. Maybe older. He looked and acted older. But there was a difference in an old man with a sedentary lifestyle of retirement who did nothing except eat, sleep, and watch television. That wasn't Bill. Bill's face may have run a few extra laps around the track of life, and it may have even stumbled over a hurdle or two. But his body had not yet raised the white flag.

He had once been an avid weightlifter and had won a few trophies. Not a bodybuilder, but a weightlifter. He had been after explosive power, not definition. That meant mass, not art. Vincent figured that at Bill's youngest best, he probably couldn't stand on anyone's competitive bodybuilding stage. But that didn't change the fact that he probably could've body slammed Arnold Schwarzeneggar. He probably still could. *And he certainly could body slam him.*

Bill walked ominously toward Vincent. "You son of a—"

"Grandpa," said Danielle, with her hand on his thick arm.

To his credit, Vincent stood his ground. His hands were at his sides, fingers outstretched, ready to grapple the man off balance and hopefully to the floor—without him. *If he went down with this mountain, only God could get that man off of him.*

Vincent's eyes were wide with adrenaline, his weight leaning heavily on his back foot for leverage. Bill reached over without taking his gaze off of Vincent and placed his hand atop Danielle's hand. This helped him remember why everyone called him *Pastor* Bill. He was a man of God. He was nearly beside himself with anger, but that was no excuse to act like He didn't know God.

"What have you and Heather done to our granddaughter?" Bill demanded.

Vincent swallowed to buy time. But the tense split-second offered nothing.

"I told them everything, Dad," said Danielle. "Everything." She looked at her father. "You promised me you'd do the right thing. You didn't. You lied. So I told Grandma and Grandpa everything."

Nancy walked to the bottom of the staircase. "Heather, I know you hear us. Come down here!"

There was no sound from upstairs.

"Heather!" Nancy yelled. "You get yourself down here. Danielle's told me everything you and Vincent's done to Becca. Heather!"

Still no sound from upstairs.

Nancy was in a fog of heartbreak. She was so ashamed of herself for failing God and Becca. One moment, her grief and shame were trying to push her to sit in dejection on the bottom step. The next, it was telling her to forget about her hip and get up those stairs and get that daughter of hers downstairs, even if she had to drag her by her hair.

"God, I'm sorry. I've raised a monster." Nancy's hands went to her face. "What did I do to make her this way? What did I do to make my daughter a cruel person?"

Faint memories started surfacing in Nancy's mind. Heather's pregnancy. The dream. Heather on a table at an abortion clinic. Little Becca in the womb fighting for her life. The abnormally long pregnancy. It all made sense now. That child knew her mother was trying to kill her, and she did the only thing she could do. She tried to hide. That's why the pregnancy went so long.

Nancy raised her head in a scream, emotion carrying her like a mad locomotive. "Aaaaaaaahhhhhh, how could you?"

On a small table along the wall of the staircase was a beautiful vase. Nancy picked it up with both hands and smashed it to the floor. She saw a plant. She smashed it to the floor. A mirror hanging on the wall. She picked up a small lamp with a heavy base and through it against the mirror. It shattered and fell to the floor.

Bill and Danielle hurried to the ruckus. Vincent didn't. He wouldn't stop her if she burned the house down. He was tired.

"Grandma," Danielle's voice whimpered.

Bill hugged Danielle to his side and pressed his big hand against her cheek. "Let her alone, Danielle," he whispered. "She'll drop dead if she can't get to the bottom of this."

"I'll go get Mom," said Danielle.

"Mom!" Heather partially yelled from the top of the stairs. "What are you doing?"

Every eye looked up at her. She looked pathetic. Not physically. Physically she looked fine. It was something else. Something obviously fake. Like a white woman at the checkout counter of a store trying to convince the clerk and police that the Chinese guy on the debit card was in fact her.

"You know exactly what I'm doing. And you know why I'm here. Now are you going to get yourself down these stairs, or are you going to make me go up there?"

Heather thought of her mother trying to climb the stairs and grimaced inside. She came down the stairs, but she was clutching that Chinese debit card. "What is this all about, Mom?"

Bill went to Nancy and placed his hand under her arm. "Let's go sit down. We can talk in the living room.

Vincent was sitting on the edge of a chair with his elbows on his knees and his fingers interlaced under his chin. He stared straight ahead at them.

Bill, Nancy, and Danielle sat on the sofa. Heather sat on a chair that matched her husband's. She took a quick look at him and felt not the slightest confidence in his demeanor. He looked like he couldn't wait to spill his guts. Sometimes he was so weak. It was one of the things over the past few years that made her loathe him.

They had agreed *together* to have the abortion. Then he comes rushing in at the last possible moment to stop the abortion. He had stopped the abortion and stopped her life. He was a doctor and she was a paralegal clerk with a law degree. He had his career. Living his dream. And what did she have? Nothing but children! She was just what Dad had said she'd become. A stupid woman with nothing but a house full of children.

She took another glance at her husband. This look was hard. *And now you sit there trying to convince yourself that you're the good guy and I'm the bad guy,* she thought.

"I told them everything, Mom," said Danielle.

Heather's face tightened, but she said nothing.

Nancy looked into her daughter's face. She knew Danielle was telling the truth, but she was holding on to the barest of hopes that like Lazarus coming out of a stinking cave after four days of death, her daughter would offer some rebuttal that would clear the air of the stench of cruelty, and give her reason to hope for a resurrection of their family. But Heather offered nothing except a tight face of defiance. *Oh, my God, it's all true*, Nancy painfully admitted to herself.

The next hour was an extremely one-sided activity. A non-stop barrage of questions and accusations and yelling on the side of Bill, Nancy, and Danielle, and short, evasive, non-explanatory answers from Vincent and Heather. The cornered couple posed a united front, even when it came to their behavior at the school musical. No one believed for a second that Vincent had suddenly gotten ill and that Heather was simply following him to make sure he was okay.

Bill, Nancy, and Danielle had all agreed to not tell Vincent and Heather that Becca had gone to an abortion clinic. That was a situation they hoped looked worse than it was. Maybe Becca wasn't there for herself. Maybe she was there with someone else. In any event, in light of what Danielle had told Bill and Nancy, there was no way they'd tell her parents that she had gone to an abortion clinic.

But Heather and Vincent were being so surprisingly stubborn in their lies, and the pieces of the puzzles were connecting so perfectly, that Nancy changed her mind about telling them. She wasn't going to let her granddaughter live another day in this home anyway. So what did it matter if they knew.

Plus, she was enraged at what they had done to Becca, and how they were still lying about it—right here in front of Danielle! She had to break through the lies. And it was her guess that it would be Vincent to break. Because although Vincent and Heather were lying like they were Mafia talking to the FBI, she saw sadness and regret in his eyes.

"You remember God gave me a dream when you were pregnant?" said Nancy.

The change in the room's atmosphere was immediate. So immediate that Nancy wondered what had taken her so long to get here. There was almost an audible crack in Heather's icy heart. She looked at Vincent with an expression that seemed to shout, "Don't go wobbly on us!" Vincent looked at her as if to say, "Can't you see it's over?"

Nancy thought of what she was about to say and for a moment thought of asking Danielle to leave the room. *No, Danielle is already in the middle of this mess. She knows what's going on more than I do.* "The Lord showed me that you were pregnant and that you were planning to abort the baby," said Nancy.

Danielle gasped.

Vincent did, too, but inside.

"I told you what the Lord showed me, and you swore up and down that you weren't even pregnant. Well, time showed that you were. I told you then that God knew you were planning to kill your baby."

Heather tried her best to maintain the façade, but she looked as exposed as she felt.

"I wrote it all down, Heather. In my journal. It's all there. I write down my dreams, and I know exactly what I told you." Nancy didn't want to ask. She knew the answer. Heather's and Vincent's expressions were confessions of guilt. But she had to hear it out of Heather's mouth. "You tried to abort that child, didn't you?"

Heather commanded stillness in her body. No trembling. No crying. No wavering. She looked her mother in the eyes. "No, I have never tried to abort Becca."

Vincent had a look that wasn't there, but it wasn't altogether vacant, either. His lips moved as he looked at the floor. There were two roads before him. At the end of one was a bear. At the end of the other was a lion. Both were hungry. Was there a path other than these two roads?

"Dad, say something," Danielle pleaded.

He looked up and moved his mouth to say something—what, he didn't know—but fear had a club in its hand. It beat his words senseless, leaving him with confused, halting mumbles.

"Danielle got a call today from Chelsea Women's Medical Clinic," said Nancy. "A lady using Becca's phone said she was there and had some kind of panic attack. Poor child was laid out on the floor. We went to pick her up, but she was already gone."

Bill looked at Vincent. His eyes mirrored the suspicion in his voice. "Becca doesn't have panic attacks. What a coincidence that she has her first one at an abortion clinic."

No, there was no other path. The lion and bear were upon him. Vincent's face went pale. "Chelsea?" he said.

"Yeah, Chelsea Women's Medical Clinic," said Bill, his voice gruff. "You know the place?"

Vincent closed his eyes and gripped the sides of his head with widened, tension-filled fingers. He moaned through the unnatural pressure in his throat, "What would make Becca go back to that awful place?"

"What? What did you say?" said Danielle. "Go back? Is that what you said?"

He didn't hear her. He stood and looked around at each of them with an open mouth and no words. He dropped his head and said too low for anyone to hear, "Oh, my God. Becca, what have I done? I've ruined you." Then he opened the front door and walked out.

At first, no one said anything. But when he walked past the window, Danielle jumped up and ran after him.

Bill and Nancy turned from the window to Heather.

"Why, Heather? Why would you abort your baby?" Nancy shook her head in shameful disbelief. "Why, oh, my God, why would you treat that poor girl so badly all these years?"

Heather's arms were crossed over her chest. She was still seated. Tears rolled down a face that didn't reveal whether the tears were from regret at her behavior or regret at being caught in such behavior. She answered in a low voice that made Nancy and Bill shudder. "I tried to abort her so I could live."

Danielle came back running and crying. She thrust her hand forward. "He gave me this. He said he keeps it with him all the time."

"What is it?" Nancy said, as she took it from Danielle. Her mouth dropped open.

"It's a sonogram of Becca," said Danielle. "Look at the date stamp."

"My God! It's only a day before God gave me the dream!"

17

Ta-Nisha walked into the house behind Crystal and Becca. She immediately looked at the statue on the mantle over the fireplace. "Thought you were going to get rid of 'em, Crystal." She was talking about Shiva. "You ain't hardly 'bout to get rid of a man with four hands, and you know it." She looked at Crystal with a mischievous grin and added, "Freak."

Crystal ignored Ta-Nisha. She and Becca sat on the sofa as though they'd just run a marathon. They sat on opposite ends, with their arms stretched across the top.

Ta-Nisha dipped her chin at Becca, and said with raised eyebrows, "And speakin' of freak. Girl, what was that all about? You were lookin' at that woman like she was Chinese Frankenstein or somethin'." Ta-Nisha stretched out her arms and walked a few steps like Frankenstein.

Crystal would've given Becca more time before asking her about what happened. Or she would've left it alone and just let her talk about it whenever she wanted to talk about it—if ever. But Crystal knew Ta-Nisha wasn't like that. She'd get into your business four-feet deep after only a few minutes of knowing you, if you let her. And she didn't see it as nosey because she didn't mind people being waist-deep in her business. If you wanted to know, ask her. If she didn't want to tell you, she wouldn't.

But, honestly, Crystal wanted to know what happened just as badly as Ta-Nisha. So instead of asking her to back off, she looked at Becca with an expression she hoped shielded her curiosity.

Ta-Nisha continued. "Remember when I met you, the first thing I said was, 'What kind of mess you in?' See, I know what I'm talkin' about. Crystal is the guardian of Gotham City."

Becca looked thoughtfully into the floor. She shook her head, trying to figure out what had happened. She'd been on this track since they had left the abortion clinic. "I've never freaked out like that before in my life." She thought deeper. Weird things did happen to her with her parents. But she'd never had something like *that* happen. "One minute everything was—no...no, that's not true. I started feeling funny in the parking lot. That's why I didn't go in."

This confirmed the change in Becca that Crystal thought she had seen in the car in the clinic's parking lot.

"I felt sick. So I stayed in the car. But a little while after you two went in, I felt a lot better." She shook her head like something didn't make sense. "Then when I got out of the car, I felt really dizzy. Honestly, I don't even know how I made it from the car to the waiting area. It was like hands were holding me up on both sides and guiding me inside. That's when it got really weird."

"Who you tellin'?" said Ta-Nisha. "You looked like you was in a horror movie."

"I was," Becca said flatly.

Silence.

"The doctor looked like a monster. That's why I was trying to get away."

Crystal looked intently at Becca.

"I don't know why. It doesn't make sense. But when I saw that doctor, an overwhelming feeling of dread came over me. I *knew* that woman wanted to kill me. I felt like she had already tried to kill me." Becca shook her head and shrugged, looking at Crystal. "I mean it doesn't make sense, Crystal. Right?"

"Yeah," said Ta-Nisha, "you crazier than me and my two sisters." Her nose turned up in thought. "Naw, maybe not crazier than Deandra. She a crackhead to the max. But Momma got her on the church prayer list. She gone be alright."

Crystal nodded. But as crazy as today had been, there was something about Becca's fit that wasn't as crazy as it looked. She recalled Becca's nightmare. She recalled the scissors and monsters and *Highway to Hell*. She recalled what Becca had said about how her parents treated her. She compared all of that to what had happened today. They were weird pieces of the same puzzle. She was sure that once they were properly fit together, the picture would become clear.

This is where it got as interesting as it was weird. The morning that Crystal had nearly got into a bloody fight with the black guy, once it was over and she couldn't think of anything else to yell out at the guy as he had walked away, she saw Becca standing there with an open mouth, frozen in place. Something strange had happened to Crystal the moment she saw Becca. She wasn't sure whether it was a voice or a really strong feeling, but something had communicated to her. The communication had bypassed her mind and gone directly into her gut.

Take care of her, and I will remove your pain, it had said.

"What do you think that means?" asked Crystal. "You've never been to that place before. Right?"

Becca pulled her chest back. No, she had never been there. Nonetheless, she was as sure as her name was Becca that she *had* been there. "Crystal, I don't know how to answer that. I've never physically been to that place. I've never been to an abortion clinic, period. But everything in me says that I have been there. And that doctor. Oh, my God, that doctor. It's like on TV, when some woman has been raped by a guy wearing a mask. Then she hears his voice. She knows it's him."

Crystal stiffened at the imagery that poured into her mind. She shut it down by focusing on Becca's problems and how she could help her. Like a fish swimming beneath the water, but close enough to the top to be seen, that strange voice rose from the depths of her soul.

Take care of her, and I will remove your pain.

The girls talked for several hours before Crystal looked at her phone and saw it was time to put her plan into action. "Look, Becca, I'm going to take Miss America back home. You—"

"Miss Universe," Ta-Nisha corrected.

Crystal looked at Becca and opened her mouth wide and stuck her finger halfway in a couple of times like she was gagging. "You need to stay here and chill out." She saw Becca about to object. "No, really. I've got something I need to do. I need to do it alone. Somebody may come by later to pick you up and bring you to me. You need to come." She looked intently at Becca, the lightness gone. "You *need* to come."

Actually, the thought of having the house to herself didn't sound bad. "Okay, I'll come," said Becca.

Ta-Nisha beat both of them up from sitting and surprised Becca by hugging her as she got up. When she let her go, she said, "I don't know why your parents don't like you. Besides being crazy, you ain't half-bad."

Becca laughed. "I'll take that as a compliment."

"It is. It is," said Ta-Nisha. As she was turning away, she added, "Could use a little make-up, but that ain't none of my business."

"That's right, Ta-Nisha. That's none of your business," Becca laughed, having gotten to know the girl with no boundaries better.

The three girls walked onto the porch. Ta-Nisha took one of Becca's hands. "Becca, we all messed up. You, me, Crystal—even though she got her problems locked up in a safe. Maybe she'll give *you* the combination," she said, looking accusingly at Crystal. "But things gone get better. We just gotta trust God."

"You believe in God?" The question came out of Becca's mouth automatically. She wondered if her tone sounded disbelieving.

"What? Because I cuss, fuss, fight, and freak. You can't judge a hoe by her hair." Ta-Nisha said this as she tapped at the itch under her braids. "God's working on me. He's workin' on you, too." She hugged Crystal. "He's even workin' on the ice queen here. He ain't forgot us."

You can't judge a hoe by her hair? Becca was stunted by the analogy. Who would call herself a whore? Was she still doing that? Didn't Crystal run over her pimp? He rides a chair now. She's trying to get an abortion. She does drugs. And what does being a whore and a hairdo have to do with one another?"

Ta-Nisha looked at Becca and laughed. "Look at yo' girl, Crystal. She tryin' to figure it out. It's in her eyes."

Becca was aghast that her expression had betrayed her. "No. No. I don't—it's not— I mean…"

Ta-Nisha laughed.

Crystal grinned.

"Look at her. Mary Poppins can't even get the lie out her mouth," laughed Ta-Nisha, as she went down the stairs. She waved her hand in the air without looking back. "Don't play God cheap, Becca. He got yo' back. You just gotta trust Him."

Crystal looked at Ta-Nisha waiting by the car, then looked at Becca with a smile. "You can't judge a hoe by her hair," she said to her with a chuckle, and went down the stairs.

Crystal drove off weighing the risk of her plan. Becca was her friend, and her friend needed help. That was enough to outweigh the risk. Becca needed to know the truth of what happened to her, and Crystal was going to get it for her. The truth was the only thing that could help her.

But there was a fear lurking on a ledge. If the truth was what she thought it was, it could have the opposite effect and send Becca into a tailspin. The coin had two heads, and still Crystal was unsure of what call to make. She made the call. She'd need help for her plan to work. But that was one of the benefits of helping a lot of people. She had a lot of people willing to help her.

Becca's phone rang. She looked at the number. She wasn't answering calls from anyone she knew, especially Vincent, Heather, and Danielle. The call was from Crystal. "Hey, Crystal."

"Becca, someone will be there in less than a minute to pick you up. Listen to me, okay? I'm doing something very important. You need to do exactly what I tell you. Do not look out the window for the car.

When the car comes, do not look at it directly. Do not look at the person directly. Approach the car with your hand to your face covering your eyes."

"What?" asked Becca. She liked Crystal, but she was still a stranger. And now she was sounding like a criminal. She was about to pass on this ride.

"Do you want to know why you fell out at the abortion clinic? Do you want to know why you think that doctor tried to kill you? Do you want to know where your nightmares are coming from?"

Becca grimaced. "Yes…yes…but, how…" she whimpered.

"Then do what I say, Becca. Don't look at the car or the driver. Don't say anything to the driver. Just get in and look away until you get here. The driver's going to drop you off and drive away. Do not look at the car when it drives away. Okay? You got that?"

"Yes."

"Okay. The driver should be there. See you when you get here."

Crystal was right. The car was there. Its lights shone down the dark street as it parked in front of the house. Becca turned on the porch light, made sure the door was locked, and put her left hand to her lowered head as she walked. She got in the car as she looked away. She closed the door and immediately buried her face into her lap. She knew the vehicle was a dark-colored sedan, but that was all. And all she knew of the driver was he or she was human—presumably.

For the next half hour or so, Becca cried into her lap without once thinking of lifting her head or of how odd this arrangement was. What was odd was to be hated all her life by those who were supposed to love and nurture her. What was odd was to live with a haunting, hollowness inside that made her feel like the slightest wind could blow her away. What was odd was to have a father who hated being in the same room with her, and to have a mother who only acknowledged her existence when forced to do so. What was odd was to have a family and yet feel so alone. She had seventeen years of odd. So an odd car ride was barely noticeable on her radar. What was a big blip on the radar was Crystal talking like she had found out information about her that she hadn't been able to figure out all her life. How could she do that? What kind of connections does she have?

The car slowed, then stopped. The driver hadn't spoken the entirety of the ride, and he or she wasn't saying anything now. So Becca didn't know if they were at a light or if they were at the destination. Her phone rang. She got her phone with her head still in her lap.

"Yes."

"You're here," said Crystal. "Get out of the car and come in the front door. And don't look back."

"I won't."

Becca turned to the right and opened the door. She closed it and kept her head lowered to the right as she walked toward the front door of the house. She heard the car leaving. She got to the front door and it was only then that it dawned on her what she had just done. But it didn't freak her out, as she thought it might. Instead, she felt empowered. As weird as it had been, she had done something to reclaim her life. She didn't understand what. But she was doing something now to reclaim her life. It felt good.

The door opened when Becca was several feet away. Crystal's hair was under a shower cap. She didn't smile, but Becca knew she was happy to see her. Crystal pulled her into what appeared to be a totally empty home. "You okay?"

"Yeah, I'm okay," said Becca, feeling stronger already than she had felt since she didn't know when. She looked at Crystal's hands. She wore latex gloves.

"Here, put this cap on, and these gloves."

Becca did so without asking any questions.

Crystal looked at her. She could tell she'd been crying. "You don't want to know why I asked you to put this crap on?"

"You'll tell me what I need to know?" Becca was happy with her answer. More than once she had looked weak around Crystal. She didn't want her to think—or to know—she was weak. For once, she looked strong, unafraid. She saw that Crystal was also pleased with her answer, but she told her why.

"I don't want any trace that you or I were here. No hair. No fingerprints."

An alarm went off inside Becca. She didn't let it show on her face.

"We are going to go into the basement. There's a pop-up black curtain separating the room. We're on one side," Crystal looked at her friend, hoping for approval, "my friends and Dr. Li are on the other."

It took a few seconds for this to sink in. When it did, Becca asked, "Dr. Li, as in that lady at the abortion clinic?"

Crystal gripped Becca's arm. "Yes. But you don't have to be afraid. She can't hurt you."

Becca lowered her head and rolled her eyes from side to side, studying her body's sensations. "I'm not afraid."

"That's good," said Crystal. "Questions?"

Becca looked at her with a grimaced face wet with tears. She shook her head.

"She's going to answer some questions for my friends. They know what to ask her. They're wearing ski masks. So she doesn't know what they look like. She doesn't know you and I are here. She knows somebody's behind the curtain, but she doesn't know it's us. They told her if she goes on the other side of the curtain, she dies." Crystal waited, watching for Becca's response.

Die?

The word snapped Becca out of her trance like a hypnotist waking someone under his spell. Now all at once she understood that she was in a house full of killers.

Crystal was a killer. The people in the basement were killers. And if that doctor downstairs was killed tonight, it would be because of her. She'd be a killer. She didn't want anyone to *die*. But if she backed out, would they kill her?

Crystal wouldn't kill her. That was a ridiculous thought. But what about the people downstairs? It wasn't ridiculous to consider being killed by them.

Crystal saw the battle in Becca's mind. "You're a good girl, Becca. This lady downstairs, she's an abortionist. She's killed a lot of people, but you don't want her to die. I don't want her to die, either. Nobody here *wants* her to die. But nobody here wants to go to prison, either. So we had to make it clear to her that if she goes on the other side of the curtain…"

Becca's expression didn't reveal her fear of backing out, or of the bloody civil war that was raging in her morals. A woman had been kidnapped, probably at gunpoint, and she was being held captive downstairs—for her.

The woman was here because Crystal thought the woman had information that would help her. Why did she think that? Because of what she'd told her about knowing the woman? She'd never seen this woman.

Why had she told Crystal that? This woman was a prisoner because she had had a panic attack at her clinic. What if it was the panic attack itself that made her think that? Oh, God, what had she done?

But then another line of reasoning shoved the other thoughts to the back. What if this doctor does know something? What if—the thought was utterly ridiculous—her parents had gone to this woman for an abortion?

Unfortunately, it wasn't the thought of them trying to abort her that was ridiculous. It was all of the sci-fi stuff that went with it. How did it all make sense? But even if she couldn't make sense of it all, what if that woman could tell her something that would pull up even one of the weeds of death that was suffocating her?

Becca thought of the poor woman downstairs. Even with all of her own problems, and even with the possibilities of lessening them, if only a little, she pushed her conscience forward. She wanted to say, "No, I can't do this." But a bullet from the barrel of her pain hit her conscience between its eyes.

"She's going to go to the police the moment we let her go," said Becca.

"No, she's not," said Crystal. "Dr. Li's made some videos down there that will show up on the Internet if she says anything. She knows to keep her mouth shut. Anyway, even if she doesn't, she hasn't seen anyone's face. She doesn't know where she is. What's she gonna say?"

"Okay, Crystal, I want you to give me your word that they are just going to ask her questions, and once we're through with her, we're going to let her go. Is that what we're going to do? Can you promise me we're not going to hurt Dr. Li? Killing her won't help me. It would just make my life worse than it already is. I don't need guilt on top of my pain. Crystal?"

"Don't say anything when we go downstairs," said Crystal. "No matter what you hear." She put her finger in Becca's face. "Nothing. No matter what you hear. Can you promise me that?"

"Yes."

"You keep your mouth shut when we go down there. That woman stays on the other side of that curtain. We don't have a problem."

"Okay," said Becca, tears suddenly streaming out of her eyes as if knowing horrible news was waiting for her downstairs.

Becca's steps behind Crystal were slow, heavy, and torturous in the large, multi-roomed, finished basement. The idea of learning the truth —whatever that truth could possibly be—despite whatever relief that may bring, had lost its luster the moment Becca's foot came off the last step and landed on the carpeted floor.

There was no way she could have coincidentally landed at *the* abortion clinic that— And that's as far as she could get with that thought.

The abortion clinic that *what?* It just didn't make sense. None of this made any sense at all. She had had a panic attack at an abortion clinic that she never would have gone to had it not been for a girl she'd just met. And now she was *seriously* entertaining the crazy thought that Heather had taken her there to abort her, and somehow the visit to the clinic triggered memories of her being taken there in her mother's womb? Was this her own thought? Or was she riding piggyback to Crystal? What was she doing here in this basement?

The closer she got to the black curtain, the more she focused on the impossibility of her thoughts. But what if it were true that Heather had tried to abort her at this clinic? What would it mean? How would it help to know this? Or was she foolishly about to sit in on her own mental autopsy?

Crystal peeked at the woman from the edge of the curtain. Her back was to her and she had been instructed to not turn around. Two men in black coveralls and black ski masks stood before her. Crystal couldn't see Dr. Li's face, but she could tell from the woman's shaking body that she was terrified.

"No, we're not going to kill you. Don't ask me that again," the shorter of the men ordered. "Answer our questions and we all go home."

"What questions? What questions?" Dr. Li yelled in confusion, unaware that she was yelling at her kidnapper.

"Your business. Your clinic. How long you been doing abortions?"

Dr. Li looked perplexed. Why would these people want to know this? Her eyes widened. *Oh, my God! They're anti-abortion fanatics!* "Nineteen years."

"Dr. Li, I want you to give a lot of thought to what I'm about to ask you. Seventeen years ago."

"Seventeen years ago?" she asked incredulously. "You want me to remember something from seventeen years ago?"

"Nancy, you're going to remember. You're going to remember a lot of things. Year by year until we get to this year." The scheme was to get her to talk about every year just in case she did go to the police. Better to have the cops focusing on seventeen or eighteen years instead of one.

She swallowed hard. "Okay," she submitted.

"Seventeen, maybe eighteen years ago, a woman came in for an abortion and changed her mind." The shorter of the two men peered at her. "We want to know about that."

"A patient who changed her mind? Seventeen or eighteen years ago?" Dr. Li started crying again. She knew there was no way could remember something so old. "You know I can't remember something that old. You're not going to let me go."

"It's not my decision whether you go home or not, Nancy. It's up to the person behind this curtain. If that person hears what he or she wants to hear, you go home. Simple as that. Now tell me something that'll make the person behind the curtain tell me to let you go home."

Dr. Li dropped her face into her hands and spoke through tears that sprung from a fading hope that she'd be let go. She shook her head. "I can't do it. I can't do it. There's no way I can—"

An angel of truth lightly touched Dr. Li's head.

She raised her head with an expression like she was looking at a movie. "They came in twice."

"Who came in twice?" asked the man.

Crystal looked back at Becca and hurried her over with her fingers. Becca reluctantly obeyed.

"A white couple came in twice for an abortion. The first time the woman changed her mind." Dr. Li's face showed that the memory was getting stronger. "Them!" she said angrily.

"Who?" one of the men asked.

"I will never forget that couple. They came in the second time. The woman came to one of the patient rooms. Once inside, she was adamant that she wanted the abortion. I remember her for several reasons. One is that I rarely have a woman come in and ask me to kill her baby. No one says, kill my baby."

"She said that?" the masked man sounded shocked.

"Yes. She said, and I quote, 'Dr. Li, I need this baby dead today.'"

"The mother said that?" asked the kidnapper.

"Yes," said Dr. Li, "that's exactly what she said." This lady was trying to remember herself away from a shallow grave.

Becca gasped and covered her mouth. Her knees felt weak.

Crystal whispered in her ear, "We don't know that that's your mother she's talking about." It was too late to stop this thing now, but she felt her own stomach getting sick.

"I picked up the scissors to eviscerate the fetal matter."

Becca flinched when the doctor said scissors.

"All of a sudden music started blaring throughout the whole clinic. It was *Highway to Hell*."

"*Highway to Hell?* Are you sure?"

Dr. Li looked at the man like he was nuts. "How would I forget a song with those kinds of lyrics coming out of nowhere while I'm preparing to do an abortion? I still don't know how that happened. Our intercom system hadn't been hooked up yet. How do you forget something like that?"

Becca stumbled backwards, clutching her chest. Her face was a mass of tears.

"Are you having another panic attack?" whispered Crystal. "I can get you outta here," she said, at the same time trying to guide her away.

Becca wouldn't go. She couldn't talk, but she shook her head that she was staying. She stood with both arms partly extended toward the black curtain. Crystal wrapped her arm around her friend's waist. She felt tears rolling down her own face and was glad she did. Dead people didn't cry.

"I left the room," Dr. Li continued, "to find out where that music was coming from. When I returned," the doctor shook her head as though she still couldn't believe it, "I'll never forget. I was trying to apologize for the interruption. The woman said, 'Dr. Li, I don't mean to be rude, but I don't want to hear it. What I need is an abortion. I need it now. I need you to take this baby from me.'"

"She called it a baby?" asked the taller of the kidnappers.

"She called it a baby. Yes."

"Do you remember the lady's name?" The kidnapper who asked looked at the other one like, *Why not ask? She's remembered all this.*

"I remember both of their names." She paused.

Becca and Crystal stretched their necks toward the curtain.

"Heather and Vincent Simmons. I banned them both from ever stepping foot in any of my clinics."

Becca's heart didn't stop. Her brain waves didn't stop. Her lungs didn't stop. But she did something she didn't think she could do again. She died. Her arm went limp and filled with pain. More pain than she'd ever felt in her arm. She would have screamed had she not been in shock.

She looked into Crystal's tear-filled eyes with her own dazed eyes and bobbing head, and asked softly, "Will you please take me home, Crystal? I'm dying, and I don't want to die this close to my parents."

18

Cystal sat on the edge of Becca's bed, watching her and wishing she could do more. Wishing she could do *something*. She was an expert in feeling hopelessness, despair, and pain, but an apprentice in dealing with them. At least she had not yet found a way that didn't simply cover the problem for a while. Or worse, a way that didn't ultimately make her problems worse. This was her assessment of herself, and time had killed all contrary arguments.

Her hand rested on Becca's knee as she watched her slowly rock back and forth with eyes shut tight from pain. She watched the nonstop trail of tears with sad eyes. She felt so totally useless. Her friend needed her, and all she could do was pat her on the knee, hurt inside for her, wonder how long her friend would hurt like this, and at the same time try to deal with her own depression. *Why did the cloud of darkness and gloom have to drop on her now? Of all times, now, when her friend needed her so desperately!*

Becca pulled her head up and stopped rocking. Her closed eyes were level. Hearing the abortion doctor confess that her parents had tried to abort her—twice!—had thrown her like an explosion scattering debris.

The explosion was now gone. The ringing in her ears was gone.

The confusion and feeling that she was about to pass out were gone. But she was emotionally in a crumpled heap, and the residue of the explosion was in her flesh. She grimaced as she rubbed her limp arm.

Becca knew Crystal was watching. She knew she wanted to help. She knew Crystal couldn't help. "I'll be okay," Becca said, without opening her eyes. She tried her best to mask the pain that sawed her arm in at least ten places.

Crystal's face turned up into an unconvinced half-smile. *Your parents hate you, and you just found out that they tried to abort you twice. You're not going to be okay, Becca.* "I know you'll be okay." She watched her for a few seconds, not wanting to leave her for one moment. *One moment was a lifetime if you needed someone and no one was there.* She knew this from experience.

But her own depression had descended upon her, bringing the outside night into her soul. She felt it thickening and coiling around her neck. "Becca, I won't leave you. I just need to go to the kitchen for a minute. Okay?"

"Okay," said Becca, her eyes still closed.

Crystal reluctantly stood up. She'd hurry, she told herself. She took two steps.

"Crystal," said Becca, as she rubbed her arm deeply, her grimace showing more of itself.

Crystal turned and looked at Becca's clinched eyes. "Yeah?"

"Bring me some."

Crystal was glad Becca's eyes were closed. So many things went through her mind at this request, and each of them took turns arranging its own expression on her face. Her first word dragged. "I'm…going to get a drink."

"Okay," said Becca.

Crystal paused, wondering. She turned to leave the room.

"And Crystal?"

Crystal turned, wondering what Becca would say next. Her closed-eyed friend said, "Do you have any more marijuana?"

Again, Crystal was glad that Becca's eyes were closed. The weak thought was buried too deeply beneath heavy layers of her own emotional baggage to qualify as clearly discernible, but something inside of her sent a shadow of a wisp to her mind. *Whatever you think you heard about this girl helping you get rid of your pain is crazy? She can't help herself. She's going to go down fast.*

"Yeah, I have some. It's like water," said Crystal. "It's important to stay high-drated."

A pretty smile broke through Becca's grimace. "That's clever, Crystal—even for you." The smile disappeared. "Think you can help one of your dehydrated friends?"

Crystal looked at Becca and felt a sadness come over her. It wasn't the sadness of her own depression. In the couple of seconds between Becca's request and her answer, she heard herself kidding with Becca about being a nun. Without trying to analyze anything, she knew that was where the sadness had come from.

The voice had said Becca would help her get rid of her own pain. But Crystal knew it had been speaking of the girl she had nicknamed the nun. And now the nun was asking for alcohol and marijuana. She wanted to warn her. She wanted to say, "Drugs and alcohol are lame! They won't do anything but wrap a tourniquet around your problems! You keep the tourniquet on too long and you lose a limb!"

But as deceptive as a tourniquet was, looking at her friend, how could she say no? Tourniquets had their place. They stopped the immediate bleeding. They kept you alive for a little while longer. Maybe Becca was stronger than her. Maybe she wouldn't kill the rest of her soul by depending too heavily on tourniquets. Maybe all she needed was to stop the bleeding while she sorted things out.

Could she help one of her dehydrated friends? she thought. "You have to be there for your friends," she said to Becca. She turned and left the room. She was ashamed that despite her momentary reluctance to give her friend alcohol and marijuana, there was something inside of her—something shameful—that seemed to like the idea of Becca becoming more like her.

Something that told her if good girl Becca was leaving, maybe bad girl Becca would stay.

"Stronger and stronger we get," said Unwanted to Alone, sharing his attention with the angels he called the three stooges. "Look at them, Alone. They don't know what hit them."

"She doesn't know what hit her," he said with glee, speaking of Becca. "Don't you just love it when they use our tools to try to fix their problems?" He shook his head, finding it hard to believe. "You'd think they'd learn. *Drugs* and *alcohol?*"

Unwanted pointed to Gabron, Justis, and Krasa. "You'd think those clowns would learn. Six thousand years of warfare over these worthless people—" He stopped and looked hard at the fourth angel that suddenly appeared to the other three.

The demons watched for a minute.

"I don't like it," said Alone. "The antsy one who's always trying to get his hands on you looks too giddy. What do you think that angel of truth is yakking about?"

Unwanted's face twisted. "Truth, what else? Let them talk about truth. Does it look like our girl is getting any closer to the truth?"

A slow smile crept onto Alone's face. Then a wicked laugh joined it. "No. The only thing she's getting closer to is alcohol and dope."

It was Unwanted's turn to try a smile on a face naturally built to resist smiles. "That's not the only thing she's getting closer to."

"She's going down fast," said Alone, with refired confidence.

The girl's conversations bounced all over the place. Compliments of marijuana, alcohol, and two tortured pasts. One of which was discussed in detail, and the other discussed only in the vaguest of terms.

Becca took a long hit off her joint and rested her arm across her knee, which was propped up on the long bench she and Crystal sat on.

Crystal rested both elbows on her knees as she leaned forward, looking sideways at Becca. Her long jet-black hair hanging and partly covering her eye. "You know, you may want to exhale sometime tonight."

Becca choked out a laugh and dropped her foot to the floor of the deck. She was more choking than laughing, which made her laugh more, which in turn made Crystal laugh.

"Crystal!" Becca exclaimed once she got the last cough out. Her hand was on her burning chest. "You're trying to kill me."

Crystal took a swallow of her drink. She slowly rolled her head as she spoke. "I don't think you need any help with that one."

The demons didn't agree with that statement.

They appeared to be standing across and down the street. In a certain sense, they were; in a literal sense, they weren't. They stood in another dimension. Their distance from the girls they looked up at wasn't measured in human feet or yards. It was measured in something that was often a mystery even among demons and angels. It was measured in righteousness and sin and mercy and judgment and freewill and sovereignty and...well, who knew what else?

The point was she was either tantalizingly within their grasp or frustratingly out of their reach. These things could change in a flash. One had to be ready, positioned.

The best Suicide and his demons could do this moment was to keep watching the girls.

"You know all that stuff I said about you being a nun?" said Crystal, with a crooked grin.

Becca looked at her with a combination of a smiling *I tried to tell you* and a *I know what you're going to say* look. "Yeah, yeah, yeah."

"I take it all back."

"I told you I wasn't a nun."

Crystal looked at her friend with a little grin and thoughtful eyes.

The playful tone of her voice didn't betray the depth or seriousness of her thoughts. "Oh, I'm through with that nun crap." Her eyes narrowed into mischievousness. "You know what I think you are?"

Becca turned her head sideways and dipped it toward her shoulder in an exaggerated pose, as though she were a model going for a sultry look. "What am I?"

Crystal downed the last of her drink and put the glass down by her foot with a heavy clunk. "A madam."

"Madam?" Becca did a half cough and left her mouth wide open. "Madam?"

Crystal bounced her index finger. "Not just any madam. A murderous madam who's the kingpin of an international syndicate of sex traffickers and assassins who launders hundreds of millions of Columbian and Mexican drug cartel money," she paused, thinking, "…through your own bank. That's how you launder the dirty money. *And* extortion. You've got your hands in everybody's pockets."

Becca broke in. "*And* when I'm not doing all that stuff, I'm sitting on my best friend's deck smoking all her pot."

Best friend.

Crystal thought on this. What did that mean? *Best friend.* She'd known her what? Less than a week? How could she be her best friend? People threw that word around too easily. "And drinking all her liquor."

"And drinking all her liquor," said Becca.

"And eating all her food," said Crystal.

"And eating all her food," said Becca. "Geez, what a leech."

Crystal heard the humor in Becca's voice, but she saw questions in her eyes. "Friends take care of their friends," she said. "Whatever I have is yours. I told you that. Don't worry about anything. Money's never an issue with friends. The only thing that's ever an issue is whether someone is a true friend or a friend in name only."

"You are *serious* about friendship. I've never heard anyone talk about it like you do," said Becca.

Crystal's face went serious. "You called me your best friend."

Becca suddenly felt awkward. Honestly, she didn't recall ever referring to Crystal as her best friend. But she sure wasn't going to admit that. Not to Crystal. She tried to smile her way out of this embarrassing situation.

Crystal seemed to read her mind. Her face softened. It wasn't Becca's fault. She was only seventeen and didn't know what true friendship meant. "Sometimes I can be a bit literal. Spooky intense, you know? Gotta learn to lighten up. Trying to keep up with the new queen of the marijuana buffet table's not helping any."

Becca had observed Crystal and pieced together enough of her cryptic comments to know she was in constant emotional torment. She didn't know what the cause was, but she thought it may have something to do with men, since she was so angry at them, and friendship, since she was so fanatical about it. She was trying to kid her way out of a vulnerable moment. "I've never met anyone like you," said Becca.

"Yeah, well, you're only seventeen. You got time to get luckier."

"No, seriously Crystal. I've never met anyone like you. You care about people. You care about me. I know you do. And all you know about me is I'm screwed up. How can—?" Becca stopped.

"How can a stranger love you and your own parents don't?" Crystal finished.

Now it was Becca's turn to think on Crystal's choice of words.

Love.

What did she mean love? Was Crystal saying she loved her? Or was she simply saying that Becca was thinking that thought? She thought it better to keep this reasoning to herself. "Yeah, I guess so."

Crystal looked at her young friend with a warm heart. She thought the warmth came from her feelings for Becca rather than the alcohol. "Becca—"

"Crystal." Becca spoke at the same time Crystal spoke. "Sorry. Go ahead."

"Madam's first," said Crystal.

Becca smiled. "Okay. I just want you to know that I appreciate everything you're doing for me. I don't know what I'd do if you weren't here for me. Some people," Becca shook her head, "some people would take advantage of a girl in my situation. It's dangerous out there." Becca took Crystal's hand and smiled with tears that sat on the edges of her lids. "I know that I'm safe here. I know that even though you don't know a lot about me—well, no, actually you know a lot about me."

They both laughed—for different reasons.

"I'm stammering all over myself," said Becca. "I guess what I'm getting at is," her mind sought for and found an awkward but supporting idea, "I've gone out with a lot of guys, and one way or another everything always led to sex. No matter how sweet or kind or supportive they were, they always had an end game. An agenda. You know what I mean? I know the analogy doesn't make sense here. It's just that where do you find people like you? Someone who cares for people just because they're a good person?"

Crystal turned her face away and thought on Becca's words. Her hand felt awkward in her hand.

"I know what I'm saying when I say this, Crystal. I'm your friend. I don't have much, but whatever I have is yours. I love you," she said, and hugged her. *I love you* were probably not the right words, she thought, but Crystal was a special human being. A one of a kind person. *Her best friend.*

"I love you, too," said Crystal, with an ache in her heart and a ball of confusion in her head. They pulled apart from one another and Crystal felt like her soul and Becca's soul were one and that pulling away had torn it. She had never felt a need like this for another person—male or female.

"You were going to say something before I stepped all over my tongue," said Becca.

"You're a special girl, Becca," was all she could say. "Thanks for being my friend." She stood up. "I'm feeling a bit sick. I'm going to lie down."

Becca jumped up and hugged Crystal again.

Crystal closed her eyes and didn't try to understand the deep hole she had fallen into. All she knew was that now something *else* was wrong with her and she was at a new level of lostness. "Goodnight, Becca."

"Goodnight, best friend."

Becca sat back down and purposefully listened at the muted sounds of people walking and driving up and down the night's street. She was less than half a block away from Euclid Avenue. It had a handful of small restaurants and a few bars, but she figured the increased traffic was probably a show at the *Variety Playhouse*, a concert venue that had been converted from a movie theater.

She took a deep breath of the crisp March air and felt good.

Then she felt bad.

Suicide and his demons were crossing the street.

19

"Look who's here," said Self-Pity, looking to his left as he, Hopelessness, and Suicide crossed the street. "What do you think attracted Perversion? You think Unwanted invited him? I don't know how strong the stronghold is, but if Perversion joins…and if he can get his hooks into her…" The spirit's voice faded as he noticed evil approaching from several directions. "Looks like he's not taking any chances. Look at all these demons."

Perversion was a twisted mess of a demon. His large body had the appearance of a gorilla-like monster who had been created in a hurry with parts that didn't match. Even the placement, shape, and color of his eyes didn't match. He could turn his thick neck only so far. It was easier to turn his whole body. He did, looking around at demons approaching from every direction. Some walking. Some hungrily running, as though the last of their favorite dish on the buffet table was being scooped up by others. Some swooped in from the air.

"He sees something in the girls," Suicide said of Perversion, "especially Crystal. I saw it, too."

Self-Pity switched subjects. "I don't see any problem with me, Suicide, but I don't think Unwanted's going to be happy to see you."

Hopelessness wasn't a part of their conversation. He was lost in his own dark thoughts. He ignored the growing numbers of demons and Suicide's and Self-Pity's conversation. He was thin, but exceedingly heavy with darkness. He labored his heavy feet up the porch steps and into the house, ascending the stairs to get to Becca.

"And what about you?" Suicide asked suspiciously.

"Same thing I told you before we entered the girl in East Atlanta. It's why no one likes you. What sense does it make to burn down your own house?"

"Yeah, well, I'm a suicide spirit. What in the darkness am I supposed to do? Pass out energy bars?"

Self-Pity turned to him and they both stopped at the first porch step. "Look, I understand that you can't help yourself. It's your nature. I know. I know. But some of us get tired of having to find a new house every time you kill our host. It's not easy, you know."

"I know," Suicide said, with a tinge of regret.

"Just try to control yourself," Self-Pity encouraged. "Try torment."

Suicide's big head went back.

Self-Pity saw the argument that was coming. "I know. You're not a spirit of torment." Self-Pity raised both palms and placed them on his friend's wide shoulders. "Just try it. Stretch it out. Kill her little by little instead of all at once. Maybe you can even kill her without actually killing her."

A large, red, circular eye that was high and just to the left of the center of Suicide's scaly forehead, and a smaller, oval-shaped pure black eye looked back at Self-Pity. Suicide's blinking eyes were uncoordinated. "I'll try."

Justin, Krasa, and Gabron watched with peril what could only be accurately described as an invasion. Demons were coming from every direction to get to Becca. And they paid as much attention to the angels as they did to the fallen leaves on the ground.

"They're everywhere," said Gabron. But his sword and dagger were still in their sheaths. A sign that he understood more perfectly his warfare. Demons had as much access to a person as that person allowed. He thought of the words of the blessed book, *Neither give place to the devil.* If Becca put the devil's name on her lease, angels had no right to keep him out of the house.

Justis was about to comment on the invasion. Gabron had learned a lot, but there was still much to learn.

Mark, one of the three truth angels, appeared before them. He began where Justis had planned to begin. "Perversion is here because of Crystal's love for Becca."

Gabron's eyes got large with the thought of such a sin. "Is her love sick?"

"Sin is sick," Mark answered. "Everything about sin is sick. Everything about the sinner is sick."

"Is she planning such a lewd offense?"

"Crystal's plans? You do not ask about Becca's plans? The plans of a seed mean nothing if the soil is poisoned," Mark answered. "The heart is deceitful above all things and desperately wicked. Who can know it?"

Gabron looked at Krasa and Justis with troubling questions that pushed his eyebrows together. "We have been with her all her life. We have seen no such evil." He looked at his friends for assuring expressions. He didn't find them. His insides shifted downward like a mudslide.

"To the pure all things are pure," said Mark. "You do not see evil in Becca because you desire Becca to have no evil. It is the error of many sons and daughters of God. They see, and yet don't see. They hear, and yet don't hear. Their pure hearts and desire for their loved ones to serve the Lord do not allow them to acknowledge the truth about the spiritual condition of rebels they love. Of course, you do not pray for the salvation of those whom you believe already possess it. So it is an eternal tragedy."

"But...?" Gabron hung his head, his one-word sentence never coming together in his mind.

"The sons and daughters of Adam were not created for rejection. It is as unnatural for them to live in rejection as it is for them to live under water," said the truth angel.

"The whole world lives under this curse," said Gabron.

"And each person deals with it in his or her own way," said Mark.

"Becca? And Crystal?" Gabron asked, pondering the conclusion of this troubling conversation.

"Perversion was attracted by the growing soul tie between Crystal and Becca. They are both hurting. They are both empty. They are both lonely. They are both hungry. They are both available." Mark's face was tranquil as he studied the trouble on Gabron's face.

"Would Crystal do such a wicked thing? Would Becca do such evil?" Gabron hated his question. *He knew the answer was yes.*

"Sinners like to think they have morals, but it's an illusion," said Mark. "They are dead in trespasses and sins. They walk according to the prince of the power of the air, the devil who now works in them for disobedience. They are by nature the children of wrath. When they do evil, they do what they are. Under the right circumstances, they will do whatever the evil one tells them to do."

Gabron was stunned. But it wasn't the truth that affected him so. For even among those who had never worked so closely with the sons and daughters of Adam, it was known that humans were evil beyond comprehension. Rather, the dazed look on his face, and his wooden couple of steps to the side, was because of the closeness of the tragedy. It was the difference in hearing an explosion from a mile away, and having that same explosion happen six inches from your ear. Same explosion. Different effect.

The warrior angel didn't want to ask the question, but he needed to ask. He swallowed the bad taste in his mouth and exhaled with a pained look.

The truth angel waited for the question that he knew Gabron had to ask.

"Will Perversion prevail?" he asked.

"Time will answer this question, Gabron."

The most successful demons operated in teams. Suicide was immensely successful. His team consisted of two circles of spirits. The inner circle was the one closest to him, and the one with permanent members who traveled with him and worked with him on every case. There were only two: Self-Pity and Hopelessness.

The outer circle were various demons who came and went, depending on what kind of condition Suicide needed to create to kill his victim. The regulars in this group were demons of depression, self-hate, lying, and delusion. Suicide had found that it wasn't necessary to have depression demons in his inner circle because one always showed up whenever Self-Pity opened the door for Hopelessness. Nor did he always need a demon with special lying abilities because Self-Pity made people highly susceptible to believe obvious lies without special assistance.

Hopelessness stood next to Becca's bed and looked at her with dark, brooding eyes. The demon wasn't literally dark-colored, but the energy he carried made him appear dark. He turned and looked at Self-Pity with an impatient expression. He pointed his head toward the victim.

Self-Pity got busy, and Hopelessness followed closely behind.

Suicide stood at the foot of her bed with his heavy arms poised on his wide waist, waiting for his door to open.

It had not been Becca's first time drinking alcohol. She had done so several times at parties. She had even smoked marijuana once, if taking one hit counted. The effect of that one hit had scared her—she thought it had been laced with something—and she had made up her mind that she was sticking with alcohol. But things had changed. That was the old Becca. The Becca who naively clung to the hope that being good, whatever that was, would make her parents love her.

The new Becca—and she knew it was a radical new Becca—had grown up once and for all the evening Vincent and Heather walked out on her at the school musical. Well, there had been one foolish moment of fantasy afterwards when she had asked Crystal to take her back home.

A wave of anger washed over her, leaving a stench like untreated sewage over her memory of the event. She'd never make that mistake again.

Her thoughts took an abrupt turn from anger to self-pity. Hundreds of thoughts dropped on her like cluster bombs exploding all around her. Not a square inch of self-esteem or certainty was left untouched. Becca shook her head under the barrage.

Why did they do this to me? Why don't they love me? It's never going to get better. They don't treat Danielle like that. I did all the right things, and look where it got me? What does everyone think of me? Think of all the people who were at the musical. There must be something wrong with me for my own parents to treat me like this. I can't stay with Crystal forever. What am I going to do when she gets tired of me?

Becca's mind focused in horror at the words she had heard come from the abortion doctor's mouth.

"They came in twice."

"The woman came to one of the patient rooms. Once inside, she was adamant that she wanted the abortion."

"I need this baby dead today."

"Dr. Li, I don't mean to be rude, but I don't want to hear it. What I need is an abortion. I need it now. I need you to take this baby from me."

"Take this baby from me."

"I need this baby dead today."

"Take this baby from me."

"I need this baby dead today."

Becca suffered through this tormenting loop for three hours. Finally, mercifully, she was at the point of escaping the voices by falling asleep. But just when her eyes fluttered for the last time, Hopelessness shouted, "There is no hope!"

Then his loop of dark lies began.

20

Becca rolled right and left and right again on the mattress. She pounded the pillow twice with an open palm as though the problem was the pillow. It wasn't. She turned over onto her back and opened her burning eyes. Sleepless night number four.

The misery of sleep deprivation wrapped around her like a mummy's cloths. She couldn't take it off no matter what she tried. And she felt heavy. Like her bones were made of solid lead. She stared at the ceiling with a blank stare. Sad, teary eyes replaced the blank stare once the voices started up again. Was there no end to the voices? Was there no new depth of pain and loneliness and despair she couldn't experience? When would it end? Would it ever end?

Vincent and Heather. Vincent and Heather. *Vincent and Heather!*

She was tired of thinking of Vincent and Heather and why they did what they did. Why they were who they were. Why they hated the way they hated. She was tired and fed up with where these thoughts took her. It was like being nearly drowned in mud only to be pulled up at the last moment so the tormentor could do it all over again.

The mud of misery was in her lungs. No matter how hard she tried, it was too deep to remove. Heavy tears rolled from the corners of her eyes. It was too much. She couldn't handle it any more. It had to end.

———

Self-Pity looked at his friend with widened, concerned eyes. "Suicide," he said.

Suicide didn't answer.

Self-Pity saw the glazed look in Suicide's eyes. He looked at the light stream of heavy dark liquid coming from the sides of his mouth. He saw his heavy chest rapidly rising and falling. He knew what this was! "Suicide!" he yelled.

The big demon was fixated on the girl. His wide eyes bore into hers as though his sight was drilling through solid rock. It wasn't rock, however; it was her mind. He was cutting through her defenses. *He had to kill this girl.*

"Suicide! Suicide! Stop it! Control yourself!"

Suicide's large head went forward a few inches.

Self-Pity pushed the thick demon's shoulder. *Snap out of it!* he thought.

Suicide didn't feel the smaller demon's hand on his shoulder. He didn't see the demon. At this moment, all he saw was a girl he had to kill.

———

Becca pulled her heavy body and sat up on the mattress. Her thoughts floated around the house. They took her to every room. The house seemed ten times as large as it was and as a hundred times as empty. Crystal had been gone for three full days and hadn't called. Her only explanation before she left had been, "I gotta work on something. If you need me, call or text."

There had been something about the way she said, "If you *need* me," that had kept Becca from calling. It was like she was saying, "If it's an emergency, call or text." Becca hadn't seen it that night on the deck, but she saw it on Crystal's face when she left. She seemed really depressed and distant ever since they had last sat on the porch together. Of course, Crystal was always distant. But something was pushing her even deeper into her shell.

Becca felt something cutting the cords to those thoughts and leading her into another.

———

Self-Pity watched in horror as Hopelessness spread his webbed arms and leapt onto Becca, wrapping his arms around her arms and his legs around her torso. Hopelessness squeezed with all his strength. The girl's mouth went wide with a gasp, and so did Self-Pity's.

———

Crystal's room. Look in Crystal's room.

Becca was in the mud again. Thrashing. Legs kicking. Arms outstretched in panicked flails as her body sank, looking for something solid. Anything that might help her escape the thick, dark liquid of a suffocating grave. The thought was the branch she needed. *Crystal's room.*

She stood up from the bed and walked in a stupor down the hall and into Crystal's room.

Under the mattress.

Becca looked at the high bed. She walked directly to the left side as though guided and reached her hand between the box spring and mattress. Her hand felt something solid. It was like ice in her hands, even though it was nestled. Why wasn't it warm?

A faint perception answered her question. *Guns are cold.*

Becca pulled the gun out and looked at it, handling it as clumsily as would a child. It was heavy and black. Why would Crystal have such a heavy gun? She looked at its side. It was smooth. Not like the guns with the big thing on both sides. She couldn't see the bullets. They had to be in there. Somewhere.

She stared at the gun in her hand as though waiting for it to speak. She thought of sitting on Crystal's bed, but something inside recoiled at the thought. She didn't want to violate Crystal's space. Her mixed up state didn't let her consider that she had already done that.

Becca took the gun and walked down the hallway toward her room without taking her eyes off the trigger. She didn't feel the floor beneath her feet as she approached her bed. She sat. She cried. Each tear a bitter reminder that she was alone and unwanted in the world. It would never get better. It would only get worse. She was already dead, but without the peace. Why not end the torment now? No one would miss her.

No! No! No! screamed the thought inside. *You are loved by God your Creator! Don't look to people! Look to Me!*

Becca heard the foolish thought. There was no God. She put the gun to her head. She put her finger on the trigger. She closed her eyes. Her finger pressed, then stopped pressing. The gun dropped to the floor before she did. She crumpled beside it, motionless.

A Few Seconds Earlier

The angel of the altar positioned the bowl of prayers. "Are there any tears to mix with the prayers?" he asked.

"There are tears," answered an angel. He approached the angel of the altar and gave him a small container filled with tears that had come from Bill, Nancy, Danielle, and others.

The angel of the altar mixed the tears with the prayers and asked, "Are there cries and groans and travail of spirit to mix with the prayers?"

Three angels approached, each with his own container.

The angel of the altar examined the contents of each container for purity. He mixed the contents into the bowl of prayers. There was yet one thing missing. The angel lifted an elaborately embroidered vial and tilted it over the bowl. A single drop of blood fell into the bowl. A mist arose and filled the air with a sweet smelling aroma. The angel looked at the Lord God Almighty, who had been watching the activities from His throne. He approached God.

"Lord, I present prayers on behalf of Becca. She deserves judgment, but the saints cry out for mercy. She is but a moment from death, but the saints cry out for life."

As Becca Pressed the Trigger

The large fist came from behind Suicide and struck him on his right jaw. The cracking sound filled the room as the demon's large head pressed violently against his thick neck. He fell on the side of the bed and tried several times to get up before falling limp on his back.

Hopelessness heard the cracking sound and turned his head toward it. He was still wrapped around Becca. He froze when he saw the big mercy angel. He was careful to move nothing but his eyes. He looked at Suicide. *Oh, my darkness. This is it.*

"Do you want me to stop?" Hopelessness asked with a quivering voice.

The mercy angel's big head turned in every direction, surveying the crowded room. They had him outnumbered maybe a hundred to one. His murderous eyes were cold and inviting. He couldn't find any of the demons to give him eye contact. Apparently the crowd had heard enough about mercy angels to not take the bait.

"You may continue," the mercy angel answered Hopelessness.

"What about the rest of us?" asked another motionless demon with his head bowed.

"You may continue," he answered.

A drowsy voice came from the side of the bed. It was Suicide. "What about me?"

"The prayers of the saints have given her a time of rest from you," he answered.

Suicide labored to talk through his pain. "How much time?"

The mercy angel disappeared.

"How much time!" Suicide grabbed his face. "Ohh, I think that thing broke my jaw."

Something froze Becca's hand and the gun dropped to the floor. She fell beside it, her body drained of energy. *I can't even kill myself,* she complained. *What do I have to do to find peace?*

A demon of rebellion kneeled beside her and whispered into her ear. *Why should you kill yourself? Why should you make it easy on them? Aren't you tired of being the weak one? Can you imagine them at your funeral? Standing there with fake grief. Pretending to be heartbroken. Don't let them win. Show them that they don't control you any longer.*

Becca lay on her side for several minutes ignoring the spirits of truth, but listening to spirits of rebellion, anger, hatred, unforgiveness, and false comfort. The more she listened to their ideas, the more empowered she felt. She got off the floor and put the gun back under the mattress.

Becca looked into her darkened soul and saw her parents abusing and ignoring her. She saw herself trying like a desperate fool to win their love by being good and smart. Well, she may have been a bit desperate at the moment, but she was no longer a fool. They'd never have that kind of power over her again. "Your little pathetic, good girl Becca is dead," she said. She smiled as she embraced the darkness. They'd see that she was no longer weak.

21

Becca stepped out onto the upstairs deck and quickly stepped back inside. She didn't mind cold weather, but she did mind freezing. But freezing or not, this was the fifth night being alone in the house. Just her and her voices. She had to get out, even if it was just sitting on the deck freezing her butt off. She returned with a drink in one hand and a light blanket draped over her shoulders and back. The drink would warm her belly; the blanket would warm her back. She sipped and was satisfied with the hot sensation in her chest.

She hadn't actually stayed in the house the entire time Crystal had been gone. She'd gone out walking, getting to know the area, and checking out the small indie shops. There were over ten bars within walking distance of Crystal's house. That wouldn't have meant anything a couple of weeks ago. Alcohol wasn't then much on her mind. School. Studying. Sports. Practice. That's what was on her mind a couple of weeks ago.

And Vincent and Heather.

But they were now nothing more than bad history, and she wasn't living in the past. It was about the future. And the future was about her, not them. *Not them!*

Becca sipped her drink again and frowned on one side of her face.

What did ten bars mean to her? She was seventeen. She couldn't order alcohol. And Crystal had surprised her when she told her that good fake IDs were a lot harder to get than happened on television—unless the thrill of getting an illegal drink was worth several hundred dollars or even more than a thousand. Plus, Crystal was right. A person would have to be blind to think she was twenty-one.

She sipped again. *Well, no one can stop me from drinking here,* she thought. She took two big gulps and put the glass down. The sound of the glass hitting the wood did something to her. It made her feel grown and in control. It didn't make sense. It was just one of those things.

Becca got a thought. She hopped up and went and got her phone and returned to the deck. She scrolled through her calls and texts. She must've gotten more calls and texts than the president. She had deleted hundreds of calls without listening to them. Each time she saw Danielle. Delete. Friends. Delete. Even Grandma. Delete. She didn't want anything to do with that life any more. *She wasn't weak any more.*

She looked at her phone's screen and poised her finger to delete Grandma's latest text. She didn't. Instead, she resisted her first inclination and read it.

Becca, I had a dream about you. I saw you at the zoo climbing over the fence to play with the lions. Then I saw you and a snake talking to one another. You're in great danger. Come back—

She stopped reading and jabbed her finger hard on the screen. *Delete!*

Becca didn't want to hear this. She was never going back. She hardened her heart. She had to. It was the only way to stay strong.

But your grandmother loves you. You know this, Becca. Talk to her, came the angel's thought.

A demon countered. *Your parents try to kill you twice while you're in the womb. You live almost eighteen years in pure hell. And now that you're free, Grandma has a dream? It's a little late for dreams, isn't it?*

Becca's eyes tightened. Yes, it was a little late for dreams. It was a lot late. Too late!

This didn't stop her mind from tossing her onto the giant, sticky flypaper of her grandmother's words, especially the part about the talking snake. Becca remembered the story of Adam and Eve and the Garden of Eden. She didn't need a Bible story right now. She needed to get her life together.

But the more she tried to ignore the story, the stickier it became. She couldn't kick it loose. Satan had spoken to the woman through the snake. He had excited her curiosity and then offered to satisfy it. He had deceived her into disobeying God.

"He did this by getting the woman to talk to him," said the angel of truth. "Her first mistake was talking to the deceiver. Don't talk to the devil, Becca. He is too crafty for you. The more you talk to him, the weaker you become."

She looked out into the night's darkness with angry, impatient eyes.

"All you seek is found in God," said the angel.

That's it! Becca had had enough of these thoughts about God. Where was He when her parents were trying to kill her? Where was He the seventeen years that Vincent and Heather were killing her through silence and neglect? Where was He when they walked out on her at the school musical in front of everyone?

She hopped up. Her words carried the pain of love betrayed. "I'd rather serve the devil than a God who stands by and watch innocent children treated like this by their parents. At least I know what I'm getting with the devil."

She wiped her eyes, which suddenly had filled with bitter tears. "God, if You are real, listen to me this one time. I tried Your way." She shook her head. "I tried being the good girl. It doesn't work. Crystal is right. The world wipes its butt with nice people. I'm through being toilet paper. I'm through with You. Now, please, I want you and

Grandma, and everyone else who tells me I need to do more—I want all of you out of my life."

She looked at her phone with a frown. A teenage girl, a minor, runs away from home and is only thirty minutes away. A thousand calls and texts, but where were the cops? Couldn't they locate her by the GPS on her phone? Her angry lip turned up at the corner. But that only happens when someone wants to find you, doesn't it?

Becca grunted. *She had done it again!* She'd let herself drift off into wondering if Vincent and Heather were looking for her. She knew they weren't. Why was she so weak?

She disposed of the urge to throw her phone into the street. That wasn't the answer. The answer was to stop these pathetic inner monologues. She thought of her musings in a mocking voice.

I'm not weak any more.

I can drink if I want to.

I don't need Vincent and Heather.

I'm not trying to win their love and approval any longer.

Good girl Becca is gone.

That last one. If that were true, where was the proof? Sure, she'd smoked some marijuana and drank some liquor. But the pain in her gut, the pain of being nothing and invisible to those who should have celebrated her life, mocked her declarations. She'd been threatening it to herself. It was time to act.

"No more talking. I'm going to *do* something," she promised.

Becca left the deck and went to her room. It was odd to be left alone in someone's home for such a long time, but compliments of Vincent and Heather, she'd had lots of training being alone. She let herself plop onto the mattress. Immediately Danielle popped into her mind. Immediately she tried to push the thought out of her mind. It didn't budge.

Danielle must be worried sick about you.

Becca thought of a string of words that she felt would have rivalled even Crystal. After she blurted out the angry words, she was both glad that thoughts of Danielle vanished, and that Crystal hadn't heard her attempt at poetic cursing. Maybe she should stick to regular, uncomplicated, straight line cursing.

She smiled. Clumsy or not, the cursing felt good in her mouth. It wasn't the first time she had cursed. Every now and then she said hell or damn, mostly to fit in. But that was about the extent of her part-time career in cursing. To be honest, she'd always thought hardcore cursing was beneath her. Why would an intelligent person with a good vocabulary regularly talk like that?

But this time she hadn't tried to impress someone with a half-hearted hell or damn. She had energetically strung together every curse word she knew into one long tirade. And clumsy or not, she had done it for herself.

She laughed out loud at how silly she sounded trying to curse like Crystal. In that department, Crystal was a starting all-star pro and she was a bench-sitting third-stringer

. Her laughter stopped as she thought of Vincent and Heather. Then the happy expression left her face. She'd love to curse out Vincent and Heather.

Your grandparents love you.

"Oh, my God!" Becca exclaimed impatiently at the thought. She swiveled and torpedoed herself backwards into the mattress. "I am not even going to listen to this."

She wondered at the feeling that she was being watched by something that wanted to touch her. But the alcohol allowed only a few moments of uneasiness before it put her to sleep.

A new demon stood next to Becca's bed. His whole body was wet with a sticky, jelly-like substance that dripped onto the floor as he watched the girl. His eyes travelled over every inch of her body. He couldn't touch her now, but if their plan worked, her body would be his in a little while.

"Lust, I'm glad you could make it. Perversion's already here trying to get in," said Unwanted. He stood a good distance from the sticky spirit. "If Suicide doesn't kill her first, you'll have a nice new home. God's granted her mercy for now. So we have some time before he can kill her."

"How much time? Is it going to be worth the effort?" Lust asked.

"You see the girl. You tell me," said Unwanted, his smile going to the depths of depravity.

The sticky demon's pale gray eyes hungrily scanned her body again. "Thank you for inviting me. How soon before he arrives?"

"This pathetic, one-armed dog will be yours before the sun rises."

Lust looked at her again. "Excellent."

Becca's eyes popped open from her dreams, but not before being eaten by lions. Her face frowned when she realized she had dreamed Grandma's dreams. She rubbed her burning eyes. How long had she been sleep? She searched the bed with her hand and not her eyes. She located the phone and looked at it. It was after 2:00 a.m.

She closed her eyes and recounted the dreams. Not because she wanted to, but because they had been so vivid. In the dream, she had fought past zoo guards to get to a high fence that separated the people from the lions. Somehow she had scaled the fence and jumped over. She pondered something weird. The zoo guards all had odd names.

Mercy.

Goodness.

Longsuffering.

And the lions. There were three of them, and they all had names. The lions were named *Selfish Desires, Sin,* and *Death.* It was the first lion that had caught her attention. He was mesmerizingly beautiful and alluring. There was something so mysteriously fascinating about this lion that his beauty covered the fact that he was a lion. When he roared at Becca, she looked at him and focused exclusively on his beauty, ignoring the large teeth she had clearly seen when he roared.

In the dream, she climbed the fence, all the while staying intensely focused on the lion named *Selfish Desires.* Once across the fence, she balanced herself on the thin ledge and walked sideways as she pressed her chest hard against the fence to keep from falling backwards into the twelve-foot deep pool of water. Upon reaching the end, she positioned herself into a crouch and leapt onto a roof that provided shade for the lions.

Becca was surprised when out of nowhere another guard appeared to stop her from leaping from the roof to get to the lion named *Selfish Desires.* Somehow she knew the guard's name was *Grandma's Prayers.* He rushed and tackled her. They rolled from side to side in a furious tussle of strength and will. He was strong. Much stronger than she.

But she found that the more she desired to be free, the stronger she became.

She struggled to her feet and struck the guard senseless. He was dazed on one knee trying to clear his head. She picked him up and threw him from the roof across the lions' pool and over the top of the fence. He landed hard on the concrete at the feet of people who were watching the whole thing.

Becca looked at the crowd and yelled, "I must follow *Selfish Desires*. I've been denied all my life, and he wants to be my friend."

"Don't do it!" pleaded the guard she'd tossed across the fence. "It's a trick, Becca. What you need can only be found in God!"

"No," Becca yelled back, "it hurts too bad to follow God. I have to go my own way. I have to follow *Selfish Desires!*"

"No!" screamed the guard. He watched in horror as Becca got on her hands and knees and hung from the twenty-foot roof and dropped the remaining twelve or thirteen feet.

She landed hard, badly twisting and spraining her ankle, as the guards grimaced. They always landed hard. They always faced the lions as cripples. And amazingly they always did what Becca was insanely doing now. They always used their remaining strength and mobility to hobble or drag themselves toward *Selfish Desires*.

Becca was no dream interpreter, but even she could figure this one out. She didn't like it. She tried to will away the rest of the dream from her memory. It only became more vivid.

She saw herself hobbling after *Selfish Desires* into a cave. The lion named *Sin* jumped on her and mauled her. Then the last lion, *Death*, jumped on her. All three lions ate her until nothing remained but bones and a bloody carcass.

Becca sat up in anger. This was Grandma. This was her doing. Her text. She had fallen asleep with that text on her mind. That's where these weird dreams had come from.

Dreams. There was another.

In the second dream, she was talking to a snake that was as beautiful and mesmerizing as the lion, *Selfish Desires*. The snake saw her looking for a precious coin she had lost. He offered to help. She accepted. Then she discovered that during their search, she had lost another precious coin. They looked for the coins together. Then she discovered that during the search, she'd lost her gold necklace. They looked together for the coins and gold necklace and she discovered that now she had lost her gold ring. By the time the search was over, her body was covered in tattoos, and she had lost every piece of jewelry, every piece of clothing, every strand of hair, and even her soul.

Becca stood. The alcohol had closed her eyes, and the dreams had opened them. Wide. She knew her body wouldn't let her go back to sleep any time soon. She'd take a shower and surf the web until she got tired. Maybe doing something dumb would help her fall back asleep.

She walked down the hall to the one shower upstairs. What was the moral of the snake dream? She huffed and said, "Don't talk to snakes."

Becca knew she was the only one in the house, but she still felt like something was watching her.

23

Becca took off her clothes and left her bra and panties on. She slipped on her shower slippers, grabbed her Grady High School shorts and top, and walked down the hall to the bathroom. Although it wasn't really a bathroom. It had no bath, only a shower. A house this size and with so many bedrooms should've had more than one shower. It was the one complaint that Crystal had about the house that Becca agreed with fully.

Who designed this house? Becca thought as she stepped inside the no bathtub bathroom. She looked into the mirror. Her face frowned a little. She blew breath into an open palm. She smelled like liquor. Drinking alcohol was one thing. Smelling like alcohol was quite another.

She trotted back to her room and got her toothpaste and returned to the bathroom. She brushed her teeth and turned on the shower. She stuck her hand out under the water and stepped inside when it felt good. Becca soaped her body and turned her face up into the soothing, warm water. It. Felt. Soooooo. Good.

The sound of the plastic toilet seat hitting hard against the seat cover opened her eyes. Her eyes widened at the strong sound of a seemingly endless stream of— Not turning around yet, she thought, *Urine? Someone is peeing? A man is peeing? A man is peeing!*

A man. That's what froze her in place. A flurry of thoughts shot across her mind like fireworks against a night's sky. First, the obvious. She was alone. She was naked. A man had broken into the house.

Then, the not so obvious. Was he there to steal something? Was there more than one? What would he do to her? Was she going to be raped? Murdered?

Another thought fought for her attention and got it. The guy hadn't said anything to her. Why? Even if he was high, she was only six feet away from him and the water was on. He had to hear it. There was no way he didn't know she was in the shower.

Becca mustered enough courage to wipe the clear, but steamed shower door just when the last of the man's stream ended. Her mouth dropped open and her knees almost buckled in fear. *He was totally naked!* Her mind called a strike. It stopped working, offering her nothing but rape, murder, and a meaningless eulogy for its thoughts.

She watched him, with the foolish thought that maybe he hadn't seen her after all. Maybe he was on drugs and was out of his mind. Maybe that's why he didn't know she was there. Then fear followed that thought. If he was on drugs. *Oh, God*, she thought.

The man shook himself. She watched his hand. It was like watching a 3D movie in slow motion. She would have gasped, had she had a gasp left. He finished. She didn't know it, but her eyes lingered where his hand had been. Her eyes widened even more. She could almost feel the pain he'd inflict on her body. Rape would be horrible enough. But being raped by *that?* There was just no way.

Yet, fighting him was out of the question. She didn't see anything she could use as a weapon, and he had so many muscles. They were everywhere. His chest. His arms. His abs. His legs. And he was tall. Maybe six-one or six-two.

She stilled her breathing. He was through using the bathroom. For some reason, he didn't know she was here. She'd wait until he left and she'd—

"Hey, Crystal," said the naked man.

Becca's body went rigid. She saw the man turn his whole body around and look from where he was into the little clear spot she was peering through. Her eyes found a way to get even wider. He called Crystal again and started walking toward the shower. Becca crossed her chest and pressed her back against the wall. Fear held a hand over her mouth, forbidding her to say anything.

The door opened.

The muscled, naked man let out a low curse that lasted at least three seconds. "You're not Crystal."

Becca looked the man in the face. The only reason she didn't crumple to the shower floor was that her muscles were stiff with fear. If her mind would unscramble and her tongue would stop ignoring her, she would say, "No, I'm not Crystal. Will you please get out of here?"

"You're Becca," the naked man said, now flashing perfectly even, sparkling white teeth. "She told me about you." He nodded his head twice. "She likes you a lot. You're in good hands. She's good people."

Becca looked pleadingly into the naked man's eyes. Her tongue was still not working. Finally, her fear allowed her to think beyond immediate survival. *Why is Crystal's boyfriend standing here talking to me like we're not naked? Why doesn't he leave?*

"Oh, I'm sorry," he said, with a smile that Becca thought awkward and disloyal to acknowledge as beautiful. "I'm standing here in my birthday suit talking to you like we're friends."

Friends? You mean lovers, don't you? thought Becca.

He stretched out his hand. "I'm Gerald."

His name meant nothing to Becca. She looked at the naked man's hand. Was he for real? She was standing there scared to death in the shower, and he wanted to shake hands? Maybe he was on drugs. She didn't want to antagonize him. She stretched out her hand.

The man took her hand, but he didn't shake it. He took it gently into his own and pressed his other hand lightly on top, sandwiching it. He grinned. "Crystal didn't tell you about me?"

Now that Becca was apparently not going to be raped and murdered, her tongue wrestled free of its paralysis. "No. She didn't tell me about you." Her voice was light with tentativeness. "Can we finish this conversation later? Like after I'm dressed." Then she added, "And after you're dressed?"

The naked man lowered Becca's hand as though he'd just been stricken by the light. "Oh. Oh. Oh. Oh. I apologize. I'm so sorry. My bad." He let go of her hand and backed up. "I, uhh…we're kind of free-spirited."

Becca plastered her arm back across her chest. *We?* she thought. Did he mean Crystal? Did Crystal walk around like this? She'd never seen her walk around naked. *Thank God! And who is this guy?*

"I apologize. Really," said the naked man, as he backed up. "I thought you were Crystal. We can talk later. Maybe in the morning." He smiled and left.

You thought I was Crystal? How long does it take you to see that I'm not Crystal? She felt herself wanting to explode into tears. She cupped her face in controlled cries. But she had no confidence that she could continue to muffle her crying.

She turned the shower off and got out. She haphazardly rubbed the towel over her body, quickly put her shorts and top on, and peeked her head out the door. She didn't see the man.

She ran to her room and closed the door and locked it. She grabbed a pillow and sat on the floor against the dresser and pulled her knees up to her chest. She buried her face into the pillow and burst into tears.

After several minutes of crying into the pillow, she raised her head. "Oh, my God. *That's* Gerald?"

"Yes, Becca," Lust answered, moving as close to the bed as he could get before hitting a barrier. Droplets of sticky jelly hitting the floor as he moved. "This is Gerald. Beautiful, isn't he? He's going to help me get my hands on you."

Knock. Knock. Knock.

Becca was dead tired. It had been impossible to get the images of Gerald out of her mind. It had taken her an hour to fall asleep. And even then, she saw the beautiful man in her dreams, doing all manner of things to her. In fact, the knocking on the door rescued her from the muscled man in her dream having his way with her again. Although, honestly, in the dream it was difficult to see who needed the rescuing.

"Becca," she heard through her grogginess. "I've made you breakfast."

Her eyes opened. She used a few seconds to get her bearings. There was a light tapping on the door. "Yeah?" she answered.

"I've made you breakfast."

That. Was. Not. Crystal's voice. It was him! Becca popped up on the bed. *What do I do? What do I do?* She looked at the sliding lock on the door. That little lock wouldn't stop a man like him. It was more for privacy than anything else.

"You've gotta be hungry," he said.

"Umm...umm..." she stalled.

"Becca," he called.

"Yeah?"

"I'm fully clothed." He waited through a long pause.

"You sure?"

On the other side of the door, a slow grin on his chiseled, naturally tanned face formed. "I'm sure."

"What does fully clothed mean to you?" she asked, now standing at the door.

He smiled with a closed mouth. "Pants, shirt, boots."

Becca leaned heavily with her back against the door and closed her eyes. She wasn't in any danger, she told herself. If he had wanted to do something, it would have been when they were both naked in the bathroom. She took a deep breath and let it out. *But I have to get that image out of my mind.* She slid the little bolt and slowly opened the door into a crack, hoping he was being truthful about being fully clothed.

Thank God! He was clothed. Relief flooded her. But when she saw his smile, she knew she was in danger. It must've been her fear when he had entered the bathroom that let her only see his beauty. But now that she knew he lived here with Crystal, her mind was functioning without the dread of contemplating rape and murder. This guy was absolutely gorgeous. Like some kind of god in human form.

"I'm a great cook," he said, with a smile that was doing funny things to Becca's insides.

"Uhh, okay," she said standing behind the door and talking through the crack. "I'm going to put some clothes on." She blushed at her own words. He had seen her totally naked. They had had a conversation without one square inch of clothing between the two of them.

I really had no choice in that, she thought. *I do now.*

"I understand," he said, with that smile again.

She closed the door and leaned her back against it and lightly bounced her head on it. She had to recover. She tried her best to not think anything about Crystal's boyfriend. She failed. *Who is this guy? Is he even human? Okay, Becca, get a hold of yourself. He's just a guy. And he's Crystal's guy.*

The last thought brought a sense of calm to her. He was Crystal's guy! There was absolutely no chance of anything happening between them. She let out a sigh of relief. She'd never admit it to herself, but there was also a tinge of regret.

She put on some clothes and reached for the bedroom door knob. Her phone rang. She looked at the phone with attitude, ready to push *Delete.* Her eyes lit up. "Crystal! Hey!"

"Hey, girlfriend. You been good?" asked Crystal.

"As good as I can be without you here to keep me straight," Becca kidded. "Are you ever coming home? What *are* you doing?"

"Yeah, well, I needed to get away for a while. I didn't plan to be gone so long."

"Have you been good?" asked Becca.

"You know me, Becca. I try my best not to be good. Been partying with some friends."

Becca's brow furrowed, forming temporary crinkles at the bridge of her nose. "Friends? Without me?" It was said as a joke, but Becca felt a real slight.

"Loud music. Flashing lights. Hot bodies. Bad boys. Naughty girls. I'm in Miami. I'll be back some time tomorrow."

"Oh," said Becca, "okay. I'm glad you're having a good time." She didn't sound convincing. "I just miss my friend." She waited for Crystal to respond with similar sentiments. She didn't. "I met your boyfriend."

"Come again."

"I met your boyfriend. Gerald. Last night. Scrawny little Gerald." She dropped the description there. There was no way she'd recount everything Crystal had said about him.

"Oh, that boyfriend."

"Yeah, that boyfriend," said Becca, smiling. "He's not exactly as scrawny as you described him."

"I hear he's put on a little weight since I described him to you," said Crystal.

"A little," said Becca.

Crystal knew she couldn't let this drop as a joke. She had deliberately lied to Becca. "Look, Becca, I don't want to make any excuses about lying to you. I shouldn't have done it. But I did. I lied because I didn't want you to leave. I thought if I'd told you Hercules lived down the hall from you, you'd leave."

Hearing Crystal tell her she didn't want her to leave made up a little for the slight she felt for her going off to Miami with other friends. "He's your boyfriend, Crystal. Even a no-nun nun like me understands that."

"Why do you think he's my boyfriend? Remember I told you he's a male whore?"

"Yeah," said Becca, mentally scratching her head.

"That part was true."

"Oh."

"No, it's not a problem," said Crystal. "That's his thing, and he's upfront about it. But unless you're into open relationships—I mean *really* open relationships—he's nobody's boyfriend."

After a pause, Becca said with widened eyes, "Whoa."

"Now, why did you think my whore friend was my boyfriend? Because he's gorgeous?"

Becca wondered whether she should be truthful. "Have you— I mean, no. No. Not have you? I mean—"

"We're friends. If he needs me, I'm there for him. If I need him, he's there for me. It's no big deal. It's just sex. No strings. Friends taking care of friends. Doesn't even happen as often as you'd think it would. He's hardly ever at the house. And believe me, he's got lots and lots and lots of friends."

Becca didn't know that one side of her face had twisted. This was nasty and empty. It sounded like animals going at it. *Just sex? How do you give yourself to someone so intimately and call it just sex? What about love? What about God?*

Becca snapped out of it. The first part was her. That last thought, however, was a leftover of going to Grandma's church when she was several years younger. Would she ever be able to totally forget that Bible stuff? She didn't even recall ever memorizing the Scripture that was emblazoned in bright lights on the wall of her mind.

Marriage is honorable among all, and the bed undefiled; but fornicators and adulterers God will judge.

"So why'd you think Gerald is my boyfriend?" Crystal asked again.

Becca gladly left the irritation of that Scripture. "He, uhh, I was in the bathroom and he thought I was you."

Crystal didn't know whether to laugh or curse. "Oh, God, he pulled that lame crap again? That's the third time."

"What?" asked Becca.

"You were taking a shower, weren't you?"

Becca's eyes narrowed. She answered in a long, "Yeah."

"Let me see. You were taking a shower. He walked in on you and he thought you were me."

"That's—yeah, that's what happened."

"Was he naked?" asked Crystal.

"Yeah."

"Did anything happen?"

"No! No!" she answered more forcefully. "Nothing happened."

"He's not my boyfriend, remember? Everything's cool. I just—that snake—" Crystal shook her head. "I'm sorry, Becca. I told you when you first came over that he's a whore. I should have told you he's a tricky whore. He's done that naked man, *Crystal is that you?* routine before. He knows I'm in Miami."

Becca let out a stream of curse words and ended with, "Why would he do this?"

"First," said Crystal, "don't curse in public. Okay? You're not too good at it. Second, do I really need to answer that for you?"

There was a pause.

"Don't take it personal, Becca. Gerald really is a good guy. If you're his friend, he's there for you."

"Yeah, you told me."

"No. No. I don't mean like that," said Crystal. "I mean besides being a tricky whore who's always using that bat of his to hit homeruns, he's a good guy. He'll do anything for you. You just have to know what you're dealing with. And he'll be straight up with you."

"Like he was straight up with me in the shower?" asked Becca.

"He's a whore, Becca. That's who he is. Everyone has to choose their own friends. If that's not something you can deal with, don't. There's some people I won't deal with. They just don't fit. Maybe Gerald's somebody you don't want to deal with. That's cool. He'll be cool with it, too."

"Really?" asked Becca.

"Really. Like I said, he's got lots of girls. He's got 'em everywhere. Every city he plays, he's got girls."

"What do you mean, every city he plays?"

"He's got a band," said Crystal. "That's why he's not hardly at the house." She added, "If you didn't fall for that shower crap, that's the strongest you'll get from him. He'll never cross the line, if you know what I mean. He'll never try to force you or slip something in your drink or something like that. But!" she said with emphasis, "he will give you what he calls 'every opportunity to go to bed with him.'"

Becca felt like she was driving a car and had hit a patch of ice and was trying to recall whether to turn into or out of the spin. Should she brake or not. Doing nothing didn't stop the car's spin and momentum.

"But, Becca, I do need to tell you something," said Crystal. "You're not like me. You've been hurt, but you still got some heart left. I know you may not see it that way, but I'm pretty good at reading people. Gerald's not like a regular lay, okay? He's," she searched for the word and couldn't find it, "*different*. It's easy to lose your mind with him. That'll only happen though, if you still have some heart left. My heart's been gone a long time. So I'm safe. It's just good sex for me. But it'll be like heroin to you. Remember the story of Adam and Eve in the Garden of Eden? Sometimes it's best just to ignore the snake or to tell it to shut up."

Becca looked at her phone. Of all the examples in the world to use. Adam and Eve and the Garden of Eden? "So, are you telling me to not have sex with him? I mean I wasn't going to. And I don't even know him."

"I can't tell you or Gerald what to do. You're both grown. Do what you want to do, Becca. Just do it with your eyes open. Zombies like me live off of eating death. You're not a zombie, girlfriend. Eating death may kill what little life you have left."

Crystal was glad this had come up. It wasn't her nature to tell people how to live their lives. Everyone had his own life to live. But she felt responsible for Becca in a way she'd never felt responsible for anyone else. Plus, through some way she couldn't explain, she felt her fate was linked to Becca.

"Your food's getting cold," Gerald yelled upstairs.

Becca opened her door. "Okay, I'm coming. Just finishing a call." She returned to Crystal. "Your tricky whore boyfriend made breakfast."

"Slam him about that shower crap he tried to pull."

"I can do that?" asked Becca.

"Yeah. He won't get offended. He'll just laugh. Look, I gotta go. I'll see you tomorrow night."

"Okay. Bye," said Becca.

She went to the kitchen. There he was. Sitting at the table. There were two plates of food. He hadn't touched any of his.

"Good morning. I didn't want to eat without you. It's nothing fancy. Just a veggie omelette, hash browns, or you can do grits if you want. Or both. Wheat toast and juice."

"Good morning," said Becca. She wanted to be angry with him, but his smile was so beautiful. It could've disarmed an army of mad women. She wondered what she could say to him. Crystal said he'd just laugh at her. Oh well. "You're quite clever," she said, with a pleasant smile.

"Breakfast is an easy meal," he said. "I can reheat your food for you if you'd like."

"I'm not talking about breakfast."

"No?" He sipped his juice and put the glass down. "What are you talking about?"

"That was Crystal on the phone," she said innocently.

"Uh oh," he said, with a twinkle in his eye.

"She said you knew she was in Miami."

A faint smile crept onto one side of his face. His brown eyes squinted a little.

"Why'd you come into the bathroom when you knew I was taking a shower?" she asked.

The moment she asked the question, she wished she could take it back. This wasn't going as she had envisioned. Crystal had said he'd laugh. But she'd asked the wrong question. Oh, she didn't know what she was doing! She was way out of her league. She'd be eighteen in a few weeks, but this guy was probably five years older than her. She wanted to push away from the table and run upstairs and start over.

No, I'm not hungry. Thanks, but no thanks. Keep the lock on the door. Stay in her locked room until Crystal returned.

"If you talked to Crystal, we both know the answer to that question." He wore a short-sleeved shirt. He reached across the table and held her hand. He looked into her eyes. "And we both know why you asked...don't we?"

Becca dropped her eyes from his to break the spell. Her eyes fell upon the tattooed snake that twirled around his thick forearm. The snake's head rested on the back of Gerald's hand and was pointed at her with its mouth open.

Don't talk to the snake! she heard the angel's loud thought.

She pushed the chair back and abruptly stood up. *I have to get out of here.* Becca hurried out of the room.

Gerald smiled and said nothing. He continued with breakfast. He knew she'd be back.

Lust could have made his move before Becca pushed away from the table. But he was like a cat playing with a captured mouse. Oh, he was most definitely going to gobble her up. But he wanted to toy with her for just a little while. He'd show his power over her compromised will by making her come back to his man. Right there in that kitchen. She'd return like the slut he knew she was.

He let her get to the top of the stairs. "Call her," he said to Gerald.

"Becca." That was all Gerald said.

When the words entered her ears, Lust swung a tool that resembled a long club with a long, pointed iron hook on the end that was shaped similarly to that used for hunting seals and dragging them off. But Lust wasn't hunting a seal. He was hunting a girl.

Yet, in one way this was like hunting seals. It wasn't much of a hunt for a man to walk up to a dumb seal and crush his skull and then slam the hook into the carcass and drag it off.

That's what Lust was doing here. The girl was dumb and defenseless. She'd been warned. Several times. Had she listened? No. She deserved exactly what she was getting and more. For at least the seal would have tried to escape had it known the danger. But Becca had received warning after warning and rather than run away in terror, she had found the danger fascinating.

The long hook penetrated Becca's back and came out through her heart. Lust jerked hard on the tool. An eruption of lustful thoughts exploded in her mind. Becca stood at her door with her head lowered. Lust jerked hard again, but he was surprised that she didn't move one inch. He jerked and jerked and jerked. She didn't budge.

Rebellion stepped in to help. "How long are you going to live for other people? You said you were going to live for Becca!"

A lying spirit added, "This will help you. It's like Crystal said, as long as you go in with your eyes open, you'll be alright. You owe it to yourself."

Rejection spoke up. "This beautiful man wants you. You saw how he looked at you. How would it feel to be loved by this man? You need to do something to fix the pain in your heart."

"There is no good reason to not have good sex, Becca," said the lying spirit. "Maybe you and he can be friends…like he and Crystal are friends. Wouldn't it be good to have someone you can give yourself to?"

"This man wants you," said Rejection.

"Come talk to me, Becca," said Gerald.

Becca remembered the snake on the back of his hand. She remembered the dreams. She remembered the school musical.

She went downstairs.

Gerald swallowed the food he was chewing when he saw her. "Sit down, Becca." His words were tender, his expression inviting. "I'm glad you came back. I want to answer your question."

She sat down.

"You asked me why I entered the bathroom knowing that you were in there taking a shower."

Lust regurgitated into Gerald's mouth. Gerald spoke with an anointing from hell. He took his time explaining in great detail what he was going to do to her body and how she'd respond.

"Last chance, Becca!" screamed the angel. "Flee fornication! Flee now! I'll help you!"

Becca didn't want help. God had let her suffer enough. It was time for Becca to start living for Becca.

A bright orange flame erupted on her head. Another erupted on her chest, her crotch, and her buttocks. Then her whole body. She was gone. Engulfed in a flame of selfish desire and rebellion.

24

———

Gerald had expertly proven that he was as much magician and machine as he was man. He had also proven that he was a prophet. He had confidently told Becca what he would do to her body, and how desperately she'd respond. And he'd told her something else that at the time seemed pure masculine foolishness, if not comedy. He'd told her that he'd change her body's chemistry to crave his touch.

Three months later, the comedy wasn't funny. It wasn't even a comedy any longer. It was a psychological suspense. The question was no longer, *Is this guy serious?* It was, *My God, what did he do to me?* But although she did crave his touch, she knew it wasn't because he had changed her body's chemistry.

She wished it were biological. If it were, she could see it as a drug addict's craving. Serious, yet not necessarily incurable. But this was something far deeper than a change of chemistry. It was a change of whatever was at the core of her being.

That's what had changed only minutes after giving herself to Gerald. She had become in minutes all of the things she'd been promising and threatening to become. And now, even if she wanted to go back, she couldn't. Like jumping out of a plane. Even with a parachute, she could only go where the wind took her. And no matter how scenic the journey and exhilarating the ride, that inevitably, was down.

Crystal watched Becca toy with her turkey sausage. She'd barely touched her breakfast. She knew Becca saw Gerald's face in her plate. "How'd you manage to get Friday and Saturday off? That's like unheard of, you know? And why would you want to? Fridays and Saturdays are money nights. You don't like money any more?"

Becca knew Crystal was looking into her soul. She couldn't hide anything from her. She was like an urban mystic or something. But she liked it. It was nice having a friend so close that she knew her heart.

But right now, she didn't want the mystic looking into her soul. She didn't want to talk about it. It hurt too badly. She tried to deflect Crystal's small talk with a smile that had all of the substance of a skeleton. It could only be seen by imagining it.

"That is one sick smile, girl," said Crystal.

Becca rearranged the skeleton.

Crystal's face took on a studious expression. "Oh, I see it now. You're either smiling or about to throw up. You want to talk about it?"

"No."

"Good. Let's talk about it."

"I thought I said no," said Becca.

Crystal stretched her lips and eyes and shrugged. "That's for other people, not me." She turned her head sideways as she scanned Becca. "You know you're losing weight."

Becca pushed the sausage one way, then the other, but didn't say anything.

"Becca, you know I'm all into letting people have their own space."

"So I'm not a people?"

"No, you're not a people. You're a person. So you don't qualify."

Becca pushed the sausage away and put her fork down. She folded her arms over her chest and rested her chin on her forearm, looking at Crystal with the saddest eyes ever.

"I guess that's progress," said Crystal. "This problem started with sausage. I told you before you went to bed with him that he was different." Crystal really, really didn't want to do the *I told you so* thing, but she was as angry with herself as she was frustrated and heartbroken for her friend. Why did Becca have to go to bed with him? And why hadn't she done more to stop it from happening?

"I've never known a man like him," Becca whimpered.

Crystal thought on that one for a while. Her thoughts showed on her face.

"What?" asked Becca.

Crystal turned her face in a slight grimace as she inhaled deeply and exhaled. "A virgin hooking up with Gerald. That's like an Indian jumping into a swimming pool full of booze." She shook her head. "You never stood a chance. I tried to tell you."

"But it's not just sex, Crystal. It's more."

"No, Becca. It's not." Crystal's words were sharp. "Look, I'm not trying to be mean. And I'm not trying to kick you when you're down. But. It. Is. Only. Sex. I told you that before you went to bed with him, Becca. I told you that Gerald is a whore. Gerald told you that he is a whore. Now you want him to—what? Be your faithful boyfriend? You can't change the rules in the middle of the game."

"But I—"

"You what?" Crystal's words were sharp again. "You what, Becca? You love him? Is that what you're going to say?"

"Yes!" Becca snapped. "I love him! What's so wrong with that?" Then she added weakly. "I love him, Crystal. Why are you so angry that I love him? Do you have feelings for him, too?"

Crystal gave her head several short shakes in disbelief. "I told you that other girls had lost their minds after going to bed with Gerald. I never thought you'd be one of them. Are you serious?" She sounded exasperated and irritated. "Do I have feelings for Gerald? Of course, I have feelings for Gerald. I love him like an incestuous brother. He's got a big, soft heart and a big, hard bat. He hasn't made any promises, and I don't want any. And even if he did, he's incapable of keeping them. He's honest about that. So why would I care where he's swinging his bat?"

That is just sick, thought Becca. "Well, I don't want to be his incestuous sister," she said testily.

"Yeah, well what do you want to be? His one and only?"

"Is that too much to ask?"

"Yes, Becca!" Crystal answered sharply. "It's too much to ask."

"Why?" Becca demanded.

Crystal looked into Becca's soul again. "Let's get something out in the open here. Okay? I love you, Becca. You're really special to me. If Gerald makes you his one and only, you don't ever have to worry about me. It's not like he's my only option."

"You'd do that for me?" Becca asked, with watery eyes.

"Yes. I would. But listen to me, Becca. It's never going to happen."

"Why? Why would you say that? You think he's too old for me? I'm eighteen now. He's only five years older."

"Becca, why are we having this conversation?"

Crystal pulled her chair around the table to where Becca sat and turned the chair so its back faced Becca. Crystal sat with her arms resting on the back of the chair. But one of those arms was used to jab a finger at her friend as she spoke.

"We are having this conversation because you have forgotten everything I told you before you pulled the lion's tail. We are having this conversation because you have forgotten everything Gerald told you before you went to bed with him.

The reason it will never happen—listen to me Becca. I'm going to say this really slow. Gerald is a beautiful guy with a large heart. But he is a whore. This is what I told you before you went to bed with him. This is what I'm telling you now. Nothing's changed except Gerald has screwed your brain loose."

Becca dropped her head in thought. She said nothing for a long time. "But he's been so good to me."

"Oh. My. God. I am going to scream," said Crystal, her voice in a low monotone filled with frustration.

"No. No. No," Becca urged. "I'm not talking about the sex."

"I know what you're talking about, Becca. You're talking about him celebrating your birthday by inviting you to *Bismark's*, and then surprising you by having the band sing happy birthday to you. You're talking about him letting you use his car. You're talking about him bringing you back rum from Puerto Rico. You're talking about him getting you a job at a restaurant where you make two hundred dollars a day in tips. You're talking about him looking deeply into your eyes and talking to you as though you're the only person in the world.

"You're talking about him telling you how beautiful you are. You're talking about him walking by and putting those strong hands on your shoulders and tenderly squeezing them, and sniffing your hair with his eyes closed, and saying, 'Mmm, you smell so good.'" Crystal widened her eyes. "Am I anywhere in the right neighborhood?"

"Not just the neighborhood. You're in the house. That's exactly what I'm talking about. Why would he do those things if he doesn't feel the same way about me?"

"Becca, I already know the answer to this, and not because I've talked to Gerald. I haven't. I just know Gerald. I know he's done all those super sweet things to you and for you. But think hard." Crystal's tone had softened. She wasn't trying to hurt Becca. She was trying to get some sense into her head. "Has he at any time told you that he loves you?"

"What do you mean?"

"Other than being stupid enough to think you're the one girl in the world who can make Gerald a one-woman-man, we both know that you're not a stupid girl. So let's try being literal. Has he at any time told you that he loves you?"

Becca pushed air out as if this was a ridiculous question. "Crystal, he doesn't have to—"

"I'll take that as a no."

"No, he hasn't said with it his mouth that he loves me, but—"

Crystal finished her sentence for her. "But I'll say with *my* mouth that he loves me because...?"

Becca's brow furrowed at Crystal ignoring the obvious. "Because of everything you said. Crystal, he doesn't have to say it to feel it."

Crystal was already sitting close to Becca. She scooted her chair closer. "Becca, let me tell you something. A man will tell you that he loves you for one of two reasons. To get in your pants, or because he truly loves you." Crystal pulled her index finger back and rolled the fingers of both hands on the top of the chair's back.

Becca thought on Crystal's words. She'd gone to bed with Gerald without him telling her that he loved her. If Crystal was right, he'd tell her that he loved her only if he truly loved her. But she didn't want Crystal to be right. She needed to believe there was another possibility. "But why would he do all those things?"

"Because he's a good guy, Becca. And because he's so beautiful that he doesn't have to lie to girls to get them into the sack. If anything— and I've been with him to see this—he's got to lie to girls to get out of having sex with them. Maybe if he was average or ugly, he'd lie like every other guy. I don't know. I just know that he does those things because he's a nice guy. And he loves women. He likes doing things for them." She laughed to herself. "He likes doing things to them."

She shook her head at some of her own memories. "But he really loves women. So when he smells your hair, and when he gives you all of his attention when you speak to him, and when he makes a big deal over your birthday, or when he brings you back a gift from a trip... Becca, he's sincere. But don't interpret that as love. Don't ever assume that a man loves you."

"But if that is true, wouldn't he do that to every girl he goes to bed with?" asked Becca.

Crystal grinned and stretched her neck. "What you really mean is, why doesn't he do these things for me? Right?"

Becca's eyes widened in alarm and her mouth opened guiltily. "Crystal, I didn't mean—?

Crystal shook her head. "Pitiful. You can't cuss. You can't lie. You can't handle good sex. What's left? Guess I just have to grade you on the curve."

"Really," said Becca, still clinging to her lie, "I wasn't talking about you."

Crystal smiled knowingly. "Uh, yeah, right. The reason why he doesn't do that thoughtful, romantic stuff for me is I can't handle that crap. Messes with my mind. All I can handle is the sex. And sometimes, to be honest, if he catches me at a weak moment…" She shook her head. "It can be too much. So I just tell him I don't want to hear any of that lovey-dovey crap. Just screw me and hit the door. I mean, like I said, I love him like a brother, but I don't need a beautiful man whore sniffing my hair and telling me how beautiful I am. That crap ain't right. Messes with your head. Look at you. Perfect proof of what I'm saying."

Becca could hardly believe what she had heard. She looked aimlessly around the kitchen as though she were trying to connect dots.

"What?" asked Crystal.

"It's just that I never thought of you like that. I didn't think any guy, even Gerald, could mess with you like that. And what about what you said about being a zombie?"

"Look," Crystal's eyes narrowed into girlish mischievousness, "you and I both know that Gerald is not human. I don't know what he is, but he ain't no man. Probably was created in a government laboratory and they use him to bang secrets out of foreign female agents. If he catches me at a bad time, it can make me forget that I'm a zombie."

Becca reached over and rubbed Crystal's arm. "You're not a zombie, Crystal. You may sense nothing but death inside, but you're not a zombie. Zombie's don't feel pain. And I know you're in a lot of pain."

Crystal kept her game face on. But she thought, *Where did that come from?* And why did she suddenly feel like her secret had been exposed to the world. She felt the cloud of depression closing in on her. She had to get to her room. "Becca, give it up. Gerald loves you the way he loves every girl. You're only going to get hurt if you pursue this." Crystal stood. "I'm going to my room."

"I'm going to talk to him, Crystal. I'm going to tell him how I feel."

"What is the matter with you?" Crystal yelled. "Did you not hear anything I said? I am trying to help you."

"If I talk to him—"

"Stop it, Becca! This isn't television. It's not *The Bachelor.* This isn't about getting a rose. It's about you getting crushed." She shook her head with a grimaced face. "I'll tell you what will happen if you talk to him about this. I've seen it before, Becca. If you go to Gerald with this monogamy, *I love you, do you love me?* crap, he will cut you off like a cancer.

"Oh, he'll still be courteous to you because he's a nice guy. But you will have to wear a coat when he comes into the room, it'll be so cold. Is that what you want? You want to go from having a friend like Gerald to having him say hi to you just to be nice?"

Becca frowned as she shook her head. What Crystal was saying had to be false. She was making a mistake. Gerald loved her. If he only knew how she felt about him, he'd tell her that he loved her. He'd probably even ask her to marry him. She was only eighteen. So she didn't know how she was going to handle that. Maybe they could have a long engagement. There was no need to rush into marriage. But she would ask him to let her join the band. That way she could see him more.

"He wouldn't do that, Crystal."

Crystal wanted to scream some sense into Becca, but time was running out. The heaviness was already upon her and everything was already getting dark. She tenderly placed her hand on the side of Becca's face. She didn't smile, and she didn't try to fake a smile. It would have required too much energy. Energy that was draining out of her by the second.

"Becca, I wish I could help you more. You're going to be hurt. You're going to be hurt real bad. I should've done more earlier to keep this from happening. I'm sorry I didn't. Please forgive me. When it happens, I'll be there for you. Okay?"

"It's not going to happen like that, Crystal," Becca softly answered, terrified at Crystal's prophecy and hoping it was false.

Crystal felt the heaviness on her flesh now. She had to go. "Just remember what I said. I will be there for you. Don't do anything stupid after you talk to Gerald. Don't hurt yourself."

"Why would you say that?"

"I have to go." She turned and walked away, carrying an obese and suffocating spirit named *Trauma* that sat on her spirit.

"Why would you say that?" Becca asked again.

Crystal continued silently and darkly up the stairs in silence.

The angel who had warned Becca through Crystal left.

25

Boss Man's lucrative career in pimping had literally come to a flying stop when he had landed twelve feet up in a tree, compliments of Crystal Manning, or whatever she'd changed her last name to. He had briefly tried to reclaim his women, but found that niggas laughed at a broke-down ex-pimp who couldn't stop a dog from peeing on his paralyzed leg. And hoes didn't fear a nigga they could get away from simply by walking faster than his scooter could carry him.

Boss Man was pissed off!

Going after Ta-Nisha wasn't on his agenda. She wasn't the one who dropped him off in a tree. It was that crazy white girl. Besides, Ta-Nisha wasn't a good hoe anyway. And her brothers, Jolly and T-Bone, were out of prison. *How you gone kill somebody and be out in three years?* No need in getting those crazy niggas stirred up, especially with him sitting on a scooter. But if and when they went down, he was going to teach her a lesson.

But that white girl was a different story. She'd put her car into his business, and now his street name had gone from Boss Man to Scarecrow because of how he landed in the tree. Some nigga even got video of him hanging there and posted it online. You could hear the dude in the background laughing at him and cracking jokes. That's where the name Scarecrow had originally come from. Unfortunately, the video went viral and the name stuck. Now even the hoes called him Scarecrow.

That was alright, though. When his brother and his friends finally caught up with that white girl, he was going to make a scarecrow out of her. His brother had bumped into her at a restaurant at Ponce City Market. So he knew she was still in Atlanta. She was a bartender.

Atlanta was big, but it wasn't Chicago or New York City. They had a list of areas that had a lot of bars close to one another. Midtown. Downtown. Virginia Highland. Little Five Points. Hopefully, she was at a stand-alone bar and not a bar in a hotel or restaurant. They couldn't check every restaurant and hotel, but sooner or later they'd find her.

He thought he had her when he got a call one night from his brother. The car had rolled into the garage. The door lowered behind it. Boss Man had been sitting at the door in the kitchen and looking at the car. He had wanted that white girl to see him waiting on her.

The guy who had put the gun to her face jumped out and opened her door. He grabbed her by the hair and pulled. "Get out!"

Rachel's legs were so weak with fear that she had to struggle to stand. She felt a helping punch just above her eye. It didn't help. She fell back onto the seat. Two strong hands grabbed her roughly and jerked her up. She was manhandled forward. The blindfold came off. A man in a wheelchair was peering at her with a frown.

"Who are you?" said Boss Man.

"My name's Rachel. They think I'm Crystal," she whimpered.

"Say what?" said Boss Man's brother. "This ain't Crystal?"

"Naw, that ain't her!" he spat. "How you get the wrong girl?"

"Look at her hair and make-up, man. I was in there. I heard them call her Crystal. Look at her name tag."

If Boss Man could've walked, he would've stuck his foot knee deep in Jason's behind. He looked left and right about ten times in frustrated rage before he screamed, "I don't care what her name tag says. I know that hoe's face, and that ain't it!" He wheeled his chair backwards and slammed the door.

"I told you I'm not Crystal," said Rachel, with the barest hope that she'd be let go.

The three thugs looked at each other in shocked disbelief.

"I do not believe we got the wrong hoe," said one.

"You better believe it. She looking right at you," said another.

Rachel's trembling was strong. It was in her bones and it was in her voice. "What are you going to do with me? If you let me go, I swear I won't say anything to anyone."

The one who had put her in the car stepped forward with those same cold killer eyes. "I just got out of prison, sweetheart. I ain't going back."

Crystal had been lucky that time. Matter of fact, she had the kind of luck that was driving him crazy. They'd watched that bar several nights before finding out that the day they had snatched Rachel had been Crystal's last day on the job.

But her luck was running out. Boss Man could feel it. Just not in his legs.

Alone's eyes focused on the bubble-eyed demon who was running toward him and Unwanted like his life depended on it. He hit Unwanted on the arm, turning him around. "Trouble!" he said. "Must be those truth angels. The way he's running, maybe even mercy angels."

Unwanted's insides tightened. He looked at the demons atop the outer wall of the stronghold. They were calm. He squeezed Alone's arm and held it. "No. It's something else. Look at the outer wall."

"Yes," he said. "They're calm. Then what has spooked him like that?"

The running demon tripped over something thirty yards away and planted his face into a large rock that was half buried in the hard ground. He got to his feet and looked woozy, fighting comically not to fall out.

Unwanted and Alone watched this misfit with scorn.

"Eventually we'll find out if the idiot doesn't kill himself before reaching us," said Unwanted.

The demon finally reached them. His breathing was heavy and blood oozed from his forehead into his right eye. The spirit paid too much attention to the sledgehammer pain pounding his head. He took too much time trying to wipe away the blood that dripped into his eye.

"Well, what is it?" barked Alone. "And watch where you're flicking that worthless blood."

"I'm sorry. I'm sorry, my lords. I didn't mean—"

Alone snatched a knife from the sheath on his side and put it hard against the demon's throat. "I'd just as soon slit your throat for wasting my time as for being clumsy."

"Speak, you idiot! What's wrong?" demanded Unwanted.

"Inspection," he answered nervously, as he looked down and sideways where he felt the blade at his neck. "Stronghold Assessment Team...coming."

Unwanted's and Alone's eyes bulged.

"A SAT inspection? When? When?" yelled Unwanted.

"Speak, you idiot!" ordered Alone, his blade slicing a half inch into the terrified demon's neck.

"Now," the demon answered.

"Now?" yelled Unwanted and Alone.

"And we're just finding out?" hissed Alone. "How long have you known of this?"

"Only two minutes, my lord. The inspectors were asking me questions."

"Two minutes?" said Alone. "We should have known a minute and a half ago." He pressed his blade into the demon's neck and ripped backwards.

The unlucky demon dropped to the ground on his knees. He grabbed hard at his neck with both hands as though he could stop the torrent of dark liquid from pouring out.

Unwanted and Alone walked quickly toward one of the doors of the wall.

"What do you think brought this on?" asked Alone.

"Probably was that Elsie woman. Rumors are that when that fear stronghold fell, they started talking about increasing SAT inspections," said Unwanted. "I was hoping we'd have a little more time with Becca before we popped up on their list."

Alone looked up at the wall as they walked and lowered his head. "Don't look up," he said under his breath. "They're up there. Looking at us."

Unwanted couldn't help it. He snatched a quick glance. "Darkness!" he spat.

"We should pass the inspection?" said Alone. His words sounded like a plea for assurance.

"What more can be done?" Unwanted answered his unnerved friend. "We've done our part, and we've done it well. The only wild card is Nancy and Bill, and now Danielle."

Alone grabbed Unwanted's thick bicep and stopped. "That's enough of a wildcard to cause trouble."

"What can we do about praying Christians, but try to make them stop praying?" said Unwanted.

"That's not our area of responsibility," said Alone.

Unwanted's eyes bulged twice. "Exactly," he said. "Stopping prayer is not our responsibility. Our responsibility is this stronghold. We've done everything by the book."

They resumed walking.

I hope so, thought Alone.

Unwanted and Alone entered the dark entrance and took their strategic time walking up several flights of stone stairs. They whispered back and forth until they neared the door leading to the dimly lit hall. Unwanted reached for the door. It swung open before his hand touched the handle.

In the hall awaited a short demon wearing a costume fit for a circus. That was Unwanted's assessment. Alone's thoughts weren't too dissimilar from his friend's. He looked at the little demon and looked at Unwanted.

The little demon looked at Unwanted. "Who are you?" His question was filled with disrespect, if not outright contempt.

"I am Unwanted."

The demon looked into Alone's face and went down to his boots before restudying his clothes and landing on his face again. "Who are you?"

"I am Alone."

The little demon looked at them both. "Unwanted and Alone. Of course, you are. What else could you be?" He spun on his heels. "Follow me." His short legs took off in strides that under other circumstances would have earned a snicker from Alone.

Unwanted and Alone followed after the mouthy little demon.

Unwanted bent his neck toward Alone and whispered, "Looks like an extra from some two-bit Vegas show."

Alone whispered back. "I'd like to cram my boot up this midget peacock's mushy butt."

Unwanted smirked darkly. "He's a hybrid. Peacock and Leprechaun."

When they got to the door where the meeting was to be held, the little demon stepped aside. He motioned for Unwanted to go in. He did. Alone went to follow and the little demon put up a hand. The demon took the door's handle and looked around at questioning faces as he backed into the hall, pulling the door shut behind him.

Alone wondered why the midget wanted to talk to him in private.

The little demon looked up at Alone saying nothing, as though he was waiting on something.

Inspection or no inspection, five seconds of standing in the dark, locked in eye-to-eye combat with this footstool was enough for Alone. "Is there something on your mind?" said Alone, with only the faintest veneer of respect.

"Is there something you'd like to do?" said the little demon.

Something I'd like to do? What kind of a crazy half demon is this? Yeah, thought Alone, *I'd like to—* He stopped, wondering.

The little demon sensed his wonderings. "I can assure you, Alone, that it will be a lot easier for you to cram your boot up my mushy butt than it'll be for you to get it back. You can donate that leg now, if you'd like."

Alone knew he had stepped on a big pile of it this time. He would love nothing more than to gut this little peacock and to stuff an apple in his mouth. But it was always a horrible idea to get into it with an inspection team member. "I'm sorry if I offended you," he offered. "I guess it's just the suddenness of the SAT inspection that's got me on edge."

The apology had the effect of magic. "I understand," said the little demon. "A bad enough SAT score can cause blood to be spilled. Let's have a good inspection."

"So can we keep this indiscretion between us?" said Alone. "You won't tell the chief inspection officer?"

"Of course. Our little secret."

Alone let out the breath that his career was holding. *Close call*, he thought.

The little demon opened the door and extended his arm toward the room. Alone entered and went his way and the little demon went his way. Inside was a long rectangular table. Alone was surprised to see most of the chairs filled with demons from their stronghold. This was most peculiar.

Usually, inspections began with the inspection team giving an inbriefing to the stronghold commander and his number one demon, and perhaps one or two of the stronghold's key demons. Afterwards, the inspection team would visit various parts of the stronghold. They'd ask questions and observe demons in action. They'd also conduct various exercises concerning the stronghold's defensive capabilities.

Something different was going on here. The room was filled with maybe twenty of their own demons. They were seated on both sides of the table. One of the odd things was that members of the inspection team were on both sides of the table, side-by-side stronghold demons. Was this some new intimidation technique?

Another odd thing was that the seat that was saved for him was between two inspectors and directly across from an inspector. Unwanted was two chairs to his left.

Alone took his seat. *Hmm,* he thought. It made sense now. The inspectors had upped their game. They had representatives of every part of the stronghold here. They'd ask questions and get answers on the spot without giving him and Unwanted the benefit of communicating with stronghold officers and deceiving the inspection team.

"I am the chief inspection officer. My name is Carir-qilla. It is only a coincidence that my name sounds like career killer."

Alone heard the voice. His eyes widened. He slowly turned his head to the right, towards the voice. *The midget peacock was the chief inspection officer!* The only thing keeping him from turning to look at Unwanted was the inspector seated between them.

The first hour of the inbriefing was unlike any that Unwanted and Alone had ever seen. It wasn't an inbriefing. It was an oral castration and crucifixion of both of them, with Alone being the main target. Stronghold officers watched in stunned silence, wondering whether the chief inspection officer was saving any of this surprising rage for them.

"Someone better tell me something to convince me that the rest of this inspection isn't just a formality before we give you a failing grade." The chief inspection officer peered at Alone. "Because I'm inclined to believe that this stronghold is not up to standard."

A thousand questions. A thousand answers. None satisfactory.

Chief Inspector: "Tell us again, Unwanted. What is the overall stronghold strategy?"

Unwanted: A sigh of dejection. "Chief Inspector, the strategy is by the book. Becca was raised in an environment of extreme rejection. Some of it we caused. Some of it we facilitated. All of it we've used to remind her every day that she is unwanted and alone. We've made her believe the lie that God doesn't care and that He doesn't want her."

Chief Inspector: "How?"

Unwanted: "We keep the pain so bad that she can't think straight."

Chief Inspector: "What about the truth angels? We know they're trying to undermine you. What are you doing about them?"

Unwanted: "Lies. Do you want our officer—?"

Chief Inspector: "No! I don't want to hear from a lying spirit. I want to hear from the commander of this stronghold. What lies are you telling her?"

Unwanted: "We've deadened her soul and dulled her mind with the pain of extreme rejection. We've convinced her that if God loved her, He'd never allow this to happen."

Chief Inspector: "And she believes this? She doesn't blame us? She blames God? What about the cursed book?" He flipped through a pad. "She's read some of it. How can she get that conclusion from the cursed book? The book exposes us and sin as the problem."

Unwanted: "She's only read a little of it. Mostly years ago when she used to go to church with her grandmother. She's like most people. She ignores us and blames God for what we do."

Chief Inspector: "Wonderful history, Commander. But history is not strategy. I want to know what you're doing about today and tomorrow." His eyes focused on Alone. "What about you? Are you as much a history teacher as your commander? Or can I get a coherent two or three sentences of strategy from you?"

Alone: He fought against the dizzying swirl in his mind. His lips were dry and licking them didn't help. "We are using her pain to push her farther away from God and deeper into sin. When she was little, she did go to church and read the cursed book. But the older she got, the more she started disregarding God's Word. We have taken that natural rebellion and have convinced her that the bad things that have happened to her justify a life of sin. With the help of Lust, we have set her on fire and now she burns with our desires day and night. Unwanted and I are using the fire of lust and the hole in her heart to set her up to be crushed again. This time we'll not only deaden her soul. We'll rip it out of her body."

The chief inspector gazed at Alone for several seconds. "You surprise me." He looked at Unwanted. "You see? A strategy. Not history. Strategy. That wasn't hard at all." He looked around the room at his inspection team. "Maybe we'll have a good inspection after all. Let's get out of this room and inspect this stronghold. We'll see for ourselves whether Unwanted's stronghold is worthy of the name *stronghold,* or whether we've been talking to two lying spirits."

Unwanted and Alone fumed in silence at the laughter and

bouncing shoulders of inspectors who thought the jokes of their little leader were hilarious.

The inspection was over.

Unwanted knew from the little leprechaun's half grin that he wasn't going to like the score. He took the paper from his hand and looked at his friend, Alone, before studying the paper for its most important score. He knew it wouldn't be a hundred. No one got a hundred.

Chief inspectors knew how the game was played. When a so-called stronghold was certified as impregnable, and subsequently was badly damaged or destroyed by love, forgiveness, prayer and fasting, or some other wicked device of the enemy, the first question asked was, "Who certified the stronghold?" So, uh uh. No...way...Jo...se. A hundred earned you a ninety-nine. If the inspector had been burned in the past, maybe even a ninety-eight or ninety-seven.

Unwanted's eyes glared at the two digits. He felt the whole room full of inspectors and stronghold demons focus on his trembling hand. He tried to steady his hand, but the score of 89 before his eyes and on that official document was like touching a live wire.

Anger, no, it was rage, shook his powerful arm. He saw himself beating the little peacock to near death, then tearing open that stupid orange and green jacket. He'd stick his blade into his fat belly and slowly rip upward. He'd reach into the open wound and pull the little peacock's skin apart, allowing his innards to—

"Unwanted!" the chief inspector yelled again, interrupting Unwanted's murderous thoughts.

"It is an 89," Unwanted said, his voice low and foreboding. "You gave us an 89."

"Eighty-nine!" screamed Alone, jumping up.

When he jumped up, every inspector jumped up. In response, the stronghold demons jumped up. Nervous and calculating eyes surveyed the threats on their left and right as their backs tried to find a wall. Fingers wiggled, as if in a state of deliberation. The inspectors and stronghold demons watched one another, wondering who would make the first move.

"Do you really want to do this?" asked the chief inspector.

Unwanted pressed past his fury. "Sit," he said to his demons without looking at them.

They looked warily at the inspectors.

"Sit," the chief inspector said to his crew.

The stronghold demons and inspectors sat.

"You gave us an 89," said Unwanted. "It takes at least a 90 to qualify as a stronghold."

The peacock spread his wings. He stood as tall as he could as he glared up into Unwanted's scowling face. "I did not *give* you an 89. You *earned* an 89." Unwanted opened his mouth and the peacock cut him off sharply. "This girl has prayer support! And there are angels of truth everywhere! She's down, but she's not out!"

Why you little piece of crap, Unwanted thought in silent fury. "We have no control over prayer or truth! You're not here to grade us for what Nancy and that bunch does! Or for what a blasted angel of truth does! You're here to grade us for what we do! What—we—do!"

The peacock knew that he had to cover his butt. Unwanted would definitely appeal his rating. "The *structure* is not a total loss," said the peacock. Unwanted could've spit on the little monster for calling his stronghold a *structure*. "But as you know, a large part of your grade is based on an assessment of your defenses. You deserve credit for the damage you've done, but tell me—no, tell us what you will do when those prayers and angels of truth directly attack your…*structure?*"

Unwanted stood there in front of everyone, unbelievably feeling smaller than the demonic runt he towered over. He had been bested by the little creep. The stronghold hadn't yet been directly attacked. But it was just a matter of time. Those truth angels were proof of that.

"I will take your silence as your reluctant agreement that although Becca is in bad shape, she's not as bad as she needs to be." The peacock's eyes narrowed. "You were correct about prayer and truth. *You* can't stop them." He paused. "But Becca can. God won't force her to be free. You need to hit her so hard that she refuses the power of prayer and the light of truth. Do that and you'll get your stronghold status back. We'll be back in ninety days for the reassessment."

Unwanted looked at Alone and said to the peacock. "We'll have it done in a week."

27

Crystal had asked Becca why she requested to be off Friday and Saturday—the money days at the restaurant. Becca gave no details, but she had plans. Big plans. That's why. She stepped into the tattoo parlor with that plan.

"Becca," her name sounded the moment she entered.

Becca smiled widely with bright eyes. It was Elana. The tattoo artist she had spoken to the first time she'd come here.

The angel of truth didn't touch Elana with his hand, but he was touching her with his presence. He followed her movements a few feet from her, speaking to her heart and using painful memories to stir her emotions.

"I'm back," said Becca. "I told you I would be." Becca wondered at the expression that flashed across the girl's face and disappeared before she was sure of what she was seeing. Was it a look of sadness? Regret? Disappointment? A mixture of all three?

"*Hel-lo.* You did," said Elana. She approached Becca with her own wide smile and her arms spread as though she were greeting a long lost friend. The girl's arms wrapped around Becca in a tight hug. "I've been thinking about you off and on since you came in."

Becca's eyes twinkled at the greeting. The girl had greeted her this way when she had first met her at the shop a couple of days ago. She had thought the instant rapport behavior a bit odd, but then she saw her greet other people similarly. Like she was great friends with everyone, even strangers. The girl's warmth made Becca dismiss her misgivings about the odd expression she thought she had seen on Elana's face a few moments ago.

"You have?" asked Becca. "You've been thinking about me?"

"Yes, I was wondering whether you'd return."

"Oh, yeah. I'm doing this," said Becca, smiling and looking for that automatic seller's smile and nod from Elana.

That odd expression flashed again. Or did it?

Elana looked at her warmly and reached out and squeezed Becca's shoulder. The girl smiled softly. But the smile seemed to be sending a masked message. Like a kidnapped hostage trying to communicate her position to others in the presence of the kidnapper. "Come with me," she said.

Becca followed her down a hall, wondering at the girl's appearance. Elana was a couple of inches taller than the typical Polish female at five foot seven. Her shoulder length hair was as black as could be. She was beautiful, and had an accent that Becca knew must've driven guys absolutely insane with desire. Compliments of a short, sleeveless dress, Becca looked at the girl's bare back and legs. A tattoo artist with no tattoos. That was really different.

Elana sat before a computer, and with a smile she pointed to the chair next to her desk. She punched a few keys and pulled up a folder and clicked on it. She double-clicked an image and a slideshow of tattoos began.

Becca's breath quickened. Her eyes fastened on each image as though selecting the right one would give her Gerald. The last image grabbed her eyelids and yanked them wide. "That's it!" she said, with a gasp. "You did it! You're brilliant!"

Elana smiled and turned her head slightly in disagreement. "This is not a tattoo. It is a picture of a tattoo. You gave me the picture," she said, with a thrust of her head. "I just modified it some."

Becca pulled out her phone and pulled up a picture. It was a picture of Gerald's arm. She'd taken this photo of his tattoo when he had fallen asleep after one of their marathon sessions. That night, as she watched the beautiful superman of a man sleep, she knew that she could never live without him. He didn't just fill her body; he filled her soul. He plugged the hole from which her life leaked. So she had decided to get a tattoo that matched his.

"Yeah, but it's perfect," Becca said dreamily.

The angel of truth placed his hand lightly around the base of Elana's neck and spoke closely to her ear.

"You still want to surprise him?" asked Elana. "It is a huge decision to get a tattoo. Tattoos are permanent."

"My feelings for my fiancé are permanent."

"What about his feelings for you?"

The question surprised Becca. She was here to get a tattoo, not to be counseled. "Elana…" Becca was sorting her rebuttal.

Elana smiled understandingly and rolled her chair closer to Becca. She took Becca's hand. Becca looked at her with surprise. Elana was maybe twenty-five years old. Yet Becca felt as though her hand was being enveloped by a loving mother or grandmother, full of wisdom and love.

This is nuts, thought Becca. *I just want a tattoo.*

"You are spending good money, Becca." Elana squeezed her hand. "I am very expensive. You know this. You can get a good tattoo at *Mystic Man* or *Magic Ink* or *Joe's Ink & Piercings* for half the price. You came to me because quite frankly I am the best. You see how my customers love me. They love me because of my skill and because I love them. I love my customers. That is why I am nosey." She smiled and shrugged. "I am a sensory artist. I need to feel what you feel. I turn your feelings and desires into a beautiful image."

Everything Elana said was true. What she left unspoken was that the moment she had laid eyes on Becca two days ago, it happened all over again—in a moment's time.

She was back in Vegas. Lying on the floor, sobbing at his feet and literally begging him not to leave. She'd been willing to do anything to keep him. Even trade her dignity for the scraps of his leftovers. He didn't want her, and her refusal to admit this to herself cost her her self-respect and almost cost her life itself. It had been the darkest episode of her life.

And for some strange reason, this customer, Becca, revived the memories and pain of a time she couldn't forget and of a wound that wouldn't heal. Perhaps even more strange was the near irresistible urge to share her experience with this girl.

"I understand," said Elana. "You came for a tattoo. You did not come for counseling."

Exactly right, thought Becca.

"If we do your tattoo—"

Becca panicked silently at the *if*. What did she mean *if*? She *had* to get this tattoo!

Elana continued, "—it will be with you the rest of your life. I don't want you to have any regrets."

Becca felt like she was now auditioning to have this girl do her tattoo. This was crazy. She had the money. She was there. Why was she having to talk her into taking her money? "I won't have any regrets. He's my fiancé. We love one another."

"Does he know he's your fiancé?" she asked softly.

Becca was devastated by the question. Elana's voice was soft and her words meant well. But they were like beautiful flowers in a heavy vase accidently knocked off a three-story ledge. The flowers landed dead center on Becca, not killing her, but knocking her totally senseless.

She knew what Becca's silence meant. "I have a tattoo," Elana said to the girl whose head was spinning.

"You do?"

"Yeah. It's in a place you cannot see."

Does he know he's your fiancé? rolled noisily in Becca's mind like a wagon half-filled with empty tin cans and hitting every bump in the road.

"I wish I could get rid of it, but I can't. It's with me forever." *It's branded on my heart. Killing me. Suffocating me. Laughing at me as its hands are wrapped around my throat and squeezing the life out of me.* "Tattoos often last longer than relationships. That is why I ask you these questions. I want you to be happy with my art."

Becca shook herself inwardly and hardened her heart. She was going to get Gerald with or without this tattoo artist. If she didn't want her money, she'd go somewhere else. "I'm sorry to hear that. I want the tattoo of this snake wrapped around my whole arm, just as we discussed. I want his mouth opened wide on the back of my hand, just like Gerald's snake. I want *Gerald's Girl* put where we discussed. Can we get started now? I need to have this done in time for his show."

"It is an open wound," said Elana.

"You have an open wound," the truth angel shouted to Becca.

The flower pot hit Becca again. *She saw them walking away at the musical. Every act of their indifference to her. Every act of ignoring her. Both attempts to kill her at the abortion clinic. They all were wrapped up in that one humiliating night of them leaving her there on stage.* She felt the beginnings of a low throb in her arm.

"I do *not* have an open wound, Elana. I'm just a customer who wants tattoos." Becca's voice was more defensive than she realized.

Elana looked at her quizzically. "Open wound? I did not say you have an open wound. Your tattoos. You asked could they be done in time for your boyfriend's show. *Tattoos* are open wounds. You have to take care of them, as I explained when you came in the other day, or they will not turn out as well. If you don't take care them, they can get infected and even cause serious health issues. They'll have to be bandaged. And we'll anticipate two to three weeks for proper healing. But you'll be able to remove the bandages in two to four hours and show them off."

The angel of truth lifted something to Becca's ear that resembled a bullhorn. He hoped that he'd be able to cut through the noise pollution of her pain, lust, and growing rebellion. "You have an open wound, Becca!" he screamed. "You are infected! You have to properly care for it! You can't get rid of the pain of sin by adding more sin! The way of the sinner is hard, Becca! Cry out to your grandmother's God! He is gracious and full of mercy! It is written, 'When my father and mother forsake me, then the Lord will take me up! Now is the day of salvation! Do not harden your heart! Becca, how shall you escape if you neglect so great a salvation?"

In accordance with the laws of God, the angel lowered the horn. Any more and he would exert too much influence on her will. He could help her, but he couldn't coerce her. He was an angel, not a demon. So as it was recorded with King Hezekiah in 2 Chronicles 32, he left her so that all that was in her heart would be exposed in the light.

Becca wondered at the competing thoughts.

Go after God.

Or go after Gerald

.

28

B ecca was going after Gerald.
    She had to have him.
He filled the hole in her heart.

Becca knew how Crystal felt about her going after Gerald. *Don't do it! You're going to be crushed!* she had told her a hundred different times and ways. She knew Crystal loved her and didn't want to see her hurt. *At least there was one person in the world besides Gerald who cared about her.* But Crystal didn't understand. She and Gerald had something special. She looked approvingly at the snake that wrapped itself around her slender arm. His open mouth and bared fangs on the back of her hand evoked a smile.

Becca missed Crystal whenever she disappeared on one of her mysterious trips. She still didn't know how her friend got money. It had to have something to do with her trips. But that was for another time. She was just happy that she was gone and that she wouldn't have to endure another scolding from Crystal. The last time it had gotten completely out of hand and they'd both said things they regretted.

Becca put the suitcase into the car. Her car. Formerly Gerald's car. He could've asked for more, but he hadn't. She smiled. Crystal just didn't understand. She closed the trunk and felt the warmth of the metal. She rested both palms on its warm top and let the warmth against her hands feed into the warmth of seeing Gerald, of surprising him in front of everyone. She didn't know that her thoughts had closed her eyes. She inhaled a deep breath of happiness and after a few moments of fantasizing, it dawned on her that she was standing behind her car with closed eyes and a large smile on her face.

Oh, baby, I'm going to make you pay for what you're doing to me, she thought, envisioning things that would've broken her grandmother's heart. Becca hurried around the car and hopped in. She thought of the suitcase in the trunk, and what must have been an invisible Crystal, said to her mind, *What in the world are you doing with that suitcase?*

The invisible Crystal had a point. Maybe it was a bit presumptuous, but she had to anticipate that Gerald may be so happy with her surprise that he'd ask her to stay with him for the remainder of his Charleston gig. He may even ask her to stick around for the Charlotte gig. Maybe even longer. She'd have to be ready.

The car started. She looked at the snake's open mouth, put the car in gear, and pulled off.

It was time to prove Crystal wrong.

Crystal saw the suitcase from half a block away. Alarm seized her heart. She knew exactly what Becca was planning. She had to stop her! She went to floor the gas pedal.

The angel of truth touched her ankle.

Crystal didn't understand the feeling that fell upon her. It definitely wasn't peace. It was more like a calm regulating her fear, telling her that she mustn't interfere. She'd told Becca repeatedly that the light she saw in the tunnel was an approaching train. But somehow Becca overlooked the rumbling on the tracks and the deafening sound of the horn and found a way to interpret the train's light as a lighthouse, beckoning her, reaching out in the darkness to save her from her dark wanderings and from crashing against the rocks of emptiness.

It went against every natural tendency Crystal had to help her friends. *Friends didn't forsake friends!* But as she watched her friend lean against the trunk of the car, she read the look of foolish bliss on her face. There was no way to stop a person from believing a lie if they were determined to do so. The only way to save Becca—hopefully, that's how it would end—was to leave her alone. She had to let Becca enter the dark tunnel and see for herself that the light she saw was a train and not a lighthouse.

Crystal had already pulled the car to the right side. Now she parked in front of the house. She watched Becca drive toward her. She lay across her seat to hide from her. But she knew that Becca was in a world of fantasy. If she couldn't see a train, she wouldn't see her car.

She was right. The car went by her. She raised and looked in the mirror at Becca's car. Her chest heaved and tears poured out. "It's a train, Becca. Please don't do this."

———

Gabron's eyes communicated his thoughts and fears. He didn't have to say anything.

"Gabron," said Mark, the truth angel that sometimes appeared to him and Becca's other two angels, "you are concerned for Becca."

"She is headed for disaster," said Gabron. "Why did Alphus stop Crystal? She might've been able to stop her."

"You can only slay the dragon you know of," said Mark.

Gabron's intense eyes begged for more.

"King Hezekiah was a good man of God. He served the Lord faithfully and loved Him," said Mark.

Gabron nodded with a smile that was just beneath the surface of his face. "It is amazing that such a good king was able to come from such a wicked father as Ahaz."

"But even the great Hezekiah had weaknesses."

Sadness pushed itself onto Gabron's face. "Pride."

"He did humble himself before the Lord and recover," said Mark.

"Eventually. Hezekiah didn't know the pride was there until God left him so that all his heart would be manifest."

Gabron thought of how God filled everything. He wasn't like angels who were either here or there. His Spirit was everywhere. And besides his own experience, there was the testimony of the blessed book. Hadn't David written in the psalm, "Where can I go from Your Spirit? Or where can I flee from Your presence? If I ascend into heaven, You are there; if I make my bed in hell, behold, You are there."

Mark saw the ponderings on Gabron's face. "Yes, Gabron, the Creator is everywhere. We know He does not come and go as you and I. I am speaking of His manifest presence. Think of His dealings with Abraham and Moses. He visited Abraham and ate a meal with him. He met with Moses in a burning bush and later on the mountain.

Gabron looked at the truth angel, reaching into his own memory to discover what he was overlooking. He knew of no such visitation of God to Hezekiah. So how could God have left Him. "The king had wonderful answers to prayer...and Isaiah... I still do not see where God left Hezekiah."

The truth angel's eyes brightened with the intensity of revelation. "God's manifest presence can be literal, as it was with Him eating a meal with Abraham or with Him meeting with Moses in the darkness of the burning, smoke-filled mountain. His manifest presence can also be the peace of His fellowship you feel in your soul. It can be the inner witness telling you throughout the day that you are His. It can be the Holy Spirit reminding you of the words of God. It can be many things. The point is that if He stops manifesting His presence to His servants, they can no longer serve Him on the strength of what they feel or sense."

It clicked.

"They'd have to walk by faith," said Gabron. "'We walk by faith, not by sight,'" he said.

The angel of truth nodded. "Yes. 'The just shall live by faith,'" he added. "Most sons and daughters of God know that He can and does use hard times to test their faith. Yet, only a few understand that He also uses good times and blessings to try their hearts. Blessings are just as lethal as curses. Most people fail the test of prosperity. God removed His manifest presence from Hezekiah and left him with nothing but prosperity. This condition exposed the dragon in Hezekiah's heart."

Gabron didn't know which to ask first. How did prosperity reveal Hezekiah's dragon? Or, what did that have to do with Becca? "But prosperity...I don't see how prosperity—"

Mark interrupted. "Gabron, my brother, it is not about prosperity or poverty, blessings or curses. It's about what a person does when he or she is left to follow his or her own heart. Becca will never learn of the dragon in her heart unless she sees it. And she will never see it unless it is forced out of its cave."

"But if the dragon is forced into the open..." Gabron shook his head in thought.

"Yes. Dragons are dangerous. But ignoring the dragon of sin is never an option, Gabron. Becca must be allowed to go her own way and to see the evilness and emptiness of sin. Only then will the truth be revealed. It is the truth that can set her free."

"Will she see the truth?" asked Gabron. "Will the truth set her free?"

"Bill and Nancy and Danielle are praying for her," said Mark. "Angels are working to force her to see the truth."

"So she will be saved!" Gabron said, hopefully. "Once she sees the truth..." Gabron gave short fist pumps to himself.

The angel of truth straightened himself, standing more erect. "The preaching of the gospel is to those who perish, foolishness, but to those who are saved, it is the power of God."

Alarm returned to Gabron's eyes. "But surely after seeing the truth, Becca wouldn't consider it foolishness. No, Mark. No!"

The angel seemed to grow in height as his posture got even more erect and rigid. "To some, the gospel is a sweet smelling savor unto life. To others, it is the stench of death. The truth will be to Becca what she allows it to be."

"But the prayers?" Gabron pleaded.

"The prayers are to delay God's judgment while the angels work with the Holy Spirit to open her eyes to the truth. But once her eyes are open, it is up to her to choose life or death, blessings or curses."

"I hope she chooses life," said Gabron.

Becca's face carried a smile for three hundred miles. She couldn't get to Charleston fast enough. When she saw the *Welcome to South Carolina* sign, she screamed. When she entered Charleston, she screamed again and kissed the snake on her hand and yelled, "Oh yeah! We're here, baby!"

Becca had never been so excited. Tonight her life was going to change forever. In front of everyone. She knew that thoughts of Gerald asking her tonight to marry him in response to her surprise were wild, but they wouldn't be tamed. She ignored them as best she could and tried to focus instead on just being his girl, going on the road, maybe singing some, and just having a great time with a great guy.

There was one thought, however, that elbowed its way to the front and gained a ready audience with her. *Her family didn't want or love her, but someone did.* Becca's face hardened in anger and resolve. She parked the car on Battery Row across the street from its famous waterfront antebellum mansions that overlooked the meeting place of the Cooper and Ashley rivers.

The next time they saw her, they wouldn't see a helpless little girl holding her aching arm and begging for love. They'd see a strong, independent woman with her own life. She couldn't wait to show them all how strong she'd become. And when that day came that she and Gerald did marry, they wouldn't be invited to the wedding—not that they would want to come anyway. But she'd be sure to send them all plenty of pictures. She'd send them pictures of their grandchildren, too. Grandchildren that they'd never touch. *Monsters like them can't be trusted. They don't deserve children or grandchildren.*

She made this declaration knowing that her parents wouldn't want anything to do with her children. This only infuriated her more. How she hated them!

Something tugged at her heart. *Something for them!* She screamed curse words at the monsters who wouldn't get out of her heart. *Why won't this feeling leave? I don't need them!* She thought of how she'd been ignored and despised by her own parents all her life. She thought of how vulnerable and helpless she'd always been. She thought of thousands of times she'd ask herself in tears why her parents hated her. She acknowledged in horror and shame that there was still something inside of her begging for their acceptance and love. *Get out of my mind!* She clasped her head. "God, please make them get out of my mind," she begged.

Gabron's head whipped around in every direction. He looked momentarily at Krasa and Justis. "She asked for help." He looked toward the heavens and shouted, "Mercy, Lord!"

The response from heaven was immediate.

"She will receive mercy tonight," a voice sounded from the sky.

29

The last residue of anger and self-pity disappeared from her heart when Becca saw the sign of the club from across the street. For a moment, she simply stood still and looked, enjoying the breeze that circulated the evening's seventy-eight-degree temperature.

Kenny's Place.

She smiled and looked both ways and crossed the street to join others who were in a short line waiting to show their IDs. She'd gotten a decent fake ID, compliments of one of Crystal's friend of a friend of a friend connections. No *I paid fifty bucks for this fake crap ID* for her. The extra money she'd paid had been well worth it.

The bouncer looked at her Georgia's driver's license and her confident smile and said, "Enjoy your evening."

"Thanks. I will," she said.

Wow. The place was huge. She wondered that a city like Charleston could have a place like this. A big city, yes. But Charleston? She looked at the dancing bodies. People totally absorbed in the music that was coming from *her boyfriend's band.* How cool was that?

Becca looked at her fiancé on stage and almost couldn't believe that he belonged to her. He was so beautiful. He had let his hair grow until it reached his wide shoulders. Hadn't she mentioned to him when his hair had been shorter that she'd love to see it longer? Now it was. And it was hot! He was hot!

His tight, black, v-neck t-shirt displayed his large, well-defined muscles. His bicep bounced every time he bounced his mic hand. Thick thighs pressed mercilessly against his tight black pants that hugged a narrow waist.

Becca was mesmerized as she watched the object of her hypnosis. A hard blink and she snapped out of it. Good thing, too. It was dark in there, but the whole idea was to surprise him. She lowered her head and found a seat. Everything was going great. She rolled up the long sleeve of her black blouse and looked at the most beautiful snake in the world.

"Hi there," she said to it.

Don't talk to snakes.

Her eyebrows moved with her narrowed eyes. Where had she heard that? The memory escaped her. Whatever. She was ready. Her black blouse and black pants and black shoes and black jewelry matched the all-black attire of Gerald's band. Now all she had to do was wait for the right moment. She smiled at the idea that popped into her excited mind. *Yeah, that'll work.*

She studied her fiancé's every sexy move with an approving grin.

The three angels searched the club for any sign of mercy angels.

"Where are they?" Gabron asked. "I don't see anything but demons. Becca has suffered so much. She needs mercy."

"That doesn't mean they aren't here," Justis said. "If God said they'd be here, they're either here, or they soon will be. We have to trust the word of the Lord."

It was time.

Becca's moment of truth.

Rejection and pain had been her past.

Love and joy would be her future…in just a few minutes.

Intermission was almost over. Becca was just about to get up and head for the stage stairs when she had an overwhelming feeling that she was being watched. She looked in every direction.

There were at least two sets of male eyeballs fixed on her. One of the guys was hot. She smiled inwardly. He was a birthday candle. But Gerald was a flaming torch. *Already taken,* she thought warmly.

Becca walked toward the stage stairs and froze when she saw the big bouncer standing near it. How had she not seen him? She looked to the left. Another one! *Oh no! Just like that? It's over? How am I going to get past them?* thought Becca.

Birthday.

Becca's sinking heart grabbed a vine to pull itself out of the swallowing quicksand. "Yes. Yes. Yes." The words blew out of her mouth in a low rush. "That's it." She didn't want to do it, but time was running out. She had to get up there. She pulled out her phone and punched the numbers. "Please, Danny. Please, Danny. Please, Danny. Just answer. Don't say anything. Just answer."

"Becca?"

"Danny, does Gerald know it's me?" she asked with enough anxiety to pop a blood vessel.

"Naw, he's helping Casey. She's sick as a dog. I can get—"

"No!" she screamed in a hush. "It's a surprise. Please don't say anything."

"Okay. What's up?"

"I'm here."

"Here, where?"

"Here. *Kenny's Place.* At the club. I'm here."

"You serious? Are you freaking serious?"

"Danny, please don't say anything to Gerald. It's a surprise," she begged.

Danny rolled his hand over his greasy spiked hair. He couldn't believe their luck. He walked to a corner and spoke low, but excitedly into the phone. "You're here. In the club. Right this friggin' minute? *Kenny's Place?*"

"Yeah," she said. "I need to get onstage. I have a surprise for Gerald."

"Oh, yeah. Oh…yeah, you can get onstage. Everybody's in the back with Casey. She's throwing up everything that ain't nailed down. You've been wanting to sing with us. Guess what, girl? You're taking Casey's place. I think you know all but two of the songs we're doing. We can change those. You know *Just Gimme Love?*"

Becca could've fainted from joy, but she wasn't going to. This was going better than she could have ever planned. "Yeah!" she said, pumping her feet on the floor like pistons.

"What about *Only You Will Do?*"

"Yeah. I know that one, too. I can do them both."

Danny whipped his hand furiously back and forth in his hair. He cursed with relief. "I just can't believe this. Somebody must be living right." He laughed. "It sure ain't me." He paused. "What are you wearing?"

Becca smiled. "Black pants." She paused. "Black blouse." She paused. "Black shoes." She paused. "Black jewelry."

Danny was silent for a few seconds. "Are—you—serious?" He yelled a curse word to himself. "Girl, you came ready. I'm going to ask Gerald tomorrow what color panties and bra you had on."

She smiled mischievously. "Black and black."

"Well you just bring all that black stage left," said Danny. "I'll meet you there."

Danny snuck Becca into a side room and kissed her on the forehead. He looked at her one last time and pinched her arm, then his own, and left shaking his head disbelievingly. "God is good," he said.

Gerald looked across the stage and gave Danny a look that was both desperate and hopeful. He had worked hard to get this gig and now it was sinking fast. But tough guy Danny had gone from nearly crying like a little girl to acting like he was Batman. "Everything's under control, Bro. I got this," he had said.

Danny looked at his nervous friend, winked, and blew him a kiss.

Uh huh, said Gerald's expression. He looked at each member of the band. Sheila was nervous. She shrugged and made a weird face. Blake was mouthing, "What the—?" *Exactly,* thought Gerald, joining Blake's silent cursing. Nice to know he wasn't the only one nervous. Danny was the only one on crack.

Gerald saw in his mind's eye Redd Foxx playing the character of Fred on *Sanford and Son* clutching his chest and looking up to heaven with a raised arm, saying, "Oh, this is the big one! You hear that Elizabeth? I'm coming to join you, honey."

Gerald didn't clutch his chest. He just shook his head. *Whatever,* he thought. *It is what it is.* He lifted his hand, knowing that when he brought it down, the band would be skiing downhill with a missing ski. A last, desperate, *if we weren't best friends since the third grade* look at Danny before dropping his hand.

Another stupid, "Trust me, bro," smile from Danny.

Gerald looked at the mic stand where Casey was not. His hand came down. A black blur streaked from the back and snatched Casey's mic from its stand. It was a girl. She doubled over and bounced her shoulders and wiggled her hips with the beat. Long black hair hung from her bobbing head. Gerald still couldn't see who the girl was. *Who the heck are you?* his burrowing eyes asked, as his mind searched for possibilities.

The girl's face was hidden by her swinging, bouncing hair. Behind the hair a long, deep growl exploded into a soulful cry.

What kinda love is this?

A look.

A touch.

A kiss.

Gerald should have immediately known by the long black hair of the tall girl who it was. But the predicament he was in had blocked his mind. And Charleston. They were in Charleston, South Carolina! What in the world was Becca doing in Charleston?

She looked at him with a sexy smile and sang, "It's everything I miss."

Who cares what she's doing here? thought Gerald.

Crisis over!

The cavalry was here!

Gerald and Becca bounced with the beat, their faces nearly touching as they sang:

What kinda love is this?

A look.

A touch.

A kiss.

It's everything I miss.

Becca turned and bounced her butt at him in time for him to smack it when they both sang the next line.

Want me some midnight bliss.

Perfect chemistry. Perfect timing. Perfect spontaneity. The only thing that could make the night more perfect was her surprise.

Perfect love.

––––––––

After the third song, he rolled his eyes at the *Happy Birthday* tune he heard. He looked at Danny and said with his lips, "I'm going to kick your —"

Danny gave a wicked grin and put his hand to his ear and stretched his neck in Gerald's direction. "Can't hear you, Bro," he shrugged with his hands.

"Yeah, right," said Gerald, suffering through it. He was the happiest man alive when everybody stopped singing *Happy Birthday. Thank God birthdays only happen once a year,* he thought.

At the last *Happy Birthday to you* Becca started clapping. The large crowd followed her lead. Gerald waited for the clapping to end.

When the clapping ended, Becca stepped closer to the edge of the stage and bent forward toward the audience. "And now for the presents."

Gerald looked at Danny.

"I have no idea," Danny mouthed.

Gerald saw that Danny was serious. He glanced at Sheila and Blake. They didn't know anything either.

Becca turned to her fiancé. The man she loved, and the man who loved her. Tonight, she'd give him what he wanted right here in front of everyone. The smile she wore rolled back the torturous pregnancy she had endured inside of her mother, two near abortions at her hands, and eighteen years of desolation at the hands of both parents. She unbuttoned her wrist and rolled up her shirt sleeve.

Becca had imagined this event a thousand times. She had imagined excitement and nervousness, but she hadn't anticipated the sudden feeling that she was in a fog and trying desperately to be someone she wasn't and to get something she could never have. She pushed past the terror that washed over her soul that carried with it an incoming tide of reality. She couldn't stop now. She wasn't weak any longer.

Vincent and Heather couldn't be allowed to win.

How was she able to experience so many emotions and fears and deaths in one second on stage in front of hundreds of people? In front of Gerald? She felt like a girl who had stolen Wonder Woman's outfit and had put it on and now thought she was Wonder Woman. But it wasn't the outfit that made Wonder Woman who she was. It was her power. Power that Becca didn't have. She barely had enough power to keep standing.

The torturous second wouldn't end.

Vincent and Heather were sitting in the audience. Waiting for their chance to do what they did best. Abandon her. Reject her. Humiliate her.

Was that pain she felt in her arm?

A little girl trying and failing to get a man.

A weak girl trying and failing to be strong.

A good girl trying and failing to be bad.

No! Becca screamed inside. *I'm not their doormat any more! I'm not a weak little girl trying to win their love by being good!*

Becca steeled her resolve and put a pillow over her good girl's face and held it fast until the struggle was over. She held out her tattooed arm to Gerald. "What we have is special," she said, with confidence she was drawing from emotional adrenaline. "I got a tattoo that looks just like yours."

Danny's face turned grim. "Oh, s—" He'd seen this before. He rubbed his face and pushed sympathetic air out of his inflated jaws. *I hope this isn't what I think it is,* he thought. But the way that girl was looking at Gerald... What else could it be?

Gerald noticeably stiffened. His smile was stiff, too. If that's what was on his face.

"And," she held the word in her mouth, "I got another one that says *Gerald's Girl,*" she looked into the audience, "but I can't show you that one here on stage."

The whistles and hoots and "Whoas" from the audience weren't shared onstage. Becca didn't see the pained expressions on the faces of Danny, Blake, or Sheila. They all liked Becca. And that's why any one of them would've pulled the building's fire alarm if they could've to save her from being embarrassed.

"Gerald's girl?" said Gerald, letting out a breath of exasperation, and hoping Becca didn't notice. She was a really nice girl. Nicer than she wanted anyone to know. Nicer than she wanted him to know. There was no way to end this without her being hurt, but he didn't need to humiliate her. He wouldn't humiliate her. "Okay," he said, with a smile. He looked at the audience and said, "I love the snake tattoo, but I can't wait to see the other one!" He knew he would never see that tattoo.

"Midnight bliss!" somebody shouted from the crowd.

"Midnight bliss, baby," Gerald said, for Becca's sake.

I can't wait to see the other one, reverberated through Becca's body and soul. It was like she was in a giant tuba hearing it declare Gerald's desire for her. And somehow her deep rejection had interpreted, "I love the snake tattoo," as "I love *you.*"

Everyone in the band sensed this moment of opportunity to put this train wreck in the making behind them. They made their moves, but Becca made hers quicker. "And I want you to know that I love you." She exhaled. It was out. Finally. In the open. She felt free. So free that she couldn't be quiet. "I love this man," she said to the crowd.

Half of the crowd clapped and shouted encouraging things. The other half seemed to sense that something wasn't altogether right on that stage.

"Okay, let's do the next song, Becca," said Sheila.

An angel of truth walked through the crowd.

A woman shouted out, "Tell her you love her!"

"Yeah, don't leave her hanging like that!" another woman shouted.

Both of the big-mouthed women were close to the stage. Their smiles were big and glazed. They had that alcohol induced lit up look about them. Gerald wished they'd shut their drunk mouths, but he couldn't say that. So he hoped his silent, tight smile would outlast the women's long noses.

"Go on, man" said the first woman. "The girl loves you. She's got your snake on her arm."

Becca was the only one on the stage who didn't feel the arctic chill. "I'm waiting," she said playfully, looking back and forth at him and the two women with the big mouths.

Gerald knew what he had to do. Anything less and it wouldn't end. He'd had one crazy stalker. There wouldn't be another. *I tried, Becca,* Gerald thought, now angry. He couldn't say anything to feed into her infatuation. "I appreciate your assistance, ladies, but it's not like that." His smile was handsome and hard. "We're just close friends. She's got friends. I've got friends. Friends with benefits. That's all it is."

"Now let's hear some music!" Danny shouted.

Blake heard the silent message loud and clear. He started drumming a song that was almost all instrumentals. Sheila could carry if she had to. The crowd started bouncing with their hands in the air. Just like that, Becca's big surprise was over.

Becca looked into Gerald's dark eyes and felt the full impact of the cold train Crystal had warned her of. It rumbled across her soul with the same ferocity of that horrible night at the high school musical. She felt badgered, gutted, and dizzy. Gravity tried to pull her body to the hard floor. Something held her up.

Something was Gabron.

30

The angel could not feel Becca's crushed heart the way the Lord felt the pains of His people. The Lord was the infinite, all-knowing God. There was nothing He didn't know.

Yet His unfathomable love and mercy had compelled Him to come to earth and to live among His own creation as a limited man. He experienced every burden, hardship, and temptation of human life.

By doing this, He demonstrated in flesh what He knew by divinity, and thus became a faithful High Priest. Faithfulness borne not only of His divine nature, but of the fellowship of suffering He had literally shared with His creation.

Gabron could never know Becca as the Lord knew her. Nonetheless, he sensed her agony. She was lost. It wasn't merely the absence of eternal life that he sensed. It was the absence of her soul—not literally gone, but so damaged as to be only a shell of what it used to be. Like a building hollowed out by a bomb. Walls still standing, but ready to crumble.

The angel was nearly as shell-shocked as Becca. How did this happen? The Lord had spoken from heaven and promised mercy. It had apparently been a mistake to interpret that as a promise of mercy angels. For unless they were hidden, they hadn't seen the slightest sign of them or of their work. But the word of the Lord was sure.

So where was the mercy? Had it come and they missed it? Was it yet to come? What was it about the mercy of the Lord in this situation that they didn't understand?

———

Unwanted and Alone had been standing by at the ready, daggers in theirs hands. They went into a rabid frenzy of stabbing and slashing. Unwanted focused on her arm. Alone, on her heart.

———

Becca tried to make her mind focus. It wouldn't. Her equilibrium was off. Her legs felt shaky. She was spinning. Battered and broken thoughts struggled to climb from under the rubble of her foolish dreams. Their weak voices escaped the debris and tried to steady her.

You're not a weak little girl any more. Don't break down on this stage in front of all these people the way you did at the musical. Grab the mic stand and sing. Don't let Vincent and Heather win. Just—sing.

Becca grabbed her arm and let out a tortured wail that froze the band and every person on the dance floor. She fell to her knees and screamed at the top of her voice, "Why do you hate me? Why? Why?"

Over and over her anguished screams filled the place.

No one in the place moved for several moments, paralyzed by the drama of the moment. The recovery began onstage. Danny went back to blowing air out of inflated jaws. Blake was shaking his head and mumbling something about Gerald driving girls crazy. Sheila looked at a stiff Gerald, who looked like he had died of embarrassment and had gone into advanced rigor mortis. Someone had to help the poor girl. Sheila moved toward her.

"I got this, Sheila," yelled a woman who was walking toward the stage. Her face wet. Her heart broken. She got to the first stair.

Sheila's eyes widened. "Crystal?"

Gerald shook the rigor mortis off. He frowned his face to the nth degree. "What—the—*heck?* Crystal?"

She looked at him as she walked past. "We'll talk." That was all he was getting right now. That's all anyone was getting. She had to get her friend off this stage. She got on her knees and hugged her sobbing friend. "I'm here, Becca. It's Crystal. Come on. I'm taking you home."

———

Becca sat on the passenger side of her own car and dug her fingers into her aching arm, trying to massage away the pain. But a part of her welcomed it. It gave her something to think of other than how pitiful and stupid and empty she was. "Where are we going?" she asked Crystal, her voice void of energy.

"I got us a hotel. We're staying at a Hampton Inn."

Becca didn't look at Crystal as she spoke. She was too ashamed to look at her. She asked softly, "What are you doing here?"

"You are what I'm doing here."

"How'd you know I'd be here?"

Crystal navigated through the intersection's traffic and said, "I saw you driving off with a suitcase. You're hot after Gerald. Gerald's in Charleston. Not hard to figure out. Becca's going to Charleston."

"You followed me?"

"No. You followed me. I've been here since three."

One of Becca's cheeks went up in a question. "I don't—three?"

"Yeah. They've got these things called airplanes. They can get you places a lot faster than cars."

"You flew?" asked Becca.

"You're connecting the dots, Becca." Crystal's tone was characteristic banter. It didn't carry the anger that boiled in her chest. But she would rip Becca a new one later. Right now she needed a friend.

"Last minute flight. That's expensive." Becca paused. "Thank you. I appreciate it."

"You ought to," said Crystal. "You're paying me back." She reached into her pocket and pulled out the airline ticket receipt and tossed it onto Becca's lap.

Becca picked it up. "Four hundred bucks."

"Hey, it's expensive being crazy," said Crystal, with a smirky, side glance. "No days off until I get my money back, girlfriend. Be happy I'm not charging for the Uber."

Tears started rolling down Becca's face. "I remember when I first met your friend, Ta-Nisha. She said something like all of your friends had problems. What's my problem?"

"I don't know," said Crystal, wishing she did. An angel of truth touched her. Next thing she knew, she was saying, "You got a raw deal from your parents. They gutted you. There's nothing inside. You're empty, and you're trying to fill that void. Only God can help you." Crystal squinched her eyes and frowned her face into a big question mark. *Where did that come from?* she wondered.

Becca's mind was numb. The God comment was muffled and lost, but she heard everything else. "You think I'm one of the craziest girls Gerald has ever had?" asked Becca.

"I don't know. He's had a lot of 'em." Crystal chuckled. "But I will say this. You are by far the single most crazy, disturbed female I have ever known. Crazier than me. And *that's* crazy."

Becca heard the humor and though dark, appreciated it. Two depressed people wouldn't help any. *Oh, what had she done to deserve a friend like Crystal!* But she admitted sadly that the humor was based on reality. Crystal was right. Nobody could help her. She was again standing on the high ledge of a burning skyscraper. Death behind her. Death before her.

Death was inevitable.

The only question was when, where, how, and what she would do before she left this cruel, godforsaken world.

Vincent and Heather would finally get their wish.

Becca's eyes narrowed as rage draped over her. They weren't the only ones who would get their wish. *I'm going to get something, too,* she calculated coldly.

It wasn't just Gabron who had questions. So did Justis and Krasa. They all had heard the heavenly voice promise mercy. The closest thing that looked like mercy was Crystal showing up to get Becca off that stage. But that was after the fact. The damage had been done, and the angels had watched in horror as Unwanted and Alone used the incident to strengthen the stronghold. Demons were swirling around her rejection and pain and landing on Becca like bees on a hive. She was covered with them.

The angel of truth looked at Gabron.

Gabron got right to the point. "Where was the mercy? The stronghold is stronger now than it has ever been."

"The suicide demon is all over her," Justis added with urgency.

"And there's murder in her heart!" said Krasa. "We have to respond! We have to do something quick!"

Mark looked at each angel, pondering their perspectives as guardian angels, and appreciating their love for this daughter of Adam. "God's actions are never truly reactive," he said, with a peace that injected a needed dose of calm.

"Blessed be the name of the Lord forever," said one, then all of the angels, acknowledging what they all knew to be true. *In a way that no angel understood fully, the Creator was the Alpha and Omega, the Beginning and the End, the First and the Last. Though His actions happened in real time to angels and people, everything had been settled in the mind and heart of the eternal God long before the creation of angels or people. God was not reacting to the creation; the creation was reacting to Him.*

Yet, the truth angel would share with the guardians as much as he knew. "Except a grain of wheat falls to the ground and dies, it remains only a single seed. But if it dies, it produces many seeds."

"But how many times must she die?" asked Gabron. "Hasn't she suffered enough?"

"What is enough?" the angel asked.

Prior to the recent interactions Gabron had experienced with truth angels, he had never personally spoken with one. He knew they had a reputation for being uncompromising and forthright, but *What is enough?* Becca had barely escaped being murdered in the womb. She had been treated like garbage all her life. She had been humiliated on stage twice in four months. *What is enough?* That's enough!

"You have questions?" Mark said to Gabron.

"The Lord is perfect in all His ways," said Gabron.

"But?" asked Mark.

"But there are others...people who hurt people. People who prey on others. Rapists. Child molesters. Murderers. People who love to do evil. Their feet are swift to shed innocent blood..." Gabron's words trailed off as he thought of horrible scenes he had witnessed.

"Why is Becca suffering more than others who are more wicked?" the truth angel asked.

"The Lord is perfect in all His ways," Gabron repeated. Then he said with the emotion of one who was trying to stop a tragedy, "Yes, Mark. Why should a child who has suffered so terribly through no fault of her own, suffer with such intensity? And for so long?"

Mark looked briefly at the demons atop the tall, fortified wall of the stronghold.

Gabron sensing that he was finally about to get some answers, said, "We can move farther away from the wall...to make sure they can't hear us."

"Seeing, they see not, and hearing, they hear not," said Mark. "The wicked are full of darkness and cannot see what is right before them. Besides, I am not going to share anything with you that isn't in the blessed book."

Gabron looked at his guardian friends with a tinge of curiosity and disappointment. He understood a glimpse of how the wicked could be blinded by their evilness. But he and his friends loved the Lord and Becca. So what could possibly be preventing them from understanding?

And the reference to the blessed book? Angels of truth were known to speak as obscurely as did the blessed Creator when He was in His flesh. Gabron didn't want to be left with a parable or a Scripture. He wanted to know why Becca was suffering. *Her suffering was not fair!*

The truth angel saw the disappointment and anger that the guardian was trying to respectfully hide. He knew the angel's loyalty was not disloyalty to the Lord. The guardian was merely doing that for which he was created, as was he.

"Why do the righteous suffer? Why do the unrighteous prosper? These questions have been asked since Cain murdered his brother. Enoch and Noah and Joseph asked them. Gabron," said Mark, "it is written in the Psalm, 'Do not fret because of evildoers, nor be envious of the workers of iniquity. For they shall soon be cut down like the grass, and whither as the green herb...Do not fret because of him who prospers in his way, because of the wicked man who brings wicked things to pass...For evildoers shall be cut off.'

"And again it is written, 'But as for me, my feet had almost stumbled; my steps had nearly slipped. For I was envious of the boastful, when I saw the prosperity of the wicked...When I thought how to understand this, it was too painful for me—until I went into the sanctuary of God; then I understood their end. Surely You set them in slippery places; You cast them down to destruction. Oh, how they are brought to desolation, as in a moment! They are utterly consumed with terrors.'"

The eyes of the guardians went wide. This was not the first time they'd heard these sober words. But spoken out of the mouth of the truth angel, they were more than words. They held a presence. His Presence. The Lord God Almighty was in these words.

"The Creator has favored you," said Mark.

Before any of the three angels could ask what this meant, they felt something strip off of them like an onion being peeled of its skin. Immediately, they were somewhere else. Where, and in what dimension, they didn't know. But wherever they were, the awfulness of the dark place violently and hungrily pulled at their beings, trying to separate them from their sanity.

They tried to release their excruciating pain and waves of horror by screaming into the thick darkness. But when they did, the screams left their mouths taking nothing with them. It was a torturous vacuum of absolute darkness and absolute terror.

The angels writhed and screamed and thrashed futilely in the dark wrath of God for a time so long it could not be measured. Then it got worse. A thousand-pound rock of realization smashed into them from above, obliterating anything that resembled the desperate hope of the eternally damned.

This will never end!

The truth angel waited until the light over each guardian dimmed until completely gone. "Gabron. Justis. Krasa."

Whatever was holding up the guardians, stopped. They crumpled to the ground. The truth angel waited, knowing it would take a while for their strength to return and for the horror to leave their souls. One by one, each fought his depleted state to get to his hands and knees.

"Gabron," the truth angel spoke, his voice deliberately low, not wanting to startle him.

"AAaah!" Gabron screamed, as he flinched and covered his face with his forearm to protect it from another painful blow.

"You are not in danger. It is Mark," said the truth angel.

Gabron looked at the being standing before him, his mind finally allowing him to see that he was no longer in that horrible place. He pulled his leg up and rested his elbow heavily on one knee. Then he cried. Hard.

Justis and Krasa had a harder time coming out of their horrors. In a minute, they did…and immediately were overwhelmed by deep sobs that pushed them back to the ground.

The guardians finally recovered themselves enough to converse with Mark.

"That…place," said Justis.

"It is the place of the damned," said Mark.

"The damned?" said Gabron, wondering why the Creator would send them to such a place. "Hell? How long were we there?"

Krasa looked around. "We were there for such a long time, but everything looks the same."

"You were only there a moment," said Mark.

"A moment!" said all three guardians.

"Yes, a moment."

"But it felt much longer. Trillions of years—eternity!" said Gabron.

"Why did the Creator send us there?" asked Justis.

All three guardians awaited the answer, confident in their moral perfection. But more confident in the Almighty's love and wisdom. He would do nothing so dramatic except for a critical purpose.

"You have questions about the Lord's dealings with the girl you guard." Mark looked at Gabron. "The Lord has answered. He has allowed you to experience one moment of the damned to help you see beyond Becca's immediate safety. Her immediate safety is not the most important issue. The most important issue is that she be saved from the wrath to come."

The guardians thought of their moment of hell. The thought of their Becca spending eternity in such a place tore at their hearts.

"How does her present sufferings fit in with the Lord's efforts to save her from eternal damnation?" Mark asked rhetorically. "Satan means her sufferings for evil, but God means them for good. The enemy tried to destroy Joseph through hardships, but the Lord instead turned Satan's attack into deliverance. He can do this for Becca."

"How can any good come of what Becca has been through?" asked Gabron. He shook his head and grimaced. "Her parents. They have done her much harm. They tried to kill her! And these humiliations she endures..."

"See the big picture, guardian," said the truth angel. "It is better to suffer now than later. What is it to you if the Almighty saves Becca by fire? The Potter knows His clay. Have you never read, 'Blessed are those who mourn now, for you shall laugh'? What will it profit her if she gains the world and loses her soul?"

"I see," said Justis. "I see the truth. When our Lord was told that

Pilate had murdered the Galileans and mingled their blood with the temple sacrifices, the Jews expected Him to condemn Pilate. Instead, He said, 'Do you suppose that these Galileans were worse sinners than all other Galileans, because they suffered such things? I tell you, no; but unless you repent you will all likewise perish.'"

The angel of truth didn't smile, but his eyes revealed his appreciation for Justis's revelation. "Yes. They were focused on how badly the Galileans were treated. The Creator sees every injustice, and He has appointed a day of judgment. But He made them focus on eternity."

Justis's head swiveled in quick, jerky motions from one angel to the other. His eyes were light with understanding. "Gabron. Krasa. This is why the Creator showed us the place of the damned. We are guardians. We see the dangers that are right before us. We have been so concerned about her present tragedy that we have forgotten there is a greater tragedy to come. An eternal tragedy if she doesn't turn from her own sins."

Krasa looked at his ancient friend knowingly, but saying nothing. The after-effects of his moment in hell were still heavy on his mind and commanding his attention.

Gabron knew his terrifying moment/eternity in hell had forever changed him and his perspective of the war. And though he was unsure whether his bones would ever stop trembling at what he had experienced, one of his questions still lingered. "Mark, you have spoken of the seed dying that it might live again. Becca. She's died so many times. I do not understand. Is she so wicked that she deserves such intense suffering?"

Mark moved closer and put his hand on Gabron's shoulder and squeezed. This surprised the guardian. He knew truth angels could be severe, but what he felt was comfort. "Gabron," said Mark, "All sin deserves punishment—what you experienced in the place of the damned."

Gabron shuddered.

"But these sufferings are not because of her wickedness. They are because of her prayers," said Mark. "And those of Nancy and Bill."

The angels' faces went from deep, inquisitive interest to stupefying bewilderment. They were aware of Nancy's and Bill's prayers. They had used them several times to protect Becca. But what prayers of Becca was he speaking of? She had prayed some when she was younger. But with the exception of her asking God why her parents hated her, or her asking Him to make them love her, her communication with God had stopped years ago when she started doubting His existence. *There was no room in her understanding for a loving, all-powerful God and the rejection and pain she was suffering.*

"What prayers?" asked Gabron.

"Before Chelsea," said Mark.

Before Chelsea? Before Chelsea? Before—? "The abortion clinic?" Gabron asked.

"Becca sensed that she was unwanted and alone," said Mark. "In her destitution, she cried out to the Creator. He is answering those prayers."

The guardians looked at one another, sharing a common thought. *How could we have forgotten the prayers of her earliest trial? When she was in her mother's womb?*

"But so much has happened since the trials of her innocence," said Gabron, fascinated and in awe of the mercy of God. "She has sinned much since then."

"It is written," said Mark, "'If we are faithless, He remains faithful. He cannot deny Himself.' If the Lord only answered the prayers of the faithful, few prayers would be answered. Mercy rejoices over judgment."

Gabron asked the question that was pressing hard against the chests of his friends. "So Becca will be saved?"

"Satan is trying desperately to destroy Becca, but the Lord has chosen to use her troubles to open her eyes. It is written, 'It is good for me that I have been afflicted, that I may learn your statutes.' And again, 'I know, O Lord, that Your judgments are right, and that in faithfulness You have afflicted me.'

"In mercy, the Creator is allowing the devil to show Becca the evil that is in her heart, and the wickedness and emptiness of this present age. At a time appointed, He will require her to decide one way or the other."

"Life or death," Gabron mumbled heavily.

"Life or death," said the truth angel. "She will choose her own destiny. Hopefully, she will look beyond her pain and bitterness and choose life."

31
____

Jason was coming off his meth high, and he didn't like it. The fact that he was nearly broke made the fact of his fading high that much more unacceptable. The thought of having to knock someone over the head for some money, or having to break in someone's house didn't excite him. He didn't mind doing either. He was a criminal. That was his career choice.

The problem with those options, however, was they were high risk, low reward. You robbed some mark on the street and what? A hundred, two hundred bucks? Oh, you could take her to an ATM and hope to get more. But now you've turned a robbery into kidnapping.

There was nothing wrong with kidnapping. But Georgia gave you a mandatory minimum sentence of ten years. If you caught the judge on a bad day, she could give you twenty-five. Again, there was nothing wrong with kidnapping—if you did it right, like they did that Rachel girl. Problem was when you randomly grabbed someone off the street, a lot of random crap could happen.

Random crap. He was the random crap king. That's why most of his life had been spent behind bars. What he needed was a low risk, high reward score. Something that could give him some breathing room without putting him in an orange jumpsuit.

He didn't know how Boss Man was still throwing down the way he was, but he was—hard. More money fell out of that cripple's pocket than were in his own. *What's his game?* he thought in envy as he looked at the bar's sign. He looked both ways and trotted across the street. Boss Man was giving a ten thousand dollar bonus to whoever found Crystal first. "That's my money," he said, then entered the bar.

He smiled inside as he thought of how easy it had been to get a fake DEA badge. It had been like Christmas when he opened the package and examined the badge. It looked just like pictures of real ones he'd seen online. He went back to the site to order an FBI badge only to find this message: "This domain has been seized by the Federal Bureau of Investigation." Well, at least he got a good DEA badge before the feds closed it down.

Jason scanned the place. Lots of people at the bar. A handful sitting at tables. The girl at the bar wasn't Crystal. That's okay. Doesn't mean she doesn't work here. Or that someone here doesn't know her. Bartenders know bartenders, and alcohol drinkers know bars and bartenders. Somebody in here was going to help him get that ten grand. *He could feel it.*

Jason sat on a tall chair between two guys. He heard the guy on the right order a Roy Rogers. A feeling of revulsion went over him. *Wuss,* he thought. *Probably an alchy trying to get as close as he can to his old love without falling off the wagon.* He started his questions with the guy on the left. No luck.

"Whaddaya have?" asked the bartender.

Jason's head popped up, annoyed that she had come to him so quickly. He wasn't here to drink. He was here to get ten grand. "Gimme a beer."

He looked at a sign that must've had thirty beers. He gritted his teeth, smiled, and ordered one of the expensive craft beers as an investment into getting his ten grand. The girl probably wouldn't be too helpful if he ordered a Michelob. She returned with the beer.

He paid and included a big tip. He pushed a picture toward the bartender. She looked at it and looked at him. "I'm—*we're* looking for this woman. Does she look familiar to you? It would really be helpful if she did."

According to the bartender's expression, he was not on the fast track to becoming friends with her. "Yeah, that's Amy Winehouse. You're *looking* for her? She's dead."

Jason groaned inside. *Idiot!* That ten grand was messing with him. He raised his palms up halfway and laughed. "I'm sorry. No, I'm not looking for Amy Winehouse. The girl I'm looking for does this Amy Winehouse look alike thing." He motioned with his hand. "Got really long black hair. Wears it like her. That big beehive sh— style. Wears her make-up like her." He pointed to Amy's face on the internet photo. "Black eyeliner like that." *Please, please! Gimme something!*

The bartender shook her head. "Sorry." She started to walk away.

Jason could've kicked his own butt. *How do you forget that?* "Her name is Crystal. She's tall. Got lots of tattoos. She's a bartender." His voice was anxious with need.

"Haven't seen Amy or Crystal. Sorry."

He watched his ten grand walk away. He guzzled down half the beer, took a couple-of-seconds breather, and finished it off. He put his elbows on the counter and buried his head in his palms.

The man to his right studied him. He had been listening to his conversation with extreme interest. He rested his elbow on the counter and rubbed the stubble under his chin. "Hey."

Jason saw the man's interest. "You look like you wanna say something," he said.

"I heard you talking about this Crystal girl."

Jason straitened up. "You know her?"

"She's in some kind of trouble?"

"Look, do you know her? It's very important that I find her."

The man looked intently into Jason's eyes.

Jason waited, hopeful that his ground pounding was coming to an end.

The man flicked his hand backward. "Naw, I don't think I know her." He didn't sound convincing.

This man knew something! "Look man, this—" He changed his choice word for women. Who knows? This guy could be someone who likes her. "This girl, she's into something that could get her hurt."

"Something like what?"

"Something like some people are angry about something she did and they want to hurt her. I need to get to her before they do."

"You a friend?"

That's why you ordered the badge. "No, I'm DEA."

"Drugs? She's into drugs? Crystal's…I mean, this girl, she's into drugs?"

I knew it. You know this b— "It's an ongoing investigation. I can't tell you any more."

"How old is she?" the man asked. "I mean it would help to know how hold she is."

"How old is she?" Jason's irritation couldn't be hidden. "What the… she's…I don't know. Early twenties. Look—"

"If DEA's involved, it's serious—and dangerous. I don't know if I want to get involved with something like this." The man drank some of his drink and went to stand up.

Ten thousand dollars was about to walk out the door. He didn't think about it. He just did it. Jason grabbed the man's arm and pulled him back. The man looked down unappreciatively at the DEA agent's hand on his arm. An arm whose muscles had been deliberately torn down thousands of times to allow them to grow back bigger and stronger. He sat back in his chair.

Jason was relieved that his DEA strong-arming was working. Jails and prisons all over America had financed his exercise program. So he could probably take him if he had to. But the guy's arm felt like solid steel, and they were in a bar full of people. What was he going to do? Beat the information out of him in front of everyone?

"Let me see your badge," said the man.

Jason confidently flipped it out. Once the man was through examining it, he put it back. "Now, what do you know about this girl?"

The man glanced around the bar as though someone may be eavesdropping. He spoke low. "How long you been DEA?"

"What difference does it make?" Jason was impatient.

"It makes a difference to me," the man snapped. "You're not the only one looking for her. So, you answer my questions, or DEA or not, this conversation is over without a warrant. These guys don't play. I don't want to end up on the wrong side of the fence."

What the...? This guy's scared of somebody. "Okay," snapped Jason. "Ten years. I been DEA ten years."

"Okay, so you'd have a 5T rating," the nervous man said. "I'm not talking to any special agent who doesn't have at least a 5T rating. I'm not getting screwed."

He said special agent. This guy's been around. He cursed. *I gotta watch what I say. What the heck is a 5T rating?* "I said ten years. Of course, I have a 5T rating. Who else is looking for her?" Had one of the others come by? They weren't supposed to. This was his area.

"You guys always carry your gun, right?" The man again glanced around the bar. "I'm an ex-con. Can't carry unless I want to go back to prison."

Jason was getting as nervous as this guy. "Yeah, I got my gun."

"Show me."

Jason gave him an *Are you serious?* look.

"I'm not talking unless I know there's at least one gun between the two of us," the man said.

Ten thousand dollars. Ten thousand dollars. Ten thousand dollars.

Jason inconspicuously looked around. The guy to his left was lost in conversation with a woman. Jason turned his body and faked like he was stretching his lower back. He pulled the gun from his waist and kept it under his shirt as he brought it to his lap.

Left-handed, the other man noticed.

Jason showed him the gun. "Satisfied?"

"Yeah. You got a car in case we have to get out of here in a hurry?"

"Yeah, I got a car." *But you ain't gettin' in it,* he thought.

"What kind? Where is it?"

"You ask a lot of questions." Jason's face was hard.

"I didn't start this conversation," said the man. "You did."

Jason and the man locked determined eyes. "Across the street in the lot," he said, through clenched teeth.

"You got a key FOB?"

Jason made up his mind right then that if he ever saw this man again after today, he was going to put a bullet in his head. "A key FOB? Yeah, I got a key FOB," he said icily.

The man looked suspiciously around the bar. He got up. "I'm going to the head."

"*We* are going to the head," said Jason.

The man entered the restroom first. He looked under the two stalls. No one. He pulled out his phone and unlocked the screen and put it on mute. He put the phone back in his pocket and went to the urinal.

"Hurry up," said Jason.

"Between now and the time it takes me to finish peeing, she's not going anywhere."

Ten thousand dollars. Ten thousand dollars. Ten thousand dollars. It was close now!

The man finished and took his sweet time calmly washing and drying his hands. Gone was the nervousness. He was whistling a tune like he didn't have a care in the world. Was he bipolar?

Jason's face twisted in anger. He closed the distance between them. He couldn't believe this man's behavior. Crazy or not, he was going to talk. "I don't have all—"

Jason's throat exploded when the man whipped his muscled arm from his opposite hip and sliced through his neck with a palm strike that felt like a helicopter's blade. He clutched his throat with both hands, gasping for air that found no passage. Jason's eyes watered. His knees buckled.

The man needed Jason's big, bald head to be closer to his elbow. He made it happen with a powerful kick to the shin. Jason let out a scream that was muffled by his own choking from the chop to the throat. Another powerful kick to the opposite knee and the big man was on his knees. Excruciating pain from three locations blocked any thought of reaching for his gun.

The man stood before him. "You're not going to die. It only feels like you're going to die. That girl you're looking for is a very popular girl. She has something that belongs to me, and I can't let you get in the way of that."

The man got behind him and reached into the small of Jason's back and pulled out the gun. "I don't know who you work for, and don't care. I do know you don't work for the DEA. There's no such thing as a 5T rating. Or if there is, I've never heard of it. And standard issue for a DEA special agent is the 9mm SIG-Sauer P228 pistol, not a what I'm guessing is a stolen Smith & Wesson."

The elbow strike to the base of the big criminal's skull wasn't designed to kill him. Only to put him to sleep long enough for the man's ad hoc plan to be put into place. He removed the bullet from the chamber and all bullets from the magazine. He inserted the magazine back into the gun and put it back into the small of Jason's back. He reached into his pocket and got his keys. He exited the restroom and headed for the parking lot across the street.

All he could do now was hope that no one needed to go to the restroom. And why should they? Could it be because alcohol was a diuretic? *Just give me a couple of minutes,* the man pleaded. He pressed the FOB a couple of times as he trotted.

Beep! Beep!

It was right in front of him. A black Audi. He popped the trunk and pulled the tab to lift the carpet and found a secure spot. He put the carpet cover down and shut the trunk. He ran back across the street and slowly entered the bar. Everything looked normal. That either meant no one had found the guy on the floor in the restroom, or that he was up and trying to get himself together. Or he was up and waiting for him.

The man opened the door and looked through the crack. The guy was in the same spot. Either still out, or pretending to be. He entered, watching him for the slightest move. How did he know whether or not the guy had another magazine? He hadn't checked him.

Jason was on his belly. One hand was beneath him, unseen. The other was away from his body, like he was waving. The man watched the elbow of the unseen hand and moved forward. He knelt down and touched the small of his back. The gun was still there. He let out a breath and put the man's keys back in his pocket and left.

Now all he had to do was wait.

32
____

Becca sat in the car of the Chelsea Women's Medical Clinic for two hours. She massaged her aching arm. Her eyes were dull with the fatigue of hopelessness. She watched them come and go. Teens, twenties, and thirties. A couple of them may have been older. Women getting rid of their Beccas. What did it take for a woman to pay someone to kill her child? *Why'd you try to kill yours, Heather?*

Becca's thoughts were dark with condemnation. The abortion doctor had said Heather tried twice to abort her. The first time, she had changed her mind at the last minute. The second time... Becca's thoughts paused.

The second time didn't make sense. The doctor had explained Heather's intent to get rid of her in the most bone-chilling details. So why had she changed her mind the second time? What had stopped her? Conscience? Compassion? No. She was incapable of neither. *Heather was a monster.*

What about Vincent? Had he objected at the last moment? *Who am I kidding?* she thought. That would require two things he didn't have. A backbone and knowledge that she existed. She thought of his weakness when it came to Heather. She thought of how thoroughly he ignored her as his daughter. *No. He definitely wasn't the reason for Heather changing her mind.*

Becca was ashamed of her weakness. Her eternal groveling and humiliating eagerness to grasp at the flimsiest vapor of a possibility that the monsters might have some semblance of microscopic feelings for her. *Even now. Ugh!*

She opened the glove compartment and placed her hand on the cold steel. She closed her eyes and wrapped her hand around it. The monsters would soon know what pain felt like. And everyone would soon know what pain the monsters had inflicted upon her.

She drove away from the abortion clinic's parking lot with her right hand. Her left arm dangled in paralysis and pain.

———

Becca looked at Elana, not believing what she was hearing. "You're serious. You're not going to do it?"

Elana's eyes were soft with sympathy. She shook her head. Her face carrying the wisdom of dashed dreams and heartbreak. "No, Becca, I'm not going to do this." Becca looked around the shop, as though help may be found at another workstation.

Elana's voice was low and soft. "No one here is going to do this. You will regret it."

Becca's look was pained. She clutched air through her barely parted lips and held the breath, pleading with her eyes for Elana to relent. The artist was adamant. Becca released the breath in defeat. "I have to do this," she said, as she turned and walked away. *What does it matter? It's true. I am unwanted and alone.*

"You only have one face," yelled Elana after her. "This thing you want to do to your face. It is insane."

Insane or not, it didn't take long for Becca to find someone to take her money.

Next was the hair. It had to go.

Crystal had expected Becca to be messed up after Charleston, and she was. Becca had all but stopped eating—three days now. She walked around like a zombie, held up by instinct, and barely speaking. Her eyes stayed red and puffy from crying. She drank more and smoked more, trying to deaden the pain. She slept more than she was awake.

Crystal was an expert in depression. Becca was definitely depressed, but there was something else going on. Something worse than depression.

"Under your mattress," said the truth angel.

Crystal looked from the upstairs deck at the tree in her front yard with new focus. Alarm fell upon her. She jumped up and hurried to her room and stuck her hand under the mattress. *It was gone!* She swept her full arm forward and backward. The gun was gone. Becca had it! Who else could it be?

Crystal's hand fell upon an envelope under the mattress. She pulled it out and opened it. Twenty-one hundred dollars and a letter.

Crystal

I'm sorry. I took your gun. The money in the envelope is to pay for it. Whatever's left over is yours. I owe you more than I could ever pay with money. You're the best friend I've ever had. I don't know what I would've done had I not met you when I did. I didn't have anywhere to go. Of course, you were right about Gerald. I shouldn't have done that. It was stupid and desperate. Apologize to him for me when you see him. I tried to write a letter for him, but I can't find the words. Just tell him I'm sorry and that nothing that happens to me is his fault. This is between me and my parents. I do love him...with all of my heart, but I see now they are the real reason I went to Charleston. I was trying to get him to do something he's incapable of doing. Just like Heather and Vincent. I've been trying to get them to do something they're incapable of doing. But it ends now. On my terms. They tried to kill me in the dark, and they did kill me a million times in the dark. But it's all coming to the light. Everyone will know the real Heather. Everyone will know the real Vincent.

I love you, Crystal. You were truly my friend.

Becca

Crystal's mind shot out of the gate, like greyhound dogs at the race-track. But her dogs were jumping the fence and sprinting in several directions. "Chill!" she ordered herself. "Crystal, just...chill!" Crystal waited for clear directions to pop into her survivor's mind. Only a few seconds passed. Too long. How many seconds did it take to pull a trigger?

Becca had written, 'You were truly my friend.' *Were.* Past tense. Not *are.* Crystal closed her eyes and lifted her hands nearly to her face, palms facing one another and trembling. She felt like an old ex-champion boxer who was in the ring well past her prime. She knew the environment, but she couldn't respond like she used to. She could see the punch coming, but the reflexes to slip the punch were no longer there. It landed in a belly she thought was forever hardened by repetitive trauma, but instead found she'd been softened by compassion. Crystal's hands clutched her face and she dropped to the floor in deep sobs.

Remembering...

"But, Mommy, you're not supposed to take baths. Remember? You told me."

Pamela smiled. "You're right. I did tell you that. Thank you for reminding me. Besides being my pretty little daughter, you're my wonderful little friend." She rubbed Crystal's face and kissed her on the forehead. "Mommy's just so tired. She needs to relax. Can I just take a short bath? Daddy's downstairs. If anything happens, you can get him. Okay? How's that?"

Crystal folded her arms and pouted, looking down. "You said it was dangerous."

Pamela sighed. She was beat by a six-year-old. "You're right, sweetie. Okay, Mommy won't take a bath. I'll take a shower."

Crystal looked up at her beautiful mother. She was her best friend, even more of a best friend than her school friends, Charlotte and Tiffany. The best friend and the best mommy in the whole world. "Okay, Mommy, I'll let you take a bath."

"You will?"

Crystal's little folded arms pressed hard against her chest. She made a serious face. "But I'm going to sit here until you finish."

"Oh, that's so sweet of you."

"I'm your little friend. Friends are there for their friends," said Crystal.

"That's right, baby. Friends are there for their friends."

Pamela ran the water into the large tub and poured a generous amount of Japanese Cherry Blossom bubble bath into it. Once it finished, she disrobed and entered the water. Oh, the hot, sudsy water felt so good around her.

Crystal was sitting on the closed toilet seat. She turned the big page of her book and looked at Mommy and smiled. The suds were all around her. Mommy took a mountain of the bubbles and put them on her own head. She looked at Crystal with a smile that was cut short by a violent jerk that snatched her under the suds. Mommy thrashed, her mouth involuntarily open under the surface taking in water that choked her, causing more water to find its way down her throat.

Crystal sat in rigid fear. Terror clutched her throat and squeezed. Nothing could come out. Mommy's body bounced up and down and from side to side like the cartoons when they touched electricity. Water splashed onto the floor; some onto Crystal. Mommy's head was beneath the suds. Her thrashing not totally ceased, but enough for Crystal to break free of terror's cold grip around her throat. Mommy's arm reached for her little friend. Crystal jumped up and stared wide-eyed at Mommy's clawed hand.

"Daddy! Daddy! Daddy!" she screamed, as she ran down the stairs. "Mommy's under the water!"

Raymond heard the sounds. The sounds of death. First, the big one. The sound of an improvised explosive device (IED) blowing up near a convoy truck. Then the sounds of machine gun fire from everywhere. They were in a kill zone. "Go! Go! Go!"

The convoy raced back to base without further incident. They were lucky this time. Minor damage to the big truck, but no casualties. But this was Kandahar, Afghanistan, a stronghold of Taliban activity. A lucky roll of the dice didn't mean the house wouldn't eventually win. Two hours later, the Taliban came to collect.

Raymond was an infantryman of the 101st First Brigade. The moun-

tainous terrain around them was close to Pakistan, which made it easy for insurgents to come and go. Today his platoon was assigned to patrol polling sites for upcoming provincial elections. Insurgents attacked from the surrounding mountains.

Crystal stood next to the sofa, looking at Daddy. He was shaking like Mommy. Daddy and Mommy were shaking. Daddy couldn't help Mommy. Mommy couldn't help Daddy. She didn't know what to do. She shook Daddy.

His eyes popped open. "Get down!" He grabbed Crystal and threw her to the floor, shielding her body with his own from incoming fire. Ben was hit and couldn't move! He had to protect his buddy. He had to get him out of there. Either they'd both live, or they'd both die. He wasn't leaving him. He crawled across the living room floor on one elbow, dragging Ben by the collar.

"Mommy's under the water!" Crystal screamed.

"Hang in there, Ben. We're almost—"

"Daddy!" Crystal smacked Daddy hard across his face. "Mommy's under the water!"

Raymond stopped his low crawl. He blinked several times. He looked at his little girl. What was she doing here? Wait. I'm not in Kandahar. This isn't Afghanistan. "Mommy's under the water," he heard. He jumped up.

Crystal pushed the back of his thigh. He took off up the stairs. He'd been awarded the Army Purple Heart for injuries received during combat, and the Pentagon's Valor website recorded his heroism and Silver Heart for the world to see. But none of that mattered when the ambulance drove away with his dead wife in a body bag.

He had risked his life to save a war buddy, and had dragged his little girl around the living room ducking and dodging ghosts and bullets that weren't there, while his wife was having a seizure and drowning in her own bathtub.

Crystal didn't try to shake the guilt of killing her mom or of making Daddy leave her with his sister. It was later that she learned his medical discharge from the army was more psychological than physical. That's when she understood more fully that not only had she betrayed her mother and caused her death, but by doing so, she had pushed her father over the edge. His post-traumatic stress disorder couldn't handle the fact—as he saw it—that he had let his wife die while he was fighting insurgents in the living room.

Crystal didn't blame him for her mother's death. How could she? She was the one who had let Mommy die, not him. The older she had grown, it had become more painfully clear that Mommy was dead before she had finally run downstairs. She had promised Mommy that she would be there for her. She had said, 'Friends are there for their friends,' and then stood there and watched her drown.

No, she'd never try to shake the guilt. It was right for her to feel the full weight of her betrayal. To do otherwise would be the same as saying it was okay to stand there and watch Mommy drown. And as much as her heart hurt for her dad leaving, that was her fault, too. How much could one person be expected to carry? She'd made him leave. He had to, to save his own life.

But as much as she wanted to take full responsibility for the things that had happened to her at her aunt's house, and later at the foster homes, something primitive in her rebelled at being intimidated and blackmailed into doing sexual things for her perverted cousins and their friends. And she sure wasn't going to feel bad for what she did to Mr. Archie.

Her bedroom door opened slowly. The squeak was gone. He must've oiled it. Not that the squeaky door had helped her the past year; it hadn't. As the old man entered and closed the door behind him and leaned on his cane, Crystal thought it hard to believe his wife had slept through his regular nightly trips upstairs to her room for a full year. She knew what this creep was doing, and she let it go on.

Come on in, Mr. Archie, thought Crystal.

"Crystal, it's time," said Mr. Archie.

Yes, it is, thought Crystal. She lay on her side under the cover, watching him take labored steps toward her. For an old man with a bad leg due to a stroke, he sure found strength every night to drag his old butt into her room. "I don't want to do this any more, Mr. Archie."

He took a deep breath in preparation to lower his stiff body onto the side of the bed. The sound of the old geyser having to work just to sit down was nearly enough to make Crystal throw up. "Now we've had this conversation before, Crystal. It won't take long. It never does, now does it?" He put his hand atop the cover where her backside was and took liberties.

Crystal was fourteen. But she wasn't confused and terrified. She wasn't helpless and trapped. She had grown, and not just her body. Some kind of self-defense, environmental evolution mechanism had jumped a few rungs. Mr. Archie was going to stop. He was going to stop tonight. He just had to be convinced.

Mr. Archie wasn't convinced yet. There was simply too much blanket between his old wrinkled hand and that young girl's butt. He pulled the cover back. His eyes widened. In his foster child's hand was a knife with a blade about the third of the size of a knife she would get later. But it was long enough for Mr. Archie's mind to go through the fight or flight process. He was too old to fight, and he was too old for flight. He looked at the animal-like expression on the young girl's face.

They made their moves at the same time. She jumped up with a screech and landed on her knees in the bed. Her arm was drawn back wide to the right. Crystal's attack screech temporarily healed Mr. Archie's stiff leg. He would've made his physical therapist proud of him. He pushed his cane hard to the floor and planted the good leg and jumped up. Crystal's arm swung around him as he started for the door. She was behind him and aiming for his groin. The plan was to cut it off.

Old or not, Mr. Archie wasn't going out like that! He got in one good long stride toward the door before the crazed, diving girl behind him wrapped her arm around his hip and sank her knife into his inner thigh, missing her primary target. He yelped and kept going toward the door. She fell on her belly to the floor. She charged the back of the fleeing old man on her hands and knees.

The old pervert was fast! Was there anything even wrong with his leg? He was getting away. She jabbed hard just as he put his panicked hand on the doorknob. The blade sank deep into his butt. More adrenaline made his healing more complete. Mr. Archie dragged his dead leg as fast as any able-bodied person could move down the hall. He somehow hopped down the stairs two at a time and disappeared into his bedroom.

Crystal pulled herself out of those memories and onto another even more painful memory.

"You're my little girl. But I'm not well. Daddy can't trust himself right now. Sometimes Daddy thinks he's still in the war. I have to know that you're

safe around me. I'm going to come back for you when I get better," said Crystal's father.

"I know you will, Daddy. I trust you."

"Guess you're still not well," Crystal said bitterly, her words dripped with heart blood. "Must be on the twenty-year rehab plan."

Crystal squeezed her eyes shut, smothering the gathering moisture. She focused on someone who needed her. Becca.

Becca had the gun. She had told her to apologize to Gerald for her. She wasn't going after him, thank God. But she was going to do something to her parents. Kill them? Would Becca kill her parents? She wasn't the killing type. But what did she mean by 'it ends now'?

She had to find Becca. Her friend needed her. And this time she wouldn't fail.

33

Vincent drove his car into the thick spiritual darkness and parked in the lot, as he had done several times since Becca had left, and since he had moved out of the house. He turned the ignition off and looked resentfully at the sign. *Chelsea Women's Medical Clinic.* He looked at it as though it were a shady realtor who had sold him radioactive property.

But he knew the truth was it wasn't the abortion clinic's fault for being an abortion clinic. He had known their promise of freedom was radioactive. That's why he had stopped the abortion. And now, here he sat nearly two decades after the fact feeling sorry for himself and apologizing to the air.

A drunk driver standing before a judge and jury, crying and apologizing for plowing over and killing a family. A Nazi death camp official chased down and captured, and now apologizing for his cruelty. *A father (it was a farce to call himself a father) sitting in the parking lot of the very place he had tried to kill his daughter...* He was worse than the drunk and the Nazi.

The most irresponsible drunk driver would never deliberately run over his own daughter, but he had run over Becca thousands of times. The most cruel Nazi would never shove his own daughter alive into an oven, but he had routinely and cowardly shoved his own daughter into an oven.

Chelsea Women's Medical Clinic.

Vincent looked at the sign. His anger and loathing bounced off it and returned to him like a boomerang with a mission. He saw it coming, but did nothing to dodge it. It struck him hard. What was left of his self-control shattered into a million pieces. He gripped the steering wheel with both hands and rested his head on it. He cried until he could cry no longer.

When he finally lifted his head, he knew that he wasn't going to the cabin. Nancy and Bill and Danielle had been badgering him about his decision to move out of the house. He was surprised that he had resisted their strong-arming him this long. Good thing he had. It was way too soon to start thinking about going back home. He thought of the inevitable. *If I ever go back home.* Besides, they were like South Korea and North Korea. They'd been in a progressively deteriorating cold war for years. A cold war that had turned hot the day Becca ran away.

The more he thought about it, the more comfortable he became admitting the truth to himself. Not only was he not going to the cabin for this futile family group hug. He was never going back to that house. How could he? He hated Heather as much as he hated himself.

The angel of truth watched and listened to Vincent's heart and considered.

Heather's blood boiled.

It was a betrayal. A family trick on the scale of Bernie Madoff. She threw stuff into her suitcase as she spoke to herself. "First, he encourages me to get the abortion. Then he stops it at the last moment. Then he acts like the girl isn't his child. Runs out of the room whenever she comes around. Now the spineless wimp pulls her sonogram out of his pocket and gives it to Danielle, and he's suddenly Abraham Lincoln saving the Republic."

Why was she even going to the cabin? It would be a total waste of time. Vincent had done what he did best—run away. Did she really want a reconciliation? A reconciling of what and what? Good guy Vincent and Heather the witch? No, it was better that he was gone. Nevertheless, she knew she had to go to that cabin.

Her mother had bitten into her butt like a pit bull. Mom was angry, aloof, and scolding, to the point of threatening to legally take Danielle from her.

Dad was so disappointed in her, he couldn't look at her without shaking his head. He had nothing to say to her that didn't include Becca's name and what a shame it was that she had parents like her and Vincent.

And she had totally underestimated Danielle's loyalty and love for her sister. Her silence and coldness toward her hadn't diminished one bit since the musical. And she appeared to be serious about suing for separation from her and Vincent. Heather had to go if she didn't want to fracture the relationship to the point of no remedy, if she hadn't already done so.

There was another reason she couldn't skip out on this meeting. She was lonely and isolated. How much more persecution and humiliation could she stand?

Heather threw something else into the suitcase. "Mom, there are better ways to resolve problems other than manipulation and trying to steal my child." She slammed the top down and pushed the short, silver arms until they clicked shut.

Becca wasn't going to be there, *and thank the good Lord for that!* This torture was going to be bad enough without her. But as relieved as she was that Becca wouldn't be there, wisdom that was unrecognizable and unaffiliated to her caused her to shake her head and say, "How much can be done without Becca being there?" Then her own wisdom took the mic. "But she's the problem. Good thing she won't be there."

The angel of truth watched and listened and considered.

"You bag all your stuff, Bill?" asked Nancy.

Bill took a deep breath and rolled his eyes around in his head, going over everything he had packed. "Yep," the long one word answer sounded like he was shoveling gravel. "Now it's time to bag some devils."

"Danielle?" said Nancy. Her granddaughter sat on the very edge of the sofa. Her knees touched one another and her head was lowered, but it wasn't in prayer. Not with that horrible look on her face. "Danielle, everything's going to be alright."

Danielle looked up with teary eyes. She shook her head. "No, it's not. It's not going to be alright. It has never been alright. Forcing them into this meeting isn't going to change one thing. My sister is still out there, and they still hate her."

Nancy would've loved to have been able to say without lying, "Danielle, you're being ridiculous. Your parents don't hate Becca." But with the way her daughter and Vincent had treated the poor girl, it was ridiculous to think anything other than they hated her. Nancy looked at Bill. Her throat was suddenly too fatigued to deliver empty words to her mouth.

Bill walked over to Danielle and sat next to her. He took her hands into his and kissed her on the forehead. "It's okay to cry. Tell you the truth, it's okay to worry."

The new crinkles at the corners of her eyes showed she didn't expect such advice from him. She'd been going to their church faithfully since she moved in with them, and all he seemed to preach on was loving God, living right, and having faith.

Bill's meaty face smiled. "Oh, I'm not talking about that kinda worrying, where folks wallow around in the mud of unbelief—"he gave the air a slow wave, like he was leveling wet cement—"acting like God's a midget and the devil's ten feet tall. I'm talking about being honest with yourself. You see, you can't have true faith until the fears and unbelief are dealt with. Lot of folks think if they stick their head in the ground and pretend the problem's not as bad as it is, it won't be. I can tell you from experience, that'll put you in a mighty bad predicament.

"Others think if they ignore the butterflies in their stomach and the poop in their pants and quote a Scripture or two, everything will turn out fine in the end. Well, truth is, God is gracious and merciful. Lot's of times after we strike out, He'll run us around the base like we've hit a home run. Give us a standing ovation. You can't get too used to that though. He wants us to grow up and use the tools He's given us. So sooner or later those victory handouts dry up and you have to fight the good fight of faith."

Tears rolled down Danielle's face. "I'm trying to believe the Scriptures, Grandpa. I really am. It's just so hard to do when I think of how big this mess is."

Pastor Bill loved preaching, but sitting here ministering to his precious granddaughter one-on-one was the best feeling in the world. "That's some hard business there."

"What?"

"Trying to believe God. Doesn't work for me. Wears me out. I gave that up a long time ago."

Danielle wiped an eye with her fingers. "What do you mean? We have to believe God." She looked at Nancy. "I mean, the Scripture you had me memorize, 'But without faith it is impossible to please Him.' Right?"

"Right," said Bill. "But there's faith and trying to have faith. Trying to have faith is not faith. It's *trying* to have faith. Without a mercy handout, that won't get you very far."

"What's the difference?"

"The difference in killing Goliath and having him rip you into two or three pieces. Do you have faith in me and your grandmother that we're going to stick by you in this mess and do everything in our power to help you?"

"Yes. Of course."

"Why?"

"Because you and Grandma love me. You've always loved me. You love Becca, too." She gave a slight frown. "We just—we should've visited more and gone to church with you more often."

Bill brightened and looked at Nancy. "You're right. You're guilty as sin. Both of you. And don't you forget it, young lady."

Danielle smiled broadly. "I won't. I'm sorry."

Bill squeezed her hands. "Aw, don't go cutting your wrist. I can't help myself. I'm a hunter. I can't help but take the shot when I got it." He took a deep breath and exhaled. "Now back to what I was saying. What about the neighbors on both sides of us? You've met them. Do you have faith that they'll look after you? They're good people."

"No."

"Why not?"

"I don't know them. We don't have a relationship. We do. We're family."

"Young lady, I can stop right there, and you'd still owe the church a double tithe. Think about what you said." He waited, giving her time to think about it. "You see? You believe in me and your grandmother because you know us. You don't believe in the neighbors because you don't know them."

Danielle slowly nodded. "But I was serious when I went down to the altar. I gave my life to Him. That's why I was so eager to get baptized."

"I'm not talking about salvation and *serving* God, Danielle. I'm talking about *knowing* God. You can get just enough revelation about your sin and God's grace to repent and serve Him, but still not know Him enough to have faith in Him for anything other than making it to heaven. But remember this, granddaughter. The problem is never not enough faith. The problem is not enough relationship. Intimacy. That's what it's all about.

"Faith comes from walking and talking with God. It comes from being in His presence and giving Him enough time to love you in ways you deeply sense and feel and experience. If you try to serve God without this, or you face the devil without..." He shook his head. "Well, that's why it says, 'The letter kills, but the Spirit gives life.' It was talking about the Bible, you know. Imagine that—the word of God bringing death instead of life."

"You understand what he's saying, Danielle?" asked Nancy.

"Yes, I think so. My faith in God's promises can't go farther than my intimacy with Him. If I try, it won't work. That's why Grandpa said it'll wear you out. But if I really *know* God, it'll be easier to have faith in Him."

Nancy looked at her husband. "Bill, I think she's got it. I think you can skip your closing remarks and shut down this sermon. We've got to get up there to that cabin and make sure they don't burn down the place before we get there."

Bill looked at Danielle and shook his head, his eyes twinkling. "Perfect example, Danielle. If Nancy's relationship with God was sweeter and a wee bit deeper, she wouldn't be so nervous about the devil getting the victory." He winked at Danielle and looked up at Nancy. "You can't rush the Holy Ghost."

Nancy put her hands on her hips. "Yeah, well last time I checked, your name wasn't Holy Ghost. I'm going to get me some sweet tea. Have that sermon wrapped up by time I get back or it's going to take the Holy Ghost to get me off of you."

Bill smiled. "Put your hands over your ears, darling." Danielle smiled and covered her ears. "Woman, you just gave me all the motivation I need to keep talking." He looked at Danielle. "Okay, you can take your hands from your ears. You didn't hear anything, did you?"

"What? You flirting with Grandma? No." It was nice to be in a home where people loved one another, even if it was dressed in banter and empty threat. What she wouldn't give for her family to have a home full of love.

"I better wrap it up before that Pharisee tries to nail me to the cross," said Bill. "There was a fella named Jehoshaphat. Got himself in a world of trouble. A few countries declared war and surrounded Judah. They were outnumbered. Wasn't a whole lot they could do. Jehoshaphat did something that people with real faith do. Danielle, hand me that Bible over there on that table." She got up. Bill looked toward the kitchen. "Hurry, Danielle, she who seeketh my soul cometh."

"Here, Grandpa." She sat back down.

He flipped the pages. "I've got to hurry. You don't know her like I do. She can be a violent woman." He found his page. "Second Chronicles, twentieth chapter." He read a little to himself. "Danielle, this man, when he saw that he was surrounded and on the verge of annihilation, he didn't pretend like the problem wasn't real, and he didn't try to make it seem smaller and less threatening than it was."

Bill bounced his index finger in the air. "And he didn't try to quote Scripture's he didn't believe in in the hopes that something good would happen. He acknowledged the threat, Danielle. A lot of Christians think if they tell the truth about the threat that they're not in faith. They think if they're truthful, God will see this as a lack of faith. They don't know that God's not dumb. Well, I'm getting ahead of myself. That grandmother of yours has got me all mixed up."

Suddenly, she was there. "What was that about her grandmother?"

Bill's head snapped up. "Oh, help me Holy Ghost. The enemy is upon me."

"Oh, go on, Bill," said Nancy, "but do you think you can limit your sermon to one closing instead of your customary three or four?"

Bill slowly turned his face from Nancy to Danielle. "Well, I'll be. Maybe she does know Jesus. Believe it or not, Nancy, I'm at the end of my one and only closing."

"Uh huh," said Nancy.

"Danielle, King Jehoshaphat was scared to death. Anybody with good sense would be. But he took that fear and let it drive Him to God. He got everybody together and they fasted and prayed. He stood up in the midst of everyone and reminded God of their relationship. His whole prayer was based upon relationship. Then he said something that you should never forget. It's what we're going to pray to Him today about these demon possessed—" He stopped himself. "I'm sorry. That was uncalled for. Let me just read what he said.

"'For we have no power against this great multitude that is coming against us; nor do we know what to do, but our eyes are upon You.' Danielle, earlier you said that when you look at how big this problem is, it makes it hard for you to believe God's promises. Let's do something. I'm not going to ask you to take your eyes off the problem. When you've got an army surrounding you, or there's a cancer eating your liver, or you've got parents acting like yours, it's impossible to not see it.

"We're not going to pretend this problem is small. And we're not going to throw a couple of Scriptures at it and go watch television. We're going to look at this problem and tell the truth about it. But with a little twist. We're not going to tell ourselves about it. We already know it's bigger than us. That'll only cause our faith to leak out our shoes. And we're not going to tell our neighbors how big the problem is. They'll just agree with us and help us wave a white flag. We're going to tell God."

Bill closed the Bible and stood. He had fire in his eyes. "Up, up," he said. "We're going to take this situation to God and tell the truth about it. God it's impossible. There's not a thing in the world we can do to fix it. But our eyes are upon You."

It didn't take much to get Nancy going. One of Bill's faith sparks landed on her and she caught fire. "Alright, Bill, that's enough yakking about prayer. Let's pray." She began to walk around the living room, waving a hand across her chest emphatically as she prayed. "You knew that loser, the devil, was going to attack this family before the world began. You've put the answer in motion before we had good sense to pray for it. I am a priest of the Lord Most High, and I come boldly to the throne of grace to obtain mercy to help in this time of need. I lift up Vincent. I lift up Heather. I lift up Danielle. I lift up Becca—"

Danielle interrupted with a loud, desperate plea. "Father, this is too much for me. It's killing me. It's killing me. It's killing me! I can't stand watching the devil destroy my family! I don't know what to do. Oh, will you please help me?" She fell to her hands and knees, heaving great cries and wails of pain, each birthing another and another and another.

Bill looked at her sympathetically and got on one knee beside her and put a hand on her back. He rubbed gently and said, "That's it, Danielle. Let it go. This is real faith. Pouring your heart out to God. Talk to him about the mountain. Tell Him how big it is. Tell Him how much you hurt. Tell Him what lies the devil has told You. That's what they did in the Psalms. That's what they did in Kings and

Chronicles. That's what Jesus did in the garden of Gethsemane. That's what you have to do. Then when your heart is empty and you've said all you can say, listen to the Comforter, the precious Holy Spirit. He'll talk to you. When you hear His words in your heart, faith will come. Then you won't have to try to have faith. You'll just have it."

Bill rubbed her back some more and stood up. He rubbed tears from his eyes and gave Nancy a strong, full-bodied hug.

"The poor girl needed this," whispered Nancy.

"You do, too, Nancy."

In a moment, Nancy was sitting on a chair, with her elbows on her knees and her face buried in her hands. She was crying as hard as Danielle. Bill sat on the sofa. Soon his big body was bouncing in convulsive cries. He and Nancy finished crying before Danielle finished. They sat quietly and prayed under their breath as they watched Danielle's crying come to a slow stop. Nancy went to get some tissue to take care of the long trail of mucous that hung from both of Danielle's nostrils. She caught the trail and wiped Danielle's nose.

"Just take your time, sweetie," said Nancy. "Don't stop until you hear the Holy Spirit." Nancy stood back to her feet.

Bill and Nancy didn't see when Danielle texted something on her phone and raised her face and pointed her finger at the invisible dark powers. "In Jesus's name, let my family go! In Jesus's name, let my sister go! In Jesus's name, Becca, get yourself up there to that cabin! It ends today!" Danielle looked at her grandparents. "I sent her a text. She'll be at the cabin."

"Danielle, she doesn't answer phone calls or texts. I doubt that she'll even see it. What makes you think she'll show up at the cabin?" asked Nancy.

"Because I heard from God. He said, 'Behold, I am the Lord, the God of all flesh. Is there anything too hard for Me?'" Danielle looked into the eyes of two stunned grandparents. "You told me not to stop praying until I heard from the Holy Spirit. Right?"

Bill and Nancy didn't answer.

Danielle turned and headed for the door. "Come on. Let's get to the cabin. I want to see my sister."

Nancy whispered to Bill, "What do you think happened?"

"I think the Holy Spirit happened."

"Something's going to happen at the cabin. Something big," said Nancy.

34

The Comforter had begun His work in Danielle's broken, fearful, and faith depleted heart before she had anything that could remotely qualify as faith. The God who had inspired the prophets to write, "Without faith it is impossible to please Him," and, "A double-minded man is unstable in all his ways. Do not let that man think he shall receive anything from the Lord," had used Bill and Nancy to preach the word of faith to her. He then took the seed of the word that He had planted in her heart and watered it with His tears that fell from her eyes and His desires prayed through her mouth.

Planting.

Watering.

Harvest.

It was time to reap.

"In Jesus's name, let my family go! In Jesus's name, let my sister go!" were Danielle's words that echoed in the *Hall of Confessions and Declarations* that was located in the vast throne of the Almighty. The words would be examined, and if approved, they would be spoken out of the mouth of God for execution.

The words were like thunder spoken distinctly. They rolled back and forth in the heavens above Atlanta, shaking everything that could be shaken. Every angel stopped and followed the words with their heads as though they were following a divine tidal wave. Demons in the area felt a short, but terrifying and disorienting shaking deep in their bones. Those that were flying fell to the ground to join those who were already laid out and holding on to whatever they could for dear life.

The words stopped. The shaking stopped. Demons found their way to their feet. They'd heard a deep, penetrating sound that had weakened and disoriented them, but had no idea what the sound was, other than it was something from heaven.

The arrows brought more clarity.

Becca's three guardians looked in awe at the company of archers on the horizon walking dramatically toward them. Their powerful, golden bows were pulled back and at the ready. They had long hair and were dressed in the whitest of white garments. Their hair and garments blew in a wind that appeared to affect nothing and no one but them. They leaned forward as they walked. Their strides appeared contested, but irresistible. Whatever was trying to stop them was failing.

"Look!" shouted Gabron. "Finally! The time of Becca's deliverance is here!" He looked excitedly at Justis and Krasa. "Deliverance for Becca is here! Who are they?"

The angel of truth appreciated the excitement and hopefulness of the guardians. His face, however, was expressionless business. "It is written, 'God will shoot at them with an arrow. Suddenly, they shall be wounded.'"

Justis's excitement lowered to meet the truth angel's gaze at the archers. He looked at the approaching warriors, then looked thoughtfully at the truth angel. "Mark, what is that wind blowing against them?"

"The wind is the Holy Spirit."

"Why would the Holy Spirit slow down the warriors?" asked Krasa.

"It is not the wind of the Holy Spirit that slows the warriors. It is the power of darkness and Becca's will."

"But they march on!" said Gabron.

Mark looked intently at the guardian. "Strongholds are called strongholds for a reason. Our rejoicing must be timely. We will rejoice if Becca is saved. If she gets past her anger, there is hope."

If? thought the guardians. They watched in silence as the archers began their assault.

The company of angelic archers separated into four squads of five angels. They took strategic positions and began shooting arrow after arrow. Each one finding a demon that didn't see it coming.

Thinking things through, Justis asked, "What is the immediate goal of the archers?"

"Danielle's words," answered Mark. "To make sure Becca gets to the cabin."

Heather couldn't enjoy the beautiful July weather. Nor the scenery of the north Georgia mountains. They'd had a few really hot days, but Mr. Southern Summer hadn't yet decided to be tormenting or not. The car's windows were half down on both sides, allowing a refreshing breeze to noisily drown her unwelcome thoughts as she drove up and down the heavily forested, hilly two-lane highway to get to the secluded, large luxury cabin. She wondered whether their cabin was the only one in the area unable to get a cell phone signal.

The car reached a summit that would in five hundred feet turn into a decline that would lead into the valley. She could actually see the cabin from her position. Even from this distance, it appeared large.

On a whim, she decided to stop and look at it from the lookout point. Maybe the calm scenery would help her anxiety. She looked ahead two hundred feet to where the street hugged the mountain as it turned right at the bend. She turned left, crossing the double lines and came to a stop in one of the lot's lined parking spaces.

Heather got out of the car and went a few yards to a big stone that had engraved atop it the history of the valley. She leaned against it and looked at the wide expanse of trees and mountains. Her wide sunshades and baseball style cap hid her eyes from the glare of the sun. But she couldn't escape the glare of her memories.

"What are you doing, Heather?" her daddy's accusing voice called out from another room.

"Nothing," said the little six-year-old.

The hard, worn carpet muffled her daddy's steps. "Heather! Didn't I tell you to bring me a beer?"

Heather was at the kitchen table with crayons and a coloring book. She jumped at the sound of his angry voice. His large body filled the doorway. Her young age didn't filter his expression or replace its meaning with something naïve. Daddy didn't like her. He'd never liked her. But maybe he'd like the picture of him she was coloring. If he liked this one, she'd color the one on the next page. It was one of a man holding a little girl's hand. Daddy could be the man, and she could be the little girl.

Daddy looked at her. She had a guilty look. What was the worthless little rat doing this time? "I thought you said you weren't doing anything," he said, as he walked toward her, anger speeding his steps.

Heather's eyes widened with fear. She didn't want another spanking. She had to do something. Quick. She held the coloring book's picture up. He stopped. In a few seconds, he frowned in disgust. "I wanted to give you a surprise. It's you."

"Me?" he spat. "How the hell is this me? Am I orange?" The expression he made as he reviewed the picture further left no doubt as to how he felt. He looked at the rat. "You're supposed to color inside the lines. You can't even color right. You're stupid, Heather. Just as stupid as your worthless mother."

Heather started crying. "I wanted to give you a good surprise."

"You want to give me a good surprise, Heather? Go play on the highway."

"I only wanted to surprise you, Daddy."

"Daddy? I thought I told you not to call me that. Call me Biggie."

"But you're my daddy."

"Heather!" he yelled, the alcohol taking him farther in cruelty than he had ever gone with her before, "do you know what you are?"

"No."

"I'm going to tell you. You're a stupid, used Tampon."

Heather cringed, then shrank inside. He had told her before that she was stupid—all the time. She knew she was stupid. But she discerned something this time that she hadn't understood before. He didn't just dislike her. She was so stupid that he hated her. He wanted her to play on the highway. Moving cars were on the highway. He wanted her to be hit by a car. Fear warned her to not ask what a Tampon was, but something drove her to do it.

He told her and laughed when she grabbed her heart and ran away crying.

Heather came out of the memory and found herself clutching the flesh over her heart and crying. She exhaled deeply and removed her sunshades and wiped her eyes. She got into the car and willed herself to ignore the pain in her chest. It worked. But only because the ache in her soul commanded more attention.

She drove to the cabin and slowly rolled into the large gravel parking area. She parked and removed the suitcase, pulled out the handle, and rolled it to the base of the stairs.

Heather went up the stairs already prepared to leave. This was a royal waste of everyone's time. Nothing was going to be resolved. The door opened.

"Hello, Heather."

A simple greeting. But it hit her like a simple piece of gravel hitting a car's windshield on the highway. The chill started small, but spread determinedly in Heather's chest and proceeded throughout her entire body until she felt like she was a solid block of ice.

Heather looked into the girl's glazed eyes. The smell of alcohol was strong on her, but there was something about her that told Heather she was high on more than alcohol. She was intoxicated with simmering rage.

"That's our Heather. At least you're still in character. Silence is your color."

The fuzz where long hair used to be was shocking, but hair could grow back. It was the tattoos on her face, they— Heather's mouth parted, but not to speak. She couldn't speak. Becca had tattoos on her face that said *Unwanted* and *Rejected*. One on each cheek. There was no need to ask why.

"Is that permanent?" she asked.

Becca's eyes narrowed. Her neck jutted out. "Excuse me. Are you talking to me, Heather? Did you initiate a conversation with me?"

"Yes." Heather's voice was weak.

Becca chuckled bitterly. "Better late than never, I guess. Right Heather?" Heather said nothing. "Yeah, the tattoos are permanent. How do you like them? They match the ones you and Vincent put on my heart and soul."

Heather looked at the tattoos until she had no more strength to do so. Her eyes slowly lowered, looking at the uncharacteristic clothes Becca wore. She had been a typical teenage girl. She was a shapely girl and wore fitted clothes, but she never left the house looking like this.

Heather's eyes widened when she saw the snake tattoo that wrapped around her arm and opened its mouth on her wrist. *Her wrist.* What was at the end of her wrist made her head light and her knees weak. "Why do you have a gun?"

"Get in this house, Heather," Becca ordered.

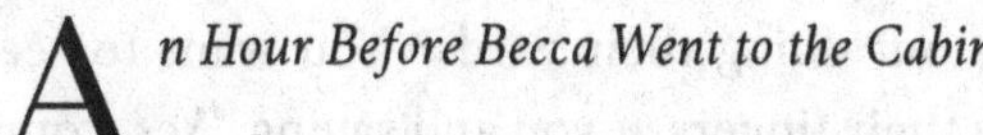

35

A*n Hour Before Becca Went to the Cabin*

Jason couldn't believe his luck! No, it wasn't luck. He must've checked a hundred bars before finding someone who knew Crystal. And the greedy dog had charged him his last hundred bucks to tell him where she lived. But what was a hundred compared to a ten-thousand-dollar bonus? That, plus the original fee…yeah, sweet! But just to make sure Boss Man's brother, Reggie, and his own friend, Dwayne, didn't have plans for that bonus, he put in a call to Boss Man. When Boss Man heard that Jason had found Crystal, he made it clear to the others that if Jason took them to the girl, the bonus was solely his. Satisfied, Jason and the crew made their way to Little Five Points.

Three men to get one girl. It seemed like overkill to Jason, but Boss Man had said the girl was like a snake and she had lots of friends. Things would get ugly real fast if they made a move on her around her friends. Reggie had tried it and it didn't go too well. Reggie said the crazy skank had pulled out a huge knife, and one of the guys with her had smiled and lifted his shirt to show his gun. Plus, someone had told Boss Man that the girl carried a gun.

The black Audi turned the corner and rolled slowly toward the second house on the right. No one was on the porch or the upstairs deck. A car was parked on the street in front of the house. Jason got antsy. "That's her car."

The men looked at the car like it was money in their pocket.

"Keep going," said Reggie. "Go to the end of the block and circle back. We need to find some place we can hang while we watch for her."

Hang while we watch for her? Jason's anger flared. Reggie was Boss Man's brother and he spoke for Boss Man, but he had found Crystal, not Reggie. "But she's in there now. I didn't do all of that work to watch her."

"Yeah? And that's why you stay in prison." Reggie's tone was sharp. "You don't see these people out doing their yards? You want to see those folks in court pointing their fingers at you and saying, 'Yes, your honor, that's the dummy who kidnapped a girl in broad daylight in front of me and my neighbors'? And my brother ain't payin' nobody nothin' for having a shootout with this girl. You feel me? Now what we're going to do is we're going to let her leave the house, and when she comes back, we're going to be in there waiting on her."

Jason held his tongue and drove to the end of the opposite block. He stopped the car. This fool wasn't messing with his money. He pulled out his phone.

"What you doing?" Reggie asked, frowning at what looked like a challenge to his authority.

Jason punched the numbers. "I worked too hard to find this girl," was his abbreviated answer.

"Yeah, you got her?" Boss Man answered Jason.

"Naw," said Jason, looking at Reggie, his contempt showing itself in his upturned lip. "And we may not get her. She's in the house. Her car's outside. But your brother wants to wait until she leaves the house so we can sneak in and wait for her." He knew he was asking Boss Man to side with him over his brother, but he also knew Boss

Man was eaten up with finding and killing this girl. "I wanna get the girl before she leaves."

"Wait, wait, wait, wait, wait," said Dwayne. "That hoe gettin' in the car."

"She's in the car," said Jason. "What do you want us to do, man? Wait for her to come back? Or follow her?"

No sound from Boss Man.

"The girl just went past us, man," Jason rushed. "What do you want us to do?"

"Follow her." Jason started turning the car around as Boss Man spoke. "Don't let her out of your sight. If she goes somewhere that you can get her without being seen, do it. This girl ain't no chump. We only got one chance at this. If you try to get her and she gets away, the hoe may disappear."

"We're behind her now," said Jason. "We're getting on Freedom Parkway."

"And Jason."

"Yeah?"

"I want that girl alive. I got some stuff I want to do to her before I kill her. But if y'all gotta kill her, go ahead. But remember, you kill her, you get half. Everybody gets half if you kill her."

Click.

———

Becca was ignoring Crystal's calls.

Crystal cursed. She waited at the light to get on Freedom Parkway. She thought of what she had done and how she would respond if someone ever did this to her. Her lips tightened in condemnation. She thought of the trouble her friend was in. Becca was going to kill her parents and herself. She had to stop her. How could she do that if she didn't know where she was? She looked at the map and the moving dot on her phone's screen. She knew she had done the right thing. It was just a GPS app.

But where in the world was Becca going?

36

Heather stepped inside with trembling legs. Becca was going to kill her. She saw it in her eyes. Anger. Malice. Revenge. They combined into one penetrating, terrifying, murderous stare. She shuddered at the change that had happened in Becca.

Becca fixed on Heather's wavering eyes as she pushed the door closed. "Go to the kitchen, Heather."

Heather heard the cold voice that came from the bald, tattooed, drug-influenced girl who once was Becca. She walked lightly through the grand room, as they called it, and went to the kitchen. Becca was a few steps behind her. Heather stared straight ahead as Becca was behind her in absolute quietness for what seemed eternity. What was she doing? Heather closed her eyes. Tears rolled down her cheeks. Becca was going to shoot her in the back.

In one moment, she saw the funeral. What would people say at the funeral? What would the preacher say? What *could* he say? It would all come out. How they had treated Becca. The whole pitiful, miserable truth. *Will I hear the gunshot? Will I die immediately? I'm going to hell.*

"Would you like some tea, Heather?"

Heather's eyes opened. She didn't move. "Um, tea?"

"Yeah, I've been smoking pot and drinking nothing but booze.

Some folks call it cross fading. You know what I call it, Heather?" Becca leaned across the sink, looking at her. "I call it a really good high. I'm going to have some ginger tea."

Smoking marijuana and drinking booze? thought Heather. There was no way she was going to say no to anything Becca offered to her, or to anything she told her to do. "Okay," she said, submissively.

"Good. Water's already hot. Why don't you have a seat?"

"At the table or breakfast bar?"

"Anywhere you want, Heather."

Heather looked at the breakfast bar and table as though there was a right and wrong selection.

"Anywhere you want," said Becca.

Heather was sure she heard menace in every word Becca spoke and the sound of a gunshot in her every movement. "Um, I'll sit at the table." She sat down lightly, as though sitting on egg shells and trying not to break them. Her chair faced the kitchen. She noted that Becca did everything while keeping an eye on her.

Becca slipped two fingers of one hand into the rings of two teacups. The gun was in the other. She put a cup in front of her mother, and one directly across from her. She went to the stove, all the while glancing at her. She put a hand mitten on and picked up the pot of boiling water. She walked slowly to the table and went first to her mother's side. Heather's eyes focused on the pot. She'd almost stopped breathing.

Becca stood motionless, looking at a spot on the table like one lost in thought. "You wouldn't have noticed, but I don't like to use the microwave to make tea. I like to use the stove."

The pot of boiling water in Becca's hand. It was the center of the universe. Heather couldn't take her eyes off it. Becca's wrist moved. Heather gasped. The water poured into her cup. Becca poured herself some water and returned the pot to the stove. She grabbed a miniature log cabin container that held a bunch of tea bags and sat down.

"Finally, we get some mother-daughter time. Just like you and Danielle," said Becca. The cynicism in her voice was reflected in her grin and dull, pained eyes. She poured the ginger crystals into her cup.

"We've never really had a nice heart to heart chat. I know you don't like to talk much. I'm sorry. I mean, you don't like to talk much—at all —to *me*." Becca's eyes narrowed as she hit the gun heavily onto the table and covered it with her palm.

Her mother flinched at the metal's thud.

"But, Heather, today you're going to talk. You're going to talk a lot."

Heather closed her eyes with a deep breath and tried hard to swallow. She couldn't.

"Where's Vincent?" asked Becca.

"I don't know. He's supposed to be here. Everyone's supposed to be here."

"Why didn't you ride together? Where's Danielle? She's the one who told me about your family fun time here at the cabin." Becca's anger rose. "I must've missed your phone calls and texts."

Heather waited until she was sure Becca was finished speaking. She was under the influence. She didn't want to further antagonize her by interrupting her. "Your father and I are separated. He moved out months ago."

Becca hadn't been ready for this. It rocked her. She tried not to let it show. She shut down her inclination to feel anything except the pain they had inflicted upon her all her life. Besides, what did she care that the two people in the world who had ground her soul into dust had separated?

"Where's Danielle? She's with Vincent?"

"No, she's with your grandparents."

"Interesting." Becca looked at her mother with a long pause. "I never thought I'd get to the place I am today. I thought I'd always be weak. Always groveling. Always begging you and Vincent for love. Always hurting. Always the victim." Her face turned grim. "I finally came to the conclusion that the pain would only end if I end it."

Heather's voice was low, but her wide eyes darted in fear. "What are you going to do?"

Becca looked at the woman who was technically her mother. She reluctantly half expected some feeling of weakness. A shameful collapse of her courage. A desperate clinging to of a relationship that never was and never could be. A latent protest against her plan. A feeling toward a woman who had never had such a feeling for her. She was pleased when all she felt was determined and burning hatred.

"I'm going to end it, Heather. I'm finally going to end it. Enough tea. Get up. We're going hiking."

Becca and Heather left out one of the back doors and walked thirty yards toward the edge of the woods. Heather knew why Becca was taking her to the woods. She was going to get her revenge. She was going to kill her for how cruel she had been to her.

Heather let go of a deep breath of final resignation. She wouldn't try to escape. *But what's going to happen to Danielle?* she thought, but dared not speed up the bullet to her head by asking about Danielle.

Becca marched her mother a quarter mile into the woods and to the base of a moderate incline. "You recognize where we are?" Becca asked, as they continued up the hill.

"Yes."

"Heather, stop," Becca ordered. She didn't yell, but she punctuated her command with venom.

Heather stopped. Her legs were weak with fear. She hoped Becca didn't tell her to turn around. She wasn't strong enough to look at a gun pointed at her. The five seconds of silence almost killed Heather.

"All my life you've either ignored me or given me one-word answers. Guess what, Heather, I didn't crash your party so you can talk to me like I'm the old Becca. Today you're going to talk to me like I'm your beloved Danielle."

Heather stiffened at the sound of Danielle's name.

Becca saw the reaction that saying Danielle's name had on her mother. The knife of rejection twisted in her heart. Her face twisted in anger. "She'll be here soon, won't she? Your pride and joy. Your *only* daughter. You'd do anything to keep her safe, wouldn't you?"

Heather turned around with tears in her eyes. "Becca, please don't hurt your sister."

"Back up!" yelled Becca.

Heather froze with her hands up, trembling palms facing Becca. "She didn't do anything. She loves you."

This set Becca on fire. She came upon her mother and grabbed a handful of her hair and jerked her face up. She stuck the gun under an eye and pushed the barrel into her. "Eighteen years of watching you walking around me like I was a piece of crap on the ground and your mouth zipped shut even when I begged you to talk to me and now"— she gripped her hair tighter and jerked her head backwards until Heather was on her back looking in terror at the daughter who was going to kill her in the woods and later kill Danielle and Vincent— "you are volunteering to talk to me because you're afraid I'm going to kill your precious Danielle."

Becca knew what she had to do when she had decided to come to the cabin. Make them talk, then end it. It was the only way. There was no turning back. But for the entirety of the trip up here, there had been whispers of weakness. Accusations from the basement of her mind like a soldier in a foxhole popping up from time to time to shoot at her.

You won't be able to do it.

You'll weaken the moment you see them.

You're still weak little Becca, looking for love. Your courage will last only as long as your high lasts.

The last accusation wouldn't take its talons out of her. But something had happened when she had grabbed her mother's hair. She had crossed an unholy, impassable boundary. Like looking at a *Keep Out!* sign with a picture of a skeleton head with crossbones on it and scaling its tall fence and jumping over anyway. She had actually done it. She had put her hands on her tormentor. The woman who had tried twice to kill her. The woman who had left her on that stage in front of everyone. The woman who hated her without a cause.

Becca's face grew dark. She twisted her mother's hair in her hand until Heather winced. "Don't you ever tell me that I'm loved! Nobody loves me! Nobody!"

Heather was deathly still under Becca's weight. Her tattoos were only inches from her own face. *Unwanted* on one cheek; *Rejected* on the other. She wanted to close her eyes from the tormenting, damning evidence of her cruelty. She tried.

The angel of truth wouldn't allow her eyes to close. He widened them and turned the tattoos into glowing, red hot brands. Heather heard the searing and smelled the burning of Becca's flesh.

"I'm not playing with you, Heather. Look at my face. What do you see?"

Heather's trembling lips produced no words.

"Don't answer, Heather. I'll tell you what you see. You see your beautiful daughter, Danielle. The one you love. The one you'd die for. We are going to take this walk. We are going to have our mother-daughter time. When I ask you a question, no matter how much you hate me, you're going to answer me the way you would answer your beloved."

Hot tears rolled down Becca's face. "Or I swear, Heather, I will stick this gun's barrel into the mouth you never used to tell me one time that you love me, and I will blow your brains out. Now, Heather, I'm ready to bond. How about you?"

Heather was about to submissively answer, *Okay.* She looked at the finality in Becca's eyes and thought better of her simple answer. She made herself smile and spoke haltingly. "That sounds wonderful, Becca."

Becca's face remained grim. Her eyes threatening.

"I'd really like that. We have a lot of catching up to do," said Heather, her acceptance of dying suddenly weak. She wanted to live.

"Yes, we do have a lot of catching up to do." Becca stood. "Get up."

Heather stood to her feet. Becca motioned her up the hill with the gun. They started walking.

"I asked you did you recognize where we are," said Becca.

The quietness of the dark woods enclosed upon Heather's nerves like the needles of a porcupine turned outside in. Everything made her jump. She tried to slow her breathing so she could answer Becca. It took several seconds to fight through her fears to answer. Then she noticed that Becca had stopped walking. She turned in three short, frightful movements, afraid of what she might see.

A tall, bald teenager with horrible tattoos on her face and a snake wrapped around her arm was pointing a gun at her face. The girl's face was wet with bitter tears. This was it. Becca was going to kill her. She'd never see Danielle again. She'd never see her parents again. She'd die estranged from her husband. She'd die stupid and a failure in every area of her life. She'd die as horribly as she lived. She raised her trembling palms.

"Becca," she moaned, expecting the bullet to slice her speech, "I'm scared."

Becca felt her own emotion, but not her tormentor's. "You're pushing me, Heather."

"Oh, God help me," Heather muttered.

Becca sent the command to her trigger finger.

"Becca, we're at the trail that Danielle and I found. She and I went all the way to the top and found a beautiful pond. We found the most beautiful flowers." Heather dropped her eyes. "Your fa—Vincent came back later with Danielle. The next day we all went back together. Me. Danielle. Vincent. We left you at the cabin. Alone."

"And unwanted," Becca finished. "That's right, Heather. I was nine years old the first time. I found out about this trail and the pond because Danielle brought me here. It's a beautiful pond."

"Yes, it is, Becca. It's a very beautiful pond. It's too bad we didn't all get to experience it together." Heather looked at Becca. The gun was still pointing at her. She hoped she had said enough to satisfy Becca's command to talk. But she also hoped she hadn't said something to get her shot. She was walking the edge of a razor blade.

Becca ended the long pause by lowering the gun. "Yeah," she said. "Up the hill."

Heather's trembling hands came down. This was not the Becca she had raised. The Becca she knew was needy and compliant and gentle. This Becca was cold and vengeful and… It hit her that she had just narrowly escaped being shot in the face. This Becca was a killer. She started her death march up the hill.

I'm not going to make it out of this alive, she thought. "Can I say something, Becca?"

"That's why I'm here."

Oh, God, help me, she pleaded, hoping that the God who had not protected her from her father's beatings and cruel words would protect her from her daughter's rage. "You said you wanted me to talk to you like I talk to Danielle. That first time, when Danielle brought me here—" She paused. This was either going to save her or get her shot. "Danielle and I, we held hands as we walked up this hill."

Becca couldn't believe what she was hearing. She stopped walking. "Heather," Becca said, from behind her.

Heather stopped walking and dared not turn around.

"Are you saying you want to hold my hand?"

Through trembling lips and an expectation of death, Heather said, "Yes." Her eyes widened and her shoulders tensed with the quick footsteps she heard rushing toward her.

Becca grabbed Heather's neck from behind and shoved her forward until she fell to her hands and knees. "Get on your belly! Get on your belly right now!"

Whimpering, Heather obeyed.

Becca had a knee in her mother's back. She pressed her face sideways into the fallen leaves. "You think I'm still weak, Heather? You think I'm still the needy little girl needing her mommy and willing to do anything for her love? Huh? Is that what you think?"

"No."

"Sure it is. Eighteen years you don't offer me the crap on the bottom of your shoe, and now that your life is coming to an end, you try something like this? *Can I hold your hand?*"

"Are you going to kill your own mother?" Heather asked desperately.

"No, I'm not going to kill my own mother. I'm going to kill you. And I'm going to kill Danielle's father and…"

"And you're going to kill yourself."

Pause. Quiet stillness.

"Aren't you?" asked Heather. "That's why you came here. To kill us and to kill yourself."

Becca stood. "Get up, Heather."

Heather stood. Leaves and dirt clung to her face. She brushed off the debris.

"I'm not weak any more," said Becca. "I don't need your love like I used to need it. If you try something like that again, I swear, I'll shoot you on the spot."

"Okay, Becca, I understand. I see that you're no longer the person you once were."

"Good." Becca was satisfied by what she saw in Heather's eyes. One of her tormentors had met the new Becca and knew that she was no longer a doormat. Becca held out her hand.

Heather looked at it and looked into Becca's face.

"You want to hold my hand, right Heather?"

Heather was afraid a yes would get her shot.

"Here's my hand. Hold it."

Heather tentatively took her daughter's hand.

"It's a shame it took eighteen years, isn't it?" said Becca.

"Yes, Becca, it is. It shouldn't have taken me this long."

"Let's go," said Becca.

———

Becca and Heather reached the top of the hill hand in hand. Heather didn't know whether or not to let go. Her daughter was high and enraged. If she let go too quickly, Becca may interpret it as another slight. If she held on too long, she may see it as manipulation. She had promised to kill her on the spot for anything resembling a trick. Still holding hands, they walked toward the pond. Heather's hand trembled atop Becca's.

"That was real sweet, Heather." Becca's voice was void of warmth. She looked at her. "Danielle must've really enjoyed her walks with you up here."

Alarm!

What do I do? What do I say? Heather's eyes watered. A tear leapt the barrier and rolled down her cheek. She wiped her eye. She knew she had to quickly speak. "She did. A lot. I enjoyed them, too. But you know I'm not very active. So I tired rather quickly. The hikes didn't bother her. She's like you. She's very athletic. She's in great shape."

She's like you. She's in great shape.

Danielle is like you. You're in great shape.

I've never told you, but you're very athletic and you're in great shape.

I noticed.

"Heather, why did you say that?" Becca's eyes were angrier. Her gun hand was twitching.

"What, Becca? What did I say?" Heather pleaded. "You said you wanted me to talk." She broke and fell to her knees. Both hands covering her face. She said through tears, "Oh God, what did I say? I don't know what you want me to do."

Becca approached her tormentor. She looked down with a hard face. "Why did you say Danielle's like me? Why'd you say I'm in great shape? Why?" she screamed. "I told you I'd kill you! I told you I'd kill you if you tried that again!"

Becca stepped back and raised the gun.

Heather panicked. She cowered with her arms raised defensively. Her body bounced with tears. "I don't want to die, Becca. Please. Please. I'm only doing what you asked. I don't know what else to do. Tell me. What do you want me to do? I'll do it."

"I told you what to do," Becca screamed. "I'm not the old Becca!"

"I know you're not," Heather whined from behind her barricade of hands and arms.

"Then why'd you say Danielle's like me! Why'd you say I'm athletic?"

"I wasn't trying to trick you, Becca. I wouldn't do that." She shook her head. "Oh God, I wouldn't do that. I know you'll kill me if I do. I said it because it's true. You swim. You run. You play basketball. You've played every sport. You're excellent in all of them. Danielle's athletic, too. She's just not as disciplined and gifted."

That was the last straw. Heather had crossed the line. Becca backed up with the gun pointed at her tormentor's forehead. Her chest heaved with the murder she was about to commit. She shook her head and knew she had to pull the trigger before Heather could see the tears that were in her eyes, ready to expose her weakness. "I told you, Heather. I told you I'd kill you."

"May I ask you something first? Please?"

Becca's finger vibrated on the trigger.

"I want to do one thing for you before I die."

Becca felt it. It was as tangible as the gun in her hand or the ground on which she stood. She'd lost control. She couldn't kill Heather yet. Heather had never asked to do anything for her and now she had. Reluctantly, she conceded that she had to let this strange and rare request play out. Whatever it was, though, it wouldn't save her tormentor.

Heather looked at the trembling gun. She looked at the strained, troubled look on her daughter's face. "Becca," she said, softly, "I don't want to die. I'm not ready. But I'm not asking you to let me live."

"What do you want, Heather?" Becca held the gun steady at her face. The moment this delay lost its intrigue, she would end this part of her plan and go for Vincent.

"You remember Danielle's princess crown? I made it for her from flowers I got from over there." She pointed. "They're in bloom now."

When Becca heard princess crown, her heart seized. She remembered. Acutely. She'd known immediately that it had been a handmade gift from their mother. The beautiful crown of flowers on Danielle's head had been to her a crown of deep thorns, unseen but not unfelt. She'd thought the thorns were gone, but Heather had just wiggled the crown deeper into her flesh.

Becca had known where this conversation could've gone the moment she heard "princess crown." But the thought had been so out of this world, so utterly ridiculous and impossible, that she shut her mind down to what could come next out of Heather's mouth. But the utterly ridiculous and impossible had hit her like a torpedo striking a ship in the dark of night. Now she was suddenly in deep water trying desperately to stay afloat.

"I know you're going to kill me, Becca. But there should have been two little girls with princess crowns. May I make one for you before I die?"

Becca didn't answer.

"Please, Becca, all I ask is that you let me make you a princess crown of flowers before I die."

Becca's eyes fluttered furiously without batting. Her face and throat tightened. Her belly bounced rapidly as she tried to control her breathing. Her body and emotions were betraying her. She was about to explode in tears. "Turn around!" she yelled. "Turn around now! Look at the pond! Do not look back, Heather, or I will shoot you!"

Heather scurried around and looked at the pond. "Oh God," she moaned, waiting for the bullet to crash through her skull, sending her to face the judgment of God.

Becca's last words to her mother had barely ended before the dam broke. She covered her mouth with a hand and ran away ten yards. She dropped to her knees and doubled over and cried bitterly into her hands and lap. She wanted to stop. She needed to stop. She couldn't let her tormentor see the power she still had over her. But she also needed to cry. She needed more than tears. She needed to moan. She needed to scream. She needed to roll around on the ground and wail until she was relieved of the pressure that was crushing her.

Heather was frozen.

Ten minutes later she was still frozen. Twenty minutes later she was still frozen. At thirty minutes, she would have looked around had she been able to overcome her fear of being shot. Her eyes did not leave that pond. Heather saw something move in her peripheral vision.

"Heather, let's get this over with," Becca yelled from the patch of flowers.

Heather slowly rose. She took slow steps toward Becca. "Thank you," she said, when she was within four feet. She looked at her daughter's head and did something that looked to Becca like a microscopic smile. She began examining and picking flowers. Every so often she'd look at her daughter's head, then she'd search for the perfect flower to satisfy the picture in her mind.

Becca studied the woman. Each time she looked back at Becca's head and then looked for a particular flower, Becca almost burst into fresh crying. Her face was deliberately stern, but her hand over her mouth was to hide her intermittent gasps of emotion.

Heather sat near Becca's feet with a handful of multi-colored flowers. She worked a couple of stems and looked up. Her smile wasn't confident. "Becca, will you please sit with me?"

This tornado was tossing and spinning and carrying Becca all over the place. She fought to get her bearing. She grasped for and found anger and hatred and revenge. Her grip was firm on her allies. The allies that had given her the power to take control of her life. But the tornado's power was infinitely stronger as it slung her and her allies. She was emotionally dizzy and compromised from its spinning.

Becca sat at an angle from her mother and wore an expression that she hoped told her she was allowing this princess crown the way a warden allowed a death row convict a last meal. The meal was for the convict, not the warden. And this crown of flowers was for Heather not her.

Heather smiled the whole time it took to make the crown. The smile was obscured by its knowledge that in a few minutes it would never be used again. Nonetheless, it was a smile. "May I put it on your head?"

Becca willed her emotions down, but she had little confidence they wouldn't break through her defenses if she slipped up. There was no way she was opening her mouth. She gave a lazy, apparently nonchalant motion with her hand.

"Thank you," she said. Then with a smile, she transitioned to her knees and placed the princess crown of flowers on her daughter. "I now pronounce you the Flower Princess. The most beautiful girl in the flower kingdom."

Becca saw Heather moving toward her in slow motion. The movement was obvious, but there was nothing in Becca's experience to allow such a reality. Then it happened. Unless, she was hallucinating, she felt it.

Heather gently cupped her daughter's face in her hands and kissed her on the forehead. "You…are…beautiful, Becca." Then she sat down and put her hands before her nose and mouth like praying hands. It was time. She opened her eyes. "Thank you."

In a few seconds, Becca's shock wore off. How could she have let something like this happen? She jumped up. "Why'd you do that? Why the hell did you do that?" she yelled, as she backed away.

Heather's moment of calm was gone. She looked up at Becca, shocked that she'd cursed at her. "I'm sorry. I didn't plan to do that, Becca. I didn't mean to push—"

"Why'd you do it?" Becca yelled. "I told you you could put flowers on my head! Why'd you say those things? Why'd you kiss me? Tell me! Tell me right now!"

"It's what I did to Danielle."

"Why'd you do it to Danielle?"

Heather's mouth opened with a quiver. She hesitated. She knew what Becca was asking. Her heart dropped like an anchor. "I love her."

Everything in Becca said don't press her for more. Be strong. Recover. Pull the trigger. Then go get Vincent. But she had let Heather seduce her. Holding hands walking up the mountain. The compliments. The smile. The princess crown of flowers. The kiss. It was all a sham. An act. She'd been played.

Becca immediately hated herself for the thought that entered her mind like a thief coming through a door she thought was locked.

Or could it be something else?

"Mom, why did you do it to me?" Becca was unaware that she had called her tormentor Mom. Or that her anger was doing a poor job of masking her need for her mother's love. "Tell me."

Heather took a deep, slow breath. She knew it was her last one. "I don't love you, Becca. I've never loved you. I tried to prevent this by aborting you, but your father stopped it at the last second. I'm sorry. I wish it had turned out differently."

Heather closed her eyes and waited for the bullet to tear through her skull.

37

Becca returned to the cabin.

Her anger and disgust for herself was beyond measurement. How could she have done such a thing? Where was the relief she thought she would now feel? The power? The freedom? She had chosen the pond because it had been denied her. She had chosen it because of the princess crown of flowers. She was going to make the monster give her a crown. But before she knew what had happened, the monster had seduced her.

Becca recalled how the monster's touch had nearly reduced her to mush. She recalled how difficult it had been not to snatch her hand away to protect her heart. But then Heather would have known her weakness. So she had held her hand like Superman gripping kryptonite to prove his strength. And like Superman, the kryptonite had drained her, leaving her depleted and helpless and with nothing but a costume of courage.

Yet, it was the princess crown and the kiss that had driven the spike of kryptonite into her heart. It had pinned her to the earth in just enough time for her to see the faint light of Heather's acceptance turn suddenly and inevitably into the thick darkness of her rejection.

Why had she not stopped her from kissing her? Why had she not anticipated such a trick? She had underestimated her. Then Heather had pounded the spike one last powerful time by telling her that Vincent had rescued her from being aborted. That had messed with her mind worse than the crown and kiss.

The tricky monster had gotten the best of her. Now she'd have to go back to the original plan. But if Vincent didn't come before the others arrived, she'd do it without him. A car sped down the long gravel path like it was being chased. Becca didn't recognize the car, but that didn't mean it wasn't Vincent. Why was he driving so fast?

The car braked and slid twenty feet to a stop. Becca hopped up, standing before the full floor to ceiling window. "This could be it, Heather," said Becca. *I can't kill you or Vincent—you fixed that!—but I can kill myself and make you watch.* "Wait a minute. It can't be," she said.

Heather went to the window.

The car's door flew open and Crystal bolted for the stairs. She ran up them two at a time. She reached for the door's handle. The door opened before she could touch its handle.

"Crystal? What are you doing here?"

Crystal froze. Nothing but her eyeballs moved. Her friend looked like Charlize Theron's character in Mad Max Fury Road, only worse. "What. In. The. World?" she said, in a flat tone.

Becca said, "What are you doing here? How'd you know I was here?" The plan was going downhill fast.

Crystal thawed and said in alarm, shaking her head, "Tell me you didn't do it, Becca. Tell me you didn't kill them."

Becca raised both palms, fighting her emotions. "Crystal, you have to leave. I need you to leave now." Her voice was scratchy and weak. "Please."

"Oh, my God," Crystal said, walking around her, fully intending to see a bloody mess. What she saw was Becca's mother looking at her and wondering whether her appearance was good or bad news. The fear in her mother's eyes was pleading with her. "This is your mother?"

"Yes. Now I need you to leave, Crystal."

"Where's your father?"

"Crystal," Becca said, her volume higher.

"Heather, where's your husband?" Crystal asked, ignoring Becca.

"He's not here," she answered, as though Crystal was the voice on the other end of a 911 call, telling her help is on the way. "Thank God, you're here. She was going to kill me. She was going to kill both of us."

Crystal's eyes turned fiery. She marched over to Heather and jabbed her finger in her face. "Was? You think I came here to save you? Let's get something straight right here and now. I don't care a thing about you. I came to save my friend. If I had it my way, I'd have you and your Father of the Year husband conveniently robbed and killed. Two worthless human beings gone, and no one looks at Becca as a suspect. Don't think I haven't thought about it."

Crystal looked Heather up and down with utter disdain. She leaned into her ear and whispered something.

Heather listened and was stunned.

"Don't think I'm not serious," said Crystal to the shocked woman. Crystal looked at Becca and the mess she'd made of her face. "We need to talk."

It took Becca a moment. Hearing someone talk about killing her parents was jarring. She closed the door and joined them in the grand room. Becca sat and Crystal followed. Heather remained standing.

"May I go to the restroom, Becca?" Heather asked.

Becca looked at her, wondering how to handle the request.

"I won't be long," said Heather.

"We can stand near the door, Becca. I'd rather talk to you privately anyway."

"Go on," Becca allowed, standing to her feet and positioning herself so that she could keep an eye on the restroom door. "Upstairs. The one with the linen shelves."

Heather walked up the stairs and into the restroom. Becca followed halfway. The door could be seen from where Becca stood on the stairs.

Nearly ten minutes of heated conversation passed.

"So that's your answer, Becca? Let me get this straight. They treat you like crap. You blow your brains out in front of them to show them how much they hurt you. The news goes viral and your parents live the rest of their lives in guilt? You're eighteen years old. *That's* your friggin' plan?" Crystal looked at a distracted Becca. "And you're going to do it with my gun."

"I bought it from you."

"Excuse me, but I didn't sell it."

Becca tilted her head and started walking up the stairs and toward the restroom.

Crystal flailed her arm. "And look what you've done to your face. What were you thinking?" She shook her head. "And you probably ought to put that gun away before you accidently shoot yourself."

"Heather?" said Becca.

No answer.

Becca turned the knob. It was locked. "Heather!" She turned the knob harder. "She's gone! Heather!" Becca reached above the door and slid her hand along its edge. A key fell to the floor. She picked it up and hurriedly stuck the key in the tiny hole in the center of the knob. "Heather!" She had to push the key's tiny edge directly into—there! Got it! She pushed the door wide. It hit the doorstop hard and came back toward her.

Heather was gone!

Becca looked at the open window. She looked disbelievingly at the bed sheet tied around a pipe under the sink. She ran to the window and looked down. *Are you kidding me? Heather? You tied sheets together and scaled down the wall?*

Becca balled both fists and let out a long scream with her eyes closed. She opened them. "No!" she yelled out the window. She scanned the woods right to left. "No!" she yelled again. She bolted out of the restroom and down the hall and past Crystal.

"Becca, let her go!" Crystal yelled after her.

Desperation compensated for Heather's exercise backslidings. She looked behind, wishing she had been more faithful to the gym and in the gym. She wasn't that far from the cabin and already her legs were threatening cramps and her lungs were a five-alarm fire. If running downhill was this difficult, how would she make it up the next hill?

Heather thought about taking a quick breather. Just a few seconds to catch her breath. She slowed and glanced behind. Becca was running after her like an Olympian. Heather jutted her neck. "My God, she's fast!"

Heather saw the object in her daughter's hand and took off down the gravel hill. In a hundred feet she reached level ground. Another two hundred feet and it was another hill. She knew she wasn't going to make it. The hill would get her.

If only Vincent or her parents would appear like in the movies. At this point, she'd even be happy with a last second rescue. But this was no movie. She could see at least a mile ahead. No cars anywhere. That was to be expected. The only cars in this remote area belonged to the handful of people renting cabins. And there weren't many cabins.

Somehow Heather willed her revolting body another thousand steps to a spot in the trees she was using as a milestone. She turned and got on one knee. The air was like a criminal evading arrest. She couldn't catch it. Speaking of criminals, her murderous daughter had gained a lot of ground. She hit the bottom of the hill and seemed to pick up speed as she ran up it.

How can you run faster uphill? Do you hate me that much, Becca? Heather stood up straight in defeat. She was beyond exhausted. She could barely stand. There was no way to escape her daughter's wrath. And, honestly, why was she running? She deserved whatever Becca did to her.

"I give...I give," she said, between hard fought for breaths, "I give up, Becca. Kill me. I deserve it."

"Heather!" Becca's voice rang out.

Heather watched her daughter closing the distance on her still target.

"You can get away from her if you run into the woods," said the angel of truth.

Heather looked to the woods on the right and left and chose left. She looked for the safest path down the slope and ran for her life.

Becca saw her disappear into the trees. "Heather!" she yelled, and stopped, wondering what Heather's next move would be. She was trying to meet up with Vincent or her parents on their way in. This was the only road they'd use. Hmm. Or she may try to double back and meet them there. There was no way she could end this in front of her grandparents. She had to catch her.

Becca took off down the embankment to save what was left of her plan. But even as she hurried down the hill, she couldn't help wondering how her life had been reduced to chasing her mother in the woods with a gun.

The angel touched Becca's leg. She felt a snag and lost her footing. She tumbled and flipped and rolled thirty feet down the embankment. She landed on her back and looked up at the light at the top of the trees. She sat up and looked at herself. The gun was still in her hand. But her very short dress that had hugged her torso and hips at the top of the hill had turned into a t-shirt that now rested above her waist. She stood and brushed herself off and pulled the short dress back down as far as it would go. Just below her butt.

Becca took off running again.

Heather had never run so much in all her life. Or maybe she had and it just seemed like she hadn't because she'd never been chased by someone with a gun. She stopped and listened. She thought she heard Becca coming. There was no way she was going to outrun this girl. She got an idea.

Heather climbed back up the hill. She had to bend forward and hold onto things to make it to the top and back to the road. She'd then cross and climb down the other side and double back and hopefully find the rest of the family. She was in a real bind, but as she climbed, she thanked God that Becca's friend had told her to climb out the bathroom window.

Heather pulled herself up the last few steps and stood up straight.

Three men stood beside a black Audi. Two were African American. One was white. All three had ski masks in their hands that were just about to be pulled over their faces. They looked at Heather. Heather looked at them. She couldn't believe what she was seeing. This evidently was the day she was supposed to die.

Boss Man's brother, Reggie, pulled his jacket back and motioned her with his other hand to come to them.

She was dead tired, and she was only ten feet way from three men, one of whom had shown her a gun. The other two were probably armed, too. She couldn't get away. And running into the woods would only lead them to Becca. She didn't love her, but she had caused the poor girl enough harm. She wouldn't be the cause of her daughter being raped and murdered. Maybe giving her life for Becca would atone for trying to take her life while she was in her womb.

Heather walked quickly to the car, determined to do whatever she could to get the men to leave this spot. She got within a few feet of the men and looked at each of their faces. Understandably, they were shocked at being in the middle of nowhere and seeing a woman come crawling out of the woods. They were also irritated that whatever mischief they were planning had been interrupted by an eyewitness. The ski masks in their hands added up to strong evidence that that's how they saw her.

A deeper wave of fear rolled over Heather as she asked herself something. What had brought men like these out here? Where were they going? What were they planning? Their car was pointed in the direction of their cabin.

"What are you doing out here?" Jason asked, holding his throat and rubbing it like it was bothering him.

She looked at him. All of the men frightened her. She saw ideas percolating in their eyes. But this one, the white guy, was really scary. He looked like he had just gotten out of prison. Tall, muscular, bald, scarred, tattoos. "I, uh, got into an argument with my driver and... well, now I'm walking."

"They drop you off in the woods?" Dwayne asked suspiciously.

"No, I," she smiled like she was ashamed to say, "had to go to the restroom."

"It's just you?" asked the bald guy. His eyes looking appreciatively at the fit of her clothes.

"Yes, just me. Would it be too much trouble to ask you to give me a ride to the convenient store back on sixty-nine? It's only about eight miles away. I don't have my purse with me, but I can arrange for payment."

As if on que, all of them looked in both directions. Seeing no cars, Jason said, "What about it, fellas? I think we got time to help the lil' lady."

"Sixty-nine? I like the sound of that," Dwayne said beneath his breath.

Reggie exhaled angrily. This thing just got messy. What choice did they have? The woman had walked up on all of them just as they had finished taking a leak. She saw them about to put on ski masks. Everyone knew what ski masks meant. They had to kill her. So they may as well use her first.

Oh God, please help Becca, Heather begged. *I don't care what happens to me. Just don't let anything happen to my daughter.* Heather smiled. "It's not that far away."

"Sure, we can help you out," said Reggie.

Heather moved quickly toward the car. "Front seat or back?" she asked.

Dwayne smiled at Jason. "On to sixty-nine."

"Your choice," said Reggie.

A female's voice yelled from the woods. "Heather, there's no place to go!"

The men looked in the direction from which the voice had come. They looked at Heather.

"Heather, I'm not going to kill you."

Reggie looked at Heather. "I bet you're Heather."

"Run, Becca! They have guns!"

Dwayne put a gun to her head. "Shut up!"

"Becca, run!"

Dwayne wrapped his arm around Heather's neck from behind and lifted her until her toes barely touched the ground. She couldn't get any air.

Reggie ran to the edge of the embankment and looked down. He didn't see anything. "We know you're in there, Becca. No need in us playing hide and seek in the woods. We got Heather up here. You don't want anything to happen to Heather, do you?"

Heather tried to free herself, but she was almost out, and the man's arm was like iron. *Please don't come out, Becca. Please, please run away.* Tears punctuated her helplessness. Hadn't she hurt her daughter enough? It wasn't enough that she was incapable of loving her. She had to also get her killed.

Becca moved from behind a large tree.

"Say what?" said Reggie, when he saw Becca. He looked at her hand and lifted his gun at her. "Keep that thing pointed at the ground. You hear me?"

Becca obeyed his command.

"Get up here. Hurry up!"

Becca did.

He stared at the tattoos on her face. Who would put *Unwanted* and *Rejected* on her face? He hadn't even seen crap like this in prison. "Give me that gun," said Reggie.

Becca handed it to him.

"So Becca," Reggie looked at Heather, "and Heather."

"I told you not to come out!" Heather protested to Becca with tears.

"I know you don't love me, Heather, but I couldn't leave. You're my mother."

"You the reason yo' daughter jacked her face up?" said Reggie.

Jason took a good look at Becca's short dress and the hump it covered. "Now that's just a shame, Heather. This girl should be loved. I won't reject you, Becca."

Reggie's eyes popped wide. "Where'd you get this gun?"

"What do you mean?" she answered."

"What do I mean?" He slammed his large hand around Becca's

neck, drove her backward, and slammed her head against the top of the car. "I mean where did you get this gun?"

Both of Becca's hands gripped the man's thick arm. It didn't budge. His grip was so tight, she couldn't even cough. He let go and she doubled over. He got on a knee beside her. "You're going to make me stop being nice to you. I want to know where you got this gun."

"My ex-boyfriend burglarized a house. It was a long time ago. He gave it to me."

He grabbed her around the throat again and snatched her up. "I don't think so, Becca. I think you know who we're looking for. Crystal. I think you're up here with her in these woods somewhere. You know how I know this? This is my gun. She and her friends took it from me. Looks like it was fate that we met today. We couldn't keep up with her, but we got you." He looked at Heather still wrapped up by Dwayne. "And we got you, Heather."

"We gotta get off this road. Anybody can come up over that hill," said Jason. His thoughts of Becca's dress taking a backseat to his three thousand dollar payment and his ten thousand dollar bonus.

The trunk popped. Jason reached inside and opened a cloth bag that had a drawstring. He pulled out two plastic ties. He put Becca's hands behind her back and tied her hands together. He did the same to Heather.

"Now it's going to be a little tight," he said. "We normally only have one person in the trunk. But, Heather," he looked at the tattoos on Becca's face, "you must be a wonderful mother to make Becca mark up that pretty face like that. Use this time together in the trunk to talk about your differences. Talk to your daughter. Get to know her. We're all going to get to know her." He smiled. "Don't worry. We're going to get to know you, too."

"Come on, man!" Dwayne hurried him.

"You got this tiny little dress on, Becca. Let me help you in the trunk."

Becca stood there with tears coming out of her closed eyes as he stood behind her and took advantage of her short dress.

"Get your hands off of my daughter!" screamed Heather.

Jason's backhand sent her to the ground. He went back to Becca and pointed his finger at her, shutting her up before she said anything in protest. He helped her into the car and again helped himself as well. He then grabbed Heather by both biceps and lifted her to her feet. He helped her into the trunk. Heather's back was against Becca's chest.

"The trunk won't open from the inside. We fixed that. So that TV stuff won't work." He looked at Heather. "I don't like you. I don't like what you've done to Becca. You need to work on this relationship."

The trunk slammed shut.

38

The trunk was so dark and cramped.

Becca's breaths were rapid with fear. That man's hands. He was going to do more. All of the men were. She and Mom were going to be raped and murdered. They'd get Crystal, too. She'd been such a good friend. The best. And now she would die. Danielle and Dad and Grandma and Grandpa. She was going to lose them all.

Would she die before them? Or would she see her family murdered? Would she see the men kill Mom? She'd thought she wanted Mom to die, but now she knew she didn't. She knew that when she'd seen that man choking Mom. She didn't want Dad to die. She didn't want to die.

Mom had tried to save her. She had warned her even though the man had had a gun to her head. She had risked her life to save her. Mom was willing to die for her. This thought did nothing to lessen the terror of the moment, but it did increase the warmth of her mother's body pressed into hers.

Heather closed her eyes for a few seconds and reopened them. It was as dark with them open as with them closed. But, emotionally, it felt darker when her eyes were open. Maybe it was because the darkness was so unnaturally dark. Yet, amidst the darkness, like the shining of a single star against an otherwise black night's sky, she saw a light. She had done something good for another without any thought of return.

Her heart warmed, then smiled, then screamed with delight as she realized she had done something even greater. She had been willing to die for someone. But not just someone. She'd been willing to die for Becca. The daughter she'd rejected even before she was born. The daughter whose existence she'd tried to pretend didn't exist. The daughter who had been chasing her with a gun.

There's something good in me, she thought. *Maybe I'm not a monster. Maybe I can be normal. Maybe this thing has lost its power over me. Maybe it's gone.*

"We're going to die, aren't we?" said Becca.

Heather hesitated.

They felt the car turn abruptly left, hit something that caused a little bump, and turn back right. Instinctively, Heather knew the driver had gone out of his way to hit some small animal for sport. That took her hesitation away. These men were evil, and they had them bound in their trunk. "Yes, Becca, they're going to kill us."

"I need to say some things—to you, before they kill us," said Becca.

A grapefruit-sized tumor of fear inflated in Heather's belly. The light against the dark sky disappeared. She was about to be reminded that she had always been and would forever be a monster. At her best, incapable of giving love. At her worst, incapable of withholding hate.

"Is it okay if I call you Mom? It's just that we're going to die in a little while and—"

"I don't mind, Becca."

"Thank you," Becca said.

"You don't have to thank me." Heather was going to complete her statement with "I'm your mother," but that was not true. Mothers didn't treat their daughters the way she had treated Becca. She braced for a verbal beating she richly deserved.

Becca said, "I went to the abortion clinic that—"

Tears jumped out of Heather's eyes. She was glad for the darkness. Glad that she didn't have to look into the pain of Becca's eyes. Glad that she and Becca weren't facing one another in this trunk. For if they were, Heather knew no amount of darkness could hide her guilt.

"—the one," Becca paused to summon strength to finish, "the one where you and Dad, um, tried to abort me."

The trunk closed in upon Heather like a car crusher at the junkyard. She was damaged beyond repair and not even good enough for parts. Guilt pressed on her with irresistible force, reducing the size of her soul by half.

"I know about your trip to the abortion clinic," said Heather.

Becca blinked hard in the darkness. Had she heard her correctly? *She doesn't know Ta-Nisha, and she just met Crystal today.* "How could you know?"

Heather couldn't smile through the stake in her heart. "Your grandmother. She loves you very much. And Bill. It was both of them. Really, three of them."

Becca's head spun, but not with possibilities. Possibilities would've required at least partial bits of information. "What are you saying?"

"I'm saying one day my parents and your sister showed up at the house. I was upstairs and Mom was screaming at me from downstairs demanding that I come downstairs. They had Vincent cornered, but there was no way I was going down there. Mom started tearing up the house, so I had to come down."

"You mean really tearing up the house?" asked Becca.

"Becca, your grandmother started breaking vases, throwing plants on the floor—she broke my big mirror I used to have hanging by the stairs."

"Grandma broke that? And it wasn't an accident?"

"You know the lamp with the heavy base that sat on the table across from the mirror?"

"Yeah," Becca answered.

"I don't know how you accidently throw that into my mirror. She broke a lot of other stuff, too. I wouldn't have anything left if I had not gone downstairs."

"I know Grandma can get feisty, but why would she do that? That sounds nothing like her."

"For you, Becca. She did it for you. Mom has dreams. It has always driven your father crazy. Years ago, she had a dream that I was planning an abortion. I denied it, of course. They never knew about our attempts to abort you. I made your father swear to never tell them. We didn't."

I was planning an abortion.

Our attempts to abort you.

Becca heard the words. They were harsh. They were deadly. But they were words spoken from her mother to her. She was eighteen years old and the conversation in this car's trunk was literally the first time her mother had conversed with her without being influenced by a loaded gun. She tore the mold off the bread and took the worms from the soup of this unlikely conversation and gladly ate. She'd eat until these men killed them.

"Then soon after you left, Danielle told them that someone called her on your phone from the abortion clinic. They told her you had fallen out and had a seizure. They put two and two together and arrived at the house."

"Someone called Danielle from the abortion clinic?" Becca knew this wasn't Crystal or Ta-Nisha. "Okay," she conceded. *But how'd they get past my screen lock?* she wondered.

"Someone probably looked in your purse and found your phone," said Heather.

"I guess so." She pondered. "But even with Grandma's dream—that was so long ago. I don't see how me falling out at the clinic would've told them that you and Dad—" Becca didn't want to finish the thought.

"That's where your sister comes in. She can be quite persuasive. She loves you more than you know, Becca. She told Mom and Dad everything. How cruel we've been to you. They asked us whether we knew of this clinic. We weren't very convincing. Did you know that your sister moved in with your grandparents to protest how we treated you? She's threatening now to sue your father and I for separation. She apparently wants to make her disgust of us legal and public." Heather's heart grew even heavier. "I think she's really going to do it."

Becca recalled when she had Crystal to take her home and she had seen through the window everyone hugging. She must have misunderstood. *Oh, what have I done? I'm sorry, Danielle.* "I haven't been answering texts or calls from Danielle or Grandma. They love me. I know they do. I closed my eyes to the truth and chose to believe a lie. Oh, God, what have I done?" She started crying. "And now they'll never know that I'm sorry."

"You're a good person, Becca. You made a mistake. It doesn't change who you are. I'm sure they know that." She thought how she wished those words were true of herself. "That's why they've been fighting for you. Mom and Dad are as disgusted with us as your sister is."

The car stopped.

Becca panicked. Something horrible was about to happen to her. Yet, the greatest fear was that there was still so much she needed to hear and she'd never get the chance. She listened for car doors opening. So did Heather.

After a few minutes of terror-filled waiting in silence, Heather said, "Becca, these moments are precious. Let's not waste them waiting to die."

"Mom."

Heather braced herself for the question she knew Becca must ask.

"Why'd you and Dad do it? Why didn't you want me? Why don't you want me now?" *Please give us time, God,* Becca begged. *I need to know.* He hadn't been real for eighteen years, but if He was real, maybe He'd at least give her this before she was raped and murdered.

Heather gathered her courage and hoped her words would help Becca. She hoped they would help her, too. "Becca, you need to know, and I need to tell."

For the next several minutes, Heather bared her soul and was brutally honest with Becca. She told her about her own painful childhood and of being abused by her natural father. "There are no excuses for my behavior, Becca. I'm not telling you this to minimize what I've done."

"No, Mom, please tell me. I want to know about your life."

Heather tried to hold back the tears. This wasn't her moment; it was Becca's. She was the one who had suffered all these years. "I'm sorry for crying, Becca, I just—" That was as far as she got before the pressure of pain broke her resistance. Forty years of pain gushed out of her eyes and mouth.

"It's okay, Mom," Becca said through tears. "You need to cry." Becca pulled against the plastic strips around her wrists until they cut into her flesh. *She needed to hold her mom!* It was impossible. Eighteen years of living with a block of ice and now that she was thawing, she couldn't touch her. *I need to touch my Mom!* Becca pressed her lips to her mother's head and kissed her again and again and again.

Heather knew they were running out of time. She fought through the tears. "Becca, I hear my father's voice in my head all the time. It torments me. Every day, telling me I'm stupid and that I'm good for nothing, but having children. I'm so sorry that I've become him. Really, I'm worse than him. I didn't criticize or beat you. I ignored you. I pretended you didn't exist."

Heather wanted so desperately to beg her daughter's forgiveness, but that would've been selfish. And deep down inside, she knew forgiveness wasn't for her. She was too bad. She'd wrecked her daughter's life. She deserved punishment, whether it came from Becca, God, or the men who had kidnapped them.

"Becca, I didn't want a baby when you came along because I was so damaged. I was convinced that I was stupid and couldn't succeed at anything but have children. That's what my father taught me. I don't know how, but there was some kind of evil power in his words. They made me believe that having a child was proof that he was right. I needed to prove my father's prophecies wrong.

"I went to law school and couldn't pass the bar examination. I failed it over and over and over. That's why I'm a paralegal." She started crying again and stopped herself. "It's okay. I've accepted it. My father was right."

Becca wanted to say, "No, Mom, he wasn't right. You can do it," but time was running out. She needed more answers. So she listened in silence.

"When you came along, in my mind the pregnancy was a sentence of lifelong failure. I know now that I was wrong, but unfortunately today's truth doesn't erase yesterday's lie."

"But why'd you have Danielle? She's only a year younger than me. What changed in a year?"

Heather breathed heavily out of her mouth. "This is not easy, Becca, but I've denied you so much for so long that I won't lie to you now even though the truth is horrible. We love Danielle now that she's here—"Heather knew she'd just hurt Becca by mentioning their love for Danielle—"but, honestly, we had her because of guilt. We were trying to do it right."

Becca was silent. Mom had been right. This was horrible.

The silence in the cramped trunk was awkward. Mother and daughter were practically welded together. They physically felt one another's tension. There was no way to hide anything. Even in the darkness.

"Do what right?" Becca asked. "You had a baby. Me. Why'd you need another baby to make it right? If one baby made you feel like a failure, how would two babies make it right?"

Heather closed her eyes tight in regret. She'd tell the truth. "Not two babies, Becca."

Becca was silent. Her eyes searched the darkness for an answer other than the one that had begun to peel the skin from her soul the moment the words had gone from Heather's mouth. "Not two babies?" It was a lament of realization, not a question."

Fresh tears rolled down Heather's face. Her words were horrible. Her behavior even worse. But she felt guilt deep in the center of whatever monsters were made of, and this was good. Maybe it was evidence of humanity. "No, Becca. I'm sorry. I thought that since I was a failure at everything else a new baby would help me."

"Why a new baby, Mom?" Becca pressed. "What was wrong with me? Why couldn't I be the baby?"

"I hated you, Becca. That's why. I hated you the moment I found out I was pregnant."

Heather couldn't say any more, and Becca couldn't take any more. Silence.

The urgency of the moment pushed Heather to continue. They'd both be dead soon, but Becca deserved to know as much as time would allow her to share. Maybe she could give her daughter a few minutes of knowing that there was nothing wrong with her as a daughter.

"Becca, I know from experience how easy it is to blame yourself when your parent treats you cruelly. It doesn't make sense, but it's how our mind works. There was never anything wrong with you. I hated you because there was something wrong with me. I don't know what it is, Becca, but I'm not right. There's something terribly wrong with me. Something deep down inside. Something evil.

"At first, the pregnancy was a threat to my success and my emotional health. Once you were born, you were the cause of my lack of success. That's what I believed. I did try to love you, but every time I looked at you, there was nothing but rage and hatred and regret. I knew this was wrong. It was evil and abnormal. I was ashamed of myself, but couldn't change.

"As time passed, it got worse. Every time you cried, every time you needed to be fed or changed, every time you said, 'Ma-Ma,' every time I heard your name or looked at your face, revulsion for you boiled inside of me. Revulsion for you and revulsion for me. I knew that abortion was wrong before I tried it. But I knew that hating my own baby was unnatural." Then barely audible, she said, "I'm worse than an animal."

Every time you cried...

Every time you needed to be fed or changed...

Every time you said Ma-Ma...

"Stop it!" screamed Becca. "Why are you telling me this? I don't want to hear any more!"

Heather felt her daughter's chest and abdomen bounce against her as she cried. "Because you need to know that none of this is your fault," she said with a true mother's authority. "You need to know that for some cruel, unfair reason you were born into the family of an evil woman and a weak man. You need to know that you are beautiful and talented and intelligent and sweet and—"emotion gripped Heather's throat, making it difficult to get her next words out—"I'm sorry that I'm just telling you this."

Becca felt like a Mexican piñata. She was dangling helplessly from the ceiling, beaten with silence and neglect until her insides had spilled onto the floor, and her mom, one of the two who had done this, was picking her candy up off the floor and telling her how wonderful it was. *This was in SANE!*

The damage was done. It couldn't be undone. But she needed to know. "What about Dad?"

"Your father has a tender heart, but he can be weak. He never really wanted an abortion. He went along with it to help me. We went to the clinic. Your father was in the waiting room. I was in the patient's room on the table. I told the doctor..." Heather paused, horrified at the memory.

"I know what you told Dr. Li," said Becca.

The darkness concealed the shocked look on Heather's face. She spun her face toward Becca. "How do you know of Dr. Li?"

Becca said, "You said, 'I need this baby dead today.'"

"Oh, my God." Heather's words were filled with grief and shame. "How long have you known? How did you find out?"

Becca thought of the futility of the questions. "Does it matter?"

"All this time, all this time, you've known," Heather whined. After several seconds, she said, "Dr. Li was preparing to begin when something bizarre happened."

"Music," said Becca.

Heather let out a deceptively low wail that sounded like her level of pain was muffled by a constricted throat.

Becca's words sounded wispy. "*Highway to Hell.* That was the song that played," she said. Its mysterious memory surfacing like a vague dream coming back. "I heard it."

Heather wailed again.

Becca looked into the dream's murky images. She saw big scissors coming at a tiny baby. Her. The scissors were closing in on her. "I see the scissors," said Becca. The baby started praying. Becca repeated the words out loud in the darkness of the car's trunk. "'Have mercy on me, O Lord, for I am weak…O Lord my God, in You I put my trust. Save me from all those who persecute me. And deliver me, or they will tear me like a lion, rending me in pieces, while there is none to deliver.' That's what I prayed when Dr. Li was trying to get me."

Heather's throat was no longer constricted. Her wails and groans and cries filled the trunk. Becca was certain the men heard her. "Mom, you have to quiet down. They're going to hear you."

It took about twenty gasps for her to stop the wails. Then a long, loud, "I'm sorry," left her mouth. "Oh, God, only the Lord could've told you that. Mom was right. She told us that if we did anything bad to you, the truth would come out. I knew from the moment I went to that hellish abortion clinic that I had made Him angry. I knew He would send me to hell for it, Becca, and I still did it. I tried to tell myself that He wasn't real. I tried to make myself forget what I had done. But every time I looked at you, my conscience screamed, 'Guilty!' That's why I hated you. That's why I couldn't look at you.'"

It was Becca's turn to wail, and there was nothing constricting her throat.

"Becca, I have something you need to know before they come. I know they can hear us." Becca continued wailing. "Baby, you need to stop. It's about your father."

This had the intended effect.

"Dad?" Becca cried. "What?"

"After the music in the abortion clinic stopped, Vincent jumped through the opening over the receptionist's desk. He tore through that place and ran down the hall and burst through the door. Dr. Li and the nurse and I looked at him like he was crazy. The doctor had the instrument in her hand. He told Dr. Li that if she twitched, he'd kill her there on the spot. I protested, but he took me out of there." Heather sniffled. "Becca, I was angry then, but I am so proud of him now. He was strong. He stood up to me. Your father saved your life."

Becca started wailing again.

The trunk popped. It was snatched up. Dwayne peered down at them. "Shut up!" Becca looked up, the terror back and fresh. She swallowed her emotions. "I come back here again, I'm gonna beat all that crying and hollering out of somebody!"

He slammed the trunk.

They waited about thirty seconds.

"Dad saved my life?" Becca whispered. "Dad threatened Dr. Li?"

"Yes, he never really wanted the abortion. Things haven't been right between us since that day. That's why we're separated." Heather knew what Becca was thinking. "Becca, there's no excuse for either of our failures as parents." She pondered. "But your father has always loved you."

Becca didn't respond to the curse words that surfaced in her mind. She didn't respond to the questions or the accusations. She just leaned back and looked into the darkness.

"Our greatest fights have been over you. Vincent is eaten up with guilt over allowing the plans for abortion to progress as far as they did. He feels that he has failed you as a father and doesn't deserve you. I looked at you and hated you. But Vincent, your daddy, looked at you and loved you. And you adored him. What he did…what he almost allowed to happen, haunts him. He believes he's a fraud. That's why he leaves whenever you're around. And that's why he throws himself into Danielle. He does love her, but like me, he felt that he could hide from his crimes in Danielle's shadow. It's no excuse for anything. I just felt you needed to know this about your father."

Heather and Becca went silent. Their hearts were not empty. There was so much that could and needed to be said. But what had already been spoken, and the accompanying emotions, demanded attention.

The truth was horrible. Yet Heather knew she had done the right thing. She could go to her grave at least with the knowledge that she had confessed her sins to Becca. She deserved to suffer and be punished for them. She knew this. She wasn't looking for forgiveness. Yet she couldn't ignore the fact that the crushing heaviness she lived with day and night since her pregnancy with Becca had lifted. She also couldn't deny the fact that despite all that had occurred today, and in this trunk, *she did not love Becca.*

Becca sorted through her thoughts like someone cutting her way through a thick jungle infested with hungry, wild animals. She couldn't handle what may be lurking in the bushes, but she had to address what was directly in her path. "Mom, do you love me?"

Heather's answer was immediate and impassioned. "Yes, Becca, I love you—with all of my heart," she lied.

Becca closed her eyes, smiled, and inhaled the scent of her mother's hair. She ignored the dull ache in her arm.

39

*L*ord, I'm sorry for lying to Becca. She's been through so much, and I've hurt her so much that I couldn't tell her the truth. I wish I could love her. She deserves a mother's love. She deserves my love. You know I've tried. I've tried everything I know, but nothing works. How does Vincent do it? Why can't I be like him? Why can't I be normal? How did I become a monster?

Lord, I'm lying next to the most remarkable young woman... I want to love her. Help me, please. I'm so sorry for trying to abort her. I'm sorry for how I treated her. I told her that it was because of guilt. I told her that it was because I was irrationally angry at her for the failures of my life. I know that's part of it. I think it is. But there's more. Something is inside of me. Something that hates Becca is inside of me. It won't let me love her. It makes me hate my own daughter.

God, I don't know what this thing is, but it's evil. I can feel its hatred for Becca rise within me whenever she is near or whenever her name is mentioned.

Heather stopped praying. How could she have not noticed until now? She hadn't felt the thing's hatred inside of her since Becca surprised her at the cabin's door and invited her inside with her gun. And she was actually lying next to Becca! How could this be? Before today, her daughter had been to her like the flu. Her physical presence made her sick.

God, what's happening? Heather resumed praying. *I'm not sick.* Heather opened her eyes in the darkness and considered how every part of her body felt. *God, I'm lying next to this beautiful child and I'm not sick. Oh, God, is it real? Will it last? Can I love her now? Am I finally free?*

Heather felt a sudden concentration of nausea in her belly spreading up and down her body. Her whole system felt comprised and weak. Strength escaped her pores like sweat on a hot day. The shaking queasiness that moved through her abdomen and chest like an earthquake threatened to empty her belly in the car's tight trunk. Something inside of her was enraged that she wasn't facing her daughter. It wanted her to vomit on her daughter. No, *it*, the thing inside of her, wanted to vomit on her daughter.

Nooooo! Why now? Lord, I've been with her for hours and felt nothing. I felt fear, but only because she had a gun. I even felt fondness. Why is this happening now? These men are going to kill us any moment. Will I leave this world hating this precious child?

The crushing heaviness was back. Heather lay under its suffocating weight, resigned to leave this world as a monster, and straining with everything in her to hold down the volcano of vomit that was pushing upward. The most bitter tears of her tormented life burned trails down her face.

God, why am I like this? If You are real, if You hear me, have mercy and help me, she prayed.

The answer from heaven was immediate. It was a thought flash, but was like a super concentrate that carried a gallon on a teaspoon. Heather saw and heard the event as though she were at the center of a giant sphere with theater screens that covered its entirety and thunderous stereo that came from every direction.

Heather was ten months pregnant and sitting at home at the kitchen table. She held a sonogram of Becca in her hand. She looked at it with a look of utter scorn. "Why did he stop the abortion? I don't want you! You're ruining my life!"

Another scene immediately followed that one.

Becca was six months old and in her crib. Heather stood at the door. She had just learned that she had failed the bar examination again. "I hate you," she screamed. Becca's little body went rigid with fear. "You've ruined my life! I hate you! I hate looking at you! You make me sick! Every time I look at you, every time I get near you, every time I hear your name, it makes me sick! You make me sick, Becca!"

Heather remembered. Clearly. How could she have been so evil? What kind of person would say something that cruel to a baby? The finger pointed at her. *She would. She did.* Her thoughts were interrupted by something her mother had told her years ago.

"If you give yourself over to your sin, God will give you over to your sin. He'll turn you over to a reprobate mind. You don't want that to happen, Heather. The sin will become your master, and you'll suffer the consequences."

It clicked.

She remembered. That's when the sickness began! The very first day. She had been feeling fine until the very moment she spoke those words.

Oh, Lord, I see it, she prayed. *I see what I've done. Please forgive me. I'm sorry I said those awful things. I don't want to leave this world without loving my daughter. Please, please, please...Mom says You're a merciful God. I need mercy. I can't face You like this.*

Heather felt something tug gently behind both of her shoulder blades. It wasn't physical; it was spiritual. She wondered at the sensation. *Yank!* She felt something inside of her tear. Then the tear proceeded slowly along the lining of her body or spirit or something. It wasn't painful. The closest thing she could liken it to was the inside liner of a jacket being removed.

She sensed a swirling sensation coming toward her, like a small tornado. *Swoosh!* It entered her. A slow smile came to Heather's face. The sickness was gone. That was fantastic! But this wasn't the reason why her mouth was wide open.

"Becca."

"Yes, Mom?"

"I love you."

Becca smiled. Her face quickly becoming a mixture of emotions—all good. "I love you, too, Mom."

"I love you," Heather said, again. "I *love* you." She started laughing. "I love you. I love my daughter. I love my daughter!"

Becca laughed and cried, not understanding what had happened, but sensing that this was the moment she had desired all her life.

Heather and Becca heard a clicking sound. Their mouths shut. This was it. They looked in fear toward the place that a man's face would appear. Maybe all three of them would be there, looking down at them with lust and murder in their eyes. A minute passed. Two minutes. Heather pushed the trunk with her head. It raised. She waited for someone to rush to the back and scream at her. No one came. She looked through the opening of the trunk behind the back window. What?

"Becca, I don't see anyone."

"No one? They have to be there. Someone popped the trunk."

"Becca, I'm telling you I don't see anyone." Heather stuck her head out the side. "Becca! Quick! Let's go! No one's out there!"

Becca's heart jumped. "What?" she asked, as she moved quickly to get up.

Heather put her legs out first and stood to the ground. She looked at her daughter. "Come on, baby. God has set us free."

"We have to get these things off our hands," Becca said, as she got out. She stepped on something and looked down. She froze. Heather looked at it and froze, too. "A knife? Mom, it's a knife."

Heather sat down with her back to it and grasped it. She got on her knees, then stood. "Let's go."

"Wait," said Becca. "She went to the car and looked in. No keys. She put her head against the car's trunk and pushed. It didn't move. "Mom, go to the other side. I don't know what's going on, but let's close it just in case so they won't know we're gone."

They closed it and ran into the woods. They'd work on getting the ties off their hands once they were in a safe spot.

The angel of truth watched until they disappeared into the trees. Then he disappeared.

40

The men watched her from the woods.

"This doesn't make any sense," said Crystal, standing on the cabin porch and looking down at her car. "That is a good battery." She looked in the distance where the road left the tree surrounded property and decided against another search for Becca and her mother. Had Heather gotten away? Crystal's gut wrenched at the thought of Becca's stupid plan.

Becca was a naïve, impulsive, needy girl who kept things interesting, but she was a great friend—more like a sister, and she could do nearly everything. She thought of the day she had first met her. Had she really heard something? Or was she just desperate? She rolled the words over in her mind. *Take care of her, and I'll remove your pain.*

Who would remove her pain? Was it saying *it* would literally remove her pain if she took care of Becca? Or did it mean her friendship with Becca would remove the pain? A less promising thought sat rudely and uninvited at the table of her musings. *What if I'm simply talking to myself?*

Crystal looked at the car as though it were a puzzle put together with no missing pieces and still unclear. "There is *nothing* wrong with that battery." She ran down the stairs and popped the hood again.

Becca held her mother's hand and led the way through the trees back to the cabin. The hilly terrain was slower and more challenging for Heather than had they walked on the road. But the slowed pace and extra effort were worth not being spotted by those criminals.

"Are you okay, Mom?" Becca asked, as she pulled her up the final yard of a moderately steep incline.

Heather felt the strength in her daughter's grip. She looked at the front muscles of Becca's leg and her long, defined bicep as she made the last step and stood beside her. "Yeah." She took a deep breath. "You're really strong, Becca. Do you lift weights?"

They started walking. Becca again leading the walk while helping her mother's speed by holding her hand. "Yeah. Strength training helps with my sports. Let me know when you're ready to start running again."

After running for her life from Becca, and now running with Becca to save their family's lives, her lungs were on fire and her legs were filled with cement. It would be days before she'd be ready to run again. "Come on." Heather took off at a pace just below a sprint. She had to warn her family.

Becca caught up and slowed her down with her hand. "We have to pace ourselves, Mom. Control your breathing. Deep, controlled breaths. You'll get more oxygen to your muscles. It'll help your endurance."

Heather obeyed, recalling her high school track days. If only she had her high school legs. She looked at the passing trees and wondered what they'd find once there were no more trees before them. Was their family dead or alive?

The tedious cycle of running and walking finally ended behind the house. This meant another walk up a hill. Heather stretched her arm out in front of her for assistance. Becca gripped her hand and up they went. They stopped at the edge and crouched behind trees. Each with her own tree.

Becca looked over at her mom. "Those men could be in there. I'm going to go check."

Heather wasn't about to let her daughter get near that cabin without her. "I'm going with you."

"Mom," Becca said, "we don't know where those men are. They could be in the cabin." She studied the surroundings. "Or they could be in the trees looking at the cabin. I need to find out if our family has arrived. And I need to warn Crystal. If those men see me, I stand a better chance of getting away if I'm alone. Promise me, Mom, if anything happens, don't come out."

Heather's expression promised nothing of the sort.

"Mom," Becca pressed, "do *not* come out. Get out of here as fast as you can."

"If those men catch you—"

Becca stopped her. "Mom, you have to trust me. They can not catch me. *No one* can catch me."

Heather thought of her daughter's university track scholarships and how easily she had caught up with her when she was chasing her. "They have guns, Becca."

"Mom, God got us out of that trunk and left a knife for us. If He can get us out of that trunk, He can protect me from their bullets. Pray."

"How are you going to get in? The bottom door is probably locked. It's too risky going up the deck stairs and into the kitchen."

"Same way you got out, Mom."

Heather looked at the sheets she had tied together that were hanging from the window. "You're going to climb up *that*?"

"You did it."

"But that was going down. And I slid the whole way."

"Mom, at school we have a rope hanging from the ceiling. We climb it in gym class. I do it all the time. I hold the school record for the girls."

Heather's eyes watered. She recalled now. Danielle had told her about her sister's record. "I'm sorry, Becca. I never said anything to you about your record."

Becca fought the urge to hug her mom and cry until she couldn't cry any longer. But she had to think like the champion athlete that she was. *Goal. Discipline. Focus. Execution. Trophy.* "I have to go."

Heather grabbed her face with both palms and kissed her on the forehead. "I love you. Be careful."

"I love you, too, Mom." She lifted a finger. "No hero stuff this time. Don't come out."

"I won't." Heather lowered herself and watched her daughter sprint to the basement door. She knew she had given a promise she couldn't keep. She'd never abandon this amazing child again.

Becca looked in a window. Ping-pong table. Pool table. Foosball table. No men. She ran to the left edge of the cabin and looked. Heather could tell that she was pondering whether to go around farther. Becca decided against it and ran back and past the door to the opposite end. She peeked her head out and brought it back. She ran to the sheets and tugged it. She gripped with both hands and hung, pulling her knees up. It was strong enough.

Becca trotted backward several feet and ran toward the sheets. She leapt with one leg extended toward the wall and her hands poised to grab the sheets. Her flat sole touched the wall and Heather's mouth opened in awe. There were nothing but long legs and a ridiculously short dress going up the side of a wall as though gravity didn't exist. The girl was like Spiderman.

Becca's footing slipped. She dangled. Heather gasped in fear, then wondered in admiration as Becca extended both legs sideways, one tight against the other as though sitting on the floor, and pulled herself up the remaining six feet. She disappeared into the bathroom.

———

Crystal first or Mom first? the quick thought went through Becca's mind.

The basement door opened. "Mom, come on! Lock it behind you." She hurried her with a hand.

Becca raced back upstairs. She opened the front door. Crystal was under her car's hood with a flashlight. Becca opened her mouth to call her. Something directly ahead and to the right edge of the woods moved about fifty yards away and caught her attention. Three crouched men crept upon Crystal under the darkening sky. "Crystal, run!" screamed Becca.

Crystal jumped and dropped the flashlight. She turned and looked at Becca. She was pointing behind her.

"They're coming!" Becca yelled.

Crystal looked back and saw three men running toward her. *Motivation!* She took off toward the stairs.

Becca could see them more clearly now. "They've got guns, Crystal! Hurry!"

Crystal stumbled forward as she neared the steps. Her arms stretched before her to break the fall. It didn't stop the top of her head from banging into the wooden step. She lay there, not out but too stunned to move.

The men were sprinting toward them. A shot rang out. A bullet hit the door near Becca. She jumped, eyes wide, legs gripped still with terror. *Focus.* She kicked herself free of its grip and hurried down the stairs.

"Don't shoot Crystal!" Boss Man's brother yelled, as they got closer.

"Not shootin' at that hoe," said Dwayne. "Shootin' at that bald head girl trying to help her."

Becca went straight to Crystal's ankles and grabbed both. It was there. She pulled up a pant and removed the gun. She'd never fired a gun before in her life. She doubted that she could hit three moving targets in the dark, but they didn't know that. She raised the gun and started firing.

"That girl shootin' at us!" one of the men said, as they all stopped and ran back from where they had come.

Crystal made it to her feet, but was still wobbly. She leaned heavily on the bottom railing. Becca turned the gun sideways and bit down hard on the chamber and carried it with her mouth. It wasn't the safest thing in the world, but it was safer than being outside one second more than necessary. She bent down and scooped Crystal up into her arms and hurried up the stairs. Heather slammed the door behind her.

"We have to get some help," said Becca, as she got on her knees and laid Crystal on the sofa.

"Who are those guys?" Crystal said, making a move to get up.

Becca tenderly pushed her back down. "Hold up. You may have a concussion. You rocked that step pretty hard."

"You were there for me," Crystal said. "You *carried* me up the stairs?"

"I'll always be there for you." She smiled. "Friends are there for their friends."

Heather looked at Becca. She looked at Crystal. *I'll always be there for you?* Her eyes narrowed.

"Car's not working. I don't know why. You gotta call the cops," said Crystal.

"Can't. No land line and you can't get a signal here," said Becca.

"Those men are looking for you," said Heather.

Crystal sat up slowly. Becca didn't protest. "For me?"

"One of them said you and your friends took his gun," Heather added, angry that she had brought this danger upon her daughter.

Crystal closed her eyes and blew out a long breath and cursed. "Boss Man's brother. His name is Reggie. But what is he doing here? He followed me?"

"Evidently so," Heather said, shaking her head and tightening her lips in irritation.

"Mom, we make it out of here alive, we can fill in the blanks later. Okay?" Her expression was soft and understanding.

Heather nodded her head.

"Now, we can't sit here and wait for these guys to break in. And I don't know where everyone is, but we don't want them here when the family arrives. We need help. Help's not coming. We have to go get it."

"If we hurry, we can go out the back and leave the way we came," said Heather to Becca.

"No, we can't let the family walk into this. They don't know what's going on."

Heather didn't like where this was going. Neither did Crystal.

"I'm going. It's our only chance," she said, knowing that they knew she was right.

"There is another way," said Crystal, her face carrying something heroic, but sad. "I could go with them."

"Are you crazy?" said Becca. "Those guys had me and Mom locked in a car trunk. We saw their faces. They saw our faces. They want to kill all of us. Sacrificing yourself just makes their job easier." She looked at her mom. "I need you to stay here, Mom. I *need* you to stay *here*."

Crystal looked at both of them and twisted her face into a big question mark. "I know I bumped my head pretty hard. Maybe I'm not who I think I am." She looked at Becca. "Last time I saw you, you were chasing *her* with a loaded gun. What's changed?"

"We talked," said Becca. *Focus.*

"You talked," said Crystal.

"You're my best friend. Always. Forever. Gotta go," said Becca.

"Take the gun," said Crystal.

"No, use it to take care of yourself and Mom."

Heather hurried to her suitcase a couple of yards away. She plopped to her knees and rummaged through it. "Here. Take this and this." It was a pair of jeans and a light sweater. "That dress is entirely too short. It's not even a dress. And you need something for your arms."

Becca's chest heaved with emotion that wanted to push tears from her eyes. She was being scolded by her mom for wearing inappropriate clothing. *She had a mom.*

Focus.

Becca put the pants on under the dress and slipped on the sweater. She looked at the fireplace and grabbed the thick fireplace poker. She kissed and hugged her mom. "I love you, Mom." She kissed and hugged Crystal. "I love you, Crystal. Friends forever."

Becca left out the basement door and sprinted for the woods.

41

*T*rust me.

Becca heard the thought. It was hard not to hear it. There was nothing else to hear in the darkness, and—she—was—*straining* to hear. She did not want to run into those men. They shouldn't be anywhere near where she was, but it was dark, they were dangerous, and everyone's lives depended on her getting help to them in time.

She was glad Mom had made her change. She had forgotten how chilly it could get in the mountains. *Thank you, Mom.* She thought of how to best make time in the darkness of the woods. The plan had sounded plausible in the cabin, but with dark woods and a tricky ground, she'd either have to walk slowly or risk running into a tree or breaking an ankle. Or she could run as fast as she could on the road and hope the men were—

Hope the men were what? Too busy trying to sneak up on Mom and Crystal to discover her? This plan couldn't work. They'd be dead long before she could can find help. There was no warning. It hit her. She fell to her knees. Then onto her belly. Her arms sprawled above her head on the soft ground.

The emotion of helplessness had hit her with the weight of possibly losing everyone she loved. Tears poured out as her hot breath met the ground below her face. "I'm so sorry, Mom. I haven't even had you for a full day, and now I'm alone again." Her desperate thoughts turned to God. "You're the only one who could've freed us from the trunk. If it was you, why did you do it? Why did you free us from the trunk of a car and leave us a knife only to let my family die?"

Do you trust Me?

Becca didn't hear a voice. It was more like an impression against the back of her mind. Words that pressed against her the way two fingers pressed against the back of her hand would "say" two fingers. She stopped crying. Her short breaths released into the soil. "Yes. You saved me and my mom."

Go to where the men are. Do not try to hide yourself.

Becca's eyes widened. She could not have heard correctly. She was trying to get away from them, not be killed by them. How would giving herself to these men help their situation? "They'll kill me, Lord," she whispered to the thought that she could not have heard. "Mom and Crystal are depending upon me. I can't let them down."

Take the poker and go to the men.

Becca stood there like a life-like mannequin. She couldn't do it. She couldn't give herself to them. *That man's hands.* He had violated her right there in front of her mother. Becca wasn't strong any more. She was a terrified, helpless teenager, whose only idea to help save her friend's and family's lives was impossible. What was she to do?

Run, Becca! If you go now, none will be lost. But you must go NOW!

Becca ran.

The moon was out, but stingy with its light.

Becca crossed the road and descended the steep embankment sideways, faster than she would have ever tried during daylight. Hopping, sliding, navigating, like she was an extreme sport athlete navigating a crazy, snowy mountain with skis. But this wasn't a sport or game. It was life or death. The heavy fireplace poker wasn't long enough to help with footing. She hopped. The ground tricked her.

Something caught her foot in mid-air. Her momentum pushed her upper body forward. She tumbled and bounced twenty feet and landed with a thud.

Becca's eyes opened. She was on her side. It took a few moments to gather her thoughts. Then a thought gathered her.

Run, Becca, run!

Becca sprung to her feet and started running with both hands gripping opposite ends of the poker, which surprisingly hadn't been lost. She stretched her hands defensively in front of her as she ran. In a short while, she was wondering where she was. Panic shot up and down her spine and settled in her chest. "Where am I? Where am I? I can't get lost," she whimpered. She remembered the thought. *Trust me.*

A trail of desperate tears ran down Becca's face. "Okay, okay, okay. I'm trying. I'm trying. I'm trying. I'm trying so hard to trust you. I can't see. I don't know what direction I'm going. You have to help me. You have to help me, God."

Becca ran. She had no idea whether she was running toward or away from the cabin. The more she ran, the more the cause seemed lost. The men would have waited for full darkness to approach the house. How many bullets did Crystal's gun hold? How many had she shot? Three? Four? Ten? She had no idea.

A memory of a Bible story came to her mind. A story she must've learned at her grandparents' church when she was younger. God's people were in the wilderness and they needed water. They found a pool of water, but it wasn't fit to drink. God told Moses to cut down a tree and throw it in the water. He did and the water was healed.

Becca ran, wondering at the story. She heard something and stopped, moving nothing but eyes full of fear. Her silent breathing sounded like thunder to her ears. She had to be quiet. The men began arguing. They were arguing about what to do with the women—her and Mom and Crystal!—when they caught them.

The men's lustful, murderous plans made Becca sick. The only thing that kept her from throwing up was that it would get her killed. *Oh, my God! You can't let them do that to us.*

The men split up.

One came in her direction.

Everything shut down in Becca. She was so scared she could not have thrown up now had she stuck a feather duster down her throat.

Focus. Discipline. Execution.

Becca gripped one end of the metal poker and picked up and moved her leg with the stillness of a cat creeping up on a bird. Her foot touched down onto the leaves. She did this once more and she was behind a tree. The man didn't appear to have his gun out yet. If he came close enough to her, she could be on him before he knew it.

Lean the poker against this tree and walk quickly to your right. Scream when I tell you to, and I will give you the rest of your heart's desire.

The thought was loud. Not like the others. It could've come from outside of her, but she knew it hadn't. Her expression looked like she was staring at a truck that was about to hit her. *What? That is the craziest thing I've ever heard. I can't do that. This can't be God.*

The story of God healing the bitter water by throwing a tree in the pool surfaced again.

Oh, my God. Becca was trapped. If she said nothing and kept hiding behind the tree, she could make it out of there alive. But would that be alive? Hiding in the woods while her mother and best friend, who were waiting on her to send help, were raped and murdered? But what would happen if she did what the voice said? Be raped and murdered. No matter what she did, she lost. It was a no win situation.

Or was it?

She thought of how the car's trunk had mysteriously popped open, and of the knife that had conveniently been left on the ground by the car so they could get out of the plastic ties. If God could do that, He could save them from these men. But leave the poker leaning against a tree and *screaming?* That was as ridiculous as healing bad water by throwing a tree in the pool.

She leaned the poker against the tree. Lord, *I hope this tree works as well as your other one*, she thought. *If it doesn't, we're all dead.* Becca could see the man about forty feet away. She had been wrong. His gun was out! She took a deep breath and started walking quickly to her right, out in the open.

Dwayne crouched. He looked to the right. He started to shout to the others when he saw her. He stopped himself and smiled. He had a better idea. There were a lot of trees between him and the girl, but they weren't dense. He could see her clearly. He sprinted.

Becca heard him coming. *Run or stay?* It took everything in her to not take off. She turned around and looked terrified. It wasn't an act.

"Don't move!"

Becca's hands shot up. "I'm not. Please don't shoot me."

Dwayne came to a halt six feet away, gun pointing at her, and enjoying every moment of the girl's terror. He looked at her clothes. "You gotta lotta surprises, Becca. I don't like this new style of yours. I like the other one better."

Becca's lips trembled. She forgot the car's trunk. She forgot the knife. She forgot the voice. The only thing she remembered was the power she felt unleashed when she had shot Crystal's gun, and now one was pointed at her.

The man smiled, but his smile had nothing but evil in it. "You didn't hear me?"

"What? I don't know what you mean," she said. Her hands shook and her chest bounced with a hundred short gasps.

"I said I don't like your new clothes. Get them pants off."

Becca hesitated with the shock that she was about to be raped. She took her pants off.

"Get that sweater off, too. It ain't cold out here."

She took the sweater off.

"What you holding on to it fo'? You ain't puttin' it back on. Throw it down."

She did.

He looked her up and down and licked his lips. "Turn around in a circle." She did. "You look a lot better now." He looked at her tattoos. "Why you put that crap on yo' face?"

Becca didn't answer.

"Make no difference. I'm mo' interested in the rest of yo' body anyway." He glanced in the directions that he knew the other men had gone to. "Who you like better? Me or Jason? Hint. Jason ain't here and I am."

Becca had to work to make her trembling mouth move. "You."

"Told that cracker you like me more than you like him. Good. I'm gone let you show me how much you like me. Turn around and go right. We gone find someplace better. I'm lookin' fo' a special tree."

A special tree.

Tree. The tree in the pool of bitter water.

They walked into an area thick with leaves on the ground that crunched under their feet.

Becca's mind didn't shift from the gear of fear it was stuck in, but she could now hear the voice of God over its loud grinding.

Scream as loud and as long as you can and shuffle your feet in the leaves. Don't stop.

Huh? she thought.

She didn't see him, but the angel stood only ten feet away directly in her path. "Scream now!"

Becca started screaming and shuffling her feet, making as much noise as she could.

Dwayne stopped, shocked at her sudden screaming. He had chosen to walk behind her to watch her butt and make lewd comments. After a few seconds, anger replaced his shock. "Shut up!" he said, as he sped up to hit her with the gun. He flipped the gun on its side in his hand and raised it.

Whack!

The sound of metal crashing a human skull with such force was horrible. The skull cracked. The screaming stopped. The body fell into a soft bed of forest leaves, bark, and twigs. Quiet stillness fell upon the violent assault and covered it the way a theater curtain closes a show.

The man stood over the body with his weapon in his hand. He was fighting the urge to not swing again and again and again until there was nothing left to strike.

Becca looked at her father's face. His fury. The iron poker she had left was still poised above his head, as though contemplating another strike. *No, please, don't do it. Don't kill...*

She was too shocked to speak, but not too shocked to wonder. She looked at the weapon in his hand. The voice. It had promised her safety. He...God had promised her safety, and she had obeyed. This was her reward for obeying God.

Becca looked at her father's trembling hands. He was going to strike again. He reared back. She lifted her hand. "Please, don't! Dad, you'll kill him."

Vincent's gaze at the man, and his trembling overhead grip on the piece of heavy metal, showed that he wasn't in his daughter's world. He was locked in his own. A world where a worthless and weak and cruel father with a million regrets for not loving his daughter was the only thing standing between that daughter and the man who was about to rape her in the woods.

"Dad, he can't hurt me," she spoke softly, moving slowly toward him. "I'm safe now." She put her hand on his and lowered the poker. She had a million questions, one of which was, where did you come from? But she couldn't ask them now. Mom and Crystal needed help. "Dad, I'm going to take this," she said, as she removed the weapon from her father's hand.

Becca located the man's gun on the ground. She picked it up and quickly decided against giving it to her father. She pressed two fingers to the man's neck. "Dad, we have to move fast. The other men—they're two of them—they're trying to get Mom and Crystal at the cabin."

"Becca..." his eyes were watery and full of sadness and regret. He shook his head. "I'm sorry." His words threatened to overwhelm her. He saw it and knew this wasn't the time. "We'll talk." He paused, hoping. "If you want to."

She looked at him and was emotionally stumped. Wasn't this what she had begged him for all her life? Yes, but this tornado had dropped upon her with no warning. She hadn't talked with him in the cabin. Or force marched him up and down the hill. Neither had she been locked in and escaped from a car trunk with him.

But he *had* popped out of nowhere at the last second and saved her from being beaten and raped and murdered. And he *had* threatened to kill Dr. Li if she proceeded with aborting her. He had saved her life twice, and now he wanted to talk.

And she needed to talk.

"Yeah, Dad, I want to."

"Let's go get your mother," he said. "Who's Crystal?"

"A friend. Dad, don't shoot him." Becca handed him the gun. Vincent looked at the man who had tried to rape his daughter. "Dad," Becca said, again.

"Okay, I won't shoot him."

"They have plastic ties." She searched his pockets and pulled out several and shook her head in anger. She crossed the man's ankles and put a tie on it and tugged. She put his hands behind his back and did the same.

"Now can I shoot him?"

"No, Dad, you can't shoot him."

"Then let's go get your mother."

42

Jason was royally ticked off. Reggie and Dwayne were blaming him for not closing the trunk all the way. He had no idea how those women had gotten out of that trunk, but he knew one thing. He had not left it open. What kind of an idiot did they take him for? He thought of how good that sweet young thing had felt in his hand and how she wasn't waiting for him in the trunk. Her mom was a looker, too. He cursed. How'd they get out? How'd they get the ties off? How'd they get back in the house without being seen? He cursed.

He rubbed and squeezed his Adam's apple. "Ow," he said. Something wasn't right with it. His leg was messed up, too, from that dude's kick. He shook his head, then touched the back of it. Something wasn't right there, either. "Think that jerk broke my head."

Jason looked at the moon. Then he scanned the area, his criminal mind weighing options. He knew they couldn't see him. He was in the trees. He looked at the front windows and door of the cabin. The lights inside were off. The porch light was on. Smart girls. The only thing standing between him and the front door was a clearing that was illuminated with moonlight. The car was close to the door.

This whole thing had gone into the toilet. Three women holed up in a cabin in the middle of nowhere. One gun. No phone signal. Obviously, no hardwire phone. *Cops would've been here a long time ago if they had one.* And he and the blackbirds were all outside trying to figure out an elaborate way to get into the house without being heard so they wouldn't have to shoot Crystal and risk getting paid only half the money.

Jason was tired of playing with these women, and he was tired of waiting for the police to show up. He ran across the clearing to get to the car. From there, he'd run his two hundred and thirty pounds up those stairs and kick that door off its hinges. He'd done it before. He'd put a bullet in the mama, screw the girl, and drag Crystal out by her hair or ankles. Didn't make no difference any more. Half the money was better than letting all the money send him back to prison.

Heather stumbled back at the sight of the man running toward the cabin. She had spotted him from an upstairs window. "Crystal! One's running at the cabin. I think he's going to try the front door."

A loud scream originated in the woods behind Jason and filled the valley. He stopped and looked.

"There he is!" said Heather.

The two women huddled at the window.

"That's the dog who touched Becca. He's just standing there," said Heather.

"Good," said Crystal, "let's open the window. I'm going to put a bullet in his big—"

"Look! There's another one," said Heather.

Jason saw something coming at him from the corner of his eye. He turned and lifted his gun. The man charging at him didn't have a gun. Jason stretched his neck forward in surprise, then anger. He refrained from pulling the trigger. He'd wait until he was only four or five feet away. He wanted to see the effects happen up close.

"He's going to shoot that guy!" said Heather.

Ten feet. Eight feet. Six feet.

Jason pulled the trigger at the charging, suicidal fool. There was a click, but no boom. Then there was.

The charging man boomed into the stationary target's midsection. He buried a thick shoulder into his gut and lifted him high into the air. He landed heavily on top of him several feet from initial impact. The crushing blow to Jason's belly bypassed years of prison sit-ups and turned his liver, gall bladder, and pancreas into jelly. The pulverizing blow made it impossible to gasp for the air he desperately needed. But there was more pulverizing to come.

The man on top punched him twice and started raining elbows on the baldhead guy's face. The man's skin broke in two places. Blood covered his face. He turned away from a blow and put his nose in direct contact with an elbow. His nose broke and blood poured out. He turned to the side in a desperate move to try to get up and escape the vicious battering.

The man on top jumped on this movement like he had anticipated it. Like this was the purpose of the beating. Jason made it to a knee. The man's arm slipped under Jason's neck at the same time he mounted his back and wrapped his legs around his waist. He locked his hands together and pulled Jason's neck up at the same time his powerful legs squeezed the man's torso.

"You…the one…chopped me…in the neck," said Jason, his grunted words barely audible under the boa constrictor's grip.

No one else would've understood the unintelligible grunts, but the man doing the squeezing did. "Small…world," he said, his own words carrying the strain of putting a fighting ox to sleep.

He waited until the man's body went limp. He rolled him over onto his belly and looked around for threats. Seeing none, he quickly took off his shirt and used it to tie Jason's hands behind his back. He snatched off his t-shirt and tied his feet together. Then he took the gun and ran to the side of the car and looked around. He reached into his pocket and pulled out the bullets he had taken out of Jason's gun earlier in the bathroom at the bar. He released the magazine, filled it, and chambered a round.

"That guy has a lot of muscles," said Heather.

"He sure does," said Crystal. "Like watching Hercules and Samson fight."

The man looked up directly at them.

They jumped back into the darkness, wondering whether he had seen them.

They looked again and he was gone.

"Crystal, he's a new one."

"What do you mean a new one?"

"He's not one of the three guys who took me and Becca. I couldn't see his face clearly, but there was only one white guy. That's the bald-headed guy tied up." Heather looked at Crystal in disbelief. "Just how many people are after you, Crystal?"

If he wasn't one of the three, then who was he. "I don't know," she answered.

Becca and Vincent watched the entire gladiator show from the darkness of the woods. She recognized the big baldhead guy. But who was the other muscle man?

Vincent was stunned. "You don't recognize the other one?"

"No, the other two guys are black. This guy's white or Hispanic or something. He's not black. That's for sure."

Vincent blew out a breath and looked at the gun in his hand. He took the magazine out and held it in his hand, looking at it.

"What are you doing?" Becca asked.

"Guys are popping out of nowhere to get this friend of yours," he bobbed his head. "And my wife happens to be in the line of fire. I'd like to have some idea how many bullets we have."

Becca was surprised—and impressed. "Oh."

"Look, Becca, that mystery muscle man's got a gun. And the other guy out there, he's got a gun. And who knows who else out here looking for your friend has a gun. Here. Take the gun. We go to the car. I'll go to the front door first. I've got a key. Hopefully, none of Crystal's bounty hunters will shoot me on the doorstep. And hopefully, Crystal won't shoot me in the living room. Okay."

"Okay, Dad."

Becca and her dad ran across the clearing. Together.

Two minutes later Vincent was in. "Don't shoot! It's Vincent. Becca's dad."

"Vincent?" Heather yelled from upstairs.

"Heather. Yeah, don't shoot. Becca's coming next."

————

The sound of a rock hitting a back window stopped the multiple conversations.

"Could be a trick," said Vincent. "Crystal, stay here. Watch the front door. I'll go up."

Heather wasn't used to seeing her husband take charge like this. She followed behind him.

Vincent ran up the stairs and entered the first bedroom. He went to the window, opened it, and peeked out. The trees were closer in the back yard than in the front. He looked down the slope and into the trees.

"How many bad guys are there?" a voice yelled from the woods

"What?" Vincent said. He looked at Heather, who was nearly on top of him. "How many bad guys?"

"I'm here for Crystal," the voice said.

"Oh, goodness," said Heather.

"Well, that's news," Vincent said to Heather. "They're all here for Crystal." He spoke through the window without showing himself. "Counting you, four," he answered the voice in the woods.

"There's one down in the front. Any others down?" the voice asked.

"Who is this guy?" Vincent said. "You recognize his voice?"

"No, he must be the guy who beat up the other guy," said Heather.

Vincent peeked. He still didn't see the body that the voice was coming from. "Not counting the guy in the front, there's still one out there. There's another one down. Not telling you where."

"Is he the one laid out by the sheets hanging from the window?"

"Sheets?" said Vincent to Heather. "He doesn't think I'm going to hang my head out of the window looking for sheets, does he?"

"There are sheets hanging from the window," said Heather.

"There are?"

"I put them there. I'll explain later." Heather looked out. Reggie was lying flat on his back. "Vincent, that's him. He must've tried to climb in the bathroom window and fallen."

That is exactly what had happened. He had been almost to the top when Becca screamed. Gabron took her scream and put it inside Reggie's ears. The piercing scream shook his bones. He lost his grip and fell on his neck and back.

"No, that's not him."

"Then counting him, my guy in front, and the guy you took care of, all the bad guys are down."

"How do we know you're not a bad guy?" said Vincent to the faceless man.

A shirtless man wearing jeans and boots walked out of the woods. His muscled arms were stretched wide. His gun was clearly in his front waist. "Cause a bad guy wouldn't come out like this."

"Put your gun in the grass."

The man grinned. "Can't do that. Goes against my training."

"His training?" said Heather. "That explains what he did to that man."

"I'm coming in. Tell Crystal her father wants to see her."

"You're kidding me," Vincent mumbled.

"That man is Crystal's father?" said Heather.

They both walked downstairs with news they didn't understand. Vincent saw that Heather was eager with the news. So he let her do the announcing.

Becca and Crystal looked at the funny expression on Heather's face.

"What's up, Mom?" Becca asked.

Heather smacked her tongue as she opened her mouth. "Uh, Crystal, that hunky hunk guy that beat up the guy and disappeared. Well, he says he's your father and he wants to see you."

Crystal's eyes glazed at Heather's bomb. She didn't stagger. She didn't fall. But she did go deaf and wobbly. She knew Heather was still talking. Her lips were moving. Instinct turned her head left toward Becca. She saw Becca bent over and her still mouth wide open, staring at her. Crystal's body looked through her mind's self-imposed silence and mirrored her friend's position and expression. Without releasing a sound, her mouth formed, "What?"

Knock. Knock. Knock.

That was the door off the deck near the kitchen.

"That's him," said Heather.

Becca threw off her shock and hurried to Crystal's side and wrapped her arm under hers. Vincent turned the stick for the miniature blinds. His gun was partially raised, but not pointing at the man. The women studied the shirtless figure on the porch.

"Is this your father?" asked Vincent.

I sure hope so, thought Becca and Heather.

She hadn't seen her father since she was seven. Crystal looked at his dark hair. His dark eyes. His hard, but handsome face. Her eyes dropped to his chest. Over his heart was a large tattoo. *Crystal*. She was on his heart. Her hand lifted a little and flopped back down. It raised again, gaining strength and staying, defying the anger for his absence and reaching weakly for the man with her name over his heart. Tears rolled down her face. "Becca, hold me up," she pled. Her knees buckled. Becca steadied her.

"Let the man in, Vincent," Heather said, as though not doing so would kill Crystal.

The door opened wide and the tall, shirtless, muscle man stepped in. Two guns were in his front waist. Jason's and Reggie's. He had tears in his eyes. "Hello, baby."

Crystal leaned heavily on Becca. Her voice sounded too weak to carry the weight of her words. "What are you doing here?"

"I haven't been well. I have a lot of explaining to do, Crystal. I've been looking for you for a long time."

"How'd you—?" she said weakly. "I don't understand."

"I ran into the guy out front when I was searching for you at a bar. He was searching for you, too. He didn't sound like a friend. So I talked to him. I got his keys and put my phone in his trunk by his spare tire. I followed him here."

"He gave you his keys?" Crystal asked, foggily. "Why would he give you his keys?"

"I had to convince him."

Heather looked at Vincent. *Like he convinced him to give him his gun,* she said with her eyes.

Exactly, Vincent's eyes agreed.

Tears rolled down Crystal's father's face. He pinched the insides of his eyes and let the tears get lost in the young hair on his face. "Can I touch you?"

"Becca," Crystal called.

"I've got you," said Becca.

Crystal lifted two tentative hands halfway up and said through tears, "Daddy, please touch me."

Her father took three longs steps and took his heart in his arms and held her tightly. "I love you. I missed you so much," he said, and broke. He cupped the back of her head and pressed her face into his bare chest, his tears falling into his little girl's hair. "Baby, I can't ask you to forgive me. There's so much you need to know first. But I'm dying inside. I haven't been here for you. When I let your mother die, I was already not well. I was sick. That's why I had to leave the army. When I let your mother die—oh, God, when I killed her, I got worse."

This sent a shudder down Becca's and her parents' spines.

"Daddy," said Crystal.

He pulled back, arm's length, and held Crystal's arms. He didn't want to not feel the warmth and life of his little girl's body next to his, but he had to look her in her eyes when he said this. "I can't make any excuses, Crystal. I don't want to offer you excuses. I couldn't help the PTSD, but I didn't have to become an alcoholic. I didn't have to become homeless. I didn't have to become hollow. I had a little girl to raise, but I was so full of self-pity and guilt that I didn't do what I should have done as your father."

"Daddy," Crystal's face wore agony, "you didn't kill Mommy. I did. I killed her. I watched her, Daddy. I watched her die. She wanted to take a bath and I told her no. But Mommy never gets to take baths. So I promised her I would watch her so she could take a bubble bath. Then she started shaking and she went under the water. The bubbles were on top of her. Mommy reached for help from under the bubbles. I didn't do anything. Daddy, I just stood there and watched. I watched for so long. I could've saved her. By the time I woke you up, she was probably already dead. Daddy, what am I going to do? I killed Mommy."

Vincent wiped his eyes and looked at Heather and Becca. They were nearly drowning in their own tears. "Becca," he said, softly, with an outstretched hand. She took it. "Heather," he said. She took his other hand. "We need to talk." He led them to a private room.

43

It was nearly two o'clock in the morning, but no one in the cabin was asleep. It didn't appear that sleep was on anyone's list. Raymond couldn't get enough of talking to Crystal. Crystal couldn't get enough of talking to her father, Raymond. Vincent, Heather, and Becca were engrossed in deep, honest, and painful discussions in the far end of the cabin away from the grand room.

Heather and Becca were side by side on the sofa. Vincent was on his knees before them both. He held both of their hands. It may have been medically impossible for him to cry any harder or any longer. He looked at them both, took a deep breath, and gave a tight, *I'm sorry* smile.

"Dad," said Becca.

He looked at her, willing to say or do anything to make up for his years of cruelty.

"Your nose is really disgusting," she said.

Heather laughed. "I wasn't going to say anything, but I'm having a hard time not throwing up."

Becca laughed, too. "Yeah, Dad, that can't taste good."

"Oh." Vincent's hand shot to his nose, covering his face. "That is just wrong," he said. He hopped up and went to a restroom.

"Oh, Mom," Becca said, remembering something that everyone, including her, had forgotten. "Those creeps. They're still out there. We left them."

"You're right," Heather noted, with all the regret of having lost a dollar bill. "I hadn't thought about those guys since Crystal's father walked in the kitchen looking like urban Tarzan."

Becca's eyes danced. "We have to talk about this," she whispered, taking her mother's hand. "That's her *father*?"

Heather gave Becca a sly grin. "I'm just going to say this one thing, and then I'm going to leave it alone. That is one *magnificent* tattoo."

"Mom, he has her name on…his…chest." Becca had fun with the statement.

Heather turned her head sideways and lowered her chin. Her eyes twinkled. "Okay, and that is one magnificent chest." She did some gymnastics with her expression as she swiveled her head up, down, and around. "Just an honest observation."

Becca poised a thoughtful expression.

"What?" asked Heather.

"Just wondering how awkward it would be for Crystal to call me Mom or Mother. Definitely not Mommy."

"Whoa, back up, young lady. He's gorgeous, but you're eighteen."

"Mom!" Becca warned, when she saw her father coming.

"Don't '*Mom!*'" Vincent mimicked. "I know what you're talking about. The cougar and the kitten. He's not even that goodlooking."

Heather and Becca rose. "Don't call my daughter a cougar," said Heather. "She's much too young to be called a cougar." She looked at Vincent with a playful dare.

Vincent opened his mouth and said nothing for a few seconds. Both of his girls awaited his response. "You're right. I'm sorry, Becca. I should not have called you a cougar."

"It's okay, Dad," she smiled. "Smart guy."

Heather said, "We need to talk to Crystal's unattractive father about those criminals out there. We forgot all about them."

Vincent smacked his forehead and spun away from them.

Heather and Becca immediately pounced on the opportunity. "GORGEOUS!" they silently mouthed behind his back.

"You're right," said Vincent. "I guess we can suspend our discussions to gather the trash."

"And, Dad, Mom wants to ask you something, but she doesn't want to hurt your feelings."

"Oh really?" he said, seeing mischief in Becca's eyes and a question in Heather's.

"Yes, she doesn't want you to give Crystal's father a shirt."

He looked at Heather. "Is that right?"

"Oh, don't be silly, Vincent. He couldn't fit any of your shirts. They're way too small for him."

He bounced his finger at her and left the room.

Forty-five minutes later, Crystal, Heather, and Becca stood on the porch, ignoring the guy right before them on the grass that Raymond had beaten and tied up, and instead delightfully watched Crystal's father emerge from the woods carrying Dwayne over his shoulder.

"What do you think of my father, Heather?" Crystal asked, with a smile.

"Crystal, I'm working on my marriage. I can't afford to think about your father."

"What about you, Becca?" Crystal wasn't through tormenting them.

Heather answered for her. "She's wondering whether to have you call her Mom or Mother. She said Mommy is definitely out."

"It doesn't mean we can't still be friends," Becca laughed. "But you will have to clean up your potty mouth."

Crystal's eyes would probably never be dry again. She wiped an eye as she looked at the man who had in one evening unlocked her soul from a dungeon's life sentence. "I think I like Mommy."

Raymond placed Dwayne right beside Jason. "Brought you company. Your other friend's not very good at scaling walls. He's laid out in the back. Can't move his legs. Don't worry. We used his ties to make sure he doesn't disappear should he suddenly get healed."

Vincent stood next to Raymond. He looked on the porch and shook his head at the cougar and the kitten, knowing how their minds were working. They smiled widely at him and waved.

"Crystal, you mind giving me a lift to go get my car?" yelled Raymond. "And I need to get my phone. And we need to go somewhere we can get a phone signal."

"Oh, Mom," Becca said, with a big, wide-mouthed smile and sparkly eyes, "he needs me to show him where those guy's parked. Don't worry about this, Crystal. I've got it covered."

Heather smiled. "The car doesn't work. Remember? And must I remind you again? You're still eighteen. You've got college to think about. Besides, he is so incredibly ugly and puny. Sorry, Crystal."

It was all in fun, Heather acknowledged. And God knew after what they'd been through not only that evening, but for nearly twenty years, a little comic relief was welcome. But she felt regret for having missed the warp speed development of her daughter over the past several months.

A little while ago she barely had time for boys. All she had time for was homework, sports, practicing instruments, and a hundred other things that didn't include boys. Now she was joking about being with grown men. What had this child been into since she had left home? *God, please forgive me for being a terrible parent.*

Crystal hopped down the stairs.

"Her daddy shows up and she's like a little bunny," said Heather.

"It won't turn," Crystal said to Raymond. She pulled keys out of her pocket.

"Sure about that?" he said, with a grin that said he knew cars.

She held the keys up and dropped them into his hand. "Impress me."

"I aim to." He sat with one leg in the car and one on the ground. He put the key into the ignition and turned. *Vrooooooom. Vrooooooom.* The car's engine was strong and smooth.

"No f—"Crystal decided to drop the word"—freaking way! I hate it when that happens! I'm telling you, that car wouldn't start."

He lifted his left hand out the window without looking at her and rubbed his fingers together. "Ma'am, that'll be two hundred dollars."

"Mom, the car is female," Becca said, slowly."

"Apparently so," her mom agreed.

———

The police and ambulances had finally left. That left a thoroughly exhausted group of people, whose bodies and heavy eyelids demanded rest, standing on the front porch of the cabin.

And it left three angels of truth who had been quite busy in their orchestrations. One of them went into the grand room.

Ring! Ring! Ring!

Everyone heard it. No one moved. It couldn't be.

Crystal bit her bottom lip and kept the curse words to herself. "I am going to pretend that I do not hear a phone ringing."

"Well, I'm not." Heather ran inside and stopped. Vincent followed.

Ring!

Heather and Vincent bent their heads sideways and walked slowly and disbelievingly to the sound coming from the bottom shelf of one of the tables. Heather grabbed it. "Hello."

"Well, it is about time somebody picked up the phone," said Nancy.

Becca came in and stood next to her father. Crystal and Raymond stayed on the porch.

"How long have you been calling?" Heather asked.

"After our *first* flat tire. We've been trying to reach you since yesterday afternoon."

"You had more than one flat tire?"

"Heather, we have had a total of four flat tires. Three were ours and one was the Triple A man. I have never experienced anything this bizarre in all my life. Danielle—thank God for her—she kept us focused on the Lord. She said God was obviously doing something with all of you and He didn't need our help. Did Vincent show up?"

"Yes."

"He did?" Nancy turned to Bill. "Vincent showed up."

"He did?" Danielle squealed. "What about Becca?"

"Did Becca show up?" Nancy asked.

"Yes, she did," said Heather.

Nancy was silent. "She did?"

"Yes! Yes! Thank You, Lord!" screamed Danielle, drumming her feet on the truck's floor.

"My Lord, my Lord," said Bill.

"And you didn't call us?" chided Nancy. "You'd think you'd get a phone call for something like this. Or at least to check up on us. We have spent more time on the side of the highway than we've spent driving."

"We didn't hear the phone," said Heather. "We didn't even know there was a phone. When did this happen?"

Nancy looked at her husband. "Bill, I declare, this daughter of ours. Heather, we had the conversation. You and I. You don't remember me telling you that I felt like I was on *Gilligan's Island* every time we came up here. Going to the mountains is one thing. But sitting in the middle of the woods with no phone is foolish.

"Your father talked with Clarence. The guy at church who owns the cabin. Had to talk him into it. Clarence told him he wasn't spending a dime to ruin his peace, but that if your father wanted to wire it, he could. He had to pay for the wiring himself. I can't believe you forgot that conversation."

"I'm sorry. I guess I did," Heather said, still not recalling the conversation.

There was a long pause.

"Mom?"

"Heather we are passing a long line of police cars coming from the direction of the cabin. Do tell me that this family meeting was not that bad of an idea. Are you the last survivor?"

Heather rubbed her hand over her face and exhaled with a chuckle.

"Well, if that many police cars had come from the cabin, you wouldn't be laughing about it. We'll be there in a few."

"Okay, Mom." Heather looked at Becca. "Your grandparents should be here in a couple of minutes." She smiled. "And Danielle. I heard her screaming in the background when she heard you were here. That sister of yours loves you dearly, Becca." She added. "And you know how your grandparents feel about you."

Bill's big truck had barely stopped rolling before Danielle bolted and ran for the door. She looked at Raymond and Crystal. Who were they? "Hey," she said to them both.

"Hey," they said.

She hurried inside. Her parents and Becca were standing...*together.* That was odd. But not as odd as how her sister looked. She looked at the fuzz on her sister's head where long hair used to be. She looked at the two crazy, sad tattoos on her face and the snake on her arm. She stepped backward and looked at the white, skin-tight dress that barely covered her butt. She used a lot of air to whisper, "Whoooaaa. I'll be right back." Danielle spun toward the door and spun back around. She hugged and squeezed Becca. "I love you. I have to warn grandma and grandpa."

Vincent looked at Heather. "I love you, too, Danielle," he said to her perfume.

"She's just excited," said Heather. "She hasn't seen her big sister in a long time."

Becca watched the whirlwind of her little sister race out of the door and toward her grandparents. She watched through the open door as the interesting conversation unfolded. There was nothing in the world that could take away the joy she felt at being reconciled with her family.

She and Mom were talking and kidding with one another with an intimacy that she hadn't even witnessed between Mom and Danielle. And Dad couldn't stop crying and hugging her. She felt like a teddy bear in the arms of a child who couldn't get enough of squeezing it.

But for the first time since all of this craziness had begun the day before, the full realization of what she had done to her face hit her.

She could wear long sleeves and cover nearly all of the snake. But she wasn't a Muslim. She couldn't hide behind a mask. This was now her. She'd have to live the rest of her life with *Unwanted* and *Rejected* written on her face in big letters.

What had she been thinking? And what about the tattoo inside her thigh? How would she ever explain that to her husband? What husband? Who would be crazy enough to want a woman with *Unwanted* and *Rejected* stamped on her face?

Danielle came up the stairs first. She held her grandmother's hand. Bill was close behind. They entered the cabin silently. Becca stood sheepishly with her arms folded, trying to cover as much of the snake as possible. To their credit, Bill and Nancy contained *most* of their shock.

"Who are those people out there?" Nancy asked.

"Becca's friend, Crystal, and her father. His name is Raymond," said Heather.

"Well, tell them we need some privacy and close the door," said Nancy.

Vincent went out and briefly spoke to Raymond. "No problem," said Raymond. "Come on, little girl," he said to Crystal. He took her by the hand and started walking with her toward the clearing. "You're going to get tired of me."

"I don't think that's possible," Crystal said.

Vincent entered the cabin and closed the door.

Nancy looked at her daughter and son-in-law and fought a lot of ungodly urges. Bill was having the same fight. Nancy looked at Becca. "We may as well get this out in the open. There's no way to pretend you're not standing there baldheaded and with awful words tattooed on your face." Nancy looked at her arm. "Is that a snake?"

Tears rolled down Becca's face. Her answer was short and filled with shame and regret. "Yes."

"Let me see it, Becca."

Becca started crying and stretched out her arm.

Nancy lifted her granddaughter's arm and looked at it. Bill came over and examined it. Nancy looked tenderly into Becca's wet eyes. "I have always told you the truth, haven't I?"

"Yes."

Nancy's heart was broken and disappointed, but soft with compassion. "This snake is hideous. The words on your face are awful and they're lies. My heart is broken, but I know whatever pain I feel, you feel a thousand times more. This was dumb, Becca. I know you know that. I need to just put it out there because you're going to hear Satan repeat that to you until the day you die, and you need to be ready for it. I wish I could've stopped this from happening, but since I didn't, I'm going to do the next best thing. I'm going to ask God to somehow use it for His glory. Get on your knees, Becca."

Becca got on her knees and without being told, she lifted her hands and closed her eyes.

"Come on," said Bill. "Put your hands on her."

Vincent got on his knees next to her and hugged around her shoulders. Heather lay her hand on her shoulder. Bill put his hand on her head. "Danielle," said Nancy, "look in my purse and get my bottle of oil. It's in a plastic bag."

Danielle handed her grandmother the small bottle and stood behind Becca and placed her hands on both sides of her neck. She tenderly massaged her big sister's shoulders. *She was damaged, but she was her big sister, and she was back!*

Nancy prayed. Then Vincent prayed. Then Danielle cried, cried, cried, and then prayed. Nancy prayed again and ended with a favorite ungrammatical prayer of their church family, "Lord, we ask You in Jesus's name to turn this messing into a blessing! Amen."

Becca's eyes opened and she wiped her eyes with both hands. She prepared to get off her knees.

"We're not through yet," said Bill. "Raise that mess up over your head." He pulled her arm up. "You stay down there. You need a lot of knee time." Bill dabbed a little oil on his finger and used it to make a cross on Becca's arm. He looked at that snake's open mouth. He put some oil on it. "God's going to close that snake's big mouth in your life." Then he did something that made Becca convulse with tears. He said, "I bless this mess. Nothing can stop the love of God, and nothing can stop my love for you. I've never been ashamed of you, and I'm not ashamed of you now." He kissed the back of her hand. He kissed the snake! Then he did the same with the tattoos on her face.

Nancy took Becca's face in her hands and kissed each tattoo. "I break the power of these words. You are wanted. You are accepted."

Becca lifted her arm.

Nancy waved it away with a chuckle. "I'm not kissing that thing. That's what husbands are for." The chuckle was the last revolution of a car's tires before it ran out of gas. Nancy's heart was broken. She was on empty and she needed to get away from this room. Away from those horrible tattoos, and away from the people who had caused them. "Bill, I'm going to bed." She walked away.

44

An hour later everyone had gone to bed and all but one was not sleeping like overworked slaves.

Becca put on that same infamous white dress, but added a pair of her sister's jeans, which she had pushed upon her right after prayer. She took a short, light blanket under her arm and crept downstairs and exited the front door. She wrapped the blanket around her shoulders and sprinted for the woods.

Becca's guardian angels had ridden a roller coaster of dread and relief, watching the suspenseful drama. Was she going to kill her parents? Yes! Then, mercifully no. Was she going to kill herself? Yes! Then, again, mercifully no. Kidnapped! Locked in a car's trunk. Molested by a killer. Would she be raped and murdered? Yes! Then, no. Instead, reconciliation with her mom!

Would she be shot? Almost, but no. Caught again by one of the criminals. Would she be raped this time? Yes! Then no. The estranged father had stopped the criminal at the last minute. Again, the wisdom and provision of God had prevailed over the enemy.

Every enemy vanquished!

Reconciliation accomplished!

Yet Becca's stronghold of rejection appeared as strong as ever. That very moment Unwanted and Alone were on one of its thick walls and looking out at them. Other demons were mocking them by literally dancing on the walls and making lewd gestures at them.

"I do not understand," said Gabron. "This is the day we were waiting for. It is here and yet the stronghold stands. How can this be?"

Justis was more experienced than either Gabron or Krasa. Yet he, too, had no answer.

The guardians accompanied her deep into the dark woods. She unfurled the blanket from her back, placed it in front of her, and threw herself onto her belly. Moans of deep grief left her mouth before her body hit the ground.

"Look!" said Gabron.

A squad of six big mercy angels left her presence.

"I didn't even know they were there!" exclaimed Krasa.

"It makes sense," said Justis. "She's had so many close calls. Only the mercy of God could've kept her while she was in such rebellion."

"But why are they leaving her now?" asked Gabron.

The appearance of Mark and the other two truth angels interrupted them.

"What is going on?" asked Gabron. "The mercy angels have left. Why?"

"Mercy has kept her. But only truth can deliver her. It is written, 'You shall know the truth, and the truth shall make you free.'"

The guardians went silent.

Mark stepped forward, his countenance growing brighter as he spoke. "Full deliverance requires full submission. 'Thou shall have no other gods before Me.'"

"What—?"

The truth angels disappeared.

The guardians knew, however, that although they were hidden from their sight, they were doing something in Becca. They watched her and listened with great interest.

She began with a scream. She beat the ground with her feet and fists, then turned onto her back and screamed into the sky. Then she cried one way and then the other, rolling here and there. She had not yet spoken an intelligible word, but the guardians understood, at least imperfectly, the communications of her pain. They wondered at her deep agony.

Becca got on her knees. "Look at me!" Becca screamed into the sky. "Look what I've done to myself! I'm only eighteen years old. All I wanted was for my parents to love me. Now they do. They love me." She covered her face and cried into her hands. "I used to be beautiful. I had beauty and no love. Now I have love and no beauty. Oh, God, why did I do this to myself? You tried to warn me. I see that now. Elana. That was you. You spoke through her. You told me marking my face was insane. I didn't listen. I never listen to you. That's why I'm disfigured."

Becca fell over onto her side. She tried to empty her pain by crying. To go back in time by screaming. To make this all a bad dream by closing her eyes. But when she opened her eyes, the pain was still there, and she was not standing before Elana. It was a bad reality, not a bad dream.

Becca crawled onto her knees again and lifted her hands. "Oh, God, I've brought this upon myself. Grandma tried to help me when I was little. I used to love you when I was little. But the older I got, the angrier I got. I started blaming you for my problems. And all this time, you were looking out for me.

"You gave Grandma the dream about Mom and Dad trying to abort me. You sent the music into the abortion clinic to give Dad enough time to save me. You brought me to Crystal so she could take me to the abortion clinic, and to hear Dr. Li confess. How could I have been so blind?"

Mark stuck his sword deep into Becca's soul again. This process went on for hours.

Becca howled like a wounded animal. "Oh, God, I've done so many things. So many filthy things. I was even going to kill my parents. I was going to kill myself." She wailed at the picture she got of her standing over her parents' dead bodies.

The picture was too much. Becca got up and sprinted through the woods. She didn't care about the trees she could see or those she couldn't see. What she could see was the enormity of her sins, and she had to get away.

An angel's hand swiped her foot. She fell. She didn't try to get up. "God," she said through tears, "I'm sorry for what I did with Gerald. I'm sorry for turning to drugs and rebellion and hatred when I should have turned to You."

She looked up. "I'm nothing. I'm nothing. I'm nothing without you. Even with my father's and mother's love, what am I without you? I've been seeking to be loved and accepted by the wrong people. People are just people. They're sinful like me. They're going to let me down. They're going to make mistakes. It's stupid for me to try to get from people what I can only get from You. Grandma told me that a long time ago.

"I don't know what to do. I know it's too late to undo what I've done. I'm like that king in the Bible. The one who was chasing David. I've made a mistake that can't be fixed, I know. But Grandma and Grandpa said you can bless the mess I've made. I am begging. Please, please, bless this mess. I don't know what this means or what it looks like, but from this point on I'm serving you.

I'm going to church with Grandma and Grandpa. I'm getting everything I need from You. Lord, even if my mother and my father forsake, I know that You will take me up. I give you this snake. I give you these tattoos on my face. I give you the one on my leg. I don't care. Do whatever You want with me. All I ask is that You wash me clean."

Becca fell asleep.

A glowing light made its way through the woods and toward her. Inside of the light was the Angel of the Lord. He carried a container of His own blood in one hand and a cloth in the other.

The guardians sensed the rumbling in the other dimension. But they didn't have to sense it; they could see its effects. The mammoth wall of the rejection stronghold started swaying. Then suddenly the ground beneath the entire structure started rolling like an ocean wave. The structure collapsed.

Gabron pulled his sword and dagger. Krasa and Justis pulled their weapons. Behind them they heard, "Destroy everything!"

The guardians looked to their rear and saw the armies of the Lord advancing.

"Unwanted is mine," said Gabron.

———

Becca woke up in the woods. Her eyes opened slowly. *I must've fallen asleep. Woods! Bugs! Crawling all over me!* She sprang up onto her bottom and used the early sunlight to frantically wipe bugs off of her.

Raymond and Crystal were sitting on the porch doing their new father-daughter thing and enjoying the smell of *bad for you, but good to you* bacon being cooked by Danielle. Her description of bacon. The sound of screams in the woods startled them. They looked at a figure emerging out of the woods with outstretched arms. It was Becca.

"Go get her father," Raymond told Crystal before running toward Becca. Raymond scanned the woods for the threat. Another criminal? A bear? He saw nothing behind her in pursuit as he neared. She was acting strange as she ran. She was waving her arm like it was on fire. At one point, she jumped up and down, flailing both arms and twirling, then looking up into the sky with both hands high. Then she'd take off again.

What in the world had happened? What was she afraid of? Wait, she wasn't afraid. She was happy. What had gotten her so happy in the woods? "Becca, what's going on?"

"Raymond! Raymond! Raymond! Raymond!"

"Hold on," he said.

"My arm! Look at my arm!"

He looked at it. He didn't see anything wrong with it. *Wait a minute,* he thought, recalling what Crystal had told him. But Becca was gone and sprinting to the house waving her arm. She stopped dead in her tracks and turned around and ran back to Him.

"Raymond, my face?" she cried. "Please tell me He did it to my face, too. Please," she begged.

He didn't know what to say. He just stared at where the tattoos used to be. This girl hadn't been wearing temporary tattoos, had she? They sure looked real. And everyone was acting like they were real.

"Are they there?" she asked, as though her life depended upon his answer.

He shook his head dumbfounded. What else could he say? "No. I don't see anything. The tattoos are gone."

"Aaaaahhhhh!" Becca took off toward her family and Crystal, who were all outside. "Look at me! Look at what God has done! He loves me, Grandma and Grandpa! He did what you said! Look! Look! Look!"

Crystal grabbed Becca's face, grabbed her arm, then ran off screaming, "You're real! It was You! I did hear You!" She dropped to her knees twenty feet away and started crying out to God.

Vincent and Heather stood there trembling, unable to speak, but able to cry. When Becca dropped to her knees and doubled over with her face to the ground crying out to God in praise, they dropped too. Neither had ever served God, but both knew those days were over.

Bill and Nancy looked at Becca and Vincent and Heather, all praising God like they were already in heaven. Becca's friend, Crystal, was over there all alone crying out to God, and acting like stuff was coming off of her.

Bill and Nancy grabbed one another. They could see the tattoos were gone. *But was this real? Had God answered their prayers this dramatically? This was like something in the Bible.* Nancy couldn't take it any longer. She timed the bouncing around of Becca's head up and down and side to side and grabbed it.

Becca looked up, "Look at me, Grandma. Look what God has done for me. He blessed my mess."

Nancy did look at her. Very, very carefully.

"I love Him! I love Him! I love Him!" Becca was beside herself. "I'm going to serve him the rest of my life. I'm going to go to church with you. I want to be baptized. Tell me what to do! Tell me how to serve him! Can I go with you when you go on your Holy Land tour of Israel?"

Nancy heard Becca's questions, but her mind was fixed on her granddaughter's empty cheeks and the place where the snake used to be.

Becca saw her sister from the corner of her eye standing alone in happy shock. Danielle couldn't move. Becca jumped up and ran to her. She hugged her until Danielle could hardly breathe. Then she dropped to Danielle's feet and wrapped her arms around her legs and cried. "I love you. I love you. I love you."

Danielle stood, gazing at the sky, unaware of her sister's presence. She said repeatedly in a holy whisper, "Oh, my God. Oh, my God. Oh, my God."

45

The home was filled with terror.

Outside, was exactly opposite. Tall, mature trees dotted the back yards and lined the quiet Jonesboro street on both sides, providing shade for the suburban homes on their half-acre lots. Children on bicycles and skateboards took advantage of the cul-de-sac's nearly nonexistent traffic. That is, until an elaborately painted ice cream truck and its familiar music came on the scene and parked at the corner's entrance to the cul-de-sac.

Free ice cream!

Word traveled down the street at the speed of sound. In a minute, every kid playing on the block was standing in line for free ice cream. The man in the truck moved extremely slow, but he assured the waiting children that he'd be just a moment. He watched the UPS truck pass his van.

There were two marked police cars with two officers in each car following the truck. They stopped their cars in the middle of the street at the entrance of the cul-de-sac and blocked incoming and outgoing traffic. Three of the officers used themselves to create a wall of authority to keep the children or anyone else from proceeding into the cul-de-sac.

The UPS truck circled the arc and stopped in front of a large, two story home, in preparation to make a delivery. Nearby, a cable technician and a natural gas technician positioned themselves at the rear of the property to make sure that no one inside could escape the delivery.

The truck's doors opened and FBI agents poured out of it. They rushed the house and took up crouching positions. Someone shouted, "FBI!" and a helmeted agent smashed the wooden door with a battering ram. The area hit exploded into a million splinters and small chunks of wood. Armed agents rushed into every area of the home.

The basement was their primary target.

The breach had been carefully coordinated. The basement's door exploded open at the same time the front door exploded open.

"FBI! Don't move!" shouted the agent.

The man moved, too quickly, and in the wrong direction.

Boom! Boom! Boom!

The guy fell to the floor still clutching his gun.

The shocked man in the chair froze in place. Not that he was going anywhere in a hurry under any conditions. But he had enough experience with the law to know that he better not move his hands.

One agent handcuffed the sitting man's hands behind his back. Two others checked adjoining basement rooms. The agent spun the man around. "So, you are the high and mighty Scarecrow. I've been wanting to meet you for a very long time." The agent smiled. "No fancy lawyers or technicalities this time. You're under arrest for a lot of things. Drug trafficking, conspiracy, kidnapping," the agent looked at the two obviously drugged chained women, "human trafficking..."

Special Agent Williams read him his rights.

"We got two girls in here," an agent yelled from another room.

"And two in here," yelled the third agent.

Special Agent Williams looked at the women. One white, one black. "What's your name?" he asked the one who had lifted her head from the mattress. Her eyes were dazed, and her head bobbed in defiance of the drug's desires.

"Po-Po?" the girl asked in a weak whisper.

"FBI. What's your name?"

The girl fought and turned her face toward Boss Man. "Told...yo'...ra...gady a...a..." She was too weakened to finish the curse word. Her words were in a whisper. "Told you...God's not...through with me...yet."

"What's your name?" the agent asked again. Do you know who this woman is?"

"I'm...Ta-Nisha. She...Rachel. They thought...she...was Crystal."

46

*T*hank God, they're only friends! Heather breathed a long sigh of relief after talking to Becca about Crystal. That taken care of, it was time to go to the end of the rainbow.

The hand holding arrangement had been Danielle's idea. Vincent held Becca's left hand. Heather held Becca's right hand and Danielle's left hand. This way Becca was able to hold the hands of both parents. The walk up the hill had been leisurely at first. However, halfway up the hill, Heather began to cry. It was nowhere near the level of the crying that had gone on earlier that day or the day before. It was the soft sob of a hard heart made soft.

Her words choked out as she spoke, "Come on, girls. Let's hurry." Heather picked up the pace up the hill.

Becca smiled in surprise. "Go, Mom."

"Yeah, go, Mom," said Danielle.

They hurried up the hill as quickly as they could before Heather's eagerness was tempered with burning lungs and heavy legs. Yet, even then she pushed. She had to get there as quickly as possible. She had to!

When they reached the top of the hill, Heather's love overcame the fire in her lungs and lead in her legs. She ran around the pond to the patch of flowers. "Come on, girls."

The sun burst in Danielle's smile. "Come on, Becca!" she said, and took off.

Becca stood still, overcome with emotion. She knew what this was, and that's why she couldn't move. She looked at her father beside her. She didn't know what to say. Her tears tried to help. "Dad…Dad," she trembled out the words.

Danielle was seated on the grass while Heather looked at flowers, then looked back at Danielle, then picked more flowers. "Come on, Becca," yelled Heather, motioning wide with her arm.

Becca's eyes poured. "Dad, she's going to make me a flower princess."

He cupped her cheeks and kissed her forehead. "You're already a princess. Now go, Becca. You've waited a long time for this."

Becca wanted to run as fast as she could to get there. But she never wanted the moment to end. So she walked. She arrived with her hand over her heart and with sobs that threatened to double her over. She sat next to Danielle. Danielle took her hand. They both watched their mom study them and the flowers to get the perfect match for each face.

Heather sat with them, carrying a handful of colorful flowers. Becca watched the flowers as though they were the second coming of Christ. They were so dazzling and beautiful. She watched her mother's fingers tie stems together to form two crowns.

Heather looked at both of her girls. They saw the love in her eyes and felt the love in her heart. "Becca, you are my beautiful daughter. I celebrate your birth and thank God for your life." She placed the crown on Becca's head.

"Danielle, you are my beautiful daughter. I celebrate your birth and thank God for your life. And I thank you for saving my life and saving this family." She placed the crown on Danielle's head.

"I now pronounce both of you the Flower Princesses. The most beautiful girls in the flower kingdom."

EPILOGUE

S*everal Months Later*

"Who are you talking to?" Vincent whispered to Heather as he kissed her on the cheek. It wasn't like he didn't have a good idea.

Heather lowered her phone a little and playfully said, "My oldest." She shook her head and mouthed silently, "She's fascinating." Something Becca said grabbed her attention. "Oh, my gosh! Sixteen? Vincent, Becca had sixteen points and ten assists. What?" she asked Becca. "Zero turnovers. Vincent, did you hear that? She didn't even play the whole game."

He sat on one of the barstools at the kitchen counter. He had an odd smile on his face. He came over and put his mouth to the phone as Heather held it. "Don't get too down on her. Anyone can have a rough night. She's only a freshman. At least she's good in academics."

"What?" Becca said.

Heather looked up over her shoulder at Vincent. She held up the phone. "She heard that."

Vincent took the phone and sat next to Heather and put his arm around her. "Hey, I hear you're really struggling on the court. What's with this sixteen points, ten assists, zero errors biz? No steals?" He looked lovingly at his wife as his daughter spoke. Going to Stanford had been a hard decision for them to agree to, but it had turned out to be a wonderful decision. Becca was flourishing. But then that was no surprise.

Vincent nodded knowingly. "Of course…two steals…and a rebound. Okaaay, well I guess that does qualify as a good game," he said with fake reluctance. He hopped up and walked away with the phone.

"Vincent, it's my call," Heather protested. "You're on my time."

"I'll give it right back," he said. "I just need to share something with *my* oldest," he emphasized. "You didn't do this all by yourself, you know." He whispered something into the phone.

Becca screamed, then cried.

"Becca? Becca?" He heard her crying in the background. "Heather," he said, as he walked toward her. "Danielle," he called upstairs.

"Yeah, Dad?"

"Your sister's on the phone. She's crying. It's pretty serious."

Sounds of Danielle rushing down the stairs were almost immediate. Heather jumped up.

"Honey, you need to sit down," said Vincent. "Becca has something to tell you." He looked at Danielle's wide eyes and gently pushed Heather onto the sofa. "Becca," he said into the phone, "you gotta stop crying so you can tell your mom."

"What is it, Vincent?" Heather's curiosity had turned to anxiety. She had been on the phone with Becca for half an hour. She hadn't said anything was wrong.

"Yeah, what's wrong?" asked Danielle.

"Here, Becca, you can tell them now. You're on speaker phone."

"Seven," Becca cried into the phone.

Heather and Danielle looked at one another, shaking their heads.

"It's God's number," Becca said with tears. "He rested on the seventh day. It's completion. You beat it by seven."

"Beat it by seven. Beat what by seven?" Heather asked, looking at her smiling husband.

"You beat the bar examination by seven points. Mom, you're an attorney!" Becca screamed.

OTHER BOOKS BY THE AUTHOR

Christian Spiritual Warfare Fiction

The Fire Series

Book 1: Bones of Fire

Book 2: Trial by Fire

Book 3: Saints on Fire

The Demon Strongholds Series

Book 1: The Spirit of Fear

Book 2: The Spirit of Rejection

Book 3: The Spirit of Ugly

General Christian Fiction

Out of Darkness Series

Book 1: The Runaway: Beginnings

Book 2: The Runaway: Endings

Finding Angel

General Dystopian Fiction

The Great Crime Spike

Christian Non-Fiction

Deliverance from Demons and Diseases

What Preachers Never Tell You About Tithes & Offerings

Mistakes We Make When Casting Out Demons

You Can Get Can Answers to Your Prayers

A NOTE FROM THE AUTHOR

Let's Stay In Touch!

ericmhillauthor@yahoo.com

Facebook.com/ericmhillauthor

My Websites

EricMHillAuthor.com

ShortBibleStudies.com

PowerEvangelism.org

Get Your Free Spiritual Warfare Short Story!

Dl.bookfunnel.com/ajx91tx3ku

Scan now and find out why pretty boy is a fool.

Read Another of

My Spiritual Warfare Thrillers

Order From Your Favorite Local Bookstore Or Amazon

See Next Page

See All of Eric's Books

God bless you!